The Illusionists

Aden Simpson

Copyright

Copyright © Aden Simpson 2016

This work is copyright. Apart from any use as permitted under the copyright Act 1968, no part may be reproduced, copied, scanned, stored in a retrieval system, recorded, or transmitted, in any form or by any means, without the prior written permission of the publisher.

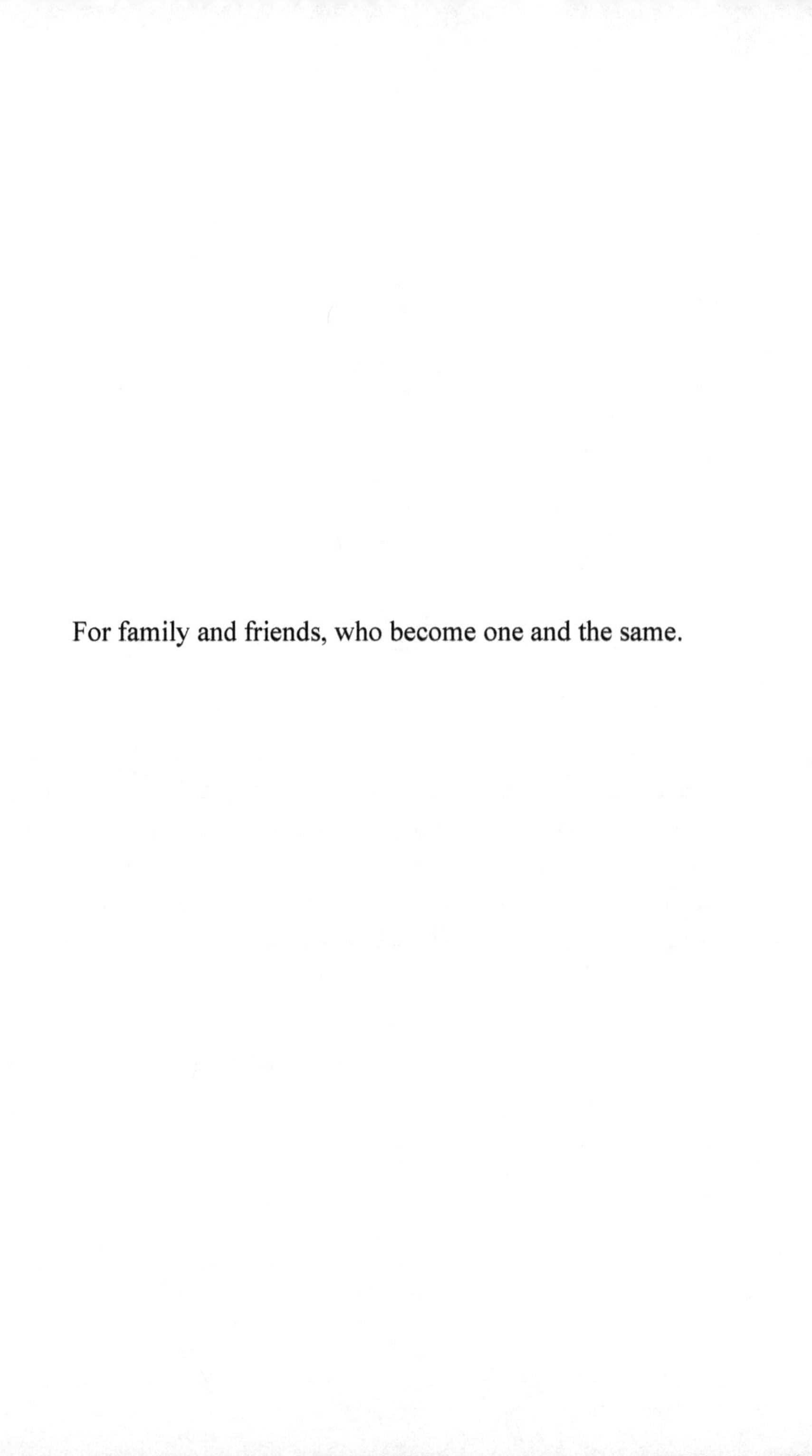

For family and friends, who become one and the same.

Author's Note

The Illusionists is a work of fiction and, with this in mind, I have taken several liberties with the geography and feel of certain, real places to suit the story. In addition to this, the towns such as Edgar, New Mexico; Derek-land, Oregon; Trent, Colorado; Holdsworth, Iowa; and Mae Si Muwang, Thailand are what I would call completely fictional. I apologise if this causes any offense.

The Illusionists

Stage I: Madness

1. Original Sin

It was all out in the open now: a softly spoken wish and two utterly devastated parents.

It was not an easy decision.

And it had not been Cole's idea to begin with.

His best friend, Peter Storrs, had wanted out. Peter's parents had been thinking of changing congregations for a while now, and Peter had been building up his courage to tell them what he thought of Pastor West. What he thought of "church" altogether.

It was a sunny afternoon when Peter revealed his plans to Cole as they walked home from school. "The other kids laugh at us," he revealed to Cole. "They say that place ain't no good. They say we're being lied to, about the whole thing."

It took a while for Cole to let it truly sink in, to even consider it was possible that there could be another way. Cole had never liked going to *that place*, it was always too stuffy in the suit and tie he was forced to put on, top button done up with intent to strangle and his mother would pinch him whenever he fidgeted (this happened to be always). Then there was Pastor West. The man terrified Cole. He was always getting Cole's parents and all the other adults riled up, condemning this and that, releasing a side to them that only ever seemed to come out when they passed that big, domineering black cross out front. It was the same pain every Sunday, where Cole looked out those church windows and was left to dream what fun lay outside while he was stuck in *that place*.

But his parents couldn't be wrong, could they? It was all for his own good, right?

"The pastor's been on the news," said Peter, "Ruby told me."

Cole didn't understand Peter's fascination with Ruby. Not quite yet anyway. He was only ten, and though Peter was only a couple of months older, it always felt like Cole was just catching up. As they grew up together and the typical milestones were passed, it would always be Peter just in front, because he had this knack for knowing exactly what he wanted and was always willing to do whatever it took to get it.

"What did the news say?" asked Cole.

"That Pastor West says evil things and that a lot of people are angry at him."

This hit Cole powerfully. Cole never really liked what the pastor said in church, or the frightful way he'd say it. The other kids in school always talked about the news, telling their teacher Miss Morales that, "the news said this," and "the news said that." Cole never watched the news but he knew it was for smart people. Sometimes, it felt like all the other kids were smarter than him. They just always seemed to look like they knew what they were doing...

Still, he had his doubts.

"I don't know, Pete."

Peter stopped walking and grabbed Cole by the shoulders. His face was deadly serious, almost angry, but Cole didn't flinch.

"Cole, my parents are leaving Free-Hill. They say Pastor West is getting too extreme. They're going to another church, but then that's just another Sunday we're wasting in church! I want to leave it all, Cole, and I reckon you should do the same."

It took a long time for Cole to say something. Church had only become bearable when Peter's family had shown up four months ago. Cole thought of Peter leaving, and it being just himself again, stuck in that awful place, no one to run amok with after service…

It was a simple thing like that, and Cole made his decision. "Will you help me?"

"Of course," Peter smiled, "We're in this together, bud. To the end."

***

When Cole finally made his announcement in the living room that following Sunday after service, his mother had just taken off her Sunday best and was preparing lunch in the kitchen and his father had just turned on the television and kicked off his shoes ready to watch the game, only to find two little boys, holding hands, blocking the screen. There was a shaking in his hands, a great trembling in his knees, but Cole did as his friend had encouraged, speaking his mind ever so quietly for the first time.

Cole's father gave him that stern look he always gave whenever Cole did something wrong, or just sat there, gazing at nothing. Whenever Cole came to after one of his "moments", it was always greeted with furrowed brows and a snapping of fingers, the lipless frustration of his parents digging into him. He never was much of a listener. He was the kind of kid who'd almost get left behind on excursions, because some little thing caught his attention and trapped his thoughts as he absorbed its existence. Their doctor thought it was Attention Deficit Disorder. Medication was recommended but his parents decided against this. It wasn't like Cole was hyperactive—he was just silently distracted; too off in his own world, likely from distaste for the real one, and this day dreaming stirred his loving but insistent parents.

Peter was sent home straight away. He put up little resistance when the face of Cole's father boiled red. A brief phone call was made in the kitchen before Cole was ordered into the car. The ride to the church was made in silence. Cole shot quick glances to the rear-vision mirror from his place in the back, briefing the eyes of his father, whose white-knuckle hands gripped the wheel in barely restrained fury. His mother did not seem as disappointed, though this was little consolation and probably just hopefulness on Cole's part. The closer they got, the longer the waves of unease tumbled in Cole's stomach, his hand clutching the armrest tightly. The bravery Cole felt in those first few moments of his defiance was fading too quickly for his liking. Separated from his one true supporter, he dreaded another visit into the heart of that clamping terror, certain it would pin him down with the force of its grandeur until a submission was squealed out.

Carved out as a place of worship for a small congregation, The Free-Hill Church stood boldly on the corner of the Los Angeles street, a lone beacon of the old ways. Cole Watts had been a regular in the wooden building with the white picket fence and the big, domineering black cross out front since before he could speak, but when his parents ushered him past all the empty pews and the grand pulpit, all sense of familiarity left him. They were taking him to the pastor's den. Cole had never been in there before, not that he ever wanted to. He'd heard the stories. When Cole was sent into that dark lair, he was sent in alone.

Little life graced the room at first. All the blinds were drawn and the air hung heavy like a fog around Cole's face. Only the sound of a soft, labored breathing penetrated its darkened state, though the boy knew this would change soon enough. He knew that the man waiting for him would rise and then the air would start to boil.

The pastor sat in shadow behind his desk. In silence he motioned towards the seat. Cole shuffled into it, finding its woolen fabric comfortable, if only for the smallest moment.

Cole started to tap his knees together, over and over. A light was turned on at the desk, the bulb angled to him like the sun, ready to interrogate. He was too far away to feel its heat but the situation got him truly exposed, as if the light was right up in his face, tending his skin, making it perspire, shrinking his pupils. All of this leading to the airing of his petrified soul.

Lanky arms, belly always round, hair already graying. A slow, deliberate stride, you'd wait for him—he'd convince you it was worth it. Cole glanced at the pastor's neck. No throbbing veins; no redness in the cheeks. No hate blasting out of the mouth, none of that just yet.

The pastor pulled his chair right up to Cole, so close that Cole could smell his breath. Cole struggled to keep it together as his insides spluttered like mice ready to flee. *Avoid the eyes*, his little brain pleaded.

The pastor spread his legs and sat back in the high-backed chair. He cleared his throat.

The room was not stale anymore. Something much worse had taken its place.

"Why don't you want to know God, Cole?"

Cole looked off to the side, avoiding those voracious eyes and that breath that threatened fire.

Remember his hand, squeezed into yours. To the end...

"Because he knows you, Cole. Knows you better than you know yourself. He has the path set for you, and I assure you, it is the light. Don't you want to feel the light, the warmth all around?"

At that point, Cole didn't want to feel any warmth; he'd had just about enough as the pressure sweated out from all over him. Cole didn't answer—he couldn't—it seemed an impossible feat.

Cole's silence did not deter the pastor. Pastor West was used to hearing only his own voice and in many ways he liked it, for he knew his voice was the Lord's voice. The pastor held those in his flock as his personal responsibility, and he'd do whatever it took to guide them through safe passage to God. He considered their failures as his own, and, to a point he never admitted to anyone in particular, it reflected badly on his standing with the Lord. Whether Cole liked it or not, the young boy was his responsibility, now and forever.

"I know what you think. You think this place is boring. Every Sunday, stuck in the same old place. You just want to go outside and play. There's nothing wrong with that—but things will change, Cole. Life will get harder, and you will need guidance. Believe me when I say there is no better guidance than *His* word. God knows what's best. Let him take you there, so that *He* can banish the Devil who makes you indecisive; the Devil, who only wants to darken the path for you, trick you into thinking there's another way. Cole, look at me. Can you honestly tell me there is another way better than God?

Cole shrunk back into his chair. *Remember his hand, squeezed into yours. To the end...*

"Do you know the Devil, Cole?"

Cole knew the Devil. Knew about hell, the fire and brimstone, the searing of flesh for eternity, not just eons but every single moment thereafter. That was a long time to pay for a mistake, pay for a life Cole hadn't yet known. He was only ten. He didn't want to know this other world that curled the bones. He only cared for the world of youth and a friendly hand.

Cole wanted to plead ignorance before he understood the word.

"I know you're scared, Cole. I know your spine retreats when I talk about the Devil coming in and corrupting us. I don't say it to scare you. I say it because I want to save you, Cole. Your parents want to save you. Don't you think we know what's best?"

Remember his hand, squeezed into yours. To the end...

The pastor's eyes narrowed. His patience had run its short course. Like a snake, his arm struck at Cole's wrist, and the boy looked up into those fiery eyes properly for the first time. The veins on the pastor's neck began their throbbing and the grip on Cole's wrist clamped down. Cole tried to squirm back into his chair but there was nowhere to go. No escape. "You're going to listen to *him*—that smarmy, little piece of shit—over your own parents? Peter's just a child. He knows nothing! Mark my word. The godless will burn, boy. All of the sinners the same."

The pastor squeezed harder. The nails began to dig in. Cole shut his eyes, trying desperately to hold back the tears.

"You think that hurts? I do this out of love, boy. How hard do you think the Devil will squeeze? Tell me, Cole. Tell me, dammit!"

As the pastor bore into his soul, Cole's mind tried to feebly escape the room but could only make it as far as the door. He thought of his parents, waiting out there, letting this voracious tongue scorch away, and doing nothing. Why did they allow this man to scream at him? Why did everyone in Cole's tiny little world insist it was all for his own good?

When the crying had stopped, Cole was walked out steadily, his feet dragging because those knees of his had buckled some time ago. He clutched at his wrist, feeling its burn radiate. Waiting outside were his parents, the concerned ones. Pastor West followed from the darkness and a hand was placed on Cole's tiny shoulder. His mother and father looked apprehensively at him, and then up at Pastor West. The pastor shook his head.

Cole felt the attention draw over him, felt the disappointment.

Progress is Painful

2. Thailand

Every day was hot. Pools of sweat would lather around Christopher Jenkins and in the beginning he often lost his grip on the machete. By the third week, the calluses on his palms had hardened and the machete had slowly come round to staying by his hand, though he still hadn't gotten used to the heat. It sent his focus in and out, no matter how much he strained to steady himself. The sweat would roll into his eyes and the salt would sting as he tried to scan the ground and trees, searching for the little insignificant creatures that carried his hope, studying their tiny trails that would hopefully lead him to *her.*

Greg Bernstein had finally found her in a nest, a gigantic mound, but Jenkins had read that other species of ants made nests in trees, using leaves as their structures. He'd examined some of these leafy cocoons, but there were no signs of *her* presence. No signs of the purple anomaly.

On this day, like all the others, Christopher Jenkins looked at his map and checked the crosses. The path not yet taken ran deep through another thicket of trees. The prospect was tiring. A grim face was sweated out once more. Jenkins regarded the lightness of his camelbak, then looked up at the sky. The heat was unrelenting. There were at least five hours before the sun went down, but even when it set, the heat would stay, the air thick with it. The map gave him at least three quarters of a mile left in this direction. He groaned. He picked up his machete and started again.

Jenkins had lost a lot of weight since arriving in Thailand. There wasn't much of him to begin with, but one notices a certain loss of one's self when all the water is drained extensively from the body each day. Buzzing through this hostile heat came the mosquitos, an endless onslaught drilling into his skin. He'd brought eight rolls of repellent with him and still they continued their bombardment. The rashes spread like wildfire, and the itching never stopped. Jenkins had never been a physical man, not in all his forty-six years, and after his first day of searching he'd seriously doubted his own survival. He was never built for the outside world, and while he knew a great deal about nature, much of his knowledge had come from scientific books he'd studied as a child.

Jenkins had few friends growing up. He was always the smart one to the others around him, a fact he grew painfully aware of. He was a different kind of creature. The others could smell it. They'd all regard him with a budding curiosity at first, but this would soon give way to isolation and in some rare cases, hatred. The kids were cruel. It was rarely physical, but the wounds ran deeper than his pale skin. The years had buried an anger that grew inside these wounds, and in Jenkins' head, he'd come to know the culprits. It was everyone else. But this never rose to the surface—no, he kept such contempt to himself. And as everyone eventually seemed to leave Jenkins alone, he took their signal and swam further out. He shunned the outside world, the one that didn't want him, and found solace in the books he surrounded himself with. Over the years he grew fond of books about men who stood above the masses. These were the thinkers, the mathematicians, the scientists, and inventors—people who imagined a better world, and were the catalysts of sweeping waves of change through their discoveries. These were the makers of progress. Jenkins had read about their works and then he'd gone to looking at their upbringings, wondering if they'd known his pain, felt his loneliness. He needed to know it was necessary. For some, little had been written. For others, he felt a connection, for they too had been misunderstood.

***

Many hours later, when the sun had begun its descent behind a thick gray wall of smoggy sky, Jenkins looked back on the path he'd cleared, and once again taken out his map. He reluctantly took out his marker and added to the black crosses. Another day lost. His feet trudged slowly back to the hamlet where he stayed.

He made his usual route through where the Mae Si Muwang village had once been. All the wooden houses in this village had been demolished and cleared since the incident. The timber had been either burned or discarded into the forest. In the day it could pass for almost peaceful, but at night he'd pick up the pace, an urgency to leave this area always rustling his bones. He'd inspected it thoroughly when he first came over, but to no avail. Bernstein's sweeps had been equally comprehensive. Now it was just an empty chasm, a black hole of dirt that held an unspoken promise: that it would take something from you if you stayed there too long. Jenkins knew this and every day he rushed through, holding his breath. Once he'd passed this ghostly void, he re-joined a rural road, avoiding the next village to reach the hamlet where he stayed. Although it would make his journey much easier after a long day of searching to go through this connecting village, Jenkins knew exactly how it would play out if he had the nerve to show his face there. They'd send him out in disgust as the bad omen he knew he'd become. They'd call on Bondok and no amount of money would convince Bondok otherwise to send Jenkins out of the district, out of Thailand.

Mae La Noi District was less than seventy miles away from the Myanmar border. Staking part of the Yuam River systems, the people in the villages and hamlets of this peaceful district used it for fishing while their main source of income came from the rice fields they tended to.

It was over an hour of heavy slumping before Jenkins found his way back to his hamlet. The house where he stayed was at the end of the main road that linked them all. There were four other houses that made up this quiet space, all in view of each other during the day. The houses were a typical mix of wood and concrete, open pergolas where the families would eat and small dark bedrooms where electricity was slim and light was made by way of candles. Jenkins was always relieved to come back in the dark, avoiding the poisonous looks of his neighbors who remained weary of his presence in their quiet hamlet. He knew they always watched, but in the dark at least he couldn't see how many eyes trailed him. Often, he wondered how long the mother would let him stay while those looks descended upon her house and spread over to her. How much money was it all worth before the stigma of letting in the bad omen became too much to bear?

The boy saw him first. "Mr. Christopher!"

Jenkins smiled. A weak smile, a tired smile. But one he would always give to Chongrak Sintawichai. The boy came racing over, his sandals kicking up dust as they snapped along.

"Did you find it, Mr. Christopher?"

"No, Chongrak. Are you ready for checkers?"

The boy nodded with excitement before a thought crossed his mind, a reminder he'd been told to give to Mr Christopher. Chongrak's English was rudimental, he never had anyone else to practice on, but he wanted to learn so that he could move from his hamlet and eventually find better work in Bangkok. Jenkins had learned some Thai in the lead up to his journey here, but Chongrak had insisted they speak English, so that he may learn.

"Mr. Bondok, he come here…looking for you! He said he come back with new visa."

Jenkins cringed. Mr. Bondok was a government district official who knew enough to know Jenkins wanted his visit to the Mae La Noi District remain a secret. He knew Jenkins was not a part of any official follow-up investigation. Jenkins was just one man and Bondok's bribe had been hefty. Jenkins tried to remain cool, "Okay, okay. Thank you for telling me. *Khop khun khrap.*"

The boy repaid his thanks. "Mother has left you rice and chicken…Mr. Christopher, she wants more for stay—four hundred thousand baht. Three days."

Jenkins tired brain did the math in his head. Between her and Bondok he'd be broke soon, and they'd be happy to see the back of him, once that paper well of his had dried.

"Okay. I'll pay her in the morning."

"We play checkers after you eat?"

"Yes, Chongrak."

A giddy smile flashed over Chongrak. The boy ran back inside to get the checkers and candles. Jenkins slinked over to his room around the side of the house and removed all the grimy clothes from his body. He then went and filled a bucket of water and cleaned himself. When he was done, he went back around to the front of the house and walked up to the raised pergola.

A bowl of rice and chicken had been left out for him, though some flies had gotten to it. Swiping them away he caught the sight of the mother lying down in the darkness of her room, her eyes meeting his, a resigned look barely made out. She nodded to the food and he thanked her. She merely nodded back. He picked up the food and took it back to the pergola where he sat off the edge and ate his cold meal quietly.

They all knew why he was here and for this reason alone he understood their contempt. Chongrak's mother had been accepting at first, the only one in the village who would. She needed the money despite the darkness he carried. When Jenkins first arrived, Chongrak had asked if he could help Mr. Christopher find what he was looking for, and in that moment his mother had exploded with an emphatic NO. Jenkins respectfully agreed, believing it was not safe for the boy to be looking for such things. Chongrak eventually accepted this decision and soon found another way to spend time with Mr. Christopher and improve his English. They played checkers. During the day while Jenkins searched, the boy would go to work in the rice fields, come home, do his chores and then start practicing his skills on the other children in the hamlet before squaring up against Mr. Christopher every night—much to the chagrin of his mother. Jenkins would always let Chongrak win at least once each day, and to Jenkins' delight, Chongrak was getting much better.

Once, when they were playing, Jenkins had asked the boy what the other kids said about him, after Chongrak had mentioned that he practiced his checkers with the two girls down at the first house.

Chongrak was reluctant at first, but the words soon found their way out. "They mothers and fathers, they say you looking for evil things… Mother says you looking for evil things… Is this true, Mr. Christopher?"

Chongrak was still holding his red piece—it's placement undecided as it hovered over the board. Without taking his eyes off Chongrak, Jenkins took the boy's hand and placed it back on the board. Chongrak did not shy away from this. He did not tense up. He kept his eyes on Mr. Christopher, patiently waiting for his answer.

"They are right, Chongrak. The thing I'm looking for is evil. It has done evil things. But I want to make it good. Do you understand this, Chongrak? I want to make it good. I believe I'm the only one who can."

They hadn't spoken of its nefarious nature since, and tonight was no different. Tonight, Chongrak perched forward in silent determination to make his piece a king and take the board. But Jenkins saw his opportunity and double-jumped Chongrak's lead piece out of contention. Chongrak huffed at this, but kept playing through, simply so that he could ask for another rematch. It was at four games in that Chongrak's mother called for him to sleep. "Okay, Mr. Christopher. Tomorrow I will beat you two times!"

Okay, Chongrak. Of course you will.

Chongrak retreated to his mother's room and soon Jenkins heard the sting of hushed words spat at Chongrak. Jenkins stood there a moment, feeling guilty and yet knowing that Chongrak's company had been about just the only good thing to come out of this wretched place so far. He considered these two things in him, wondering if he was *man* enough to go in there and defend the boy, but knowing exactly how that would pan out. So he stayed silent and turned in for the night.

Lying in his basic bed, kept awake by the heat, Jenkins found his thoughts returning once again to his internal circle of doubt, an inevitable destination he ended up every long night. Sitting deep within its familiar pattern, he wondered if what he was looking for needed to be found, if what he was doing here made sense. And on this night like many others when the doubts crept in and Jenkins had to strengthen his walls of reassurance, he lit a small candle next to his bed, got out his copy of Greg Bernstein's report and read it once more, even though by now he could sing it from memory.

Notes from Greg Bernstein (20/01/2013): *The police squad had killed all of his family members and four of his neighbors, who all acted as cover for the father, taking on all the bullets meant for him. And when all eight of them had been slain, the father finally surrendered. While in custody, the father, with his gap-filled rows of decaying teeth, talked about making the police do things for him, telling them in no uncertain terms to set him free. The man's face would strain, as if he could compel them some way to making this happen, but when nothing happened, the man would sulk in frustration. When I personally asked why this man had done what he did, his reply was simple if not vague.* พวกเขาจะไม่เข้าร่วมเสียงของฉัน. *"They wouldn't join my voice."*

There had been a slaughter in Mae Si Muwang, two villages over from where Christopher Jenkins now lay in his bed. A farmer and his family (along with four others) had seemingly snapped, playing brutal murderers to everyone else in this particular village. Nine people. All except one, a child, who had escaped and informed the people of the next hamlet over. When the authorities came rushing in, they'd found the farmer and his family en route to the other village, weapons in hand.

Greg Bernstein was CIA. He had been dispatched from Bangkok to do the fieldwork for Blackwater. The locals whispered talk of demonic possession, some kind of shamanic work at hand. It was true that the CIA had a familiar history with strange acts of "unexplainable" madness. They'd observed ergot outbreaks in France in the fifties, but there was nothing of the sort in this Thai bunch. This was different. This was a peaceful village, once. The report was of a strange madness, soon followed by a resounding obedience to the head farmer: the father. The main account of this twisted occurrence had come from the only survivor, the father himself. And by the time Jenkins had made it to Thailand, his chances of extracting blood work from the father were long gone. The man was beaten to death in prison shortly after his conviction, his remains incinerated.

* * *

The next morning Jenkins awoke in the dark. Six a.m. The only cool part of the day and a very short window indeed. The house was empty, Chongrak and his mother already on their way to the fields. Usually Jenkins would be ready by the time the heat came: a shower with the bucket, a full camelbak, and a designated search route for the day. But today he just lay there. Because those questions he'd asked of himself before sleep took him—the one's he'd asked countless times before—started gnawing away in his head with a ferocity he'd never encountered before, each question and its subsequent failure pinching hard at the brain in torturous rumination. The downward spiral began. What if the others were right? What if his psych evaluations were reasonable justification for them leaving him out in the cold to the greatest discovery of the twenty-first century—the thing he'd been searching for his whole life, something that would ensure all those years of learning within the loneliness would finally be worth it. And what if he found it (a goddamn miracle at this point) and he didn't end up like the farmer? What if he ended up like poor Greg?

He lay there till the sun rose and the overbearing heat came like it always did. He lay there staring at the ceiling while his hands gripped the frame of the bed, fingers clenched in silent, pitiful anger. It had taken them two months to find it the first time, and in those last couple of days it had been Greg searching alone, everyone else having given up. Jenkins had been here almost two months. But they were a party of fifty to begin with. He was just one person.

And when the voice inside told him to get up, to keep going, he felt its tether on him too weak. He could only see another day, sweating in the heat, surrounded by endless, mocking greenery as he tried to bear its empty promises once again. So he rose from his bed, went to his clothes bag, and rummaging through his trekking gear he dug out from the bottom a bottle of forty-year old scotch. He was never much of a drinker at all, but the very idea of opening up a bottle of refined class, a quiet celebrant for when he was finally reunited with *her*, had been a warm hope to have.

Now, with a cold, defeated emptiness, Jenkins took off the lid and started drinking.

***

When Agent Bernstein had returned from Thailand with the first samples, there was a buzz in Blackwater, and Dr. Jenkins was feeling it in every single pulse. A once quiet man in the eyes of his peers, Jenkins' eagerness to study Tyrantocillous (named for the way it made the farmer act) had exploded into this bursting enthusiasm that left his many colleagues deeply unsettled at his sudden opening up. Sure, it was an incredible breakthrough and everyone was fascinated by it—but Jenkins' eyes had the others scared, causing his peers to reconsider their own excitement, as a weary caution took its place. His eyes were too eager.

He'd had four days to examine this purple entity, found oozing like a volcano out of an ants nest thousands of miles away in a country so alien to him at this point. Four days, before he was called into his supervisor's office and told he was to be reassigned—separated from studying *her.* He was furious when told by his superior that they were suspending its study for the time being, the main line of reasoning being its high potential for danger. *But Blackwater was bio-weapons*, Jenkins had countered internally. And this had the potential to be their greatest weapon. Had everyone just suddenly gone trigger-shy? It was impossible to think that for once in their life, the uppers had realized it would be beyond their control, that curious minds had thought better of it. Jenkins remembered the desperateness in his whole being that day. He lied—what if our enemies have it? What if they get wind? We need to understand it so we can develop a vaccine. His superior looked him over with eyebrows raised. *You really think I'm buying that?*

But they had not suspended the study of Tyrantocillous. The superior—a well reasoning man—had seen something in Jenkins most unsettling; a spark in the eyes he'd never witnessed before. He'd read the psych evaluations and he knew too well about the case of Dr. Bruce Ivin, the former USAMRIID scientist who had sent letters containing Anthrax to members of congress. Everyone had missed Ivin, and this recent history played in the back of the superior's mind when he regarded Jenkins' wired eyes. Just a hunch, but it seemed enough to warrant Jenkins off the case file for Tyrantocillous.

"I'm going to be frank with you, Chris. There's been talk among the others about your…*over enthusiasm* for this case. They've brought their concerns to me."

Jenkins was beside himself, and behind those incensed brows he struggled to react to this building accusation. "My enthusiasm? Well of course I'm enthusiastic! I'm a virologist, and this is a virus that has caused behaviors in humans unheard of before!" As soon as the sentence had left his mouth, Jenkins' lips tightened back up, and he blushed—as if he'd revealed a deep secret.

His superior, having heard these words and the manner in which they were spoken, was reassured in that moment of his decision. "Chris, it looks like you haven't slept since the samples came back. It *smells* like you haven't showered either… I'm reassigning you."

Jenkins' gasped in disbelief, his insides reeling, utterly devastated. He'd blown it. He'd shown too much of his true self.

The reasoning was blunt. His psych evaluations had been cited, tied neatly with his own signature agreeing to the conditional requirements of his employment. It was inferred that refusal to comply with reassignment meant the termination of his contract. His superior then informed him that his colleagues were not to discuss the case with him whatsoever. When this barrage had finished, his superior tried to calm him down and talk about the positives; how he'd taken into consideration Jenkins' crucial work developing vaccines for the Elkins Influenza when everyone else had failed. These were the reasons, Jenkins was told, that he was also too good to lose, and would stay in the system. The anger lurched deep in his face and Jenkins was told to take the rest of the day off to come to terms with it.

***

Jenkins woke to the kicking of his feet, the soles of his shoes. His eyes rolled over to a hurried figure kneeling beside him. Chongrak. The boy turned around, a frantic flash in his eyes. The sun was going down, and as Jenkins came to realize this, he thought to himself, Another day lost, another year gone, an entire life: over.

Chongrak began shaking him.

"Mother no see you like this. Cannot, cannot!"

"It's over, Chongrak. They must've cleaned it up. I'd hoped they didn't, that they missed something, but they destroyed everything. It's all gone."

"Hurry, Mr. Christopher, Mother come soon! Please!"

Seeing Chongrak desperate, his eyes swelling, sent Jenkins into a sprawling action, if only to please the boy. He managed to stand and stumbled over to his bedroom. Before his door was shut, Jenkins scrambled to find his hidden wad of cash. He returned to the door just as Chongrak's mother emerged from the dirt path and spotted him looking guilty, as if in the act of some great conspiracy. Jenkins then forced the money into Chongrak's cupped hands and told him to leave it in his mother's room. The boy nodded and Jenkins closed himself in.

Soon there was yelling. At one stage Chongrak was pleading.

Then came the thudding of angry feet towards his door. Her silent seething of his presence in this household had gone on for too long. Chongrak's mother exploded. She barged open Jenkins door and flung the empty bottle of scotch at the wall near Jenkins feet. Shards flung around the room while the sound of the smash reached the whole hamlet.

Her eyes were a dark fire, sending Jenkins startling up into the corner of his bed.

"You! End of week, you leave! No more, no more! You bring bad spirit into this house. You bring bad things. Don't talk to my son anymore! When my husband gets home from city, you leave! You don't leave—I call Bondok. He'll make you!"

Jenkins was left paralyzed by her fury. All he could manage was a slight nod, a silent promise of compliance and a soft pleading of sorry.

She left without saying another word, slamming the wooden door shut, the force reverberating it. And Jenkins, alone once again, began to weep. Forty-six years old, and nothing he saw to show for it.

***

In the morning his bags were packed. The money he owed to Chongrak's family was paid and then some. The house was empty as per usual this time of morning. Jenkins drifted around the house, taking stock of his fruitless existence within its walls. He made his way over to the pergola and sat down along the edge where he'd once eaten his quiet meals. He looked far out into the vegetation of Thailand. So this was it. He'd done his best and he'd failed miserably. The sum of him: a large and absolute zero. He cursed this purple ghost, feeling it just waiting—begging—to be found, and knowing without a doubt that this enigma would surely haunt him for the rest of his miserable life.

But Jenkins knew he could not leave. It was really never an option, for this obsession was all he had left. It was all he was now. And by some old instinct that had stayed in him, kept this torch of his lit, he found himself setting his bag aside and pulling out his map. He opened it up and gazed not at all the crosses he'd inscribed along its weathered form, but at the small, slight trail not yet crossed off, untouched.

One last path.

He looked up again at the sprawling mass of green vegetation far off before him and those instincts, the ones that bore hope, crawled back along his spine; filling his feet with a surging energy, a pulse of possibility.

Why did he persist? Why had he flown a thousand miles away from home to look for this strange scrape of alien shit in a land that was drying him out from the inside? Why did he risk his job trying to sneak into the level four containment chambers after his reassignment, only to find his authorization revoked? Why did he think this was the solution when all the others only saw madness? Why did his eyes, his gut, everything in him, light up at the prospects? Did no one else see—were they too scared, too blinded? He'd gathered a theory, a possibility, a notion of sorts that snowballed around his head till it was all that was left. There was something in the father's story they all seemed to miss. Why had his loved ones taken the bullets for him? In those first expansive days of the discovery, those first four days he'd had with *her*, he'd asked this very question to his colleague, Theodore, one of the friendlier ones.

"Isn't the answer in your question?" Theo had replied. "They were his loved ones."

Jenkins remembered he had tried to understand this, brush off a "why yes of course that's it" look. *Of course I know that's what you do for the one's you love.* And when their small talk had ended, Jenkins sat back in his chair and tried to imagine what it would be like to have a loved one. Someone he'd take that bullet for…

But there was more. There had to be more. The neighbors had followed the father's will to their deaths. Surely they hadn't done it out of love. There had to be something in the virus that made them obey. There was something out here in this quiet stretch of Thai villages more powerful than anything else in the world.

Notes from Greg Bernstein (18/1/2013): *The child, the one who alerted the townspeople in the village over; when he was stuck in that undergrowth, too scared to come out, he told me he saw them bowing, on their hands and knees, all in a line, all facing the farmer. Listening to his every word.*

Jenkins' feet were soon moving. They marched toward the path, the only one he saw left. *She* was still here. *She* just had to be.

He would keep looking.

3. College Dropout

Before a single plane fell.
    Before the madness spread,
    Before thoughts drew blood,
    Before the gray robes made their purification,
    And before the obedience followed…
    There was a boy, a mess of a boy, sat staring at the shitty green wallpaper inside his cramped, one-bedroom apartment, wondering how everything had gone so wrong. He was the size of a man but not quite yet filled out, just a skinny frame of pasty skin. His face was stuck in a look of potent despair, every so often running his bony hands through his dark, shaggy mess of hair to scratch away at the worries inside his head. Over the years his facial features had formed into a sorry expression of doubt; his dark brown eyes perpetually squinting as windows of eternal uncertainty. But this would all change that fateful night, for this boy was right on the cusp of meeting his other half—the girl that would bring him to life and send him tumbling in the wild ocean that was love—even if at this very moment all he could see was

a slippery slope and no signs of a foothold for miles. This was Cole Watts, so close, yet so far.

He'd been drinking too much. Not today, a good thing he figured—it'd only make things worse. No, he'd been drinking too much ever since he packed his bags and moved away from his parents. He'd been staring at walls. He'd been thinking about all the wrong things. It was sometimes being lobotomized from the weed, or sometimes that usual place, that absent state of mind where the thoughts would swirl in and swirl out. Ever since he'd laid his feet on the ground here it'd been nothing but the same: drinking and smoking, looking for fun in all the easy corners. No wonder the grades had fallen. He was just hitting the same button over and over, looking to keep his mind in a perpetual state of groundhog play. For a good while, it had worked. But now, with time passing and little to show, it had all caught up and Cole was left disappointed in his circle of routine. For instance, how long had he been here and not gone out into the wide expanses of natural beauty that was Colorado? Two years of sitting in lectures—barely interested—and then washing it all down in the same bars with the same people. Then Frannie, Phil's wife (and a dear friend) has a stroke and Phil asked Cole to pick up some more shifts. What was he to do? He owed the Nixons everything. They'd become a second family to him. Phil needed all the help he could get. The Grocer struggled as it was, what with the new Walden's opening up a block down. It was Phil's livelihood; his father had passed on the shop to him.

Cole knew business. He'd studied business even though he knew he had no business doing that degree. Even if he didn't know the supposed ins and outs of the market place, it was plain as day for anyone to see that the times weren't great, not just for him. What was he to tell Phil? That this was just nature, just the market, just you're wife having a serious glimpse at the other side and now you're business is ready to do the same: *good luck with it all.*

Even if he had been so blunt, Cole knew Phil would've understood. Phil would've brushed Cole off and told him to focus on his studies. But on those quiet shifts when Cole was restocking the vegetables, he'd watch Phil milling about in the back room, a heavy heart lost in silence, a cooing animal feeling the walls of the world closing in, and Cole knew he couldn't say no.

It was wrong to think that Frannie's misfortune had been the reason Cole's GPA had taken a complete and utter nose-dive through the pool floor. It was wrong to think his own failures as a student and as a person were tied to the poor blood flow of a green grocer's lovely wife. But in some ways he couldn't help it. *If only she hadn't gotten sick...*

No, In truth those grades had been falling well before any of that happened, and it wasn't because of the extra work or the endless escapades Peter dragged him along for, it was the motivation: it had all dried up, if it was ever there to begin with. The degree wasn't for him. It wasn't even for his parents. He'd just taken it because he believed that's what you do. That's what everyone else did. And now, as most people end up doing, whether it was at twenty-one or fifty-one, Cole was sat in his shitty one-bedroom apartment with the green wallpaper peeling off the walls, wondering where the hell he was going and what the hell he was going to do...

There was a knocking on the door. The familiar three bangs then the clear impersonation of a most serious voice.

"Someone order a sausage pizza?"

Peter Storrs could be eloquent, cheeky, elitist, snobbish, charming, dazzling, athletic, superior, and caring, but he saved all his dick jokes for Cole Watts.

Through the door: *"I got lots of sausage here. Big n'juicy! Tell me where to put it!"*

For some reason, as many as twelve years ago, Peter had met Cole when they were just young sprouts in that poorly ventilated church, and, seemingly on a whim—had taken Cole for a ride. They'd gone exploring underneath the church, crawling between the many pipes that fed into the Lord's house above. They then played tag when service ended, even after both their parents had flipped when they saw the dirt that was caked onto their Sunday best. It seemed that on that day, Peter had tagged Cole and decided, "You're it buddy. We're friends for life now, right to the end." And little Cole had thought yeah why not. They'd stuck together ever since. Peter was the reason Cole had chosen Colorado University. The first time Cole tried his first beer, smoked his first joint—that was Peter. Peter was the leader, the excitement. Most of the fun things were done on his fearless discretion and whenever Cole obliged Peter's notions he'd often have a bustling new story to tell, even if they usually got into trouble for it.

But now, with a raring Peter knocking on the door, two six-packs probably in tow, Cole found himself gritting his teeth. He just wanted the lights turned out and the world to disappear. Because he needed time to think, figure out the best way to break it to his parents. He always remembered his mother's warnings that Peter Storrs was trouble, as early on as the day Cole was sitting in that car driving away from the church where that Pastor had given him the choice—*his first choice.* The truth was that things had never been the same with his parents after that. With great reluctance they'd accepted his decision that day, and while they eventually came to respect him having his own personal beliefs, for many years a young Cole was reminded of their disapproval every Sunday morning; when his parents would coldly leave the house without saying goodbye, leaving a little kid all alone.

The concept of parallel universes had a way of getting into Cole's head sometimes, especially when his world wasn't looking so bright, and in a moment of weakness Cole disregarded his best friend for the better half of twelve years and wondered what life would've been like if he'd taken the safer route: submitted to Pastor West, just like his parents had wished. Never mind what he believed, this was easier. Besides, he was already good at following the lead of others, so it seemed logical at least.

"C'mon, man. Open the door you unrelenting dong."

Cole sighed. "Yeah, all right! Fuck. Just…gimme a second."

"Quit busting one out and let me in! These drinks aren't going to down themselves!"

The door was creaked open slightly. Cole made it clear in his droopy, unimpressed face that he wasn't in the mood. He'd made it clear over the phone before, but Peter was persistent, Peter knew he could be very persuasive.

Peter frowned when he saw Cole's face. It was worse than he thought. The door was then swung fully open and the darkness of Cole's situation was thrust into Peter's slick going-out loafers. Peter's tune abruptly changed and now the good friend, the great listener, appeared from out of a charmingly sharp face. "Jesus! I knew you were in the deeps over the phone, but this looks bad."

"I fucked up. It's bad."

"How *bad* is bad?"

Cole slumped back into his couch and was soft in his answer.

He ran his fingers through his short mess of hair before scratching his head in frustration. "I've already failed every course this semester. I can't do jack shit to make up for it in the finals."

There was too long of a silence after that.

"Oh, Cole…"

"It was just…with the job at the grocer each night, I didn't have time to…and Phil needing me because of Frannie and—"

"Man you've got to tell Phil that you need more time off work. I know that shit with Frannie sucks, but this is your life, man. You're here for college."

Cole grated. They'd had this conversation before; he'd had it with himself a thousand times over. "Phil needs me. I owe him and Frannie. I can't just cut and run now, *you know that.*"

This shut Peter up. He did know how much Phil and Frannie had helped Cole along, helped him when Peter had promised just as much before Cole followed him to Colorado. But Peter had been unable to do that, and Cole understood. Peter had his own shit to sort out and he was very apologetic that he hadn't been able to help Cole fully like he'd first intended.

"Well, fuck." Peter let out after a while.

"Fuck indeed."

Peter looked around the room and took in the black hole that was becoming Cole's life, the vacuous darkness that threatened to tear all the shitty green wallpaper off the walls and suck it all in. But Peter had plans, he'd already solved Cole's immediate dissatisfaction—he was holding the refreshing solution in twelve cans and the many more that would follow down at the Rancher. He tapped the cans with a "how bout it" motion.

Cole knew his answer, and took to its predictability with disdain.

Isn't this the reason I'm in this mess—failing college—struggling through life?

"Oh c'mon, dear, don't blame the beer. At least not tonight!"

Cole dug his head into his bony hands. "What am I going to tell my parents?"

Peter rolled his eyes at this. *Tell them you fucked up, it's normal. You bounce back. It's not the end of the world.*

"I'm sure they'll pray for you—*a little extra than they usually do.*"

Cole looked up at those eyes. They had the energy of the night swelling in them, beckoning him to go exploring, even in familiar places. They were the eyes that wanted to get laid. And in their enthusiasm, Cole was left dreaming up his own possibilities for the night. This was the hook Peter always played. Cole wasn't a great wingman, nor did he really need to be. Peter was always smooth. Peter had plans. Cole's eyes took to the beer and then, like a reflex, reached out to its cold, familiar skin. Peter grinned. *Remember brother, to the end.*

And though Cole could not see it now with the darkness fogging his world, that would be the night that he met her—the girl that would change his life, explode his horizons till he saw all the great colors in their richest texture—and the end they always spoke of, well it got a little closer.

4. At First Sight

It was the burrito. Somewhere between the piling glop of guacamole, salsa, and fried potato, an unwanted guest had made a home. A microscopic bug, ready to cause havoc on those poor souls flocking to the Salsa+, craving a late night snack.

The problem, according to "Detective" Claire, was that the prime suspect had been undercooked. It had been shilled out much quicker than normal, though neither Claire nor Maddie had complained at the time. And now, in the early hours of the morning, they clutched at porcelain, removing said culprit.

"It has to be the burrito," Claire declared, as if this was the first time she'd come up with this theory.

"The vodka didn't help." Maddie added.

The mere mention of the word sent both stomachs churning, and heads were once more buried into bowls, Maddie in the washbasin and Claire in the toilet, under the burning bright light of the bathroom that gave their deeds an ugly clarity.

After wiping another round from her face, Claire cleared her throat. "Those boys were cute," she noted, slyly working her way up to a recap of the night. Maddie grimaced at this; *there's a time and a place, Claire, a time and a place.*

"…Though I wonder the look on their faces if they found us like this," added Claire.

"Lets hope the wind doesn't change on us, if that's the case."

Claire stood slowly and flushed the toilet, deciding she was done, that this little nuisance of food poisoning was gone. She took the band out of her jet-black hair, letting it all flow softly to her shoulders, and then she was waltzing out, readying herself for bed as if nothing was the matter, but that was Claire for you. When Claire left the bathroom, Maddie clawed her way over to the toilet, an upgrade if only for the fact one could sit down and get "comfortable" while the bug played hell with the stomach and the vodka made the world spin.

"Dammit, Claire. I've got class at nine tomorrow. Why do I let you drag me into these things?"

"Oh don't be that way, that place was cool. Besides, its good prep for when you finally have to front all the screaming little runts, post-hangover."

"Hopefully I won't be foolish enough to follow you by then. Lets just get through college first… Correction, let's just make it to tomorrow."

Claire returned to the bathroom, oblivious to Maddie's groaning, intent on letting her thoughts return to the boy she'd met. "So, we both know I'm going to start talking about him, and, since I've got your full, undivided attention: what do you think of that guy, Peter?"

Just as Claire asked this, Maddie was looking down into the bowl, noticing Claire had failed to flush properly. Somehow, it's always just that little bit more repulsive when it's not your own.

Another surge was forced out.

"That bad huh," Claire joked. "Well, Don't give me any shit for supposedly 'dragging' you out—even though I guess there was that point where I had to literally drag you out of bed—but so what! It was fun and don't you dare tell me otherwise. What about Peter's friend? Mopey-Dick. Seemed to light up when he saw you. What was his name?"

Without waiting for an answer, Claire was off to bed, leaving Maddie to wait it out. As Maddie sat there, she was reminded of the boy, pre-burrito, and a soft smile bloomed across her face.

Then, as if to ruin her sweet little moment of reflection, came the stomping of footsteps toward the bathroom, Claire joining Maddie once more.

5. A Brave New World

The question was why.

And to Jenkins, the answer had to be yes. It just had to.

It had to be done.

He swirled her round and round in her vial. He'd been doing this nightly for the past two months, always in the dark, always the same question, always the same answer. The time was approaching.

There were many reasons, many justifications. And every day they grew stronger. He'd spoken it to his people many times before; the earth was dying, its inhabitants in denial. How long could they make those machines, prop up those systems that bred more and more of the insatiable want, until the air was suffocated in it? The people were a hungry cancer that always demanded more—not better, but more. A cancer without eyes, eating everything. No brakes in sight.

It had to be done. The people had to be changed.

And He wasn't going to be the only one. He knew that much. There would be no parade for him—the glory would be in someone else's name. But he would know it started with him, this great change, and that had to count for something. He would know that he was saving the planet, saving humanity by transforming it. There was going to be blood. Change was never easy. It was never without sacrifice. But the ground had to be soiled, moistened for *her* growth—all of it for their own good.

The girl sat opposite him in the foyer. She asked questions, and this made him smile. She was still curious, a look of naivety still holding on in those dark eyes, even when it coursed through her veins, flooding the brain with his lengths of chain. She was the daughter of the field agent, the one from Thailand who had caught the rudimental strain, dressed in a purple liquid that did peculiar things to the brain, a most profound re-arrangement. This field agent, Greg Bernstein, was the first US citizen to catch it, but he would certainly not be the last.

Jenkins swished it around again in its vial. He felt the weight of a world on his shoulders, not the world that existed, but the possible one. How long had Jenkins been thinking about it? Contemplating its release? The ramifications, all at his finger tips.

Pandora's box,

The genie out of the bottle,

A brave new world.

He'd carried death in his hands before, the heavy hitters— covered hands in sterile labs. But those ones, the small poxes and influenzas—they could only destroy.

This was different, this purple creature. While everything else would debilitate, haemorrhage, constrict—this did not.

She was a strange exception.

The interaction caused a change in the host—a greater susceptibility—if the host survived the initial stages. Those initial stages, they were the stuff of violent nightmares, an inconsolable madness. They were not pretty, even Jenkins had to admit that. But there lay a hope behind this incessant wall of seeming self-destruction. There was a chance for a better tomorrow, and Jenkins would bring it to them.

If there was any proof it should be done, any evidence to suggest that what he was doing was not right, had to be expelled by the fact of his genes. Of all the small traces of people given the opportunity to feel it in its godly power, it had matched with Jenkins' blood perfectly.

Destiny was beckoning.

Three and a half years. Three and a half years since that fateful morning, that desperate day when he finally found her among the shrubs, like she'd been waiting all along. On his knees he'd cried that day, the greatest joy he'd ever known. It was that joy that kept him going these long three and a half years; kept him slogging toward the future he dared to prescribe.

Yet even after all the efforts at building her resilience, she was still a vulnerable little thing, and like any worried parent, he was scared about the release. There were too many variables for his liking. Even though he could now read the human mind better than anyone else, it was hard letting go, leaving her survival up to chance. He'd grown too accustomed to having a heavy hand on all the pieces.

Jenkins drew a deep breath. He carefully returned the vial into its black box and then placed it onto the glass coffee table in front of him. He took another look at the girl—her eyes still one of questioning and a very deep obedience. Rising to his feet, he left the white-walled foyer and opened the heavy steel doors of the compound, stepping out into the warm, Texas night.

There was a full moon. They say that when it was full, the moon did funny things to people. Somewhere, emergency wards were filled out, packed to the nauseating brim with the weird cases, people who knew very little of what they were doing; the Earth's magnetism misaligning their bearings, making everyone kooky and letting the kooks sing loud. Caesar was killed during a full moon. Rome was ransacked. And the people were left unaware of the beaming force hundreds of thousands of miles away that guided their tiny, strange choices.

The glint of the moonlight was enough to glance the time on his wristwatch—11:47; the clock was ticking and Jenkins felt its eternal march passing through, slowly drifting away from him. He still had time, but was weary of the numbers passing into twelve. A decision had to be made by tonight. It had been in his bones for far too long—the wrestle, long and arduous. He felt the pressure of the world in him, all its vibrations urging him onward, shaking his core.

Jenkins used to work for Blackwater. Blackwater was a small sector within USAMRIID, short for United States Army Medical Research Institute of Infectious Diseases. Its specialty was in deconstructing weaponization capabilities of viruses and tracking population spreads, specifically through vectors. Often though, Jenkins and his other colleagues would be assigned to help the wider arms of USAMRIID.

All the others in Blackwater had wanted to do was *know*. To them, the concept of bio-weapons was an ugly term, one that they shied away from. Sure, they held a lofty reverence for these molecular monsters, but above all they just wanted to know, to understand so that they could help the world through developing cures and vaccines; the checks and balances against the awesome power of nature's first critters. One could say that Jenkins was the same way. He wanted to help the world, he just believed in a different method.

Jenkins had set up his Texas sanctuary just like Blackwater. A cold gray memory of concrete and containment chambers—a miniature Fort Detrick, a one man Blackwater. In some ways he'd like to think that he'd never left, and this was merely an improvement on the old place because here he was free to run wild. Taking in that full moon, Jenkins walked further out and looked back on his sanctuary, his home. Seeing it in standing strong in the moonlight, everything he had, poised for the final step, Jenkins was brought back to where it all began, when he first felt that buzz in Blackwater during those initial periods, the birth of his dream. He was more than just younger, he was alive, and it almost felt like it was for the first time. And then, just as the eager minds had begun to study *her* in earnest, there was a death.

***

He first saw the girl at the funeral. She was too young then, and many would argue she was too young to be doing the things she'd be doing only four years later. They'd received the samples from Bernstein, and while Jenkins and the others in the lab contained themselves studying with enthusiastic vigour this tiny stretch of purple substance, Bernstein had gotten sick.

It was the madness. Somehow it'd taken a full week for the symptoms to show, a mishandling of the pure sample, not the samples contaminated with the blood of the farmer, but the ones from the anthill. The scientists at Blackwater were informed of Bernstein's failing condition. Bernstein was quarantined in his local hospital over in Langley before moves were made to have him transferred to the Blackwater facility in Fort Detrick for treatment and testing. But he never made it.

There were over a thousand people at his funeral. Popular guy, thought Jenkins. For a moment Jenkins wondered how many would come to his, but the thought was quickly discarded, too depressing to fully vex.

The toxicology report had been changed. Dengue fever. Nothing contagious. Bernstein's wife pressed the authorities for a better explanation than the one stated. Bernstein was perfectly fine for two days upon arrival. It had to be something else. But the wife got nowhere. It was all blacked out. Media ban. Everything set up to keep the noses away.

Jenkins watched them the whole time the processional continued, but they took no notice. There was a deep sadness in them both, the wife and daughter. They were lost in a sea of unknowing, an unspeakable loss. From afar Jenkins had nothing to offer them. He wasn't especially good with words and lord knows how he'd be able to comfort crying people, even though he knew a lot about the long emptiness.

The girl, the daughter of that poor field agent, still so young, would be his first. He found her on the street while looking for test subjects—people no one would miss.

At first he had done a double take, his head spun round in tight circles, wondering if it really was her. But the more he grew convinced it was Bernstein's daughter, the more poetic it seemed.

Her jean jacket was ripped, and her body itched in need of whatever took the pain away. Her lips were cracked, her eyes empty. How long had it taken before the emptiness had led her to this street? How long had she stood upright, keeping the banisters of her shaken world steady, before the grief overtook her and she just needed to escape?

She didn't recognize Jenkins, nobody would have, nor would he have expected her to. He paid for the room, throwing in an extra one hundred and forty, and as she sat on the bed, preparing, Jenkins offered her something more. A drink. A purple flavored Kool-Aid.

She waved her hand off. "No thanks—you got anything stronger?"

"This is plenty strong."

She regarded him with suspicion, her mind working out the manoeuvres for a possible escape. There'd been close calls before, but he was much older, and seemed childishly nervous, almost afraid he would hurt her. Was it a date rape drug? But that didn't make sense. He'd already paid for her. "This isn't going to put me under is it?"

"No."

This is the solution, Lola.

It took less than a week. She was more susceptible than her father. And more importantly, she survived those initial stages, the unholy sounds from within, just as Jenkins had endured. And he held her, kept her together. And with training, with Jenkins' own infected blood that reaped the gift, the power of control, he taught the girl a new world, a brave new world.

And soon she'd forgotten about her father.

She'd forgotten about the mother who blamed the government but couldn't say a goddamn word about it.

She'd forgotten about her mother taking her own life.

She'd forgotten about all the foster homes they cycled her through, after those family friends seemed to just disappear.

She'd forgotten about all those desperate nights, trying to forget.

She was taken in by a man who became her legal guardian and eventually her lover, her master.

She would come to know only his words.

And together they built their following, his small army made of nobodies, miscreants given purpose. It was not an easy task, but always the light at the end of the tunnel held firm. Some died during the transition, either during or after the madness had subsided (that came to be expected), but they passed under the radar all the same. Jenkins took out loans. He sold his old house. They pooled their money (both saved and stolen) and built the compound, his dream facility; the one he now stood by the entrance of, regarding the full moon and its maddening properties. All the way down in the middle of West Texas, where *she* could be produced in safe conditions. All two hundred and sixty-four gallons.

***

Three and a half years it had taken him since that desperate day in Thailand—where the bags were packed and he was ready to quit, and Lola, dear sweet Lola was his first and the youngest. All he needed now was someone with the right connections. Someone with the ability to plant the seeds in all the right positions before the topsoil was destroyed. Jenkins knew this person, as did most.

The time had struck twelve, and a resolution had been reached in his slight grin. It had to be done.

Jenkins returned to the foyer where the girl waited patiently. Lola knew the answer before his lips moved. He led her down the spiral stairs, further underground, past the glass containment cages where the new recruits slept, into his study. From behind, he led her attention to the corkboard in the corner of the room, every inch of it filled with the newspaper clippings.

Jenkins rested his hands on her shoulders. Lola, now seventeen, pointed to the largest picture on the corkboard, and with a look of child-like derision, cast her disgust.

It was a man with a large white cowboy hat, the photo taking him mid-sentence, his whole face snarling. While Lola did not know why his face was set the way it was, Jenkins knew.

The man was crying witch-hunt.

Jenkins had money enough to renew the complex, a former cold war survivalist bunker (that had been a feat in itself) but he needed more. He needed access to certain water treatment facilities and he needed his infiltration widespread and unnoticed. He'd also need to wipe clean whatever research those at Blackwater had made on *his* baby, including any possible vaccine. The people in the paper were very mad at the man with the large white cowboy hat, and in that snapshot, Jenkins saw a man backing up hard against the wall, looking for a solution to all his problems. Jenkins believed he had that solution.

"That's the one—he's the guy?" asked Lola.

Jenkins gaze burned deep against the cowboy. It wasn't ideal, but they didn't live in an ideal world. Not just yet, anyway. "Yes, that's our guy. He's perfect."

6. Networking

On a dirt track road, somewhere close to the middle of nowhere, West Texas, a white Cadillac streamed across the listless arid landscape. Its destination: a big concrete compound nestled into a quiet ridge. Inside the white Cadillac, the driver kept steady on the wheel. He wore sunglasses and a black suit, handgun holstered by the waist, while the owner of the vehicle sat upright in the back. The owner was known by many names, few of them good. An anxious, broad face simmered under his white cowboy hat. When the view of the compound greeted him, a single bead of sweat escaped his forehead. His heart jumped out at him. *Should have brought more than Charles,* he cursed to himself. He knew about kidnappings, had done a few training courses; a person of his stature had to know such things. At one stage or another through an illustrious empire-building career he was a board member and CEO of United Petroleum, Hydro-Electric, had previous associations with Enron (which he strictly denied) and was the proud owner of four bottled water plants. He had his own Houston Newspaper Syndicate that simmered with his calls for secession—all of this before his most recent, highly publicized attempt to embed himself in politics in the name of cleaning it up.

This had been his undoing.

It was that bastard Roland—oh he hated him with the purest of white-hot rage. Who was Roland to call him crooked—a bad businessman—bad for America? What the fuck did he know? That piece of shit was just as dirty, and worst of all, he always came out clean as a fucking whistle. Approval ratings like Viagra.

Bullshit. Roland was busting the balls of the real providers of this great country, the ones who got things done. And then there was the whole business with the tax cuts—what a stitch up! Words taken completely out of context, just like those comments he made about the Arnette Three. He didn't hate black people; his favorite running back was Reggie Bush.

He had ideas and the money, but when he ran for governor the others saw his cowboy hat and enormous portfolio and could only see a madman hungry for power, believing him to be a carbon copy of that insane Major from *Dr. Strangelove*, riding the nuke all the way to oblivion. He lost in a tight race, but resolved to try his hand in the Senate. That's how Sen. Barclay Richards found himself in Washington, ready to shake the foundations and let his voice ring loud and true. He'd seen the caricatures of his broad face, always wearing a cowboy hat that was disproportionally large (it'd cover the entire page if that damn cartoonist had his way). He'd even heard the comparisons to 'JR' of *Dallas* fame, but these were not things Richards shied away from. No, if anything it spurned him on, for in his mind, he was just setting himself further from their warped liberal ways.

It had been decided early on by existing members on both sides of the aisle that Richards foray into the political sphere was to be roundhouse kicked back to Texas. And so those federals (led by that dastardly Roland) grinded away at Richards, dragging him through the mud till the shit stuck and the media were there to snap away, dig in with their talons and blind him with the lights while his crimes were laid bear. They finally got him with the price-fixing deal in Southern California; his Hydro-Electric board giving him up as the instigator after a three year investigation. A witch-hunt he cried, but no one would hear it, no one would defend the poor, defenseless water and energy tycoon. No, everyone was all too happy to believe Barclay Richards had been handed his just desserts.

So now, three months out of his forced resignation and two weeks away from a congressional hearing clearly set up to rub salt, Richards found himself sweating away (despite the air conditioning) in the West Texas desert, going over in his head which of the two previous incidents was the tipping point for him making this bizarre, most unusual visit to a man he cursed himself for having done too little homework on.

The first of the peculiar incidents was the girl. Seventeen, young and seductive, she'd cleared all of security with little frisking (not that they didn't want to) and found herself alone in the hotel room of a man tearing his patted white hair out prepping for an interview he'd been carelessly vexed on while dealing with a divorce he hadn't seen coming from Mrs Richards number two. Those smooth, skinny legs in sultry black heels strutted across the room to the stunned former Senator; his heart racing as she sat him down and straddled against him, his nose catching that whiff of cherry that melted his knees and got all fifty-four years of him hard as he fumbled to hang up on the law-yer riling on about splitting assets and an unholy general shake down. Richards wasn't into kids but this girl was overcharged and too much in heat for him to see straight.

Her voice was soft, her lips alluring. "There's someone I'd like you to meet."

He edged backwards on the bed. "Uh, what? I mean, sure. No, wait!" His member was sinking, then almost immediately flat. He wasn't into kids. This was a trap. That bitch wife of his was trying to get him out for cheating, and though he did stray on occasion, this would not be one of them. *Get a fucking grip, Barclay.*

Richards pushed her off the bed and she fell on her ass; her short red skirt drawn all the way up, revealing black lingerie Richards couldn't help but want to devour.

"Who sent you? How old are you?" He demanded the answer to the first question and found himself a little too curious for the latter.

She shrugged off his push with cat-like recoil. "He's got what you need. A solution." she replied, a twinkle in her eye and a playful licking of her lips.

"What's your name?" he uttered in almost a whisper, his breath already spoken for.

Lola.

Richards thought of lollipops and other sucking motions. As he was twisted into these sensitive thoughts, Richards gulped, would it be so wrong to unbuckle his belt?

"I'm seventeen. All yours if you go to him."

Now Richard insides were hounding at the gates, begging him to loosen his collar and jump in—but he didn't. Her eyes had piqued his curiosity; and Richards was left trying to recall that thing she was saying while he stared uninhibited at her perking cleavage.

A solution?

"To what—the price fixing? They've got a whole army of suits and watchdogs all over me. Even 'Top Dog' Roland wants some of the action." He was now upright; all the problems right back in front of his face, rolling round his head—his brief lust burnt out and a good thing that, he reasoned. But Lola wasn't finished.

"This goes deeper than your price fixing; it's more a solution…to everything."

Now she was pulling his tie.

Richard whole body was being taken on a rollercoaster; up and down in wanting her and feeling she was crazy, a temptress, the heart of all the problems Richards had been drowning in. Yet despite all the above, he couldn't help but be awestruck by how much he was falling for her notions.

It was in the eyes. They were innocent and obedient, which in one side of him played out some sick virgin dream, but there was another side to it; a conviction in her voice that was so assured of everything it seemed to center her whole being as this unspoken, calming wave that could rest Barclay from the surrounding vultures that picked at his empire. Her presence was perhaps just that thing she was saying: a solution to everything…

Richards' distraction of daydreaming was broken with the sound of footsteps outside that sent him sprawling into action, grabbing the jacket Lola had so seductively slid off her taut body and throwing it right back on her. Richards then snatched her long strapped black purse and wrapped it over her hand.

"You tell your guy—what's his name—that I'm flattered he thinks he can help, but I'm short on time for meetings with prophets and sexed-up disciples."

Feeling a hand reaching for the golden knob outside, Richards was ready to shove Lola out with extreme urgency, but even in her high heels, Lola remained still as a statue.

"This isn't a solution just for you; it's a solution to everything, the system itself!" she forced, a hand reaching down her bra to reveal a plain white business card she then pushed against his chest, ensuring he'd take it. Just as he had done this, the door was swung wide open and Richards' fiery manager, Ben Westwood, was greeted with a flushed man and a girl too young. By the time the words "what the…" had rolled softly off Westwood's tongue, Lola had taken Richards with both arms and reached up with a full-blown kiss. Cherry.

Richards let himself go into it, this vibrant passion, and if Westwood hadn't been there he would've stayed lost with her forever. But this did not happen. She pulled away just as quick as she'd exploded his horizons. With serious eyes she told him he had exactly one week, and was swiftly out the door, brushing past Westwood who shifted aside in mounting confusion and anger. Westwood carefully shut the door before starting the ignition of his motor mouth ways. "What the hell was that, Clay? I mean for Christ's sake we've got a pressure-cooker interview in less than an hour and you're trying to squeeze out some stress with an underage honey? How old is she Clay, fifteen? Are you really trying to give me a damn heart attack?"

Richards ignored all this as he blasted open the door, his eyes darting left to right, before he screamed at Westwood to have her followed.

Looking at the business card, in plain black letters, Richards beheld the coordinates "33.5779° N, 101.8552° W".

Westwood scrambled as he often did, sending out for a tail but the scent went cold only a few blocks out.

So, his bearings now truly in a shambles, Richards had tried to forget about Lola; forget about her wild promises. He'd done the interview a little out of focus; they'd got him fumbling his words on the price fixing and the obvious fallout with Hydro-Electric (then there was the whole divorce bit which he thought was going to be off-limits), and pretty much everything else that was crumbling, but Richards got through like he always did and soon a week had passed.

Then came the other incident: the blackmail. Hydro-Electric had decided to go further into fighting Richards; their drilling proudly supported under the table by those federal rats. Richards was told the spark for further bloodshed was a security breach in the power lines that shut down the current flow of electricity. While only scrambling the operating systems, the entire company was forced to run back-ups, which then failed due to malfunctions. All up, the cost of resetting was estimated at fourteen million, and when the FBI uncovered evidence to suggest it the result of hackers, Hydro-Electric was all too ready to start a war with their number one suspect.

Richards' team of high-paid computer whizzes were working around the clock to defend themselves, checking for programs and files that would pin them as the culprits. They were left dumbfounded when presented with forged evidence of intricate plans for retaliation against Hydro-Electric from the hard drive of none other than (former) Senator Barclay Richards. The forgery was blatant, but at this point in time Barclay's reputation would be enough to hang his neck by. Despite this impending threat, it had not been sent to the appropriate executioners just yet, and equally puzzling was the lack of a demand to refrain from its release…

Of Richards' extensive team of aids, only Westwood had remembered Lola; and Richards had coolly tried to brush off the fact these cyber-attacks were dated exactly a week after their brief encounter. But the more he internally discarded this notion, the stronger the memories came back, and Richards began to feel another part of him start calling the shots. With his team running around in jittered circles, Richards had walked into his home office, taken out the business card and indulged a whiff, hoping for cherry. Leaving the sinking hole his staff were trying to dig him out of, Richards took off in a white Cadillac with only his trusted bodyguard, straight-laced Charles Bracken, straight lining it for 33.5779° N, 101.8552° W.

Where solutions promised were sure to be discovered.

***

The air was hot and dry, the sun not quite yet done for the day. The compound was all gray, a smooth concrete, and was dug into that ridge like it had been there for eons. There wasn't another building for miles. Surrounding its formidable walls were steel fences and a gate manned by two guards, both armed heavily. Charles, Richards' silent protector, concealed his terror in a professional manner as he unbuttoned the strap holding his 9mm. They rolled up to the gate and were let in without a word uttered or glances shared.

Standing in front of the pure steel doors that parlayed the entrance to all this secrecy was a man with a messy gray beard and frizzy gray hair that was tamed at the back into a ponytail, who waited eagerly for them, a wry grin on his face. The man wore sandals and khaki shorts while his dark blue shirt was left open, a skinny frame holding him up. Charles hadn't been given squat for time to screen this man; all he had going in was that the owner of the property fell under the name of a one, Christopher Jenkins.

Charles stepped out first; ignoring the beaming man's out-stretched hand. Richards then emerged apprehensively, his cowboy look more suiting this arid enclave, yet inside his bearings were shot to shit. This ponytail man on the other hand, the possible Jenkins, seemed well at home in his laid back attire, reminding Richards of one of those pesky hippies. Richards accepted the man's hand.

"Christopher Jenkins?" Richards grunted with a rough, manly voice, a lot deeper than his southern-ness usually entailed.

"Why yes I am," Jenkins replied in a sure-fire manner, his accent already more northern than Richards liked. Holding a stare as Richards summed up this man, Jenkins was eager to break the ice, a hint of excitement clear in his voice.

"Well, I know you've traveled a long way to be here and to be frank I'm a little surprised you hadn't brought a whole entourage, only Charles here." Charles flinched at his name being recognized. "But I can allay your worries right here in the now, telling you I mean no harm, whatsoever."

In his attempt to ease them, Jenkins had underestimated just how ruthless Richards was. Knowing Jenkins meant no harm, Richards then started going about asserting his dominance. First and foremost—he flatly refused to enter through the large steel doors until he had something, anything to go by.

"What would you like to know?"

"Lola in there?" he asked, finding it difficult to admit she was filling his mind up despite the presence of weapons and a hippie who was obviously a whole other level of nuts under that laid-back exterior.

"Yes, she is but—"

"Take me to her."

"All in good time, my man. However there is something I'd like you to see first."

Richards' eyes narrowed. "You're the one blackmailing me for my time. I'm sure you've got your reasons for targeting me, but I've had quite some week and I think we'd be best getting down to business only after I've fucked her sideways."

Charles was stunned.

Richards stood his ground, letting his demand sink right in.

Jenkins drew a sharp breath, he'd always considered the cowboy a sleaze ball but not to this insidious extent, Lola had really worked a number on him. Jenkins' face grew serious, and with an acid tongue boiled Richards' skin. "You'll get her, like a doll, a dirty little doll, all for your enjoyment. But if you keep that lizard brain talk up, I'll know I've made a mistake and your existence will *cease* to exist. If you listen to my offer, you will be witness to something that will take your breath away, something that will change the course of humanity forever. Better than all the Lolas of the world. Now, have I got your attention?"

Richards didn't know Jenkins was a former virologist, first with the CDC in Atlanta, then at Blackwater. He didn't know that Jenkins had worked alongside the most lethal pathogens in the world: Ebola, Yersinia Pestis, Marburg, Lassa fever and the Elkins Influenza (recently found in common Elk, discovered by a one, Doctor Elkins). Richards hadn't known any of this, nor was it really possible to know Jenkins was even in Blackwater, all that information being heavily classified. But there were more unsettling things pertinent to Richards' incomplete prognosis of the man that stood before him, tempering a quiet wrath, demanding his attention. For Richards didn't hear those dark thoughts at night, the urge to just let her loose and let the nature of man be devoured. Richards hadn't felt those many years in Blackwater, just waiting for something as holy as this to fall into a visionary lap. And most importantly, he did not see the purpose of Lola's kiss, the kiss that left him reliving it over and over; reeling for more. He did not yet know the seeds opening up inside him.

What Richards did know was that Jenkins was unlike anything he'd seen thus far, a complete opposite to himself. They were two extremes at polar ends, so why the invitation? Moreover, there was something in the eyes that played a loud tune of conviction hard to ignore. There was a truth in those eyes, just like the look he remembered Lola had given.

Yes, Richards thought, you do have my attention.

***

The inside of the compound was bare; the front room just like any other trendy minimalist place; stylish and cold. With their undivided attention, Jenkins had warmed up again and led them past this foyer that had all the markings of a waiting room. Further down the hall there were the sounds of people conversing and making their way into locker rooms, suiting up for their days work in the labs. Richards and Charles were not led down this path; they instead found themselves descending spiral stairs down to a long hallway of rows and rows of rooms, each constructed like a cross between a prison cell and an animal enclosure one would find at the zoo; a thick wall of glass giving

Richards and Charles a peek into Jenkins operations. There were people in these six separate cells, all milling about in a mindless fashion. In one cell there were two people, a man and a woman standing side by side, their skin grimy while in the far corner next to them lay the most animate of the bunch. This kid sat with both knees on a skateboard of all things, rolling back and forth, his tongue sticking out.

"Everybody, this is Barclay Richards. Barclay Richards, this is everybody."

They growled, like goddamn animals, at the sound of Richards' name, sending him reeling backwards in true fright while Charles let his hand hover over his holster.

"What are they—fucking zombies or something?" Richards cried out.

Jenkins turned and smiled. "They're angry because I told them you've been stealing their food, especially their bread. They are very partial to their bread, or at least they were when I told them that was the case." As Jenkins said this, Richards shuffled his way up to the glass window of one of the wiry males, the man's hair as wild and unkempt as Jenkins'. The man's clenched teeth were a rotting yellow and he never seemed to blink, his pupils snarling away like attack dogs. A closer inspection of the habitats left Charles unnerved, his eyes finding slices of white bread sticking out of their blue food bowls.

Jenkins leaned right up against the glass wall of the male and female. When he talked, it was as if he were addressing small children. "He did not steal your food." At this they all stopped their growling and went eerily calm, all except for "skateboard boy" who continued his manic rocking, the rolling of bright orange wheels against the smooth floor the only remaining movement of the room. Charles and Richards looked on in surprise at this kid; he clearly hadn't received the bread memo. Jenkins laughed. "That's Andrew. He's a new recruit. He's in the early stages. Obedience comes later." Richards was unsure of what to make of this show. Why? What was Jenkins trying to prove with this?

They were led to the room at the end of the hallway. Richards and Charles walked in without daring to return the hollowed looks from each of Jenkins' *things*. Inside, there was a desk and two seats awaiting, nothing special, but in the corner of the room stood a set of steel doors with a digital keypad lock, much like the entrance to the compound.

Richards gazed at the steel doors and felt a yearning build up in him. "Lola in there?"

Jenkins rolled his eyes. "Lizard brain!" he snapped with his fingers, and Richards regathered his attention. Jenkins motioned for them to sit. He then moved to the back of the desk and opened up a drawer, taking out a large black box that required a key to get in.

"We did this place on a minimal budget. Took me three and a half years to set up, had to take out several loans from the bank, sell my house. I had help from my followers. Of course, when I got it right, I wouldn't have to worry about those banks any-more…"

"You said you had a solution?"

"Yes. Right here in this box." He turned the key and upon opening it up, the case lid blocking their view, Jenkins carefully took out a vial of purple liquid. He held it out for them to gaze at, before lightly flicking at the vial, its mysterious contents swirling aimlessly inside. Richards clutched at the arms of his chair as he watched it swish around with growing panic, now certain this man was carrying something deadly. Jenkins studied their inner reproach as he did this. A slight grin broke out. He was back in the command seat, and he had them one hundred percent.

"It's called many things: Tyrantocillous, population destabilizer with a hint of flavor, the future, evolution…*my baby.*"

Richards was uneasy in his seat. He'd seen many kinds of people in his life; radical protestors, furious politicians, psychopathic prisoners, but nothing as diabolical as a mad scientist. Richards wasn't aware such a person truly existed. Yet here he was, this crazy caricature in the flesh. They stared each other down, the Southern Cowboy and the Loony Hippy with big ideas—two very strange looking bedfellows.

Charles remained fixated on the vial, his mind furiously retracing steps to plan an escape if it were to slip and break. He was not going to be a pet.

"What does it do?" Richards finally asked.

"Starts as a flutter of delirium. Much like schizophrenia. Insidious voices rattle the mind. Then come the visual distortions. Real, vivid hallucinations of terrifying things I've seen."

Jenkins saw the fear light up in their faces. This made him smile.

"You've seen these things? Heard these sounds?" asked Richards.

Jenkins motioned towards the closed door behind them, to his subjects that now sat peacefully in their cells.

"The virus does not kill everyone. Its main function, as with everything else, is to survive and multiply. It does so by manipulating the host's behavior. The dopamine receptors are rewired in a matter of days. All neurotransmitters are reshaped."

Richards shrugged, not exactly sure just what the hell Jenkins was getting at. "Turns them mad? What use is that?"

"The madness subsides, but with the dopamine receptors on the fritz, the command functions break down. Motivational cues are lost. So the virus seeks out direction from others, and the peculiar thing here—the difference between most viruses—is the reaction when this virus connects with a dominant strain, let's call it Type A. The weaker version of the virus then latches onto this Type A for the purpose of fulfilling its out-of-sync receptor system. A telepathic relationship ensues where the connections and cues of life now feed from the Type A's to the B's. One begins to see the world through their eyes. From this one could restructure behavioral learning down from years, to months, to days, to seconds. Soon everything is handed over to the Type A strain: the central nervous system, the cerebrum, cerebellum, limbic and brain stem. And when that happens, they are at your complete mercy. Now, the dominant strain is very rare. It has to do with the blood type AB and some other very specific genes…"

Richards shirked at this. He was AB. When he was younger, his momma told him he was special and that was just one of the many things that made him the way he was. Richards had built an empire out of that belief. "I'm AB," he said aloud.

"I know," Jenkins smiled. "As fate would have it, so am I…"

***

A short time later, a disgusted Richards left the place, his mind molested. Jenkins was crazy, that much was true. He had grand visions, and Richards had become increasingly uncomfortable by just how right some of his notions made him feel. But America: ground zero? Not in Texas, wasn't worth it. Call the police; ram down this doomsday conductor and his nut-bag followers. Take a flamethrower to the whole place and light her up like Waco.

Not in Texas, no way.

Richards wasn't going to have this madman running around with some zombie virus in *his* state. Richards was going to put a stop to this. Lola was never presented to him, he was sure she was already dead, but now there were more important matters at stake here.

Fucking mind control. It wasn't possible. Richards kept playing back those words Jenkins had tried to poison him with, scrambling in a bullshit reality of twisted notions that seemed to keep encircling him.

"It makes people crazy at first. They'll want to crawl out of their own skin. But this resides. The mind clears—a complete reboot—and with it comes the power to delve within, to begin the necessary changes. Telepathy. The insertion of minds into others, and the collecting of data from sealed lips. A reprogramming of the human mind, the human soul."

They were two kinds of extremes and Jenkins needed Richards to pave the way for his baby to spread. He suggested it appealed to Richards' public hatred for the federals; all that talk of secession and all.

"There will be fatalities, upwards of thirty percent—but a necessary culling in the symbiosis of man and virus. The only lasting means for extended peace… We need to start over. We need to erase these paths that create these unnecessary pieces of plastic bullshit—these destructive, parasitic ideas of getting a bigger TV, faster car, better things. Yes, there will be chaos. But out of the ashes, better leaders will be made. Better humans will exist."

Walking out the front, Charles expected a gunfight, but the two guards let them pass without incident. Shuffling towards the car, a rattled Richards kept repeating the ramblings in his head. It was all lies, the deranged spouting of a man eager to fund a cult of some sort. Something had to be done about this, and Richards knew it was up to him. He'd burn them all; a goddamn airstrike if that's what it took. Squash that hippy like the cockroach he is. *Yes*! This was going to be his new project, an Armageddon he'd rain down on Jenkins and his sick ideas.

But Richards would soon find his own circumstances taking a left turn. For he was already infected and not just with the strain that rang loops around the brain. His way of thinking was about to follow a different course…

7. Rosemary Blatt

Rosemary Blatt was tired; spent. She knew the world was sick
of her and this wore her down every day she lived and breathed
within it. Houston was a mistake, a terrible mistake she threw all
her hope into and now it all stared back at her, asking what now?
She'd filled those expectations up like nothing she'd ever considered before. She'd packed her life into a neat suitcase and once
all her necessities were lined up perfectly in her living room, she
had walked through each room of her small apartment, taking
in all her past while certain of a better future. This Houston man
was going to be it, the final hurrah; a comfortable slip into love
she had ached for her whole life. She was neither ugly nor special, her acute plainness never accepted by any potential suitors,
barring one: Chester Healy, only a boy when they met and the
elusive love she had craved in her teens showed his acne-ridden
face for only the briefest of moments, before the world caught up
to Rosemary's break and whisked it all from her.

The Houston man turned out to be a ghost, a no show, and by
default, he was nothing like the sweet gentleman Rosemary had

met in Verdana font. All the culminations of Rosemary's grand expectations were slowly cindered like the candle that killed itself as she sat alone in that restaurant, no romantic rendez-vous for her, not this time or ever for that matter. Sitting there, ordering for one, she kept telling herself this, beating down on her own prospects as they were swept away by the grim reality. Of course he didn't show; he probably had better things to do, Rosemary relented, aware she had joined the rest of the world in hating her.

***

Planes leaving. Planes going.

Lovers reuniting. Lovers departing.

One hopeless soul, returning.

The queue was long, but Rosemary Blatt didn't care. Her face mulled absent, the emptiness inside weighing her down. She always thought about it, but was always held back. *You're being selfish! Just hold out*. But there had to be a time when she had to accept facts.

No one's going to miss you, let alone love you.

She wanted to make it more elaborate than the old overdose of the countless medications she went through just to make it from day to day. A rope perhaps, maybe even a gun? But that was silly talk, Rosemary had no gun and she didn't know how to tie a noose.

The big, black security guard saw nothing of her, but Rose-mary was always too quick with the nerves, intimidated by this friendly giant as she collected her bag from the rolling table. A flimsy grab and that was all that was needed to send her cumber-some hand luggage sprawling onto the shiny floor. A large black arm pushed its way into her vision and lifted the bag for her, the big black guard smiling as he said, "There you go ma'am, don't let it get the best of you." Rosemary reciprocated the smile, touched to her core, the man's words seeming to repel her previous reductive thoughts about the universe, and Rosemary prayed that it was a sign of things to come. For the briefest of moments in her stride away from that security check, Rosemary Blatt was going to make it. She was going to get better. But a glance back at her unknowing savior crushed her, the man was now laughing with his co-workers, and old Rosemary couldn't help but feel she was the butt of the joke.

Staring out in the waiting terminal, Rosemary Blatt was sickened by all of Texas. She pretended to laugh to herself, rise above it all as the thought of living in Houston was retracted from her mind. She wouldn't have lasted in this heat, not this old girl. New York was her place, that's where she'd find her man—in her own territory, where she knew the ins and outs. She clutched her bag in her lap, holding onto this new prospect, unwilling to let it slip away as the usual armies of doubt found their way into her.

Rosie, you've been in the city for forty-four years, how is it you haven't found him yet—on your own turf as you so put it?

There it was again, the seesaw tipping back to its sinking foothold in the cold shade. How long could this go on for?

While Rosemary sulked, the pilots of Flight 34 boarded the plane. Gavin Prescott had been feeling ill the night before but had this flight earmarked for over three weeks now, eager to see his wife after an unbearable wait. His understudy had also been feeling a little strange himself, a tad flustered, but when Gavin confessed he was feeling ill and thought Krause should take the lead, Krause kept quiet about his own health. Chances to run the

show were invaluable and were to be taken with the upmost gratitude. In addition to the two pilots, others sitting in the waiting
terminal let out errant coughs, some feeling strange rumblings
in their head that kept them uneasy, yet they all kept it to themselves. Just nerves they figured.

They were boarding the plane now, a line of faces: some
nervous, some happy, one empty. Rosemary faked a smile as two
endearing attendants greeted her, their words and hers only cus-
tomary in nature. She struggled her way down the left aisle, past
the empty business class and into the lot with the rest of them,
just by the wing as she had requested, if only to feel as if she had
a choice in where she'd stew in her bitterness. A burly man sat
in her seat by the window, already settled in with headphones
and black sunglasses cutting him off from ever having to notice
her. Why did they all hate Rosemary Blatt? Why did she see it so
clearly in their faces as the pity they held for her transpired into
the familiar effort to end the conversation and get some distance
far away from her?

Regardless, this man was sitting in her seat; surely the least
he could do was help her lift her hand luggage into the overhead.
She tapped him once on the shoulder to no answer; the man was
blatantly ignoring her. The agitation she wanted to inflict on
him was brewing in her. A soft hand tapped her on the back of
her arm; it was the flight attendant asking her if she needed help
finding her seat, patronizing Rosemary like a senile old woman.
"Oh, I'm just trying to get my bag up in this compartment, my
arms don't reach that far I'm afraid."

The flight attendant responded with a youthful cheer in her
voice, sparking another temporary glimmer of hope in Rosemary.
While tucking the bag away, the man in Rosemary's seat shot a

glance of irritation at Rosemary. To him, Rosemary and the bag were the same thing. Easing her way into the seat, she felt the rough odor of the man fill her senses as he shuffled his arms to bring up a magazine to read. Watching him, Rosemary couldn't help but notice that this man, complete with a big scruffy red biker's beard and a dark leather jacket, wasn't taking off his sunglasses to read. Rosemary was soon confronted with the idea that this man had no intention of reading his motorcycle magazine, but all the intention in the world of ignoring her very existence. As she looked away, a twitch in her face kept down the outright indignation she wanted to stab him with.

She'd have to settle up her bank accounts, quit work, make appropriate arrangements…leave her will. There was a couple thousand here and there; she could leave that to Phyllis, her neighbor, one of her only true friends… All this future paperwork tugged at her exhaustingly. In fact, screw the people at the bank, why should she worry about that, she could take out a loan and put it on her party, the last laugh, or several exorbitant dinners! Yes! Her last meal, Rosemary could pick an exquisite last meal.

***

The plane was now an hour and a half into the flight, somewhere over North Carolina, almost into Virginia. Rosemary's anger had subsided into a deep sleep she had no idea she would find herself in, only to be abruptly awoken back to the cruel world that despised her. The nice flight attendant was already making the food requests. She was only a person down from Rosemary as Rosemary scrambled to reach for the menu tucked away in the back seat. "Sorry, just one second," Rosemary struggled as her eyes darted around the menu, musing over the two pictures of a roast beef sandwich and a tin foil plate of pasta. Rosemary was always a picky eater, but today she was willing to have whatever, and yet with each passing second, a distinctive pressure built in her head unlike any sort of anxiety she'd experienced prior. Everything within her senses became acutely aware of the feel of the seat and the shuffling of the other passenger's bodies on the plane. In this moment it felt like time was speeding up, as Rosemary was unsure if she herself had expanded to encompass the inhabitants of the plane, or if the inhabitants of this plane were invading her personal space, pushing up right into her, compressing. The walls of the plane seemed to close in on her, each row congesting inward until it was all swallowed up into Rosemary, filling her entire body. Inside her, she became inundated with the sights and smells of all the other passengers; their hearing and the flicking of magazine pages and the stabbing of fork to pasta amplified tenfold, ringing for miles in Rosemary's ever-expanding head. When Rosemary felt she could take no more, their thoughts came like a flood from all around her, pumping through her like the pistons of a car engine, pounding away at her in incomprehensible dribble. White-hot flashes began to fill her sight, eventually blurring everything into static. Then just like that she was back in her seat, utterly floored by this intensive invasion that had taken over her.

Still gazing at the menu, Rosemary's inaction infuriated the nice flight attendant and the burly man who now teamed up in their vicious taunts of poor old Rosemary.

It's not that hard you pitiful excuse. Choose something before I tell you to choke on it.

It was the voice of the attendant, but her lips had not moved. At the same time, the burly man was voraciously screaming into Rosemary's ear, *FUCK YOU, OLD BITCH! JUST HURRY UP and DIE! That's what's on the menu for you, bitch.* Yet there was no movement from his mouth, only the thinly concealed hatred he held for her.

It was an invisible attack from both sides and Rosemary was forced to concede. She squeaked out her choice of a sandwich. The man's order quickly followed, and in his decisive manner he showed Rosemary how it ought to be done. As the woman produced the two sandwiches for Rosemary and this awful man, the sound of his voice again drifted in through Rosie's ears, muttering all kinds of hat directed at her. Why did he persist in such ruthless manner, hadn't he said enough?

Rosemary clutched at the arm rests of her seat as the growing tension in her head made her stomach queasy. Was it something she ate—something in her tea before the flight?

Despite her clear stress, the burly man's invisible barrage would not let up, even though he appeared quiet as a mouse eating his sandwich and reading his magazine. Yet inside, all his dark thoughts festered against her, even if she couldn't grasp how she felt this. Like radiating circles of growing pain, each word hammered against her head until finally she felt the need to front this man. Her hands were shaking and in his mistake, the man's train of thought kept pounding away at her spirit until their eyes met and for the briefest of moments he felt he knew her, and she him, until Rosemary Blatt's dainty hands were sprung around his neck, a whole lifetime of lonely pain choking the life out of him.

The tranquility of the plane was broken in an instant. As if on cue, the other passengers started banging on the seat in front of them like wild children, experiencing flashes of both the pain of Rosemary and the slow suffocation of the burly man.

Flight attendants rushed to pry Rosemary from the petrified infant the burly man had been reduced to, but even as Rosemary was ripped from her seat, babbling, "I hate you, I hate you all!" in an incoherent screech, the man's trachea still lay contracted while his heart went into overdrive, unable to comprehend that it was going against its entire function by letting him die. They dragged Rosemary to the front of the plane to the empty business class seats. The US marshal on board had her restrained; still confused as to what exactly was going on. Rosemary's face was now a twitching mess as her eyes rolled lazily around as if she'd been drugged.

"What happened in there?" The marshal shouted at the nice flight attendant whose uniform was now smeared with vomit from the burly man. She was beside herself in panic.

"I don't know she was just…taking her time to order the sandwich and I pass her for a minute then she's got her hands wrapped around the guy's neck. I mean, what the fuck!"

The nice attendant was now a blabbering mess, just like Rosemary. She just couldn't bring herself to understand how those dainty hands could strike at that guy's jugular and cause so much damage. The man could've brushed her off like lint on his shoulder and yet right now his face had just turned a vicious purple as he shook uncontrollably. It was all too illogical to be happening.

Pandemonium had swept the plane, taking all of its inhabitants into a wild fix of yelling from the crew and cowering from the other passengers.

The pilots were frantically trying to get a read on the situation. "What's going on back there? We're hearing a lot of noise," Gavin the pilot snapped into his mike.

When no one responded, Gavin turned to Krause. "Keep her steady. I'm going back there."

He busted open the door and took one look at Rosemary. One long look, hearing those high-pitched screams inundate his head, twisting all his senses into a barrel roll. Gavin raced back inside the cockpit, pulling the lever for the oxygen masks to drop, before calling in whatever the hell it was he'd just witnessed.

The once burly man was now dead, choking on his own vomit whilst suffering a massive heart attack. Oxygen masks dropped and dangled like jungle vines, but the animals wanted nothing to do with it. They were beyond their own comprehension now.

The only person who was seeing things clearly was the rambling mess that was Rosemary. She had felt all those eyes trained on her as she was dragged away, taking their phones out to put on their YouTube's and other digital innovations of the modern world Rosemary had no place being in. They'd lock her away; that Rosemary was sure of. Throw her into some padded room, the whiteness of the bright lights leaving her exposed for all eternity, her self-loathing the only company available.

Rosemary didn't want to go that way. Rosemary didn't want to live with the humiliation that flushed her cheeks and begged for it all to stop. Rosemary wanted to die.

The panic of screams and flurry of confusion in economy became mute to Rosemary, as a single thought floated from her like a feather to the cockpit ahead. It passed through the door and meshed with the sweat-dripping Krause, who clung to the controls with a death grip, unsure of anything anymore. Softly, Rosemary took a hold of all of his senses.

The pilot felt Rosemary take her dainty hands and caress his face. She soothed him with his mother's voice, relaxing his insides, almost leaving him breathless. He was carefully wrapped in the blanket Rosemary had clung onto as a child, and as its fibers surrounded him, he felt Rosemary's pain and sorrow as his own, and when she asked him to end it for all of them, he did so with tears of joy in his eyes.

8. The Diner

She was naked. And so was he. He was afraid to look at first, his whole body squirming within itself, urging him to turn away, to avert his eyes and avoid the shame of knowing that she was the most beautiful creature he'd ever laid eyes on, a fact that was unquestionable and yet unthinkable. He was not allowed to witness her existence, to acknowledge it was like staring into the sun.

They were standing face-to-face, right next to each other, just within touching distance. He had no idea where they were. It was neither dark, nor light; there was only her, which made his aversion all the more difficult.

Just look at her! His insides screamed, begging him to meet her soft gray eyes and melt into one.

All right, all right! He shouted within himself.

Slowly, his neck creaked as he began to raise his head, he was going to do this, he was ready to be blinded; he knew it was worth it. As his head crept up he studied her outlines, her contours shimmering in a kind of warmth that spread from the back of his neck, making him whole. He was up to her breasts now, and was willing to take his time at this point. A small freckle right above her left areola, he'd kiss that gently, yes he would. Now her neck, he was almost there. It was a soft, elegant neck that beckoned to be nibbled and then respectfully ravaged.

When he got to her face, time became unstuck, and Cole was breathless in its grasp. The tender smile that emerged from her face made those knees of his weak and he wanted to smile back, he tried with all his might to raise those cheeks and reciprocate whatever it was she was doing to him, but knew he could never achieve this; it was an impossible feat to deliver the momentous outpouring of grace she had placed in his heart. There was movement in her feet, the right foot lifting and daintily sliding forward to him, closer. He watched the left foot follow course, and now he trembled. *She was going to touch him!* He braced for a feeling he was assured was going to break him; to split all his atoms into an explosion of melting colors coursing with the purest of happiness that he could hold onto, perhaps forever.

He looked up to meet her, a single tear escaping him; she was going to make it right. She smiled at this, her own eyes watery as she readied for contact. He felt her arm outstretch, her fingertips extending like beams of light, tensing his whole body before it was relaxed indefinitely.

He closed his eyes and waited. No breath escaped him. Two fingers, joined together, landed on the underside of his wrist. His eyebrows arched upwards in confusion as he opened his eyes, staring at her fingers lying softly still against his blue veins, as if checking for a pulse. At this he looked up at her, her face now one of a question, though her lips never moved. It was a call to action, an awakening of the soul. *Are you alive?*

***

Cole Watts lay in his regular booth at the Blackbird Diner checking his phone. This was for the fifteenth time that minute, in between the finger's tapping on the table and the toes wriggling away in his shoes while his knees played their usual fidgeting.

Maddie was late to her own meeting; she was never like that, and the more Cole thought about it, dwelled on its implications, the more he felt that pinch of white-hot pressure begin to fill his head. Looking outside his window he watched the people of his town pass by, walking off in their life circles, making all their appointments, meeting friends, greeting contacts and making ends meet. Cole would be joining them soon enough, but for now he waited on Maddie.

Madeline Bamsner. She was something else that girl, some whole different level of person Cole had no idea how he ended up with. It was an overwhelming feeling that whatever was missing in life had been found in her smile; and it was an equally overwhelming feeling that it was all too good to be true. Because these things just didn't happen to Cole Watts. He didn't think himself anything special, just a scrawny layabout of poor motivation roaming the streets of East Denver with his scheming best friend Peter, and when a peculiar oddity like Madeline Bamsner dropped out of nowhere into his universe, the first thing Cole did was scratch his dumb head.

Of course, Peter had seen her first, and at that point Cole figured it was game over. But Cole blinked in dumbfounded wonder when she first noticed him, looking gracefully past Peter as Peter hid the shock in his face. *Cole?* Peter thought.

Me? Cole pondered.

And as miracles made seldom appearances, he didn't stuff it up. It all became a juggling act really, a tightrope on an edge, the fall inevitable. Every interaction they had, Cole held his breath as if not to let the stupid out, to keep this dream alive and somehow Maddie laughed in return. Sitting in that diner as his stomach churned with bubbling angst he tried to take stock of all those brief moments they had stuck through together. Their first kiss was their third meeting (or their first date). Maddie wore a sky blue dress with sunflowers sprinkled all over. Cole was sitting next to her in the grass as they cast their eyes out across Stark's Pond, his hand so close to hers yet so far away as she eagerly told him this story about how she caught a jackrabbit when she was only ten years old just because her older brother bet she couldn't, but Cole found it hard to listen when he could almost taste that breath of sunshine inches away. When she saw how Cole's gaze dangled all over her, awestruck by everything she was, Maddie stopped talking and they both leaned in. That was the day Cole felt there was more to all of it, a purpose perhaps? They laughed freely, tangled in each other as Cole teased her with tickles in her soft welcoming bed that soon became like his home, his shelter. Peter was happy for Cole; the man now wore a smile it seemed nothing could take away.

The diner. Cole took Maddie here a couple of times before their dates to the movies and now in this anxious moment Cole sat here, batting away the creeping nostalgia that told him things were cooling off, that these warm happy memories were all he would ever have of her.

Things were changing for Maddie, she was going to graduate, but nothing was moving for Cole. He was willing to change, to do whatever it took to keep them together, but knew desperation was hardly attractive and the more things were to drag on, the more likely such a disposition would lather all over him.

The sliding of a door perked his senses. She came in that white summer dress, the one she wore when the sun shined its brightest one afternoon where they picnicked and made what Cole (in all his limited experience) could only reason as love. Light brown curls were curtains to her smile and where Cole saw a smile, he saw hope.

Maddie rushed over. Cole got up to welcome her but their embrace was over too quickly for his nervous mind.

"Sorry I'm late. I've been comforting Claire, she's still upset about Peter," Maddie blurted out as she settled into the cushioned seating.

"That's all right. It's good you're here now, anyway," Cole spoke retreating, unsure of whether he came off as nervous. "Wasn't that a month ago?" he continued, trying in earnest to maintain a fine line between supporting Claire and downplaying Peter's abrupt cancellation of their relationship.

"Yes, I know—but the way he does it—just completely cutting her off like that… I mean, has he said anything to you about it?"

Cole avoided her eyes. She knew he'd be lying. "Not much really; it's just Peter's way, I guess."

"It's just rude is what it is!" Maddie huffed as her face trained itself to the outside window.

Cole felt a rant about Peter building. At first he thought this was a chance to take the conversation away from the elephant that seemed to be hanging about in the room. But the more Maddie hated Peter, the less he could hang out with him, and the more he'd be torn between the two and the more likely she'd move on than Pete. They settled down to look at the menu. Cole would order his usual but was halted; what if Maddie was sick of him being the same?

"Well…how's everything else?" he diverted.

"Oh, you know it's all right…" she replied, her eyes once again trailing off to the outside world as a look of discomfort encroached on her face. Cole saw this discomfort and immediately felt the need to ask her what was wrong, but he was afraid to ask because deep down he knew the answer.

"Cole, what are you going to do about work…where are you heading?" The question struck him down. They hadn't even ordered. She'd been thinking about it for a while, he sensed that much, but it was the way she said it, ever so slightly suggesting whatever road he took would be on his own. Of course, Maddie had a point. So did his parents. There was no going forward for Cole, no chance at lasting happiness, that's what this young man truly thought. He'd tried another semester at Denver, maybe just to impress her, keep up the idea he was going places. But the heart was just not in it and the grades had taken their usual turn for the worse. Now it was just a couple of shifts at Phil's grocer each week. Girls like Maddie didn't stay around for that. They deserved better, and Cole knew it. Sure, Cole liked to think of himself as kind, and every so often a spark would lend him a telling observation (at least, he thought so), but with no drive, no real future plan, there would be no happy ending for the two. That was it. All slipping away right in front of him…

Cole had no money. He couldn't ask for more shifts from Phil, after that whole business of telling him he needed more time to study (if only that had actually eventuated). He struggled weekly to pay the rent in his one-room abode, and in this desperate moment, he thought of the one person who always had his back. Peter had plans, Peter had schemes; Peter could save the day.

"Peter knows a guy who could…" he started but stopped. Maddie didn't want to hear this shit. Cole felt the sweat patches starting to form all over him, under his arms, in his cramped jeans. He saw it in her eyes; the disconcerting expression that prepared to break hearts in the most humane way possible.

"Cole…"

What was he without Maddie? Who was he? Who could he possibly be? Was he just a rat, scouring the streets for the next high? Did he remember? Did he even want to remember?

Please, Maddie, don't make me go back to the way things were, don't make me go back to the loneliness, the uncertainty. I'll do whatever it is you want me to do! Please… Don't bring me to life, just to kill me now…

Cole's phone vibrated. Sweet relief if only for a moment! When he picked up, on the other line a frantic Peter was breathing hard. "They tried to hit us again—dirty bastards!"

"Whoa, Pete. Slow down there. What's going on?"

"Where are you?"

"I'm at the Blackbird with Maddie, why?"

"Are you watching this?"

"…No"

"Oh shit, ask Benson to turn on the box!" Peter was referring to the diner owner.

"What channel?"

"Any."

Cole ignored Maddie's pleas for an explanation and screamed at Benson who was busy serving a customer to change the channel from the basketball replay. "Can't you see I'm working here?" Benson yelled back, prompting Cole to run up to the screen himself, bringing over a chair to stand on in order to hit the button. Peter was never like this, never one to get riled up with the news of the world, but Cole thought little of this as the harrowing footage appeared right in his face, nearly sending him off his chair. Maddie's hand grabbed his own as all the inhabitants of the diner were arrested in dawning terror.

Splattered in great white text along the bottom:

PLANE HITS DOWNTOWN RICHMOND, VA.
TERRORIST ATTACK?

9. Long Distance

Towels not hung up. Clothes spread in neat clumps across the wooden floor. Dishes ready to be used, only after they'd been scrubbed a few times over and then completely replaced by a new set from the store. All the curtains drawn closed, leaving a gloomy feel to the place, as if it had been raining outside. There was soft pink underwear—not the sexy kind—hanging from a bedpost in the open bedroom, ready to be snatched up and thrown in the bin. The people of goodwill were counting their blessings knowing Kate Brewer was not the charity giving type. All through college she'd wondered when she was going to get cleaner, be more mature. It was always soon, just over the horizon; this perfect day when everything clicked into place, like magic. This had not transpired yet, but Kate was willing to be patient.

As Kate surveyed this current (and some would say ongoing) aftermath, she drew a sigh of relief. Her friend Sarah was right; fruit picking with Sarah's boyfriend up at Sarah's cousin's farm was just the ticket Kate needed for an escape. An escape from what exactly (well, probably herself) but who didn't need that from time to time? The air inside Kate's was stale. This would not be the case in Oregon. The air over there would be fresh and wholesome, reinvigorating her soul.

Still surveying her one-bedroom apartment, Kate checked off in her head the necessary essentials for this soul sweetener of a trip and picked up the phone, ready to break the news to her parents that no, she wouldn't be able to make it to New York for her father's birthday. Holding the phone between ear and shoulder, Kate navigated through the tiny living room into her bedroom, pulling a small bright red suitcase from the bottom floor of her built-in wardrobe. As she opened the suitcase up and readied its mouth on the bed, Kate then started grabbing skirts and shorts by the handful and stuffing them into the hungry corners while the ringing tone played over in her ear.

"Hello?" a soft voice creaked out on the other end.

"Hi, Mom."

"Oh, sweetie, it's you! (Hank it's our Kate.)"

"Hey, Mom," Kate repeated, ready to let her mom settle in by letting the questions flow.

"How've you been—oh my god, did you hear about Flight 34?"

Kate picked off the pink underwear hanging loose on the bedpost. She felt moisture in it. Definitely used, but Kate could write that off as work undies for when she was picking out in the fields. There was no need to wash them now.

"What's that? Oh yeah, I did hear. Terrible thing. Is everything all right over there?"

"It's been crazy, honey. You know it was headed for New York right? It's all everyone in the neighborhood and at work has been talking about since it happened. Have you been watching the news?"

"Yeah, sort of," Kate replied, ready to listen to her mom rehash through the phone whatever Laura Finberg of CNN had to report on the matter.

"Uncle Geoff saw it happen. He was working on a site in Tuckahoe, says he saw the nose of the bird, almost like it was heading straight for him. The thing was pretty much nose-diving, he said!"

Kate nodded away as she stepped into her bathroom, taking her hand and sweeping all the essentials into her toiletries case. She felt bad for having forgotten Geoff had moved over there a couple years back. Uncle Geoff was usually a bit of a stretcher when it came to the truth, but there was no denying the descent of the bird the way he'd described it.

They'd been playing the thing over and over on all the news channels, speculating over every little detail that was fed to them, like why the government had decided not to release the recordings of the black box. It was the usual around the clock hysteria, but this time Kate didn't want to obsess over it the way she'd done with the twin towers. She didn't want to go anywhere near that sense of true loss that had taken hold of her younger self, unable to understand that people wanted to hurt her for doing nothing but be herself.

Now she was halfway across the country and she wanted that distance to be made perfectly clear. That was why she'd done her best to stop watching after five minutes and remove its existence from her world.

"Laura said it was unnatural for a plane to do that; there wasn't a malfunction in the entire handbook that would've made it drop like that, which means, well, what Laura thinks it means, is that it was forced."

"Terrorists?" Kate asked, before half-jokingly throwing in a sharp one, "Mom, that couldn't be it, they already checked the flight manifesto: no Arabs."

Kate could feel her mom stiffen at this. As a family they had mourned just like the rest of New York, but her mom was shocked at how casually racist Kate could be sometimes.

"Kate! We thought we raised you better!" her voice snapped, and although there was only a hint of it, that authoritative clench her mother was once so expertly defined at came back to Kate in a sharp sting. Kate stopped packing as her feet tightened up on the ground. Like a long lost reflex when discomfort came, she wondered if there was time to have a bath.

"…I was only joking, Mom."

Her mother's voice soothed. "Okay, well, good. Anyways, they say the no-fly zone will be over soon, should be fine by the eighth, have you booked your tickets yet?"

Kate braced herself. "Well, that's why I called… See the thing is, Mom, something has come up."

Her mother was just as surprised as anyone. "What is it?"

"Sarah has invited me to go fruit-picking with her and her boyfriend up in Oregon for a couple of weeks."

"But it's your father's birthday! We haven't seen you since graduation. It's been four months. When are you coming home?"

"I know, I know," Kate backtracked. "And I will come, I promise—just as soon as I get back from Oregon."

"Oh, Kate…" As her mom drifted off, Kate heard a muffled voice on the other line, definitely her dad. Kate's mother barely held her mouth away from the mouthpiece—such was her ploy.

"She says she can't come, something about fruit-picking with boys in Oregon."

"No, Mom! It's not like that. It's for work, honest. Things are…expensive here," Kate exclaimed as her eyes fluttered past the bowl of weed on her glass coffee table. In the background she heard her dad draw closer to the phone—always the mediator between two strong heads. "Tell her we could help out." There he was again, always looking out for his little girl.

"No, Dad. I'm doing this on my own, this time."

Her mom gave out a frustrated sigh. She knew Kate would always strain against her, it was that way on every little thing, and as much as she missed her voice, she was fully aware her efforts would go nowhere. It was time to bring out the big guns. "I'm putting your father on the line. I know he can get you better than I can."

"Okay, Mom," Kate sighed, almost a faint shade of her mother's typical sigh whenever Dad was being overly grating. Kate knew that sigh well. "Love you."

"Love you too, Honey. Now here's your father."

There was muffled talking. Kate was sure she felt her dad waving her Mom away, *"Yes, I will! I will! We're on the same team here."*

"Kate?"

"Here, Dad."

"Good to hear your voice."

"You too."

"Now what's this I hear you need money."

"Don't worry, I've sorted it this time, as I was trying to tell Mom before she made some rather stretching assumptions."

"What happened to your job at the Juice Hut?"

"It wasn't enough. Things are expensive here," she repeated once more as the last of her wrinkled clothes were stuffed away, the suitcase ready to be clicked shut. She was making good time and wondered if a rewarding treat was in order. Would there be time for a bowl and a bath?

"Well, a few free meals at home ought to leave your wallet nice 'n full."

"Dad, it's not that. Well, it's not *just* that. Oregon, out in the sun, cleanse the soul…"

There was a long pause on the other line, "Everything okay, kiddo?"

"Yeah, it's fine. Just need some fresh air."

Colorado was fresh enough but a stink had formed in East Denver's social tethers and seemed to cling to Kate, none of it her fault, really. But it was enough to warrant an escape, at least for the time being.

"I hear it's fresh in New York this time of year," her dad joked.

"I'm sorry, Dad. I'll book a flight first thing in Oregon. I promise. Now I know I'll miss your birthday but of course I'll call."

"I'd love that, sweetie."

Kate smiled. "So, what's mom got cooking up for you on the day?"

Her Dad's voice perked up. "Okay, get this. Atlantic City. Henson vs. Marquez."

Kate laughed. "Mom will love that."

"Yeah, well it's my day; she's happy because I'm happy… and she'll be there," he said in the nicest way possible.

Kate tried to wash this down quickly. She cleared her throat.

"Who you putting green on?" she asked.

"What, me? Gambling?" her dad laughed, letting himself time the pause to his answer perfectly. "Marquez. Gonna wipe the floor with Henson."

Kate laughed hard into the phone. Her dad always held his own hilarity in high regard and she needed to soften the blow she was dealing. "All right, Dad, well best of luck! I've got to keep packing, but I promise I'll call you on the day."

"No worries, honey, look forward to seeing you when we do!"

"Say bye to Mom."

"Will do."

As Kate put down the phone, she took in her sullen apartment. Anyone walking in right now would believe they had the solution to Kate's sordid funk: open a damn window. Let the sun shine in on your shrine to slobbery. Let those crimes be aired out and exposed so that you may find the motivation to address them. Yes, Kate decided. She'd do just that, but there was no time for a clean up of this proportion, the clock said so. Sarah and Justin would be buzzing the door in less than half an hour. There was no time to reassess her life here, in the now. That would have to come later in Oregon. Now she could have that bath. She had to wash anyway. She started justifying in her head, *if I don't smoke before, I can have myself a bath; one last indulgence before Oregon.*

10. Somebody's Poisoned the Waterhole!

Jenkins had been busy. Ever since he let Richards walk out that door, a cold chill had taken to his skin, letting the sweat surface as he fought rigorously within himself deciding whether to put a bullet in that cowboy's gargantuan head and start again. Starting over was of course a difficult prospect.

The whole time Richards had made his visit, Jenkins had struggled to keep it together, not let his frustration let loose into blood. He'd grown accustomed to a certain level of control in all situations, and was left reeling completely off-balance when the meeting had not met his strict expectations. It appeared Richards had not yet succumbed to Jenkins' baby just yet, despite the sworn declaration of Lola Bernstein that the deed had occurred by way of that lustful kiss.

An entire week! Incubation periods varied from person to person but the timing of this key individual was just plain rude.

Yet despite this, at the very last second, Jenkins left it up to circumstances out of his hands and the order to kill was withdrawn. Starting over again—wasn't going to happen. Inconceivable. The wheels were already in motion. Richards would turn sooner or later.

Starting over. Well, this whole business was about that very fact, but it had to go just right, the conditions for release had to be perfect. Jenkins went inside and felt the emptiness of his labyrinth echo within its cold steel frames. The white sofa, the one he'd sat in all those nights before, beholding his vial, was inviting him to sit down and gather himself, but his brain kicked the idea away like an empty can on the street. Lying down now was fruitless to the cause.

The compound was practically empty by this point. There were no real people to talk to now; they were all positioned in strategic spots across the West Coast, tethered to white vans that held his baby in air-tight drums. Not that *she* was airborne just yet, a fact that had kept Jenkins grounded, afraid to launch. *She* loved the water and vectors (the backs of flies and mosquitoes), whose innocent daily routines into the surfaces of people's dinner left a smidge of Tyrantocillous—only a smidge, but just enough. *She* spread easily through saliva and other bodily fluids, and Jenkins was certain that with the creation of more Type A's, her spread would increase exponentially with purposeful intent.

The water was their initial aim. Reservoirs. Fountains. Jenkins' baby thrived in a liquid solution and plans had been put in place to ensure gallon upon gallon escaped the attention of the water treatment plants' scrupulous filtering. Those technicians slugging through in their underwhelming salaries—they'd get a glimmer that something was wrong, that some mild discoloring had found its way into quality testing, if that.

They could run all the tests they wanted and alert the authorities, but by then it would be too late; *she* would flow, as always intended, right into the mouths that needed it most: the ones who needed to be tamed.

Jenkins had trained *her*, a full resistance regime, an exposing of his baby to flocculation, chlorination and disinfection of both the ozone and UV kind. A thorough acclimatization, done the best he could. It was getting the jump from waterborne to airborne that had been the real problem. He couldn't generate the required mutations. It was reliant on too many factors. In three and a half years Jenkins had not once seen evidence of airborne tendencies in test samples. Despite this, he was still confident in her possibilities. He had her running at a communicability rate of sixty-nine percent—contagious enough with acceptable fatalities. Hopefully, over time and with the right amount of exposure, *she* could even evolve to be as easy as the common cold.

Lola was out there somewhere. She had not been inside the compound like Jenkins had led Richards to believe, and with their unsuspecting participant storming out in disgust at his notions, Jenkins felt more so than ever the need to slip into Lola for some lizard-level stress relief. This sudden urge was only a momentary fog in his mind as Jenkins slowed his breathing, steadied his shaking hands and reassured himself of the pursuit of a higher enlightenment. Ignoring the cool sweat that now soaked his undersides in the air-conditioned chamber, Jenkins understood a timer had been placed on his baby's arrival, and got to work accordingly.

He made calls to the hackers in Vegas, his three best tech people, giving the orders in an insistent tone that strained a little more than usual. He had brought them on-board on the premise of a challenge and they had proved difficult to deal with, but were effective so far. All Jenkins heard was an "okay," before the phone hung up, leaving Jenkins pacing back and forth, repeatedly running his fingers through his oily gray hair.

It was systematic. Up and down the West Coast. The hackers hit hospitals, blood banks—anywhere else that had digital records of blood type. Fifteen minutes later it was done, and Jenkins knew phase two was already fifteen minutes behind schedule. The calls were made to Rachel Pegg, Brett Hurst and Blake Fields in Reno, north of Las Vegas as they silently cut the wire to the Reno Water Treatment Facility, assisted by a lovesick and overly responsive guard Rachel had infected with Jenkins' baby. They rolled in casually and the guard who was once a puppy dog of a human being, barged through like a lion, staking claim to his territory. There were few who resisted and those that did were knocked out with chloroform. Brett Hurst and the lovesick guard meticulously recalibrated the humming machines that pumped out the cleaning particles, while Rachel set about infecting those at the facility unwilling to conform just yet. When everything was locked up and secure, from out of their van, two barrels were produced and carted down to those massive, gyrating filtration systems where all the purple contents were drained through. All up it had taken less than an hour.

***

Reno was sloppy compared to the way Vegas went down. Lola was in charge of Vegas. She already had forty-three people made by the time Jenkins came calling, most of them employees in the Las Vegas Water Treatment Plant. That went down smoothly. Even easier was getting barmen to drink spiked drinks and then spike others. Lola would fuck three people a day, sending them into a wild frenzy of sweat which would then be replenished by a convenient purple Kool-Aid she seemed to have plenty of in her motel room. They'd take her grape-flavored water and then return to the bed to keep pounding away. Afterwards, when their senses had return and filled them with shame, the men would go to their doctors, fearing syphilis, or whatever web MD told them had them feeling funny in the head after a dirty sex romp as dirty as that. Sometimes, the doctors would then unwittingly give it to their other patients and family. The shamed men would go home to their wives and give it to them. Their wives would give it to their children. Their children would play with others. Those others would play with others.

Little life circles endlessly linking...

Once Lola was done in Sin City, Jenkins had given her directives to make haste to California, where his other people were waiting. There were thirty to begin with, waiting with all the discipline in the world between their ears, staking out those reservoirs in Eastern and Northern California. San Francisco basin was open for business, no water treatment required because it had been accepted long ago that the waters were naturally pure due to their location in protected watersheds. Security was lax enough, and thirty-five gallons passed through undetected. Thirty-five gallons, when only a single drop was required for the pathogens to begin their journey into the minds of those who needed it. When Jenkins was told of San Francisco, he beamed in pride. It was all falling into place, the matching of his dreams and the rough, once-thought untamable conditions of reality.

Next on the list was Sacramento, which fell just as easily… and momentum was at an all-time high until Colorado Springs. It was a four-man operation at most. They had pulled up in that un-assuming white van just like they had always done. But this time the police were waiting, weapons drawn, and a frenzied firefight had gone down. The four men were part of Jenkins' original thirty and they went to their deaths, the last of them to die crawling into the back of the van and setting off the incendiary explosives, removing the FBI's best chance at studying the barrels filled with purple liquid. Twenty-eight gallons lost.

Lola broke the news to Jenkins when he finally reached her in the Holiday Inn, the agreed-upon meeting point for the LA County reservoir treatment center four miles away. Tears had been wiped from her face and Jenkins held her in a numbing shock. At first he figured it was losing James, Alex, Stuart and Crow that brought her to clench to him tightly, her stomach contracting as she began to cry again, muffled in his embrace. But looking into Lola, picking her brain as he always could, he found her bereft of mourning, strained only by the single fact that she believed there would be no upheaval; that all their work would be for nothing. He put a wave of calm into her and sent her into the other room, letting her lay down on the bed. He saw the devotion in her eyes just as he wished them closed, the sleep that took her coming at the snap of his fingers.

Jenkins then sent the two others standing guard in the room, Rachel Pegg and Brett Hurst, out to fetch them all dinner. When they left, Jenkins slumped himself down on the edge of the bed and tried to feel them, feel all those infected. He knew they were out there, that much he could sense but only the blank dreams of Lola came through him. There wasn't going to be enough. And now the Feds were onto them. Time was closing in on both sides and soon they'd be squashed, jammed in with no one to influence but the very nearly dead. Jenkins' head came up from this dreary prospect and looked at the old landline phone. He picked the phone up and let his fingers twirl through the chord curls.

He knew the number. His brain remembered things a lot better with the virus flowing through him, and this was a piece of cake. Now it was just whether to dial. He hesitated at first, but eventually relented that there was little to lose at this point. His fingers dialed away in a trance, a number he had never called before but knew off by heart. If the FBI were listening in, then they'd close in quick.

A man picked up on the other end. It was not Richards. "Hello?"

"Yes, I'd like to speak to Barclay Richards please."

"Who is this?"

"Just put him on."

"Now listen here, fuck face. If you don't tell me your name I'm not giving him—"

There was a commotion on the other line; Jenkins felt it. The man, Westwood, was heard pleading to know what the hell was going on, but the phone was snatched from him. Jenkins heard angry footsteps drawing away. An ear was eventually brought up to the receiver, a heavy breathing clouding the line. When the man on the end did speak, he was very calm. Not boisterous. Calm. "You shouldn't have called. It's not secure."

Jenkins was both stunned and hopeful. The hairs on the back of his neck danced as the goose bumps in his skin lifted. There was dead silence for a moment, only the buzzing tone of the receiver as both men thought through what it was that needed to be said.

At last it was Richards that broke the silence. "I have loyalists in Hydro-Electric. I'll give you their names. They can help you access the LA county reservoir. I take it you want me to deal with the East Coast?"

Jenkins remained silent for the moment, letting it sink in. "Yes."

"I'll need access to *her*," said Richards.

Jenkins smiled. "2017 Greenway Pass, North Houston, fourteen barrels... Oh, and one more thing. An original sample still exists in the facility I used to work for, a branch of USAMRIID. They have information detrimental to her."

"Consider it cleansed."

Jenkins beamed. "Thank you."

"See you on the other side, partner."

***

Richards had been a sick mess all the way back from Jenkins' concrete bunker. Charles kept checking every few seconds behind him, to glance at the clear sweat that Richards kept wiping away from his face. Richards was looking out the window, mostly wincing, but sometimes gazing out like an excited puppy (which Charles figured was worse). There was the odd coughing fit thrown in for good measure as well. It switched back and forth, in an endless loop, and Charles shifted uneasy in his seat as he picked up the pace.

When they arrived at Richards' mansion, aka Texas HQ, Westwood was furious before he'd even answered the door. "Where the fuck have you been? You leave as we're trying to save your career while it hangs by a fucking thread—wait, Charles, why are you... What the hell happened to him?"

Westwood's change of tone was instant as Richards slumped wearily out of the car, his arm around Charles for support. Richards was looking past Westwood, struggling to make it inside.

"My bedroom, Charles, take me to my bed."

"What is going on?" Westwood demanded to know.

Richards repeated his request as Charles pushed past West-wood, giving him a look of mounting fear. This froze Westwood; seized up all his nerves, most of all that motor mouth of his. Charles was never one to give away his emotions and Westwood wasn't even sure fear was one of them. They hobbled along together, down the long yellow hallway, the one Richards soon to be ex-wife had insisted upon. He was laid down onto the bed after Charles removed the satin covers while Westwood stood by the door.

Richards brought Charles close to him, tugging at his collar to bring those cauliflower ears right up to his now frail lips, "Get that weasel out of here… No guests," he whispered.

Charles did as he was told and forcefully removed a bum-bling Westwood out of the grand master bedroom.

"What's the big deal? He doesn't look too damn crash. Seri-ously, tell me what's going on! Should I call a doctor?"

Charles had considered this many times in their six hour drive home, but each time he insisted, Richards declined. "I don't think he wants one," Charles said, perplexed.

"Well, what the fuck *does* he want?"

***

There was a hammer being drawn down on the life of Barclay Richards. He was a child and then some (maybe about ten), standing before a committee of his peers. They were all children dressed in dark black robes too big for their bodies, in a high up bench that looked all the way down on little Clay. If he thought about it long enough, these children looked awfully silly, and in any other situation, Richards would've brushed them off and busted out of this court room in one stride, just like that. But this did not happen, because Richards was quivering in his spot, feeling the heat of their gazes pour through his skin.

You said you were special, is it not in your blood?

"Yes," he replied. (He wanted to add that it was because Momma said so, but then he'd look foolish in front of the child judges.)

Then why do you waste your time with these federals? Why do you let them push you?

"They're so big. They're everywhere. There's too many…"

Then make them small. You have us inside you now. You can be everywhere…

This went on for three days. Richards staring at the ceiling, talking, rambling, letting those judges inside his head beat him down then fill him back up—all a part of the conditioning. And always they talked about that Roland, that bastard. He was the reason everything was wrong in the world, a sick bile that had to be taken care of.

He has to go, Barclay. Make him small, make them all small.

The housemaid, one of the many, would leave food at the door and be told to leave it by a stuttering Richards on the other side. Once, she had peeked her head around the corner of the long yellow hall, but she did this no more thereafter. Only two snatching arms were seen, dragging the tray in like a hungry beast. So the maid stopped looking. Charles had been the one to take his food in at first, but Charles had called in sick for the past two days. Westwood had knocked on those big mahogany doors to Richards' bedroom every day since Richards came tumbling through them. Westwood's pacing was getting worse, he was losing his usual snazzy cool. Richards had five different meetings to attend, last of which was the congressional hearing in Washington, now only a week and a half away. Compounding

Westwood's worries was the dark cloud of this apparent framing, threatening to break and put the final nail in Barclay's coffin. They still had no leads as to who the perpetrators were and what it was they wanted, and they were going to get nowhere without Richards shedding more light on the subject. So everyday Westwood would brace the potential fury of his boss and knock three times on the door.

"Go away! Don't bother me with these trivial matters!"

"What about the board meeting in Aberdene in two days?"

"Cancel it."

"What do I tell them? Are you sick?"

"Cancel it!"

"Jesus Christ!" Westwood cursed. Richards wasn't giving him anything. Aberdene was important, Richards had built this bottled water company from the ground up and within its walls he was a legend. But it wouldn't take long for the rot to set in once you're suspected of white-collar antics. They were sticking by him for now, but how long would that last? Westwood couldn't help a man that wouldn't help himself. He needed to make a quick getaway on this one. Would a letter after four years of service suffice? As he considered all this, a strange animal-like murmur began to emit from the grand master bedroom. A letter would do just fine, Westwood decided.

***

Richards was naked, except for his underwear, which had been soiled on the third day. His eyes would constantly roll every which way while his jaw remained slack as he let all the grand revelations these past few days swirl into a coherent vision, first around him, then in front, then slowly inside, meshing with his whole body. There were strange feelings, certain things he could not explain. For instance; Richards could hear Charles, nine miles away, beating at the walls of his spartan apartment, circuits fully-blown as he paced back and forth trying to hold back a murderous rage that had come out of nowhere but refused to leave. *Why was this happening to him?* He screamed aloud to himself. The logic was there but Charles could not connect the dots, he couldn't even eat and the lack of sleep was causing distortions in his vision, his ways of thinking.

"Fucking bastards," Charles muttered over and over, not truly sure who it was aimed at—that hippy Jenkins man—maybe. "FUCKING ASSHOLE!" he screamed, before collapsing in a heap on the floor.

As Richards sat on the floor of his master room, naked except for his underwear, he closed his eyes and listened to these ramblings of Charles and was overcome with the deep need to soothe him, to tell him everything was going to be okay.

It's okay, Charles.

He felt Charles' heart stop, his eyes scaling all the dark walls. "Who said that?"

Richards' mouth blipped, his brows furrowing like he was having a bad dream.

"WHO SAID IT?" Charles roared, a gun now in his hand, aiming wildly at the silent walls.

Richards felt his heartbeat begin again. Felt the sweat run, and the shivering start. Was it possible?

It's me, Charles.

Charles legs buckled on his carpet floor. He was on all knees, still swaying his head left and right, looking for the voice that spoke in his head. "Sir?"

Richards was hesitant once again. He was just as confused as

Charles now. *Yes, Charles.*

"Where are you, sir? What is happening to me?"

At this point Richards opened his eyes. He was still in his grand master bedroom, and yet a part of him was standing over Charles in his dark apartment, watching this man tremble, scared for his life. He saw both things at once and felt compelled to take Charles to a brighter place.

I want you to calm yourself down.

As Richards said this, he felt Charles' breathing slow down to a crawl, his whole body centering into a calm mass. Feeling this most intimate control, Richards trembled in joy, and like a building wave, the possibilities came to him. He now understood the gift he'd been given. He could use this to take others to a happy place. He could obey those child judges, satisfy their quotas and he knew just exactly how to do it.

He saw the possibilities and felt the intense raw power.

Then, as if god had intended it, the phone rang and Richards answered the call. When it was over Richards called out to Charles, called out deep into his soul, and without a word, the obedient Charles got to work.

***

Richards did not make the board meeting in Aberdeen, but Charles made it to two of the four bottled water facilities along the gulf and the Eastern Seaboard, just a shade over twenty-four hours apart. First of course was the Houston division, where Charles was greeted with great enthusiasm. *Oh yes, Barclay's going to fight those claims don't you worry, you know they're just trying to shake him.*

A large, impromptu meeting was organized under the behest of Charles, sending all the workers to leave their stations, letting those machines hum on their own. As Charles conducted this meeting with a charm he was not especially known for, hired men ghosted through to the filtration machines. They carefully turned off the microns, UV and Ozone filters and let the three barrels they had dumped into the springs earlier that day run through undetected. Quality testing had already been bought off. Leaving them none the wiser, Charles departed in a convoy of straight-faced men who then drove off north, reaching Delaware just as the sun was rising the next day. It was all hush-hush, none of the board members being alerted to Richards' well-recognized bodyguard making the rounds with a convoy of shady characters. None of the workers had known Richards was absent from these high up meetings, and it seemed Charles was there just for inspection on his behalf. The barrels were either passed off as storage of a new cleansing chemical, or as part of an experimental new water flavor the company were trialing. For the plant-workers, this story went down smoothly. Sure, bottled water is big business, why not move into flavored water?

By the seventh day, Richards was up and constantly on the move, talking sporadically over the phone about a new campaign to revitalize his already successful *H2-Fresh* bottled water brand. The members of the board were bemused by this sudden burst of energy. Boisterous, he was always considered, but now, in the face of the congressional grilling, the former senator was bursting at the seams with grand intentions. Congress was looking for his head to stick on a pike, yet this man seemed to pay it no mind. Everyone was thumping Westwood with calls, only to be met by the news of his resignation. Westwood had no idea where Richards had gone, or where he was heading. There were rumors, sightings of the man with the large white hat and broad face making his way up the Eastern Seaboard with no confirmation of his attendance at the hearing. And with this lack of confirmation came the distinct calls of a snubbing, a big fuck you. Congress had heard of such a thing being tossed around the grape vine, yet could find no source confirming this impending rebellion. *If he was driving up towards us, then where the hell was he?*

Richards soon became untraceable, a digital ghost, and the NSA would have had him in a second if they weren't busy trying to figure out who had been getting into the western water supply. The Top Dog had personally demanded Richards be found and brought to Washington, but that was the day before Rosemary Blatt's flight went uppity along a main street of Richmond; before the cases began to show up in Las Vegas, San Francisco, Denver, Richmond, Vermont, Delaware, Michigan, Maine, New York, Florida, Houston, Dallas and Austin. All sight of Richards was lost in this newfound hysteria that was fast clogging up the hospitals with patients suffering from strange delusions, talking of the voices that compelled and the dark deeds that followed.

11. Wings

Men with guns surrounded the perimeter fence, their fingers primed on tempting triggers. Inside their Kevlar vests, pools of sweat gathered and drenched against the skin. The flies were early for the summer. They buzzed effortlessly at the men who wrangled within themselves to wave away at their faces the least amount possible. Orders had been to shoot on sight any trespassers. Bio-terrorists, that's what they were told to expect. The CO was puzzled by this declaration. The men were not told to wear gas masks, although many had privately taken them along, hanging them off their utility belts. There were over thirty men, set up in bushes around yellow-fried hills of dead grass. All sights aimed down at the dark surface of the Fresno Reservoir, sister site of Hydro-Electric's California pump division.

***

They kissed. Jenkins withdrew first and handed a Kevlar vest to Lola who put it on without a word. There would be four of them on this final dump. The authorities knew about Christopher Jenkins now, his face and description circulating through every database imaginable. There was also no home to go back to: Jenkins' sanctuary having been jury-rigged with an assortment of explosives. When she was turned into rubble, the FBI and local Texan authorities flashing red-n-blue had nothing to go on. There was always the possibility of Jenkins' former colleagues rallying to find a cure if they hadn't done so already, but there was nothing more Jenkins could do about that. Such unfortunate circumstances were in Richards' hands now.

Inside the motel room they loaded their weapons into duffel bags they then threw into the white van already carrying the last five barrels, while Rachel and Chris got into another car. The white van had been marked ever since Colorado Springs and now there was footage of it making the rounds in all the other watering holes. The Feds were closing in; they had everyone on the case, that's what Jenkins felt in his heart.

Despite this, Jenkins held a great deal of hope for this final mission. There had been no public acknowledgement of their deeds just yet; it seemed the military was keeping a close wrap on it all, still believing in that deeply ingrained cover-up mantra. There was a chance, and no sense in going back. Forward she must go. So that is what Christopher Jenkins and Lola Bernstein did; bumbling into the cop-magnet of a van like the two stooges, soon to become three when they picked up Tony Gale from his house.

Tony Gale was their inside man, the last necessary patsy in a world on the brink. As general operations manager of the Fresno reservoir, he had access to the treatment facility adjacent to the calm blue surface water that fed both Hydro-Electric and California's main water supply. A prime candidate for the last lap dog of Lola.

Tony's house was squared away in the middle of suburbia, and as they passed through those clean streets and orderly footpaths, Lola gazed out in bleak contemplation.

"What is going to happen to these places when the people change?"

Jenkins had thought long and hard about this before. "They'll still live in there, but those people in mansions, they will share."

"But what about us, where will we live?"

"Oh, we'll live in a mansion."

Lola's hand slyly found its way onto Jenkins' lap, lightly stroking his thigh. "Will we have to share?"

Jenkins gave her a sly smile. They took in the quaintness, appreciating the unsuspecting faces they passed; oblivious to the storm approaching.

Tony's house was typical of the neighborhood. Large trees provided consistent shade to the front of the house, which was separated from the street with a twenty-foot, upward sloping driveway, a brown station wagon parked at its crest. They rode the van up the driveway and parked just behind the wagon. A nerve then snapped through Jenkins' brain, sending Lola into a shiver. Something very bad, an unsightly act, had just occurred in Mr. Gale's once quiet house.

Jenkins and Lola shared a glance of true terror before rushing towards the front door, banging hard on its wooden frame while the bell was buzzed simultaneously. Jenkins had already seen it. They were too late. The sound of footsteps thudding from inside found their way to the door.

Tony wore a white shirt, stained thick with blood, a knife dangling loose in his hand. There was a look of dullness behind his clear rimmed glasses, an indifference to the mayhem he'd just made on his wife. Such violent stains of red.

When Tony saw Lola, his eyes sparked into life, but Jenkins was furious, throwing Tony inside, leaving Lola to slam the door behind them.

"How could you do that? Jesus Christ—you sick fuck!"

Tony cowered away. His finger raised desperately to Lola. "I did it for her! I did it for her!" he babbled.

His wife's body lay peacefully in the bedroom. There was no struggle, she didn't see it coming.

Jenkins rubbed his head vigorously, cursing over and over. This was the chaos he had calculated. The side effect he deemed necessary. But to see it, to see this man as crazed as he was, fixed on a wild notion... Whatever doubts Jenkins had about the whole thing were now pouring through like a tidal wave, crashing against his skull with no means of reproach. In that moment Jenkins thought of clotting the man's brain; trying again, finding someone else. But there was no time. They had to use him. And in a terrible, twisted way, Jenkins rapidly began his rationalization that he couldn't let Mr. Gale's wife die for nothing. Lola's face had blown a furious red, and she started smacking Tony's already flushed face.

"I did it for you!" Tony babbled over and over between the hits.

Watching Lola lash out at this man's face was justified in Jenkins' mind, but his other train of thought, the one that could not be stopped, knew that the guy was useless to the cause if he looked like he'd just been smacked senseless. Jenkins sent a calm wave through both of them, sending Tony's knife dropping.

Jenkins tried hard to slow his own pounding heart. "Okay, what you did was wrong. Very wrong. But it had to happen."

Their postures grew stiff like soldiers standing to attention and they now hung onto his words with great appeal.

"Are you disappointed in me, Master?" Tony whispered, a splatter of blood now running down the side of his face.

"No, you're fine," Jenkins lied. "Just get yourself cleaned up so we can complete the mission."

The change was immediate. Tony was now ecstatic, running into his bathroom, shouting, "Of course, of course! Oh joy!"

Now left alone, Lola had forgotten about the dead wife lying silent only a couple of rooms away, and felt an urge build up again in her. She slowly made her way over to Jenkins in that sleek way she'd perfected, and asked if there was time for some play. Jenkins measured her with a whiff of spoilt. How many men had she gone through on his bequest that it was all she was now, all she knew? Now he could only feel sorry, as she let her tongue play come hither. Yet even with everything moving so fast, her pull was hard to resist. He was about to succumb when the sound of a car door slamming outside broke his trance.

Outside, Lee Smith, deputy-head of security at Fresno Water, stepped out of his vehicle shakily; all his focus on the white van, its very existence in that driveway exhausting him as the implications came rushing up into that thick head of his. He yelled at Bradley, his subordinate who remained in the company car, to call the station and tell them he'd found those bio-terrorists. Lee tried to brace himself while internally commending his excellent hunch that had brought him here to Tony's house. Tony had called in sick the past few days, and worried words from his wife had convinced Lee something was not right.

Jenkins was frozen inside, he was watching it all blow away, seeing all the possible scenarios dissipate all at once. Lola drew her sidearm and flicked the safety off. Jenkins' thoughts focused on the van. They could not let so many samples be available to the government. When it was in people, the virus changed. But in those barrels it was unadulterated, the opportunity for synthesizing a vaccine too great. Jenkins gave Lola one last kiss then ordered her out the door. So this was how it was going to end.

Lola blazed out the door, guns up. Lee raised his, while Bradley scrambled to get his pistol out of the glove compartment.

Lola advanced, ignoring the screams of a child across the street.

Lee kept cool. "What have you done with Mr. Gale?"

Now Jenkins emerged from the depths of the house. "He's just cleaning himself up," said Jenkins, a small detonator hidden in his hand.

By this stage they were locked in a standoff, with Bradley, coughing his way out of the car, joining the party late.

"What's in the van?" asked Lee.

Hiding his fear, Jenkins managed an almost defeated grin. "The future."

Lee was not into his bullshit answer. Lee did not take bullshit. "Quit fooling and tell me exactly what's in the van. We got police on their way. There aint no escaping this!"

Lee put his beads right on Lola's head and for the first time realized how fresh-faced she was. Bradley, whose lungs remained locked in a fit of coughing, distracted Lee further as both of them tried to keep their shooters steady on the bio-terrorists.

"Picked a lovely time to catch a cold didn't ya Bradley, you lousy sum' bitch."

Bradley tried to apologize and as he did, Jenkins noticed something, a slight thing. He felt the coughing inside Bradley churning out, the lungs working overtime while the stress hormones flooded his system trying to work him into overdrive. Jenkins felt all these things, and then he knew, deep in his heart that this boy Bradley was coming down with his baby. Jenkins grinned once more and in his mind he whispered: *kill him.*

Bradley's eyes grew weak, his knees starting to buckle. He yelled at Jenkins, asking him what the hell he was talking about, before falling into another fit of coughing.

Lee was now frowning, seriously disturbed by the state of Bradley.

"What the hell you saying, man?" Bradley screamed at the top of his lungs (whatever was left of them) to Jenkins, but Jenkins could only grin in return as he felt the particles of spit fly out in the breeze and drift further away, ready to find another. Jenkins let Lola see this too, and as she peeked into its glory and came to know what it meant, she lowered her weapon and grinned just the same.

Kill him.

The sound of sirens whirling in the distance were forgotten and as Lee grew stunned by their easy surrender, he turned to see the beads of Bradley's pistol lined up on him.

"What the—"

The cops rolled up a minute later. The van was gone, yet Jenkins had removed the explosives and thrown them inside. The flames from the ensuing explosion would eventually reach the tips of leaves on the front overhanging trees, which would then jump onto the neighbor's roof. There were no signs of the bio-terrorists or Tony Gale. There was only a fat man lying dead on the lawn, smoke still rising from the hole in his head.

Driving away in a heart-pounding drench, Jenkins held Lola's hand as Tony Gale sat in the back, eyes gleaming with excitement. They would be caught eventually, probably tortured and then murdered when things were spiraling out all around—Jenkins figured that much. But by then it would be too late. He had seen enough; they had done enough. *She* had evolved in her transmission, and Jenkins shed a tear of joy. His baby had found her wings.

12. The Mechanic

Long, dirty brown hair. Chubby cheeks and a snub nose caked with black grime and dried sweat. Soft eyes.

This was Max Wilkins, lying underneath an SUV, meticulously testing the pipes of this magnificent black beast. He was alone in the garage, the other mechanics having glued their eyes to the TV long ago.

Everyone in the auto shop had grown slack in the past few days; their bodies drawn to the glare of the tiny, twenty-inch screen with the fuzzy reception out in the waiting room. They were all suspended in dread, talking about it reaching New Mexico eventually, and like them, with nothing else to go on, Max agreed. Yet while they sipped their empty coffee cups in complacent stasis, Max maintained his work on the SUV. He did so because John Foster had asked him to.

Edgar was a small town, a population of around four thousand, just northwest of Albuquerque. Smack bang in the dry, lifeless horizons of New Mexico, Edgar seemed to miss the attention of snowbirds, and so found newcomers few and far between. So when John Foster had strolled into town about two years ago, people started talking. He was in his early fifties, had dark gray hair with matching gray stubble, and bore an old scar that ran down the side of his cheek; a single white line to go with a menacing look that suggested he'd know exactly how to pull a person apart, piece by piece. When Max was still in school, they used to make up all these crazy adventures that Ol' Foster had been through, and, getting as close to looking without staring at his foreboding mug, those stories sounded eerily accurate. He was a vet for sure; they knew that much, but everything else was just conjecture.

"He's one of them survivalists," Billy Thompson had declared. "Real crazy like."

"He was in Vietnam."

"Shut up! He ain't that old!"

"I heard he killed thirty Iraqis in Desert Storm. Had a break then killed some more when we went back."

"What'd he do between then?"

"Carved his killing knife!" They all laughed at that one.

But no one was laughing now.

People were seeing something happen on the West Coast, a great and terrifying change that was lost in translation to those who weren't there. There were army trucks bustling in neighboring Gallup sixty-five miles away, going off either California or Las Vegas. Vegas, now that was a scary thought. Sure, they had a few million more visitors than Edgar, but the idea of a virus sweeping through the desert, caught in a wind across the vast expanses of nothingness, reaching its victims with invisible hands... Once a notion like that had slipped from the tongue, it was hard to retract.

Max was now fitting in the bulletproof glass, glancing towards the waiting room, wondering if he should ask for help, but then thinking against it. If he did it all by himself, if he helped Foster, then maybe the man of many myths would help him when the shit hit the fan.

The day Foster came in was just a few days after that plane crashed in downtown Richmond. Max was manning the counter when Foster strode through, citing his demands with stern vigour. His voice ran deep as any gully and perforated Max's insides—a voice that matched the myth. With misleading baby blue eyes that could narrow and strike with a menacing stare, he listed his requirements: bulletproof glass on all windows, and well…Max lost him after that.

"Bulletproof glass?" said Max, motioning to the small garage through its open door, barely enough room for four cars. "We don't really have any of that just lying around here."

Foster eyed the fresh-faced chubby kid, feeling the kid's feet begin to quiver.

"Can't you just order it?" he said.

This was an obvious answer to Max, and yes, there were certain sources he could get them from quite easily. (Not that those sorts of places were on speed dial or anything.) But letting words escape him coherently felt like an impossible feat to Max at this point. It was the overwhelming feeling of seeing Boo Radley from up close after all those stories. Eventually, Max just nodded away until a slight "yes" was croaked out. By the time he finally collected himself, Foster was gone, leaving only his high expectations screwed into the sides of Max's brain. Max stood there in a daze behind the counter, looking at the poor, hand-written list he'd taken of Foster's requirements: Bulletproof glass, Front-barrier bar. Snow tracks (as an accessory). It appeared that Foster wanted to get around like an unstoppable road warrior, and that he'd pay whatever they quoted—money wouldn't be a concern. For the rest of the afternoon, Max kept going back to Foster's last comment: *that money wouldn't be a concern...*

It was something about the way he'd said it that had Max feeling real uneasy. He'd gotten a similar feeling watching the footage of that plane crash for the first time, and it wasn't long before Max couldn't help but connect the two things. Foster was preparing for something big, and if that was the case, Max started to wonder if he should be doing the same.

***

The bulletproof glass was all in. The front bull bar was fixed in place. Foster's apocalypse death roller was ready for duty, and not a moment too soon it seemed. Terry was gone. He'd seen enough and told the guys he wasn't coming in anymore.

"What you gon' do?" asked their boss, Chips.

"Sit tight at mine. We're getting as much food as possible. I hear it's getting real bad in the west. Tanks rolling in and shit."

"We're seeing the same things you are, Terry. It's just a panic. It'll die down."

But would it? Max had seen that fight in Atlantic City. They'd shown it over and over again, almost more times than the crash. The crash was old news by this point. There were endless stories about hospitals being loaded with people coming down with some sort of madness—but that fight in Atlantic City… You knew right then and there that something was changing, something was very wrong; an unnerving snapshot of the current times crystallized in a moment of pure savagery. One of the fighters was clearly focused, the other one aimless. The crowd roared when the big guy knocked his opponent's lights out—but it didn't stop there. That was when things got brutal; that was when Max really saw just how close people were to falling back, regressing into animals. The man just kept wailing on his opponent once he was on the ground. This wasn't cage fighting, no UFC. He just kept punching… Then there was the referee; just standing there with this childish grin on his face while the guy on the floor just stopped breathing. The ref started clapping, and the crowd followed. You actually heard clapping erupt in the stands, not just from a few people but hundreds, then thousands. Soon they were all clapping. All cheering as this man's head was caved in…

News columnists said they needed to arrest the referee, arrest the judges. Arrest everyone there for letting it happen. But who was going to stop them? The police were overworked, completely stretched figuring out who kept setting buildings on fire and why so many people were just outright killing themselves. *We have a suicide epidemic—no we have a schizophrenic epidemic.* People are losing their minds, *well then who is taking them?* Collective Delusions. People on the news kept talking about things like they were sharing dreams; only it wasn't in dreams but in reality—a very twisted version of it, anyway. Things were getting off their usual, razor-edge lines. "Order" was a commodity being sold off cheap and thrown into the river. Straight-laced folk who considered themselves normal, rational human beings saw all their senses collapsing like skyscrapers on top of them. It was all hazy; the sides of buildings would melt into faces and ask questions from the other side. New Jersey became ambulance city, sirens wailing constantly day and night, but it didn't stop there. There was New York, Philly and now Boston…

For four days this went on. They were glued to that TV. Ricky, Craig, Bernie, Reggie, Max and Chips. By the fifth day, it was just Max and Chips. The main street of Edgar had been cleared out. The TV was now broken, burnt out from its round the clock running just like the viewers who suffered through it. (Either that or the spanner Chips had thrown through it in helpless frustration.) The shop was silent after that. Chips wasn't doing much now, just idling in his office. Only Foster's car remained in the garage. Chips had suggested between his long hard swigs of JD that Max go home. But Max was waiting for Foster to return. He tried not to notice the way Chips had started making drunken trips from his office across to the garage, looking at Foster's vehicle, Max's pride and joy. Letting his hands tap on the bulletproof glass, making notes, weighing things. Chips had glassy eyes and slurred in his speech; that was the drink for sure, but behind it, another tune was playing in his head. To Chips, it seemed like someone had prepared.

When Foster returned six days after he'd come in, Max was just as shocked to see Foster, as Foster was surprised to find the shop was still being manned. Max got the feeling Foster was armed. His army jacket had a bulge under the left of his rib.

Chips eyed them both with disdain from afar in his office, barely standing upright.

"You got a plan, don't you?" asked Max.

Foster looked him up and down, but avoided those pleading eyes. Here was a chubby kid with doofy long hair that almost blocked his vision—the only one still at his post. Foster glanced at Chips, taking in his oily motor-slick hair and shrewd eyes; the guy looked like a schmuck that used people. Foster could feel his greasiness from a mile away and saw plain as day the way Chips was looking at Foster's car, looking at both of them.

When Foster's voice finally opened up, it was spoken as the bare bones truth.

"Government's going to try and eradicate whatever it is. Who knows how far they will go. Isolation is the key in the early stages."

"You got a place. Somewhere that's ready for this, don't you?"

"Look, kid, go home to your family."

"Only got a grandma." (The drink got Dad and Mom left after that.)

"Well then go to her."

"She's in a home… You heard what's happening in those places?"

Foster's head dropped. He had heard about what happened in those places. The hearts of the elderly were too weak to make it past those first symptoms, and if they did, there was the privilege of catching a mental disorder from someone else's mind. It spread like wildfire in those places. Those places were going to be firebombed, Foster reckoned. *Firebomb the retirement homes—it's in the national interest!*

This kid didn't want to leave his grandma. Foster knew that. He needed someone looking out for him and now Foster could see that he was the only one left who fit the bill. Foster had kids. Two sons. Hadn't spoken to them in years. One of his biggest regrets in a long list of many, yet here was a chance to redeem… Foster reached for his wallet, fumbling for it, biding time. Foster hastily handed over the cash, almost two-grand, but deep down he knew what the kid really needed, what they were all going to need soon enough.

Max watched on from the middle of the road as Foster drove off in his newly fitted, armored land warrior. He kicked away at the loose gravel on the road, feeling abandoned by Foster's silent exit. To Max's surprise, there was a commotion down the street. A scatter of people, those brave enough to still be outside, were scrambling to rake out all the food and bottled water they could. Max thought it foolish to go in there, so he just lingered outside the front of his shop, feeling more alone than ever.

Through the window, Chips watched on with a half-done bottle of Jack dangling in his hand, grasping at a notion that Foster had just rode off with his ticket to survival.

***

It was night time when Max knocked on Foster's door. Outside, the streets were dead quiet. The streetlights were still on, there was still power, for how much longer Max didn't know. Sat beside his feet was a brown suitcase, filled with all the possessions he felt he couldn't live without, and a baseball bat lying on top of it. There was a camera monitoring the door. Max felt it zooming in. He looked up at it like Oliver Brown asking for some more please.

"Sir, It's me, Max. The kid from the mechanics." He was fighting back the tears, hiding his face behind his long hair.

"I know you don't know me very well, but like I said before, I ain't got no one else…my only close relative is my grandma. She…well, this isn't easy to say, but I can feel the winds changing, and something real bad like you said is happening. I'm too young to take care of her through this… I need to survive. I ain't lived long enough yet…"

He slumped himself down on the porch, and soon the tears came. A deep sob, the only thing his body was capable of doing. He must've been there for five minutes, just slouched in heart-breaking anguish. Then, from within the white, wood-paneled house that bore in its bones a lifetime of destitution; came the sound of heavy doors opening followed by footsteps, each step drawing closer and closer to the front door. Max stared at its wooden frame in pending hope. There was a sound of locks being drawn away, followed by the creaking open of the door. Foster, wearing an green army t-shirt and camo fatigue pants, stared directly into Max's eyes, sizing the boy up once more as the kid struggled to wipe the tears away. Foster then took notice of the brown suitcase and the baseball bat that wasn't going to hold up to much in the coming storm. The kid looked like he could barely manage a bunt with that thing. When Foster finally did speak, it came out as an order, resolute in its truth. "You step into this house, you follow my orders to the letter. You don't, then we have a problem, and I can assure you I'll be just as unforgiving as this world's going to get. Do you understand?"

Max nodded.

"Pick up your suitcase and come inside."

Inside was bereft of any warmth, with barely any furniture. As Max walked past the narrow corridor he peered into the living room, where it seemed very little life had flowed. There was an odor of sweat permeating from Foster's back. The man had been busy at work and it made all the surroundings thick and pungent, crammed right in Max's face. The kitchen was at the back of the house, its contents completely stripped. Foster opened the back door and kept it open for Max to walk through. Draped under a tarp in the darkness, sitting under a termite-riddled carport, Max identified his sleeping black beauty. "Through here," Foster ordered, turning Max's head over to a cellar door tilted on a slant up against the house. Max put his suitcase down and helped pull apart the doors, really straining himself as he tried to show his strength to a Foster who clearly remained reluctant about letting him in. Max was holding onto the fact that inside the auto shop where he worked, with cars more so than people, those hands and that brain of his worked in some kind of beautiful symphony that Max knew he could play best. This would keep him firmly as an asset to Foster. *Be an asset. Be useful! Be useful!* Max tinkered away to himself, as the doors were pulled apart.

A cavern of darkness greeted them. Foster ambled down the stairs with all the confidence in the world, all too familiar with the engulfing absence it shook into Max. Then with the flick of a light switch, the place of refuge Foster had been preparing was lit up for Max to behold. Shelves were stacked with rows and rows of canned food. Multiples of portable Coleman cooking stoves stacked well against a laundry sink that brimmed to the top with plastic-wrapped cases of bottled water. The place was cozy, and the only means of comfort seemed to be Foster's bed. It seemed his only allowance, every other inch of the digs fitted for survival.

Foster pointed over to the corner with the shelves of canned food, signaling for Max to put his suitcase down. "I'll get you a bed. Won't be comfy," Foster said.

"I can help," offered Max, but Foster said he had it. A flutter of unease crept into Max. Foster wasn't kidding about comfort if he could carry the bed by himself. Was it an outdoor camping mat? Well, shit, Max hadn't brought a sleeping bag, hadn't brought a lot of things, to be honest. He just wanted to make the decision to cut and run while he had the chance, before the knowledge that he'd left Grams in that home to fend for herself caught up to him. Shit. There he was, thinking about her again, letting it stew in. She was eighty-three years old and on the slope towards dementia. Every time it comes back at you, just remember that fact, Max told himself. Just remember that fact.

Looking around the room, there was little to console Max with; this would be his home for however long it took for this thing to blow over. He stood still, fearful of touching anything, afraid that Foster would come in and notice. There were at least two hundred cans of tuna and spam, all the base substances for the barest of living. *Bare living*. Forget about the bare part, Max rationalized; just remember the living part. Also in the room: a large green locker standing the height of Max. When Foster eventually returned with (to Max's growing unease) an inflatable bed and some cushions, Max asked what was in the locker. Foster wondered if Max was the kind of kid who asked questions about everything, then reminded himself the kid was just scared. They both were, to be honest.

"Security," Foster finally answered.

Max returned a blank stare, until it dawned on him. "Oh, guns. Gotcha."

"You're going to have to be faster than that, kid."

***

Max set up his bed, hunkering in and trying to find the most comfortable position to lie down with (there was none). He tried his best to make conversation, but Foster was conservative for the most part. Foster said very little about his past, only furthering Max's imagination about this wild, military Boo Radley. When Max asked if he'd fought in the Iraq War, Foster replied, "which one?" a smile breaking from his face, a rare sight Max had already concluded. It seemed Foster had heard the stories about him, or at least knew they existed, and found them appealing enough to let them continue.

What Foster did talk about though, and in considerable length, was *it*.

That was all the boys back at the shop had talked about. Probably all anyone could talk about right now. It was hard not to. Max had barely said a word on it back in the shop, he was the youngest and as much as they respected him as a mechanic, the matter-of-fact Ricky Voss would've drowned out his two-cents worth, no doubt about it. Max had thought about suggesting it was zombies but this was rubbished off. A population destabilizer—an accidental outbreak of some government concocted plague—that's what Foster had boiled it down to. Following a panic there'd be an economic collapse and the desperation would further propel widespread violence. *Vicious cycles*, Foster called it, and Max gulped.

At Max's request, Foster brought the TV down, but the reception was shitty. The Internet on Max's phone wasn't holding up well, either. Instead, they relied on most of their news from an old transistor radio Foster seemed to cherish the same way Max was falling for that black beauty covered in tarp next to them in the above world. The news coming from the radio was intermittent, but anything that did come through was preaching all sorts of end times, running dead-on with Foster's predictions. The East Coast was imploding on itself. Manhattan had been cordoned off to stop a mass exodus. The government was not giving clear answers as to what the hell was going on or what they were trying to do to stop it. Foster would then always interject with a comment on those bumbling bureaucrats and Max would remain silent. Closer to home was California, and what they heard about it made Nevada seem like a vacation. News choppers over California reported gigantic brush fires that fire fighters were struggling to put out. Everyone was stretched. In the cities there was constant gunfire, with few outside reporters able to comprehend who the hell was shooting at whom, and for what.

For those reporters high in the sky, what they didn't report when they came back down to the explosive earth were the voices; soft, echoing demands that came in demonic whispers, rattling around in their head. These reporters didn't mention this to anyone, not even their spouses. What they did report on was the large amount of black crosses that seemed to rise tall from the ground in the foothills of Southern California and Sacramento. It seemed that wherever these crosses arose, the gunfire ceased, and when they saw that the reach of these crosses kept spreading, the adrenaline-soaked feel the body made against the relentless violence was replaced with an unnerving suspicion against whatever the hell was restoring the calm.

For four straight days Max and Foster had stayed in this cramped shelter, listening to the radio blare on, the tone in the speaker's voice growing dimmer as the speaker found it harder and harder to account for what it was exactly that they were seeing, slowly debilitating into deep pockets of lengthy pauses as comprehension became difficult. This would dissolve into a pattern of Max getting the goose bumps running all over him, before Foster would turn the radio off and try his best to refocus that fear, talk Max down with contingency plans. Foster would spell out the scenario to Max, letting him write it down and giving him five minutes to explain, under the pump, just exactly what to do. Foster would snap at him if he didn't get it right, those veins on the side of his neck throbbing out, ready to tear out of his neck and strangle Max if he got it wrong. Such frustration was amplified in the tiny room and had the same effect as an electric shock on Max. Foster blasted this visceral kind of pressure over and over until Max learned. And he did. His knuckles cracked white like cramming for a test, and Max's focus soon narrowed into a brim collection of preparing for the worst. By the third day, Foster had opened the army locker and Max was given an overview of the various assault rifles and shotguns Foster had been stockpiling. Down the bottom of the locker, taken apart were the pieces of a large machine gun, bigger than all the others.

"What is it?" Max asked, somewhat familiar with all sorts of weapons.

Foster grinned, sliding his fingers along the long barrel. He eyed it just like he did the shitty transistor radio, full of faith in its inner workings.

"M-60 machine gun. From Vietnam."

"…How old are you?"

Foster let out a short chuckle. This was more rare than a smile.

"Not *that old*… She's too heavy if we go mobile, though I know she'd be a precious commodity for trade… This new world, paper won't be necessary for a long time."

Foster talking about the new world made Max's face drop. Made him think about all those lost opportunities; all those times he scrimped away his hard earned dollars, feverishly hoping he'd get out of Edgar and make something of himself up in Nevada. The way Foster talked about this new world, declared its existence, had Max feeling that longing pain, the one he wanted to deny with every breath in his body. There was no going back to her; that youth he thought he could hold onto for just a little while longer. He was only seventeen for Christ's sake. Helplessness crept inside and hollowed him out. The old world it already was.

***

The days dragged on in this flavor, nothing but bad news getting worse. Foster had only started this survivalist bunker as a hobby, a month before Flight 34 went down. What had started as passing interest soon became his one true passion, ending up with enough resources to last him three months on a stretch. With Max there, everything had become halved. While it was never acknowledged, every time the food was split, Max kept up that mantra of his. *Be an asset. Be useful be useful*!

Foster felt his youthful eagerness as it bounced off the ever-closing walls and tried to hone this energy into figuring out their next plan.

"We'll have to move when we're down to a week's left of rations."

"We could check Main Street pretty soon."

"No. It's too early," Foster said.

"Why?"

It was stupid to ask why. Foster had already told him a thousand times over. They had to ride out the madness. Keep quiet. Let the crazies kill each other off.

"We will go when you're ready." Foster decided.

Their talk of future plans, future movement, brought with it more questions. Once they had ridden out the madness, what then? They talked of leaving, but where to? Go to Main Street, find more supplies, consume them. Move elsewhere, find more supplies, and then consume them. The prospects were bleak. What was next? What came after survival? Max had asked Foster this, and the man who had prepared for the end of the world was found ill-equipped in comforting words of hope. Were they going to help rebuild society? Was this even possible?

***

It was on the eighteenth night (and the hundred and fiftieth game of Go Fish) when Max's silent wishing for the boredom to end came knocking on the front door. They turned to the two camera monitors surveying Foster's front door and the back of his small house covering the carport and the entrance to their bunker. Outside, knocking on the door, leaning on it when he wasn't knocking, a bottle of Jack in his other hand—light on the liquid—cut a restless figure. Chips.

Foster ordered Max to keep dead quiet, and Max obliged, now only able to hear his heart pounding away. It took a good five minutes of that sloppy knocking before Chips noticed the camera above him. There was no sound feed, just Chips waving his arms about forcefully. He then began kicking at the door, almost losing his balance and falling backwards off the porch. While his old boss entranced Max, who tried to figure out if he was sick, drunk—or both, Foster had already slid his bed out and opened a shaft leading to a crawl space up towards the house.

Before Max had a chance to comprehend there was a secret crawl space, Foster had hissed for him to stay put and keep quiet.

Keep quiet, keep quiet, keep quiet!

By the time Max had returned his eyes to the monitor, Chips had given up on the front door, Max just catching his back, freezing in terror as a shiny pistol hanging out the back of Chips' pants was flashed, if only for a brief moment. With heart in mouth, Max waited, everything in him clenched tight, pleading that the moment would pass. The screen stayed blank. Chips had given up. He'd gone away, wasn't going to hurt anybody tonight, least not them. But then, to Max's horror, he heard footsteps outside, slushing up the gravel driveway.

Now Chips had appeared in the rear screen and seemed to have found what he was looking for. The night vision on the camera was grainy, but Max was getting most of it. Chips stumbled over to the tarp covered SUV, and, throwing away his bottle, grabbed the tarp with both hands and began yanking it off. At this point he started yelling, loud enough for Max to hear.

"I know you're in there! …Piece a' shit. Hey, I got a family! Needs protecting too, asshole! Who you think you are? Keeping all the surviving…surviving shit to yourself…fucking bastard."

As he kept swearing away he began kicking at the door of the SUV, then picking up a piece of timber ply which he then tried swinging at the windows, the timber bouncing off the black tints, unharmed. Take any other day and Max would have beamed in admiration. But on this night he felt himself shrinking smaller and smaller till Foster fixed it. Max heard shuffling in the house. Foster was moving. Then the back door was swung open and Max caught the back of Foster's head on-screen as Chips reached for his pistol. A loud BANG followed.

Max closed his eyes and held his breath, suffocating in the silence that draped the now still night. He dared not open them and watch the victor still standing or stumbling. When he heard something heavy being dragged across the grass, he knew. He pried those eyes open to catch Foster methodically laying down some tarp onto the ground.

Max didn't know if Chips was sick or drunk, but he knew at that moment it was here. It wasn't just on that crappy radio or that shitty TV, but right here in Edgar. This was the new world.

13. Voices

The shops are empty. Everything's been stripped bare. Sharon got what she could yesterday; two garbage bags full of fruit, ramen and boxes of crackers. She nearly didn't make it home; a big brute of a man tried to snatch the bags from right out of her hands, but Samantha, our daughter, hit him with a loose brick from someone's previous front wall. This was only four blocks from our home. When they came rushing through the door, spilling out their story, I couldn't match up the image of Samantha hurting anyone like that. This was our sweet daughter. Everyone in the neighborhood always spoke highly of her. Samantha's a natural at sport. She may even get a soccer scholarship if she doesn't choose to focus on becoming first chair. I'm not sure why she would throw it away by assaulting a stranger like that.

Sharon is practically tearing her hair out when I ask what happened to the man. She seems confused by my concern.

"I don't know, Doug, for fucks sake! We were out of there while we had the chance."

***

It took me a whole day to bar up the house. Ran out of timber three quarters through the upstairs and had to pull out some floorboards from downstairs. Just as a precaution, the doors are sealed too, who knows if this thing's airborne? Samantha won't come out of her room. I hear muffled crying when I make my way up there, stopping myself short of opening it and seeing my daughter. I just can't bring myself to look her in the face. If I see her and then I cry it's all over. They need me to be strong, competent. I can't tell either of them I saw an invisible elephant fucking an invisible giraffe when I scurried out of the gun store. I can't let them think I've lost it. *Keep it together, Doug!* Or was it a giraffe fucking an elephant? You know what, it was probably that.

***

Sharon's glued to the TV. Those eyes of hers barely blink. She's got Laura Finberg of CNN on around the clock blasting this *thing* out into our living room. She hasn't said a word all day. Or was that yesterday? Sirens blare outside, whirling this way and that, off to the next outbreak.

They've got this lettering system: the *A*'s, *B*'s, *C*'s, and *D*'s. Laura's trying to simplify the madness, condense it into easy to digest parts for us, like CNN has turned into a twisted sesame street. The *A*'s use the *B*'s and the *C*'s are just crazy. *C*'s are just the early stages before they become *B*'s. Then there's the *D*'s. The *D*'s don't even make it to the *C*'s. They get to miss the whole show.

Even with rationing, we won't last two weeks. I'd make a run but it was bedlam in the shopping district last time Sharon spoke…whenever that was. The TV blares all the time. It bleeds the violence, and we can't stop watching.

They think it's become airborne. Laura Finberg of CNN now tells me they are declaring Martial law in fifty states. Police in riot gear flood the screen while tanks and Humvees zip past in droves. California is gone; it's all black crosses. They aren't going to abandon it they're just going to focus on smaller outbreaks—yes, that's what they're saying. That means the government is going to come and sweep all the crazies out real soon, then we can go back to being a happy family again! I will go back to work and finish the Henderson's account, Sharon will clean up this house and take Samantha to her soccer practice and we can just forget this whole thing ever happened.

The orders are clear. The army's going to go door to door—see if you're sick. Avoid drinking from the tap. Stay indoors and isolate yourself. Just wait. Just wait. Stop the spread.

Sharon's broken her silence; she started telling me she's hearing voices.

"That's one of the first signs says Laura," she blurts out to me, clinging desperately to my arms, an ugly strain in her face as tears run down them. Sharon's desperate; I can see it in her sad little eyes. She needs to tell me what she's been hearing and what the voices are telling her to do. I don't want to know, so I edge myself backwards. What if she tells me and then I catch whatever she's got?

I panic. A slap across the face and the room is silent. My hand still reverberates with the sting. In the corner of my eye I see Samantha, as quiet as a mouse, fear brewing in her tight lips as she struggles to get the words out. "I hear them too," she whispers.

I sit them down in the living room, family meeting style. I act like I haven't been listening to Laura of CNN, like I don't know the symptoms, like all I've heard for the past few days is anything but that bitch's voice. *First it starts with the paranoia. A sneaking suspicion that your world is changing ever so slightly, tilting in a direction you have no control over and feel ambivalent about. If they like you, you feel warm. If they don't like you, then they treat you like any person with the flu; all contact is broken and your world spirals into this big black mess of confusion. An endless kaleidoscope of terror, your darkest fears, scaling the skin and burning holes where they see fit, ever so gently. And when all the walls inside fall and the chains of society are no more, you will beg them to take you in—to feel that bathing glow of warmth. And we are coming, Doug. We are coming for you.*

A strange thing for a news reporter to say, don't you think? But I digress.

They remain painfully still as they sit. They avoid my eyes.

"What is it you're hearing?" I calmly begin.

They look at each other, afraid to talk. "Voices," Sharon breaks. That's all they say and in the silence I begin to suspect they're afraid to tell me because the voices are talking about me, about them hurting me.

"What is it they are saying?" I ask, trying to conceal the shaking of my hands. There is only silence as they avoid my gaze; it cuts the room open. Sharon's frantic now, she's telling me to put the gun down. I feel the coldness of the trigger as the tip of my finger twitches over it.

"WHAT ARE THEY SAYING?" I yell, a pounding pressure building in my head, filling my ears. There are drums beating all around the room, the heat all turned up and my heart struggles to keep pace. A part of me itches to end it; that it's their fault we're in this god-forsaken mess… The next thing I know, I snap back. The gun lowers slowly, and I see Samantha's face, all red and swollen in the panic, her eyes trailing the lowered gun until it is by my side. Her eyes then meet with mine. "It wants us to join them."

***

We argue openly now. Or maybe it's just me. Sharon seems to just take whatever I give to her. I don't mean to do it; it's all just spilling out too fast beyond my command. Samantha creeps around the house likes she's afraid of me. I insist that it's just cabin fever that's got me down; got me pacing all over, repeated patterns; don't touch the cracks in the floor. No cause for alarm.

Little light enters the house; we're already starting to look paler. When the slits of light we cling onto sets, I feel my eyes begin to deceive me. Shadows move in sinister ways; bony fingers like the banisters of the stairs. Have they got into the house already?

***

Sharon and Samantha left last night. Took all the food; right out the front door. My gun was lifted, right out of my pants. I would have saved them, but I was sleeping. Sleep. Hadn't been getting much this past week—or two?

The TV doesn't work. All electricity is out. But it's okay though; Samantha will fix it when she gets back.

Without the TV, I spend most of my time watching the world fall apart outside through those tiny slits between the boarded up timber panels. Some of the houses across the street have had their windows covered as well. My hands tremble all the time now. I get these inner urges trying to pull me outside, see if those neighbors of mine are okay. But of course that's just what they want me to do. Trust them. Believe we're in the same boat, they aren't infected and neither am I. It's just what they want before

I'm knocked out and being fed to their kids. You know what, fuck the neighbors, seriously. I lent Tim that hedge trimmer three months ago and it took him two months to return it—only after I asked him, of course. Fuck Tim. Fuck Tim and his hungry kids.

The government spooks keep telling us to wait it out in our homes while they seek out the people making the noises in our heads. Of course I'm furious about the whole thing. I've heard what they've been doing to those people that give themselves up. They try to put them down and then they're surprised when they resist. The government can't protect us from the voices. *I don't want them to...*

Why should I be punished—and why the hell do the walls keep breathing? It's so fucking stuffy in this house and my gut keeps rumbling, I'm so damn hungry. Sometimes all I can hear is this deep voice, beckoning me to follow him into the light. And when I close my eyes, I see this man with the deep voice. He dresses real nice. Wears a sharp suit and makes sense of things, makes sense of the world. But then sometimes I hear this other, irritably high-pitched voice that buzzes around the edge of that delectably deep voice. This whiny voice screeches and begs for me to leave his head. I don't think he realizes he's the one in control. He's always freaking out, scrambling crayon swears on the insides of his house, on the inside of my mind. The man in the suit is telling the scared one to relax. He's telling him to leave us be. I like the man in the suit. He says he likes me. But the man in the suit doesn't like the scared one. He says the scared one lives close by to me and my other brothers and sisters. He suggests we get rid of the scared one.

I like his suggestion.

Use the axe.

14. Escape

Peeping through the single slit of their house, Peter Storrs watched as the suburbs he had once bemoaned for their lack of "fun" rapidly begin to disintegrate. Smoke billowed through the air while those trying to catch a peek from behind him made wild guesses about where the fire had begun.

"It's the Wal-Mart on Belmont and Fifth," cried Claire, before her friend, Molly, added, "They've broken through the Rockies, its all around us now! We've got to leave while we still can!"

Peter stepped away from the window and watched as the others filled his space to let their minds drift further into fear. Peter knew it wasn't the Wal-Mart—the fire and frequent gun shots were much closer; it was probably the school or church only blocks away, but he saw there was no point in voicing such an opinion.

Claire turned away from the window and reached for Peter's arms. "We can't wait much longer, I don't think he'll make it," she blurted in a vain hope of scaring Peter into jumping ship, but Peter held firm. "We don't leave until he comes back. You walk out there without him and you're as good as dead."

As Peter spoke, there was the thunderous boom of an explosion nearby, shuddering the walls of their house.

"It's the petrol station on Henson Drive!" Tom Waters, by the window, yelled. Peter's eyes met Claire's. Unable to reassure her, he retreated downstairs.

Every room was filled with strangers they had picked up, everyone looking for a way out of the chaos. As Peter walked to the back door, they rushed past him in the hallway, scrambling to pack their clothes and empty the kitchen of all its useful contents. When he got to the backdoor he saw her, knees down in the grass, her body facing the statue of a baby angel.

Madeline Bamsner; an angel herself with a caring heart that sunk the fuzzies well below the skin, who could warm any room with a just a flash of her smile, had walked into Peter's life when she started seeing his best friend, Cole, the man they now waited for with each excruciating second.

Peter stood by the door watching Maddie. She was praying, an act she hadn't done since the third grade. She'd dismissed it as the purest form of nonsense to Cole, and it was the first time Cole had seen her get riled up, regardless of the fact he completely agreed with her. Yet there she was, her hands clasped together touching the tip of her nose as her mouth moved in whispered motion. Peter thought it odd she was praying to god; in times of trouble many turned to the heavens for answers, but Peter saw these recent events as proof there was no one to answer to in the sky above. Then again, maybe she wasn't talking to God. Peter's grip on the doorhandle tightened as he braced himself to interrupt her in this vulnerable state, but he was cut short by a distinctive knock on the front door. Everyone had left their rooms and now stood by their doors, their eyes drawn to the front door. Peter moved briskly past them until his face was inches from the door. He took a deep breath before opening it. Cole stood like stone, his face unmoved by the chatter of machine gun fire that filled the air of the madness outside.

"Did you find them?" asked Peter, already sure of the answer. Cole stared vacantly for a while before springing into life.

"No. They weren't at home."

"What about Phil and Frannie?"

Cole's face tightened up at the mention of their names. Phil had seen the way things were heading and had decided he wasn't going to let Frannie endure the coming catastrophe. Finding them both like that was the real reason Cole had gone off looking for his own parents. He couldn't stand to lose both in such a short amount of time. Cole did not answer the question and Peter knew enough to let it slide. Colen then looked beyond Peter to the cowering faces clutching doorframes. "Get your things, we leave now."

Without a second to lose, the heads disappeared into the rooms, picking up their bags.

"North?" Peter asked.

"North," Cole confirmed.

Maddie came rushing through the hallway and hugged Cole with everything she had.

"Please, don't leave again," she whispered between the tears.

"Never again." Cole responded.

"Your parents?"

"I looked everywhere…" Cole began, his whole face welling up, his eyes beginning to break, before Maddie tightened her hug.

"I'm sorry, Cole. I'm so sorry."

Everyone scattered out of the house as a channel chopper buzzed above them. Piling into the cars, Cole told them not to look beyond the ground in front of them. As the other cars were filled up, Peter and Maddie rushed into the front car, urging Cole to jump inside, but Cole found himself breaking his own rules; staring at the smoke he had passed on his way back. Lit up from the inside of a church, it swayed backwards and forth into the sky, holding Cole transfixed until the chopper sent the smoke swirling in all different directions. Cole then looked up at the chopper, whose dark glass eyes seemed to watch him and only him. He brushed off this paranoid feeling he'd seen the same chopper before back in California, and broken from his gaze, Cole fled to the beaten down Camry and dived inside. Peter slammed his foot hard down on the pedal as he left his parents' home, leading the charge out of a Colorado in chaos.

Even with the engine revving through the scattered debris that lined the roads, they could still hear the screams. Peter skilfully bobbed and weaved through broken down cars and crazed pedestrians, who ran about aimlessly trying to hide from the *voices*. Most people had left the safety of their houses now, those powerful urges too great to fight. Some sat on their lawns completely bug-eyed, bathing in the heat, completely oblivious to the whirling sounds of destruction all around them. Peter almost swerved off the road when he saw someone using a hedge trimmer on the windows of their house.

"It started back up again two days ago," Peter yelled back to Cole who frantically kept Maddie's head buried deep in his chest, avoiding the ghastly carnage that surrounded them. "There were explosions everywhere, we must've heard at least twenty by now. The army swooped in but I think they left when it started—OH FUCK!"

There was the screeching of tires first, then the thud of a dog smashing the front headlight, startling Maddie, who tore herself away from Cole's chest to see what had happened. An old woman had charged at the dog, her mouth dribbling as if ready to eat this scampering animal. Its escape had run the course of Peter's Camry.

"What the fuck was that?" Maddie blurted before Cole pulled her back into his warm embrace. "Just a dog," he said, "just a dog."

Making the final turn out of Peter's neighborhood, the brakes were slammed once again, as Peter's eyes radiated in shock at the sight of dangling legs hanging by a street lamp, a ladder tipped over next to the lamp.

"I don't get it… I just don't get it." Peter muttered to himself, his head tapping lightly on his headrest. The car behind beeped furiously. It was Claire screaming for Peter to haul ass. Maddie pulled herself off Cole and repeated the instructions. Breathing heavy, Peter re-gripped the steering wheel and they began to move again. They made their way through his suburb towards the interstate highway, ready to gun it northward. Hopes of an open track were immediately cut short as cars were blocked in bumper-to-bumper frustration all along the turn. Discouraged by this, Peter, Maddie and Cole watched on as people in their cars banged furiously against the windscreen and all the door windows, the screws in their heads dangling heedlessly off the hinges. Peter and Cole shared a glance.

"We can take Fourth Avenue; skip up toward Fort Collins then cross the tip of the Rockies into Wyoming," said Peter.

Maddie wasn't up for it. "That's through the rest of the sub-urbs! You think they're going to be any better than your street?"

"WE GOT THROUGH DIDN'T WE?" Peter screamed back at her, ready to unbuckle his seat and slap her across the face. Their blood ran hot and the car became a furnace boiling with frustration. Inside, they all tried to stop the retching in their throats, keep down what they'd seen.

Peter and Maddie now both turned to Cole, who tried to back away in the suffocating seat. It was life or death, Peter or Maddie. Cole wanted to crawl into the seat and blend in with the fabric. Peter was good at making decisions and his seemed the only choice, while Maddie dug into his arm, still giving no clear alternative. She was shaking, they all were. Just as Cole bumbled out, "I don't know," the frustrations of one man broke into his view only twenty yards from their car, a shotgun raised as the man tried to make space for the cars in front of him to move. The explosion of the back window of a family van was splattered with blood, sending Peter and Maddie's attention back to the shrill screams of other's fleeing their vehicles on this blocked interstate.

"Okay, just do it!" Cole finally let out.

Pulling into reverse and almost hitting Claire's pickup, the convoy turned back up into his neighborhood, running alongside the highway looking for a way across. They nicked through a crossing a few miles down.

The other side was eerily quiet. There were no people sun-bathing in the madness out on their lawn, no half-naked miscre-ants with deviant looks in their eyes. No, this quiet was much worse, sending their convoy down to a crawl in growing fear, getting this unsettling notion that the hammer was about to come down. At first Peter wanted to tell Maddie he was right, that not everywhere was as devastated as his suburb, but in all fairness Peter preferred seeing the crazies rather than feeling them lurking in the shadows.

They snaked around Longmont, gunned it through Berthoud, and then circled round Loveland; all in silence, nobody outside in the open, just the odd speeding wheels ready to make a quick getaway just like them.

In the distance, a loose hanging road sign indicated the approaching Fort Collins. Fort Collins was one of the largest towns in Colorado, and even though they had made it this far without actual harm gracing their bodies, Fort Collins remained a black hole like Denver: to be avoided at all costs.

"We go around it."

"Through the parks? Or re-join the interstate?"

"The parks! Get some altitude on this *thing*."

It was settled. They cut quickly left in a four-way intersection, almost hitting the curb with unnecessary speed, the mountains now looming in front of them. Gunning it along the empty street, they caught up to a man jogging methodically with an axe. Entranced by this individual who seemed to take no notice of them, they drew level with the man from across the street, no one in the car noticing the voracious crowd of thirty or so up ahead, their clothes visibly ripped and neglected, dragging a shirtless weakling out the front of his house where from the branch of a tall seasoned oak a noose was laid. Peter hadn't noticed their car had come to a complete stop, instead having only eyes for the axe jogger who joined this maddened crowd as they hoisted this man, kicking and screaming, into his final position. They watched on in horror as the deed was done, Claire not beeping them on as she usually did, too caught up in this twisted specta-cle. The crowd then turned to one man, previously hidden from Peter's view.

The man stood above them like he was levitating, his feet hovering gracefully by the sheer will of their collective con-sciousness. He wore a black suit and matching tie, all the attire suitable for a funeral, except for a wicked smile that was lapped up by all the other wild-eyed folk like loyal, hungry dogs.

As the words, "What the fuck…" escaped from Peter's breath, the man in the suit suddenly came to life, his stare reach-ing inside their car, making Cole and Maddie jump backwards to the far side of the back seat. The man in the suit raised his arm and pointed directly at them, sending the crowd dashing towards them in a murderous rage, weapons wailing wildly. Peter snapped into action and burned rubber, the boot of the screech-ing Camry narrowly missing the wild swing of the axe jogger. Swerving past, Claire's side mirror was swiped as a token from an emaciated girl, left growling at the cars as they made their escape.

Their hearts racing, not a word was spoken for miles. Even-tually they cleared the suburbs and found themselves climbing higher and higher up the grade, hoping that the over-hanging trees would swallow their path to all that could have followed.

It was the beeping of the last car in the tired convoy that led Peter to pull over. The sun was well and truly out of sight and darkness was beginning to descend. Ashton Gaines, the eldest of the group peeked out of his Rover, the last car of the convoy, with four others; a dried salty sweat still stuck to his skin from when they saw the hanging. They all met at Claire's middle car as Lamar, her friend, comforted her.

"We're almost out of gas," said Ashton.

Peter was curt. "How much is almost?"

Ashton paused for thought before looking at his wife, Amy, for support.

"The needle's been touching the red for a while now," he said.

There was silence as the group absorbed this fact. There was thirty miles at best when you were hitting the red. The closest gas stop would be back down the mountain and into the jaws of the cock-eyed crazies. But Amy was building up a case…

"There's a stop-over village not too far ahead. It's got a lookout area and one main street."

Peter looked at Cole, whose grip and sight never left Maddie. He then looked back at Amy.

"How you know about this?"

"I used to pass through there with my family when I was a kid."

Glances were shared between all of them, with all focus inevitably making its way to Peter. It was an obvious choice, for what alternative was there? The light was fading with every passing minute and each of their souls had been fed through a meat-grinder today.

"Well, we'll need more than your nostalgia to make it through the night, but I guess it's the best we got right now. Take the lead, Amy…"

As they returned to their cars, Peter nudged Cole off to the side away from Maddie.

"That freak in the suit; you see the way he was looking at us?"

Cole nodded, thinking back to the point where blood-curdling voices were expelled from the man's stiff finger as he tried to reach into them.

"Will he follow us?" asked Peter.

Cole was never much of the reassuring type, nor was it usual for Peter to look so jilted. Cole was drawn to Peter's hands that still shook in fear; the same hands that supported a young Cole when he needed help, leading him away from that fiery pastor. Hands that took his sulking head when he'd dropped his way out of college, and led him to a bar as good friends do.

Where he met a girl and everything changed.

Now it was Cole's turn, and he found the words as best he could. "If he does, we'll hide, we'll do whatever it takes… We're going to make it through this, Pete. *Remember: to the end.*"

That night, as they huddled into the abandoned stores on the main street of Trent, weary beyond belief, Cole began to have his dream—the one he'd have every night thereafter, only to always forget with waking eyes. The dream of a burning building, the fire lit by an old man with veins on his neck throbbing with red-hot hatred, urging Cole to join in the fun. Then, Cole would find himself standing on a throne of rubble, below him a crowd of endless faces, some he knew very well. And like a flood funneled directly into his ears came the building noise of questions.

15. The Federals

Everything was in free fall. Deep below the White House, a digital map displayed the spread of Tyrantocillous. Blinking red lights encompassed where chaos reigned, and all of the United States was lit up in endless blinking. The Commander-in-Chief was running out of manpower to command: All around the country, military units and local authorities were abandoning their posts in droves, hoping desperately to find a place to stave off infection. But there was nowhere to go, no escaping the inevitable...

The CDC needed more live specimens of Type *A's*, but not a single live one was coming forward or being caught. Nobody that powerful would be the guinea pig. The authorities knew these people existed. There was the man in New York, the woman in Boston. But these people were dead on arrival, collected after being put down by other Type *A's*. It was in the blood type and other specific genes, that's all they could discern. Everyone up to the Joint Chiefs of Staff gave blood samples with gracious hope that at least one of them, someone within their circle could potentially contract the Type *A* strain. The Top Dog was speech-less when he got his results back. Would they still listen to him? Did he have the right? They said it was dependent on the genes, well, didn't his father say he was a born leader? Weren't those the exact words bestowed upon him? *Dress me up in a suit, real proper, but what did it mean if the faith was gone? What authority could be called upon?*

Slumped in his chair, the Top Dog had slowly lifted his gaze to his second in command and thrown those lanky arms of his up in the air. Was there anyone left in his corner with the gift? *Call the Kennedy's, I suppose?*

They swiped up Type *B*'s by the thousands but no one could get a read on how their brains connected up to the *A*'s. Was it a virus that induced telepathy; that made *B*'s slaves to the *A*'s? They knew the *A*'s existed, but without a live specimen, study-ing the interaction was impossible. Whatever the case, it seemed both strains sent the host into fits of unspeakable delusion in the initial stages as this thing learned to live in their skin.

Their best chance at any kind of Intel had been offset by a renegade F-16, lighting up a small facility, a part of USAMRIID that had supposedly once held an original sample and years of research. Their best man for the job, a former chief supervisor of Blackwater, and the only one not in Blackwater when three missiles and an F-16 torpedoed through it, claimed his team had been focused on perfecting the Tyrantocillous virus before pursuing a vaccine, and even then he wasn't much use—a broken neck; a calculated murder—someone covering their tracks in the sea of chaos.

With the former supervisor gone and all his staff mangled fixtures of the rubble, there were no more experts left to consult with, no groundwork to start from. All of it incinerated, along with their chances.

Numbers. The Top Dog was being crushed by some over-whelming figures, and it was only getting worse. Like a building tsunami, the projections were rising rapidly each hour, with the numbers taking them to ninety percent as of day forty-three. Ninety-percent. That was 285 million people, all out of their heads; crumbling inside, tearing down the very walls of society that had once kept them safe. If having blood type AB meant you had the hold on people, then the number of Type *A*'s could poten-tially reach as high as 12.7 million. Everyday people plucked out of the blue, suddenly inundated with this overwhelming power and no experience in how to control the growing masses inside their head.

How would they handle it—suddenly having the will of so many others at their fingertips? That was almost a best-case scenario, because what if they were already in positions of pow-er—what if they enjoyed the taste of *more*? 12.7 million and Ted "Top Dog" Roland had a terrible feeling few of those would play nice.

Roland had his suspicions. There had been a questioning of priorities when the president ordered scores of Special Forces teams after the former senator, Barclay Richards. There were bigger fish to fry they argued, but Roland had felt enough to sense Richards had something to do with this outbreak. Word from those close to him had spoken of Richards suffering a mysterious illness before Flight 34 went down. There was also the talk of the snubbing, and whispered claims that amongst the chaos, the cowboy was moving northward, marching on Wash-ington.

All this had Roland fearing the worst. Because if he was right, if Richards did have it, then the bad times were only just beginning…

This was of course before the madness had taken Roland; had taken all of them. They had been running things from below the White House floors; securely locked in by several layers of concrete. *Her* infiltration was most likely one of the many members of staff returning from the surface, no visible symptoms showing. Once it got down there, trapped in enclosed corridors and rooms, the ventilation cycling the air through all areas, it was only a matter of time.

Roland had thought it was just a cold at first. A cold set on by the stress of every exhausted option sent crashing and burning on arrival. He had remembered feeling the soreness in his throat, the dripping of mucus slithering its way out his nose, and thought: *This! On top of everything else!* But colds didn't make you see things, hear strange voices, feel these rapturous urges…

None of this had been reported, this mad minute under the capital that spanned two days to a week for some. No one could know just how susceptible those at the top were—even in their suits and positions of power—to a bug that wasn't letting up. They did not speak of this phase at all, not even to each other. These manic hours locked away in whatever room of isolation they could afford, the fever burning out their darkest of fears which wrapped tight around the skin, removing all the barriers of sanity right before their grainy eyes. Some cried like babies, pleading for their mothers. And when it all settled and they'd regained a solid footing, they were just grateful to breathe in some semblance of logic and reason, thinking optimistically that they'd passed through the eye of the needle. Not unscathed, that much was true and always would be, but still alive.

This was the way it went, whether you caught it in the first days, weeks or months from now. But it was yours, like a rite-of-passage into the burning world. A Brave new world someone had once called it.

They had tank busters, predator drones, surface-to-air missiles, armor-piercing bullets, A-10s, F-18s, apache helicopters, stealth bombers, and nuclear warheads. They were the world leaders on major conflicts of the twentieth century, aware of all sorts of terrains and all kinds of enemies. They'd fought in jungles, deserts, the cities of Europe and they thought they had seen everything. Fighting against an insurgency in Iraq and Afghanistan was a gargantuan task, but they had stuck right up in it, slowly getting the hang of fighting invisible enemies among the civilians.

They had history, tradition—the constitution.

And then there was this virus.

This virus, plucked out from within, and all those weapons, all that training and all that history was useless when *it* was everywhere and everyone became the enemy. Roland knew the solution, knew it right from the beginning: lose. But who would be willing to accept the fact that the Type *A*'s were the only ones who could bring peace to the madness that coursed through every vein in America. Few would admit, but none could deny: they were the new world leaders.

And lose Roland would.

***

No one in the command room had noticed him walking in; somehow he'd slipped past security, past those heavy doors and strolled on in where endless chains of smoke drifted above the table seating the remaining Executive Branch and Joint Chiefs of Staff. All he had on him was a pen and a message to deliver. In an instant they were flying out of their chairs, scrambling in shrieking terror over one another to get out of his way.

There was blood, *so much blood.*

Roland felt the sweat run down his back as he crawled backwards up against the cold, hard gray wall of the command room that now looked set to become their final resting place. Amidst the broken yelps from his beloved wife filling the room, the sharp words of a dead man played repeatedly in his head.

Sir, we must do something while we have the power to do so…

Roland's hands clammed up as they brought his knees further in, ready to turn himself into a ball, rock away all his problems. He began to rock, the back of his head tapping the wall as the motion settled him in his body's last apparent attempt to keep itself together. It was the worst he had shown of himself since everything went to hell almost two months ago (not that the others had fared much better). Those close to him had seen his entire presence slowly disintegrate under the grating pressure and paranoia that blasted him each passing moment since that plane went down. Sure, he had volunteered for the job and it was known by all as the most demanding position on the planet, but if you had told him he would be dealing with a threat like this; if he'd been given a preview to the types of twisted horrors he'd bear witness to? No. He would politely decline, clean the papers on his desk, and blow his brains out. Term over.

His wife, Joint Chiefs of Staff and those of his cabinet that remained had stood by in growing concern as he stopped caring about his appearance and personal hygiene and most of all, stopped hiding the familiar passage of sweat that formed on his back whenever he found himself against the ropes. He had felt its familiar journey many times throughout his life, and as he vied hard for the position in office, he found himself concealing its presence from the furnace glare of the media, who in turn searched for a glimpse of it when pressing him with the tough issues. He always wore suits, avoided see-through shirts and showered regularly, always conscious that his enemies would be quick to feast on his fear lest they catch a whiff. As the events of Flight 34 and everything that followed unfolded and his appearances to the public had abruptly cut to zero, his state deteriorated to the point where he could not hide the fear that now covered every inch of his body and left him in that rocking position, the sweat on his back an uncomfortable reminder of problems that now seemed almost bearable to the conundrum he stared at, now leaking blood onto the cold floor.

It was his second in command, his most trusted advisor—his best friend—now just a bloody centerpiece of the bunker room. Everyone at the large oval table had flown out of their chairs, just like Roland had done, when that young staffer had come in and tried to kill him with only a ball-point pen in his soft, dainty hands. The young man would've succeeded had the president's dearest friend not taken his place, gallantly pushing Roland aside as the man swung away with a cold dead look that brought horror to everyone in the shrinking, suffocating space.

One stab. Blue ink and blood; right in the throat. His friend bled out in minutes.

Security quickly restrained the man and had him taken outside the room to be shot. As they threw him along, he put up little fight and said nothing, his empty stare through dark-rimmed glasses reaching the president from across the room and shaking him to his core as the face brought an instance of recognition to his rattled memory. The kid was a communications clerk of some sort, the president clearly remembering walking past this feeble upstart at his desk as he had passed through the communications sector of the underground complex. Putting his hand on the young man's shoulder and mustering up his trademark courageous persona, he had commended everyone in that room for working so damn hard in these times of national duress, assuring them the hard yards they were putting in would be a major catalyst in winning back the America they once knew. This young man had beamed with the most earnest of pride and gratefully thanked the president; shaking his hand with firm, reassuring support the president wished he could reciprocate with any account of genuine confidence. That youthful smile and the feel of his hand now burned holes of furious blood-bursting anger in the president's mind, overwhelming him to the point of yelping in hopeless anguish. How much was a man to take?

"Get someone in here to clean this goddamn mess up—and don't tell anyone out there what has happened!" It was his third in command, Secretary of State, Bill Macready, now taking control of the chaotic mess that had filled the room. "AND SHUT HER UP!" Macready added, ordering two suits to calm down the screaming first lady. Before the president could finish rocking himself into oblivion he felt a hand restrain him. Macready bent down to his level, and looked him straight in the eyes before he repeated the words of his late friend, the second in command. "Sir, we must do something now while we still have the power to do so…"

The president saw Macready was trying to be strong, to hold everyone together, but this was pure desperation. Macready did not want this responsibility. He just needed to believe that Roland could alleviate their woes. That the President of the United States of America could once again stand strong.

Helping the president up and to his chair, Macready ran his fingers through his hair and sat down in the seat that once occupied Roland's second in command. Roland slumped in his chair; the sticky pool of sweat that had lathered the back of the seat once again reunited with his back. Macready stared forcefully at everyone else in the room, beckoning them to return to their seats. They did so reluctantly. They remained in silence while security fumbled around getting the body out of the room. With the shutting of the door, Macready slid some papers across the desk to the president. Roland stared at it but had no intention of reading.

"Sir, these are several directives regarding the issues of national communications, drone efficiency, and the security of our national nuclear missile sites. I would…" Macready stopped as the president's attention had drifted back to the splatter of wiped-up blood at the heart of where his friend had just died. Noticing this, Macready took his blazer from his chair and rashly threw it over the mess. He then promptly slapped the president across the face. Everyone in the room froze except for Roland, who was snapped back from his daze into a resigned clarity.

"You can't do that, you know," Roland spoke of hiding the blood. "All our blood is in the open now, ripe for the taking…" Macready ignored this drifting announcement and took the papers back, reading them aloud for the whole party to hear.

"Under Article 32.6 of Operation Wounded Eagle, under duress from inside forces we determine the initiative of cutting power to all media outlets and phone lines nationwide for the purpose of removing enemy access to these resources. And with regards to our nuclear—"

"God dammit how are we going to fight back if we can't communicate with each other?" It was the Secretary of Defense, who could finally take no more of his own helplessness in trying to remedy a solution.

"Those lines of communication will be used by them just as effectively as what just happened in this very room moments ago. They will take us quicker if we leave them the technology to do so," retorted Macready, the dichotomy of outcomes slicing at the thick air of the room.

What was it going to be? A quick death, or a bleak future of endless running and hiding?

They now all looked towards the president who avoided their pleading gazes, placing his focus on the light that shone on the desk. He continued with his line of thought.

"We can't…we can't just hide what we've done, what has happened here, which we ourselves have allowed to occur. We made our play with the drones and the screenings, but it is done. These directives; we turn off the power, they turn it back on… Our hand has been played and it has failed."

As he spoke these words the final nail in the coffin had been struck, the knowledge that he would be the last American president sealed, along with the hopes and dreams of a future he had once set out for himself. Yet his face gave none of this away; as if he had shrugged off all the violence he had beared witness to these past two months, these last few moments. He stood, slowly but surely, ready for one last impassioned speech.

"You've asked me to make the decisions while we still have the power to make them. I don't personally believe the interna-

tional quarantine will succeed. The Type *A*'s will take our minds
and fight amongst each other for the power to control us. It may
not be the life many had chosen, but it may not be our end. What
I do know is that in all this conflict, cool heads may be lost and
in the near future a madman may deploy our most devastating
weapon on this great land or use it on the rest of the world. We
must ensure access to these weapons is permanently disabled.
This may be the only way we can save our people."

They knew what he meant and calls were made immediately. All over the room the sound of resignation, of closure, were
felt as thoughts of sacrifice. They heard him say he would save
the people and it truly felt to them as if it were they themselves
making this valiant act. His wife stood from around the table
and smiled until she fell into his arms, proud of him as the tears
began to swell again from her eyes. The sight of their embrace
caused a painful reminder of what the others had given up in possibly their final days. Ruing this thought, they tried to comfort
themselves in their collective sacrifice for the greater good, but
this was short-lived and very much in vain as they soon found
out. The young man's stumbling, violent foray into the most
secure part of the underground facility had not been to kill the
president, but to find him. To see his eyes light up in sheer horror
after being told his fate.

At first it came in a slight tingle—a shiver in the hands. Then
it began to course through their veins, lifting the hairs one by
one all over their bodies. They all stared at each other in utter
confusion. *Can you feel it too?* The room itself began to move
and sway as their minds sweltered under this alien presence that
reached into their souls and made them feel utterly naked until
a white beam of light surged above the table. As the light came

to focus, they all saw the face of the man that the president had thrown his growing suspicions at ever since this whole ordeal began to unfold.

Like a hologram, he hovered above the center of the round table, facing every member with gleaming eyes and a wicked smirk that slashed at their hearts, washing away any embers of hope that remained in them.

He spoke only to the President.

"Hello, Teddy," Richards grimaced in utter delight at the fear he brought to all of them.

"Look, Richards…" the president began, ready to save face—but he was severely interrupted by a man reading his thoughts before he could articulate them.

"What? Take you but leave the others alone? Oh, what a brave man! What a show you put on for these foolish yes-men, these cowards. You can't save them. Why do you think I'd let you?"

"Your issue is with me," The president quietly uttered but this only made the cowboy angry.

"No! My issue is with the whole goddamn cesspool of failed systems you try over and over to sell as "good enough" to the people. The same systems you now so desperately cling onto, even when the dawn of a new age is at hand. When we revealed ourselves to you, your reaction was typical. You saw the future and you were scared. You wanted to hold onto a power corrupted indefinitely since its inception. Now it is time for a new form of leadership, a new way of life, surpassing all the opportunities you once spoke of…"

The president held his wife tighter than ever before. "What I did to you I did of my own accord. You can't honestly tell me that your kind will be good for the country, good for humanity. When I look out there it's not our people killing each other, it's your kind laying waste to everything—absolutely everything. Only anarchy awaits your new fucking life."

This angered Richards. His face flared up and within a split second, the First Lady had been thrown off Roland and Richards was upon the president, his hands wrapped around Roland's neck in an iron grip. Security tried to pull Richards off the president but their hands grasped at thin air; unable to comprehend that the president's own body was choking on itself. The others in the room pleaded for Richards to stop, the Secretary of Homeland Security blurting out that she was sorry for what they had done; what they were still doing all across the country.

Before the government had lost most communication lines with the armed forces, the last protocol initiated was the quarantine and capture of subjects infected with the Type A Tyrantocillous virus, with termination the likely end at the hands of the CDC. Richards' escape, like so many of the others, was done without lifting a finger, and now in the final stages of his vengeance, he waited until the president's face had gone a pale blue before releasing him onto the floor.

They wanted to beg; wanted to get down on their hands and knees before him and touch his feet, promising whatever he wanted so long as they could keep breathing the air they once took for granted. It was the sight of the inside of a huge concrete facility hovering above the round table that stopped them, its hallowed walls brimming with military personnel standing to attention as stone statues. As the facility was screened into their very eyelids, Richards reappeared, coming into focus as he walked towards them much like a documentary presenter, a wicked grin held under that white cowboy hat. They couldn't look away; those that tried would merely see him when they closed their eyes. Richards was now in a secure room standing over a control desk of many buttons and flashing lights.

Roland knew the place, its purpose. He was too late.

"I'm not going to kill you—not straight away, anyway. But I can't let your kind pervert the world that needs to be rebuilt, fixed. Take a look at these walls; they will surround your final days. I'd suggest not going outside, the radiation won't be kind to your organs." Richards then allowed his hand to hover over a large red button, clichéd in its horror.

"Please. Reconsider. It doesn't have to be this way."

Richards' body extricated itself from the missile launch room and his distance from the red button caused a slight relief in the trembling audience, only for him to quickly reappear, kneeling beside the president, his face right up against President "Top Dog" Roland.

Richards whispered, but everyone heard his words.

"I want it to be this way, and the world will be what I *will* it to be. I've already pressed it. Enjoy."

And with a wry smile the foundations rocked, as the world the president sought to preserve was torn apart from above.

Stage II: Peace

16. Falling from the Ceiling

A light breeze drifted calmly along the meadows of rolling hills, making the yellow and white daisies dance. These were the good days; any idiot would tell you that. Kate Brewer would look in any direction and see clear blue skies and greenery for miles. The textures of the meadows were so vibrant, so inviting, that the sight of it alone sometimes left Kate breathless; its very existence wrapping around her like a warm blanket, telling her that everything would be all right. The sun's rays would tender her soul like soft piano tunes, each note as silent and momentous as the subtle climaxing of life all around her.

These were the fields of endless bliss that Kate was unsure how she'd come to find herself in, but was grateful nonetheless. She'd fall backwards into the soft grass with not a care in the world, magically missing the daisies by inches, only to turn her head and be able to examine the infinite beauty each little daisy held within its petals. To breathe it all in was to fully be overwhelmed by a sense of grace, a pure cleansing nothing else in Kate's life had ever brought her.

When Kate opened her eyes she was in the park, right in the center of Derek-land, amongst hundreds of others lying idle in the prickly grass that made their skin pink and itchy. Her irritation was minor, for she knew exactly what to do. She closed her eyes again, and was now with Sarah, her best friend, as they ran playfully through the meadows, laughing a laugh that echoed well beyond the horizon, a sense that this could go on forever.

***

Kate opened her eyes. She was alone in her silk-sheet bed, the creases of Derek still fresh on his side. She swooped out of bed effortlessly and wandered through the house in her pajamas to the back porch that overlooked the small haven of Derek-land. Sunny day it seemed, though when was it not with Derek? She went into the bathroom to brush her teeth and found Derek stark naked in a trance on the toilet. His face was locked in an epic strain, his stare vacant yet full of thought. When he came to, Kate's presence sent him jumping.

"Shit, baby cakes! How could you? Scaring me like that."

Ignoring this with a beaming smile, Kate sat on Derek's lap and asked him what was planned for the day ahead. Derek held her and looked deep into her hazel eyes, a soothing tone being prepared in his throat.

"Baby, I've got some things to take care of today. Listen, why don't you take the others to the meadows?"

A smile broke across Kate's face, soothing Derek in return. Kate had gone to the meadows yesterday. Kate had gone to the meadows on Wednesday. Kate would go everyday if she could, and for all she knew she did. Days were not well defined when she spent them with Derek; they blended together in a blur of fascinating colors that could swell in and out of Kate, as if she could eat them like lollies of bursting juiciness. Derek's suggestion sent her into a frenzy of excitement. Her hands met his and like a child squealed, "Oh, I love the meadows! Sarah will be overjoyed!"

Sarah greeted the news as expected. Her boyfriend, Justin, ran around the room, his arms outstretched like an airplane in a breathtaking elation of childish energy when Sarah shared this wonderful news. Leaving her overjoyed neighbors, Kate hopped around to all the other houses and the numbers grew. There was Sally Matthews from the salmon-colored house opposite Sarah and Justin. There was Malcolm Wright, an old man of undeniable spritely vigour. After him came the Mavis twins, and then the Thompsons, all from this tiny street that now brimmed with life at the prospect of an excursion to the meadows. Once Kate had spread the word through her own street, her feet began to descend down Baker Crescent to inform the other lovely citizens of Derek-land where to go.

The people of Baker Crescent were far more numerous than Derek's street, and while Kate saw less of them with each passing day, she would always make the effort to invite them to the meadows every time she went. They were Derek's busy workers and under his guidance the food was brought to the table by their wholesome hands. Kate would often ask to help them and contribute, but Derek would seldom oblige, often hushing her away as he reiterated he wanted to spend time with her. The houses in Baker Crescent were not as nice as the houses in Derek's street; many of their windows still boarded while some were smashed completely, letting in the cool breeze of the approaching fall. Inside, they were always dim lit and smelled of moldy neglect. Kate would often find herself zeroing in on Herman's place.

Herman was an old black man in his early sixties built with a ticker that just wouldn't quit and a sweet smile surrounded by freckles that always told Kate it was going to be a good day. Kate knocked on the creaky front door, her usual upbeat knock. A slow shuffling was heard from inside until a tired Herman opened the door.

"Miss Brewer, fancy seeing you here, sunshine of my day!" Herman warmed up, extending himself to embrace her bubbly tenderness.

"Herman, I have great news: we're going to the meadows today!" Kate beamed with excitement, holding his hands ready to do a little happy dance. But Herman pursed his lips, ready to disappoint Kate once again.

"I'm sorry, sweetie. Derek wants me to run a few errands today…but you go on and have fun now," he closed with a smile. Kate peered through the rest of the joyless house and saw Shaun and Bethany hanging out on the couch in an air of vacancy similar to the way Derek had been on the toilet. "What about you guys?" Kate motioned towards them before Herman interjected. "Oh no, sweet. Derek's got them running some errands today as well. We'll be fine, honey. You can tell me all about those meadows when you get back."

Kate sighed, if only for a moment. Whenever Kate asked, they always declined. She just wanted them to be as happy and as carefree as she was. Their daily refusal never got her down for too long though, for everyday was another chance to enjoy that feeling of *forever* in the meadows. She would simply ask again tomorrow. Leaving Herman's house, the sound of the work horn bellowed across the town, with the houses on Baker spewing out scores of residents as they trudged their way down to the old yellow school buses that had become their work buses. Shaun and Bethany brushed past Kate without saying hello, startling Kate who was only settled with the calming hand of Herman. "They just excited to help Derek, is all. Come on now, you best be off having some fun!"

Kate shrugged this off and was soon skipping her way back to Derek's. Sarah, Justin, the Mavis twins, the Thompsons, old Malcolm and now Betty Sue were all lined up with retro cruiser bicycles hanging by their sides.

"Ready?" Sarah gestured to Kate's bike with the woven white basket that carried apples, bananas, oranges and mangoes.

"Always," Kate enthused and they were soon off in a leisurely snake that swept out of Derek-land and into the Oregon countryside. The sun was out for all to see and its light cast a glinting of the dew that lined the fresh grass Kate and the others glided alongside. Once they were past the town's limits the world opened up and unending fields of greener pastures lay all around them. The meadows of Kate's fairytale dreams were hidden away behind a hill of small lilac bushes. They left their bicycles on the quiet road and strolled over with bubbling anticipation to the overwhelming sense of white and yellow daisies that dawned like the sun as they made their way over the hill.

Old Malcolm was the first over. "Last one in's a rotten egg!" he cheered and this was followed by a breaking gallop. Kate, Justin and Sarah gleefully chased him, springing over the hill and diving into the endless ocean of white and yellowed goodness. They rolled their way all along the soft daisies that would spring back tall and unbroken, resolute in their beauty. The flowery scent filled their nostrils and relaxed all the muscles in their body; all worries, if they ever had any, gently floating away into the sky. They laughed; they gorged on juicy apples and made daisy angels where they lay. Sometimes they'd forget what they were giggling about, but then they'd forget about forgetting and the cycle would go on and on. At one point they were all lying in a circle with their feet sticking out, and Sarah asked Kate if this was *forever*? Kate's eyes drooped in a dreamy haze and drifted off while her mind whispered *yes*. As Kate lay there in her enchanted state, Sarah and Justin undressed and started making joyous love right next to her. The sounds of Sarah warmed the group, who all smiled and nodded in agreement, and soon everyone but Kate was naked in bliss.

***

Kate awoke just as the sun was beginning to set, a cold breeze waking not just herself, but also the other, less clothed, members of the party. The Mavis twins were on top of the Thompsons and old Malcolm was hurriedly putting his shirt on, a glint of cheekiness in his bug eyes.

"That went by so quickly," Kate muttered to Sarah and Justin, who stretched out like butterflies from a cocoon made of themselves.

"There's always *forever*, tomorrow." Justin yawned, completely rested.

They picked themselves up and rode their bikes home in near darkness. Though the reflectors on their bikes had nothing to reflect in the fading light, Kate was unconcerned with trailing off and crashing, the path of the road all too familiar and watched over by Derek, who would never allow such a thing to occur.

As Kate eased over the final hill she was surprised by the darkness of Derek-land. A single, icy drop graced her spine and sent chills all over. No lights lit up the town like they usually did, and the candles that flickered through windows were restless in their dancing. Kate drew to a stop on the corner of Derek and Baker. Sarah came screeching behind her, stopping just in time. A pungent scent of dread lingered in the cold air from the people of Baker Crescent and that single, icy drop Kate had felt now swelled into a thick sheet of creeping despair that pierced through her until its grip arrested her heart. Feelings of a past life before Derek bubbled up insider her, and though Kate was curious at first, the closer these memories came to her surface, the more her mind begged her to turn and walk away.

"I think I'll see Derek now," she said, abruptly leaving Sarah and the others.

Kate felt a tension in all her muscles as she slowly creaked opened the door of their house. A chasm of eerie silence was soon broken by the sound of Derek's voice coming from upstairs. There was agitation in his tone, something Kate had never heard from him before this moment. Even downstairs, she could feel him pacing backwards and forth, talking like he was on the phone. But there were no phones in Derek-land, there was no need; everyone you could ever need was right here, thought Kate.

"You can't take my people like that… How am I going to defend myself when they come—how do you suppose I hold up my end of the economy if I don't have anyone left? …Well, how long do we have?"

At this point Derek turned around to see Kate watching Derek in a heated conversation with himself. His last words had taken the blood all from his face.

Kate's eyebrows furrowed in confusion as she approached Derek cautiously. "What's going on?" she mumbled.

Derek rushed across the room to comfort her. "Baby cakes, that was just…business."

"Well…shouldn't I know your business? I mean…we're together… I love you."

He looked deep into her eyes, and melted away that creeping fear.

"Then make love to me."

"Okay."

***

Kate awoke to an empty bed. The familiar creases of Derek were cold. She sauntered over to the bathroom and found him once again on the toilet seat, this time at least with some pants around his ankles. He looked down, locked in a gaze at the tiles on the floor. How long had he been like this? Kate felt she had seen this before, that she had scared him while he sat there on the toilet with his clothes missing and his eyes vacant. She wanted to ask him what was wrong, but instead she fell into an old comfort.

"Hey, what are we doing today?" she asked in her most innocent tone.

He wasn't shocked by her presence this time, instead breaking his trance to look into her eyes with the deepest of sadness welling at the surface. He pulled his pants up and brushed her aside as he washed his hands and his face, giving himself time, bracing himself. When he turned to her, he saw her small round nose, the freckles on her cheek, the love in her eyes. Derek wanted to spend the rest of his life with her in that room. He wanted to hold her and never let go, to run his hand through her hair and suffocate on her scent. He wanted to do all these things, but somehow he felt she would get wind of the coming storm, and this he couldn't allow.

"I'd love nothing more than to spend this day with you, but I have to prepare for things…"

Kate was left feeling anxious after this, and when she suggested she take everyone to the meadows, the question had a certain death to it, a notion that the meadows were dying somehow.

Derek shook his head. "I'm sorry, not today. Today I want you close. Go to the park. Lie down and I'll be with you."

Kate's demeanor dropped at this, and when she made her way down the stairs, she stopped at the door. Derek had started talking to himself again, but Kate didn't want to listen. Sarah and Justin waited patiently outside their house for Kate to come and tell them the wonderful news, that they would once again find themselves riding their bikes gleefully down to the meadows. When Kate ambled slowly over, hands in her jean pockets, her clothes suggested otherwise.

"The park?" asked Sarah.

Kate avoided both their gazes. "Derek wants us to be close."

Justin was like a child with no understanding of the matter, flinging his arms over in the direction of the meadows, "But it's not that far away!" he irritated. Kate could sense that both of them felt the unease of everything like she did, and while they still loved the park, they couldn't shake the feeling that the earth's axis was slowly tipping off its usual balance.

While Sarah and Justin rounded up the others on Derek's street, Kate eased her way over to Herman's house, trying to assure herself a smile from her old friend could swing it all back around. Her knock was weak and full of anxiety and when Herman opened the creaky door, that familiar smile never showed.

"Hello, Kate," he eventually let out.

"Hey there, Herman. Well, today we were going to the park

and since it's a lot closer to home I figured you may be able to come with us this time?" As she waited for Herman's reply, she noticed the empty couch where Shaun and Bethany usually sat in anticipation of the work horn. Herman was already dressed in his farmhand garb and was ready to spring the door open as soon as that horn went off.

"Unfortunately, honey, Derek has once again asked me to help him in the fields today; as you know winter is—"

Kate cut him off, for the first time tired of his excuses. He'd had one every day for at least three months now. "Where are Shaun and Bethany?" she demanded to know.

"Ah, well, they went someplace else… Derek's orders."

"But the work horn hasn't—" she was cut off by the blaring of the work horn. A crumpled farmer's hat was produced from Herman's hidden hand as he tried to pass Kate.

"Duty calls," he muttered, trying to crack a smile, but a firm hand on his arm stopped him dead.

Kate's eyes swelled in desperation, "I *insist* you come with us."

They locked eyes before Herman waved her off, and with his head dejectedly facing the ground, joined his other colleagues who now filed down their street on the descent to the old school buses. There were fewer than before.

The park was the center of Derek-land. When Derek first cast his light over the town, this was where everyone met. It formed a giant square of greenery with paths from each corner that met in the gazebo middle. Flowers lined these paths in the beginning, but neglect had wilted them down. Derek used to hold group meditations in the park, standing center stage in the gazebo, Kate by his side, with everyone else (the people from Baker Crescent,

Hobbes Drive and Derek's Street) all lying down in the grass like one big happy family. A single, all-encompassing breath would be drawn and exhaled in synchronized fashion as they watched the clouds roll by. Those were back in the early days and as Kate approached the park, the lack of people flooding its once green abundant floor left her feeling empty. She found her way in between Malcolm and Justin, closing her eyes as she lay down. The grass hadn't been cut in a while and its ticklish fingers took to Kate's arms, legs and back of her head. In a way it was a good distraction, a small irritant Kate could focus everything on before the calm of Derek's touch would take her out to sea like he'd done for all the others who closed their windows and embraced a familiar world. Soon, the itchy grass dropped away as Kate felt warm waters, waters of the tropics, bathe all around her as she floated off into a light of unimagined intensity that slowly reached to the ends of her everything.

When the bombs dropped, a bubble of silence filled the park. Outside it, every horrid thing happened and all at once. Roofs were torn off houses. Screams were muffled out by scattered explosions that filled the air, sucking the oxygen clean out of lungs. The people in the park looked over in the direction of Baker Crescent, taken aback by the commotion. At first they didn't understand the fire and smoke, they didn't hear the last sounds that humans made, or the smell of burning skin. They had no idea of what was to come—but this bubble did not last. Like a blood clot in her brain, a sharp pain coursed through Kate's head, and for a brief moment all the filters Derek had fed into her were peeled back, leaving Kate truly exposed to the chaos. She heard the shrieks now, their last cries grating every inch of her, and when she turned to Sarah and Justin their faces shook in painful disbelief, their mind begging them to turn their minds off and let them forget they ever existed.

Trembling, Kate looked to the sky, hoping maybe that the sight of clouds would carry her away from this falling ceiling. There were no clouds, only the entrails of a large mechanical bird, the culprit making its escape in the distance. When Kate looked over to the houses between her and Baker Crescent, the billowing of smoke filled her nostrils as she slowly rose to her shaken feet, entranced by the swaying of the smoke as it danced to the screams that now filled her head. Sarah, Justin, Malcolm, the Mavis twins and the Thompsons were all quick to flight, scurrying towards their homes and slamming the doors.

All alone, with the hairs standing upright along her arms like the itchy grass that once dressed her body, Kate's vision became a tunnel, hollowing itself into the direction of the corner of Baker and Derek's street, where she would come to see the truth of the world. Her feet carried her towards the sounds of pain that ripped through her eardrums, leaving a ringing that burned.

When she finally fumbled her fingers around the corner and gazed into the terror, her body was arrested by the sight: People were scattered around the jet-black smoke that engulfed the buses. The trucks that carried the food of the toils were also burning.

Standing tall before the fuming wreckage was Derek, ordering the people of Baker Crescent to rush into the burning truck to retrieve what was left of the food. They did so screaming, their clothes and soon their skin turning to black. Kate's jaw went slack and she dropped to her knees. Her sight began to fade and in its last moment, the voice of Derek filled her head, wishing her to return to his bed.

So she did.

***

When Kate awoke the next day, a splitting headache left her grasping at the sheets in agony. Once again, Derek was not on his side of the bed, but now this was no surprise to Kate. Fighting the aching throughout her body that tried to keep her restrained in bed, Kate searched deep into the fogging recesses of her memory, trying to grasp the bloody pieces that galloped and swarmed in her, trying to breach the surface. Blood-curdling shrieks drew her to people in flames; their cries edging Kate towards burning hands that reached out in charred desperation. Then the pain ran through her elsewhere, and while this world vanished, another was drawn in its place: that first moment when the silence broke. The screaming was constant. Kate tried to run, but the sound would follow her, inundating her ears everywhere she turned.

A desperate Derek moved to snuff out the screams, imploring her to forget, calling her back in. Soon, everywhere she turned Derek's face would follow until her vision was only his face staring deeply back at her, the awful noises gone. When Kate's eyes finally reopened she saw Derek sitting at the foot of the bed, looking away, his shoulders slumped.

"What happened?" she let out with a rasp in her voice.

"Nothing happened." There was a pause. Then, "Life happened. Mistakes were made."

Kate reached out and graced Derek's forearm, only to pull away immediately as coldness flooded through her, truly jolting her insides awake. Kate could take this no more.

"I want to see Baker Crescent," she demanded. "I want to see what you see. What you've been hiding from me all this time."

The faces of the houses on Baker were caved in; their smiles smashed to rubble, the structural sheeting sticking out like bone.

The work buses were now black skeletons, their contents emptied out and cindered by jumping flames. Derek's people milled about the wreckages of scorched earth; they had been working all night to save the food, to store it for Derek when he made his run, if time had still allowed him. Now, with energy sapped rigorously from them—right to the last drop—the people of Baker Crescent shuffled their feet in circles, no home to go to, no orders to take.

Derek would not let Kate see this; he couldn't bring himself to show her the truth, the damage of life happening. Holding her hand they both strolled down memory lane; the houses now perfectly restored to their original fifties style, the people joyful, the time wound back to better days. When Kate stepped over broken glass, Derek turned it to grass just like the grass of the meadows. When Kate passed by the aimless heads that swayed into nothingness, Derek pulled up their cheeks and smiles were forced. And for the first time walking down Baker Crescent, Kate did not search for old Herman, her memory of that freckle-lined smile, like his life, already gone.

It was not long before Kate had left Derek's hand and skipped away like she did in the meadows, swimming with daisies among the burnt wreckage. She skipped over lifeless bodies like she did with the stream near the meadows, with Derek watching the softness of her landing; ensuring it. She breathed in the air afresh, the pungent vapors of death overpowered by daisies.

The sound of muffled drums in the horizon broke the silence. All heads were turned to the south, all heads except Kate, who now waltzed her way back gleefully to Derek.

When they hugged, Derek took in her hair, his fingers intertwining with her smooth brown locks, knowing such a time was coming to an end.

"These past few months," he whispered, "have been the best months of my life."

"Me too," she buried her face into his shoulder, all that anger, that confusion, once again washed away. "Why are you crying? We'll always be together."

"Of course," he replied. What was one more lie?

They walked back at a slow pace to Derek's house. Sarah and Justin paced backward and forth outside their house. A beaten-up hatchback had been loaded to the brim with everything they owned, the last boxes of salvaged food squished right up the back. Justin was smoking a cigarette and Kate found it odd; he never used to do that.

"Going somewhere?" Kate asked, still unaware.

Justin ran his hands through his oily long hair before thrusting them at Kate in pounding frustration. He wanted to grab Derek and wring his neck out.

"She doesn't know yet? Why doesn't she know?" seethed Justin.

Kate backed away, the terror creeping its fingers once again around her ribcage, searching for that heart. "Know what?" she uttered as Derek broke into a rage, shoving Justin away, sending him falling onto the bonnet of the hatchback.

"I can't!" Derek screamed at Justin, before staring at Sarah and softly repeating, "I can't..."

In those words, Sarah understood. She understood Derek couldn't break the world to Kate the way he did for her and Justin. Sarah longed for the same treatment, to forget the heaven Derek had forged for them so that the fall wouldn't be so bad, but knew the heaviness in his heart could not extend to Kate. The slate would be wiped clean and Kate would never be completely sure she ever knew a man named Derek Fisher. It was the best he could do for her, and though he wasn't sure if it would stick when his heart stopped and he was no more, he prayed that by such a time Kate Brewer would be well out of harm's way.

"Why don't you come with us?" Sarah pleaded to Derek.

"We've already talked about this. It's me they want. I can only give you more time now."

Sarah began to cry, so Kate rushed to her side to comfort her, caught up in the emotion of it all with no idea of the final good-bye that was waiting.

"North?" Justin suggested, thinking it the obvious choice.

Derek shook his head. "Canada is holding the border better than expected. Besides, the people of Portland have conceded to the Puries…" Derek paused at this and contemplated his refusal to join the Puries when they had offered peacefully. Could he really have saved himself and still been with Kate?

Convert or be killed.

He brushed this away, all too late now.

"Utah is your best chance for the moment; The Mormons are ready to put up a fight…" Derek then rushed over to Kate, hesitating as he held her by the shoulders. He then leaned in for one last kiss before a nod sent Sarah and Justin bundling a confused and resistant Kate into the hatchback, her memory of Derek slowly disintegrating; their first kiss the first thing to fall off the face of her earth. The car was all screams as Kate babbled like a baby while the sight of Derek grew smaller and smaller.

Kate never saw Derek give his life for her. She wasn't there when the men and women in the gray robes finally surrounded him in the park and bludgeoned him to death. But when the final embers in Derek's heart eventually burnt out, so too did his remaining warmth leave Kate, all of it abandoning her body at once. Kate was sitting quietly in the back of the hatchback as it sped through the drier lands of Eastern Oregon when it happened. Sarah heard a sobbing from behind her and turned to see a deeply confused Kate, all her features shrivelling into small burrows to minimize the surface area of pain before taking off her seat belt and lying down in the fetal position; a chunk of her life now missing in a dark vacuum that let in a chill, hollowing her bones.

Sarah looked at Justin, her eyes dictating Derek's last wish: that Kate would never know.

17. Shopping List

The weather was getting frosty. Dampness hung in the air as two soldiers sat prone, eyes hidden behind binoculars; all attention placed on the outer rims of Salt Lake City below. Leaves of red, orange and yellow patted the soft floor around them. While the seasoned man with the binoculars kept still, his younger counterpart scratched at the side of his knee through thick pants while a single sheet of paper flapped about in the wind in his other hand.

"I think I need new pants. I'm beginning to think these ones have bugs living in them, trying to renovate into my legs."

"Why don't you add it to the list?" said the seasoned man with the binoculars, the sarcasm applied with as little effort exuded as possible.

The younger counterpart nodded and took out a tiny pencil, carefully placing the flimsy single page onto a small, flat pebble as he surgically added the necessary request to the growing list of requirements one makes when attempting to bug out.

The seasoned veteran took time from his calculating observation of a falling city below, to watch this boy make the paper maintain a smooth correspondence with the pebble that kept it flat. Even so, the handwriting was illegible.

There were seven items on the list:

— Aspirin

— Tent (already ticked twice)

— Portable Coleman gas stove (because their one had just broken)

— Food

— Information

— Guitar

— New pants for Max because the old one's have a bug infestation.

Foster turned to look Max in the eyes. "What color do you want the pants?"

"Any color will do. Blue."

"Camo would be better suited."

"Then why did you ask?"

"Let you feel like you had a choice?"

Both of them returned their focus to the city below. The Puries would be coming, Foster was sure of it. People were already scrambling out in roads not too far from where Foster and Max were lying down, fleeing off to wherever the Puries were not.

No real sense of direction, no hope.

Still, things were quiet. Not as quiet as the previous three months, but knowing that the violence was ready to encapsulate again, there could be some solace found in this relative silence, a greater appreciation before the blood flowed.

Foster thought back to when he first saw the word *guitar* scribbled on that shopping list.

"What's this?" Foster had asked, rather bemused, a rare intrigue of the lighter side leaving him briefly.

"What else are we going to do when we bug out?"

"You play?" Foster continued, his patience still not running its short course.

"Not yet. All the more reason to learn," Max elaborated.

"Shall I get you an instruction manual?"

"No need, I'll learn by doing."

Foster sighed. "I'm going to regret this."

Now, finally within reach of people, within reach of the past, Foster couldn't help but think that Max was scanning the ridges of civilisation with the sole focus of finding a music store and that precious guitar.

"I don't see why we can't find a nice deserted house and make do there," said Max. They had already been through this. The circle had turned once more.

"They'll look in all the houses," Foster repeated.

"But this would be secluded. A holiday house!" Max gestured emphatically as he was edged towards a grim prospect of spending more countless months in the wilderness with no one but Foster for company. Maybe he should add "people" to the list while he was at it…

"No buts," Foster gruffly rebuked, before reminding himself this was just a kid he was talking to. "Maybe after a few weeks, if it's safe," he conceded.

Foster then lifted himself up, causing Max to follow suit. They made their way to the black beauty before rolling carefully down the mountain. In the back seat a large dark blue duffel bag clunked away. Foster repeated the time orders, once in his head and once for Max.

"10:25—park behind the tree line by Holt Street. It's six hun-

dred yards to the camping store. Four minutes twenty seconds accounting for baggage. Meet contact behind camping store. Trade M-60 machine gun for three portable stoves. 10:32— once goods are acquired rendezvous back behind the tree line. 10:40—Max provides support from the car all along Clarence Avenue. Bug out, and continue the mission."

Max had asked before why this contact of Foster's wasn't going to come with them. The fact Foster found him raving away on some nutty conspiracy theory frequency was not the best start, but Foster had known the guy from back in his days in the military. Surely he'd be an asset, Max had argued, risking the high possibility the man was just as zealous as Foster.

"From what he used to be, it's not a long shot to guess that M-60 is part of his last rites. Don't know if I could convince him out of it. The man's a headstrong bastard."

Max didn't have a mirror to give to Foster at this point. Shoot, that was another thing he needed to add to the list.

The black beauty rolled down passed several fleeing cars, their inhabitants all adorning those precious gas masks, before going off road and clearing out of sight behind a tree line of shedding oaks and bright orange and red bushes.

"Keep your radio on at all times."

"Of course," Max uttered the obvious.

"Stay in the car. And don't move until I give the all clear. Turn the engine on when I radio in."

"Yes," Max irritated.

…

"What do you do if I don't make it back?"

"Bug out."

"…And then?"

Max paused. He knew what Foster was talking about, what he wanted him to say: continue the mission. That was all Foster ever talked about back in the cave. It was the answer to Max's question: *what do we do after surviving?* The answer had belatedly come to Foster somewhere between the silence and the approaching cold that iced their bones while they stared at each other thinking, *what now?* Out of the blue Foster had declared it, and it quickly became his great hope, as crucial as warmth in their freezing, damp cave. It was the thing Foster needed to keep his focus, to keep him going. Whenever Foster spoke of it, he spoke as if it were already the truth. *"If it's a virus, then there is always the possibility of a cure. There will be people trying to find one. They won't give up, and neither will we. These people, Max, they will need our help when the time comes to take back this country. We need to survive now, so we'll be ready when the cause needs us..."*

Max was dubious about the whole prospect. He couldn't see a cure to all this, he didn't think it possible. And even if there was, what help could they bring? What difference could they make? He doubted all this, but understood just how badly Foster needed it. So when Foster asked him to take an oath, Max knew he had to oblige.

"…What happens after we bug out, Max?"

Max felt his teeth clenching up. *Would he really go through with it, if Foster weren't there, pushing?*

Foster's eyes demanded an answer, and Max knew the right one. "Continue the mission."

Foster smiled. "Good boy."

Bracing himself, Foster took in a deep breath and was soon out of the car and swooping to the back seat for the duffel bag, dragging it out as he gauged its heavy contents and the strain he already felt in his arm. Max watched all of this helplessly. Last chance to pick up the pleasures of the past he had taken for granted all these years. An old fashioned burger with the cheese carefully melted and the freshest lettuce and tomato, or however fresh Wendy's made them (the main point was that Wendy's made them and Max didn't have to cook it himself).

A beer.

Just a little bit of time in the sun to sit back and relax, not worry if your thoughts were truly your own.

As Foster began jogging off towards the meagre remnants of civilization, Max scrambled to get his final request out. It was the only thing he felt mattered anymore.

"Bring back a girl!" he yelled, trying to make it sound like he was joking. He wasn't.

18. Trent

A cool breeze floated across the ridge, the leaves of the trees all following its gentle touch with little effort, almost playful. They would soon fall as the season dictated, but for now the afternoon sun left pink streaks in the sky, best viewed with a little bit of wine and an arm wrapped around the one you love. There wasn't much wine going round anymore, but there was someone Cole loved, and whenever she smiled back at him; he found the image perfect; the moment ceaseless.

The cool breeze was faint to all but Cole, who felt it mix with the sweat that clung to him, shivering his skin. His knees were weak, the bones in his shins feeling as if they had already started to split. On his back, a large cumbersome backpack—the kind one would take around Europe, if Europe were still Europe the way Cole thought of it. Beside Cole, in mirror fashion but with a smaller additional backpack across the front of his body was Lamar, Claire's squeeze and the strongest of the group. Trailing behind both of them was Vernon, a stocky kind of guy. He was once an insurance broker, who had drawn the short straw and won the ticket for the grueling food run. The cars had been empty for months now, any gas used for cooking. They left bicycles at the foot of the ridge for whenever the need to sneak into town came up. They had made do, better than most in fact.

The three of them climbed the familiar ridge, sometimes with their hands on the ground, crawling upward like monkeys; their backs used to the heavy lifting while the mind drifted off to watching that sunset, taking in the pink sky and falling in love. There wasn't long to go now, just past Miller's rock and the redwoods before the clearing would be upon them.

"I'm going to take Yvonne and hold her just right when I see her," remarked Vernon who counted down the seconds just before the sun went down and that magical moment held him breathless. Lamar spun a similar tale about Claire, while Cole kept his plans with Maddie to himself, although it followed in the same fashion as well.

When they made it to Miller's rock, the typical perching got under way. The bags were dropped aside the boulder unique enough to warrant a name, while the sweat was wiped off their brows and they were granted a brief respite to daydream away.

Lamar was going to spoon feed Claire the frozen meal he'd sneaked out of a heavily guarded convenience store. Vernon was going to take Yvonne to their favorite spot in the woods and take her ever so sweetly from behind. Meanwhile, Cole watched a sparrow taking its food to the young, and couldn't help notice the similarities. He'd tell Maddie about it. He'd tell her and she'd be impressed and want to make love to him right on the knoll next to the playground.

Cole hadn't watched the sparrows, or nature in general for a long time since he was a kid. But in these past few months, watching nature regrow, Cole felt it brought him closer to the earth, like he was regrowing with it.

There were questions that lingered, sure, but Cole didn't worry, he could usually hold them off; he'd just have to think about Maddie and everything in him seemed to find its place. In fact, there had only been one time when those questions had breached surface, the ones he'd asked of himself back in the diner that day the first plane went down. It happened during one of the quieter days. Everyone was sitting on the knoll, Peter entertaining them with the fluffy clouds he let swirl into animals. It had been so long since Cole had thought of that day in the diner. Out of curiosity, he let those questions wander and play their soft tune. *Who was he? Who was Cole Watts? Was he anything without Maddie?* He could barely remember before her, only the flashes of a known loneliness filling his younger self. He vaguely recalled the feelings of a sinking dread the first time he'd read his grades, as if it were the end of the world and that left him chuckling to himself. Funny, the things he used to worry about.

Then there were the dreams. The ones he always had, and always forgot. Maddie thought it was the virus. She wanted Cole to tell Kelly the doctor about it, but he had refused. He told her it was nothing—that it didn't matter—besides, he couldn't remember them anyway, and what would Kelly be able to do about it except kick up a panic?

Deeply unsettled by this at first, Maddie soon grew to accept its peculiarity. It just became one of those things. They'd all gone through something like it (the madness) early on, and they were all still alive and seemed okay, sometimes even better than before. Maddie had told him never to ask what it was she saw in her moment of madness and because he never asked, she accepted the restless sleep he could never explain. And even when it did bother her, Cole would always seem to wake up just in time and hold her, telling her always:

It doesn't matter, Maddie, it doesn't matter, because we're here, together. That's all that matters.

And he was right. Those questions and those dreams meant nothing to him anymore. He didn't have to consider a world without her, and who he would be in that world. And those dreams, well, they were forgotten the moment he woke up to her. All his answers were right there on that ridge waiting for him, and he knew he had the strength to hold on now. All he needed was her warm embrace…

Another breeze picked up across the ridge, and Cole was roused from his daydreaming. The winds were beginning to pick up, and he figured it was time to go. Yet when he went to call Lamar and Vernon, he saw they were still deep in their daydreaming, looking aimless at the sky, as if they were already up there on the ridge with their loved ones. The mother bird remained in her feeding to the younger ones, and Cole relaxed once more, figuring why not, another few minutes couldn't hurt. So he went back to watching the sparrows and thinking about Maddie.

***

The warmth they made for each other would soon be put to its greatest test. The temperature was dropping each day, the inevitable winter coming like a sheet, ready to cover everything. They'd gotten lucky with fall, but this could not hold in a place on the edge of the Rockies. They'd talked about moving on, even just for the season to pass, but they only ever got as far as talking. Even with the prospect of freezing conditions that were going to dip well below the zero on most days, the trips down to Fort

Collins below had been made to stock up for an unspoken white winter in Trent.

It was Peter who had swayed them, had built up their desire to stay in the place they had come to love, to need. Maddie had said quite rightly that the pink streaks would not follow in the winter, but Peter had put a very slick line of nerves into the group: if they left, some others could take their view and the pink streaks would be lost forever. And when Peter talked to Cole about it; making snow angels, everyone keeping warm at Pappali's, he got his hook right there. They could stay warm. Three to five months was nothing, a small blip, and then it was back to business as usual. The pink streaks once more.

Maddie took longer to convince. *I love this place too, Cole. It's where I found myself, and where a lot of beautiful memories will always be—but it's going to get too cold. It's one thing to say we can take it now, but three months, in every inch of us? We will freeze. People could get real sick.*

Before Trent, Maddie had never been much of an outside person. She rarely exercised but for her fingers on the phone, checking Facebook, scrolling endlessly. She never really posted any comments. Instead, it was a steady stream of 'likes' because she felt it was somehow safer that way. She had strong opinions on a wide variety of topics, but reserved them for only those closest to her. When Maddie did go out, it was at the strong behest of Claire, whose determination to get Maddie outside proved invaluable every time, with Maddie playing babysitter when a little too much had been drunk. That was Maddie's circle. That was all she was, and this depressed her. But when the world went to shit, and she was forced into the wild with Cole and the others, Maddie found she was more than adaptable.

She surprised herself.

Maddie could hunt. It seemed her ability to catch jackrabbits as a child had not been forgotten. She first learned how to track the animals, discovering all the nooks and crannies they inhabited. And soon enough, flimsy, basic traps and spears were honed into deadly instruments. She caught more than the rest, and her catch was able to feed half the group almost weekly. It was usually jackrabbits and sometimes squirrels. She'd even saved Ashton from walking right into a black bear at one stage. Cole had tried hunting with her a couple times, but he was always falling over or messing up traps and generally being too loud—almost as if it were on purpose. Hunting left him a little embarrassed, and in many ways he was relieved when Maddie told him not to worry about stalking the rabbits anymore. He didn't really have it in him to kill the little critters, though there was no complaining when it came to dinnertime.

Maddie had come into her own on this ridge. It showed in her hands. They were soft no more, calloused from all the coarse spears she'd carried and furniture she'd carved out of loose timber in her downtime. She'd made a bedside table and a redwood chair for Cole to sit in (and was quite comfortable once you got the hang of it). She was pulling out splinters each day till Lamar found her some gloves.

Cole remembered the sweet softness those hands had been, the smoothness of their texture when he held them with his own. He remembered (even though it were only a dream) the way her two fingers, stuck together, had fallen soft on his pulse and awoken his soul. He missed those soft hands, but seeing Maddie swell in pride at her work, the fulfillment in her being, he knew which he preferred.

It was not just Maddie that had found her calling here in Trent—all the others had flourished too. Their lives had grown simpler, and they were all the happier for it. Maddie could hunt and craft chairs and bedside tables anywhere, she knew that, but this was where they had become a family, this was their home. And when Peter said they would stay and it would bring them even closer together, everyone had come to believe it, Maddie eventually following suit.

The mother sparrow gave out a flurry of chirps before flying off. Cole took this as a sign and rustled the hefty load onto his back. He watched Lamar and Vernon do the same.

"Okay guys," Cole smiled. "Let's go home."

***

They were all there waiting on the grassy knoll when Cole and company returned. Spread out, sitting idle, taking in those pink-ish streaks, not a care in the world. Maddie was sitting further away on the bench, *their* park bench, with a spot saved especially for Cole. Upon seeing the weary travelers, Peter was the first up, calmly floating over to meet them. Lamar and Vernon perked up immensely at the sight of Peter and hugged him with whatever energy they had left.

"Fellas, please. Go to your loved ones and take in what sun remains left in the day. You've served us all too well."

At this they were off, almost sprinting. Peter's eyes met Cole's and with no words being exchanged Cole saw a favor brewing.

"Pleasant trip?"

Cole shrugged. "The catch was pretty good. A few close calls… They're stocking up as well. There are more people guarding the food now. But I think we can still get more… A couple more runs down and we should almost be set for winter."

"Good. Excellent," said Peter, but other things hid behind his eyes.

"They've started again," Cole remarked, even though they could clearly hear the rounds all the way up on the ridge. "Yes, I know," said Peter, although it seemed to not bother him that much, they'd been safe so far. Peter was good at playing calm, and when Peter was calm they all breathed easier. Still, his lips were pursing, building up to something else.

"I need you to talk to Maddie." At this Peter looked away, gazing back to the streaks. "She was gathering wood when she saw Claire and myself… I think you should talk to her, clear things up…"

A blood vessel popped in Cole's brain—*you fucking dirt bag…*

This was not the first time with Claire. Nor was it the first time Peter had slept with a taken girl in the group. But they loved him right from the get-go, all except for Maddie who had to be smoothed over whenever Cole reported such deeds in growing agitation. Now Cole wanted to punch Peter, square in the face, with all the follow through of the world behind his bony knuckles. Lamar was Cole's friend and Claire had grown on him too, but Peter had such a way with people it was almost unconscionable to hate him. Ever since Cole had met him all those years ago at that church when they were kids, Peter was always this way. He'd talked his way out of going to church, barely breaking a sweat. He skipped school whenever the urge came to him, and got away with it time after time. The one time he was caught red handed? A light talking followed by a pat on the back. *Boys will be boys,* apparently.

Now, standing before Cole on this sloped grass, Peter's eyes delegated an urge for things to return to normal. The safe bet that Cole always forgave, and Peter could carry on as he always did, leading this new congregation.

Cole relaxed his shoulders, took that deep breath once more and let the words flow gently.

"Pete, you've got to stop doing this. You know it's wrong."

"I know, I know! This is it. The last time, I swear!"

Cole looked out past Peter to see Maddie, still sitting alone on their bench, perched upright, anxious for him to join her. Easing away from this final request, Peter mentioned in a happier tone that the mural had been completed, but suggested Cole should wait till morning to see it in a better light, let the paint dry. Mustering up some enthusiasm, Cole asked if Peter decided to go with putting the man in the suit in there.

"Well, Kelly's the artist, and Grace believed it was the only way to truly captured my bravery," he grinned.

Drained from the climb, Cole only managed a tired pat on Peter's shoulder before trudging off to Maddie, "Of course, Pete, of course."

They all sat in couples on the knoll, cocooning themselves into one another while eyes were drawn to the sky and the clouds of delicious, fluffy pink swirls that soothed their souls. Claire was busy embracing Lamar, while Vernon whispered his bedtime plans to Yvonne who giggled in anticipation. Molly Waters played with her boyfriend Tom's long and knotty hair that went all the way down to his shoulders. Ashton Gaines played with an air guitar, humming out slow burners, while Amy knitted happily away on all their winter clothes. A nice bubble of warmth had taken them and when Peter rejoined them, they all let out gasps of exalted joy. Cole had eyes only for Maddie, working out the patterns of talk in his head that would ease her worries so that everyone in Trent (including himself and Maddie) could take in the fading sun and once again bask in a perfect moment as a happy family.

Maddie swept out of her seat when Cole drew close, heaving his backpack off him, almost sending it rolling down through the soft grass. Right before she hugged him, Cole felt the distress in her dimples, the strain in her curly hair and darting avoidance of her eyes.

"How was your trip?" she asked, barely moving her mouth.

"Good," Cole replied before repeating the lines he'd sung to Peter. He then grasped her gently by the arms, and looked deep into her eyes. "You saw Peter…" he began.

Her lips twitched nervously as she glanced at Peter, who entertained the others with his presence. "In the woods," she whispered, "with Claire."

Cole urged her arms softly to their bench. She silently refused, her feet stuck to the ground; too embarrassed to face Peter while they talked about him. Things had been mending between her and Peter; she was lowering her cold wall to him ever so slightly with each passing day in Trent much to Cole's wishes; slowly finding herself just short of an unexplained phenomenon of worshiping the guy that had swept through the group. In the beginning, huddled together with Cole in the abandoned upstairs storeroom (that soon became their bedroom) she'd cursed Peter, blaming him for swaying the group into staying in this one-stop rest area. Then when things got better, Maddie was lost for words at how Peter had inexplicably made them feel the way they were now. How he'd turned them all into a family and gave them a home. The man in the suit from the town below had stopped haunting them from afar; and though winter was approaching, for the moment it seemed to be held at bay by Peter's hands. Everything pointed to the presence of Peter as the reason for the weather staying the way it did, keeping as warm as it was. It was a feeling Maddie couldn't comprehend, could never fully trust, yet here was Cole, supporting Peter as he always did to keep it all stable when the truth seemed to break it all apart.

With the sun now gone, it was only minutes before darkness would take them. Looking once more at Peter who revealed to the eager congregation the story that would be told tonight, Maddie finally agreed to sit back on their bench.

"What did he say this time?" she asked.

"Said it was a one-time thing. Said he knows he did wrong."

"Said it was the last time?"

Cole's head drooped. "Yeah."

Maddie rolled her eyes.

They now sat in silence, unsure of where to go from here. Despite their frustration, they'd both relent to Peter because things were working; they were alive and they had each other. As Maddie reminded herself of this, she felt Cole's hands slid into hers, telling her everything would be all right.

***

Peter was a writer. Or he wanted to be when he grew up. To be more precise, when he grew up in a world much unlike this. When the madness in everyone had settled and the people below in Fort Collins stopped firing their guns and rounding up their victims, Peter had gazed out at the amazing view and the heavenly vibes he had created within them all and saw a chance to start that dream of writing again, even if it was only for the family.

He started with little picture books, found a couple of crayons in Pappali's. Kelly did the doodles and Peter wrote the story. Cole suggested something to do with sparrows to which Peter happily obliged.

The sparrow turned into a specific bird that belonged to a family of birds with big feet that kept them grounded at all times. Only this one tiny bird was not born with the big clumsy feet just like his sisters and brothers and mother and father. His feet were tiny and dainty, providing no defense to the ridicule and abuse his family threw at him for being different. His sister would hurl the cruelest words into his ears while the brothers held him down with their strong feet. This bird cried every night thereafter as the names he had been called would crash around in his head in endless waves. He would always look down at his feet, blaming them for not being stronger, blaming himself. Then one day this little bird got so fed up he cursed his little feet and tried to slap them with his arms. But he could not reach, he wasn't even close, and in a fix of frustration he tried over and over again until he saw the ground fall away from him. First it was the grass and then the leaves of the willow tree they took shelter in and then it was the entire ridge they lived on! He soared majestically and flew to many different lands; the Sand lands, the Salt Lakes. His eyes boggled in utter amazement as he was graced with sights he'd never thought possible to exist. And when the sun that had blinded him like never before made its travels downward, the bird returned to his home at the base of the willow tree to explain to his family the brilliant and amazing things he'd been blessed to experience. He gathered them around, his voice deep in confidence as he recounted the winds at high altitudes, the space, the freedom, the tops of trees and the feeling of seeing out into the horizon, seeing the great beyond. He spoke it all at once and was exhausted by the time he'd finished, sucking in big pockets of air into those tiny lungs of his. Puzzled looks dawned on all of them. When the questions came, they came with a gust of indignation that blew the little bird off his high perch.

"How did you do that?"

"What do you mean Sand Lands? There is nothing past the willows!"

"Are you insane?"

They circled him, their questions turning to snickers and soon it was back to the name calling; a complete disregard for anything this little bird had said, simply because he lacked the strong feet of the others. Their shadows loomed over him, ready to envelop. After reaching such heights he was now trapped by the rules they had set out and felt it tying up his insides.

"Prove it!" they jeered, but his wings were too tired, and when he couldn't, they began pecking at his wings, torturing his bones. When they all stood back with those big feet of theirs; his wings were utterly broken, his chance at freedom shattered.

No matter how many times Cole heard that part, readied himself for it, he'd clear his throat and the next time he blinked his eyes would begin to swell up.

And then Cole would begin to feel the goose bumps, first in his arms, when the mother, who had stood by in her chamber of bitter self-preservation, finally took pity on her tiny, outcast son. Those goose bumps would then spread across the entire back of Cole's neck when the mother started feeding this tiny little bird worms from her catch, even if it meant she ate less, helping him one day at a time push through the pain of being in their cage. It was five grueling months stuck in that nest, resting those wings when he knew they were meant for better things and when he finally stood up on those tiny little legs of his and slowly flapped his wings, feeling that strength again, he took one last grateful look at his mother before shooting away into the sky, just as he was always meant to.

The little bird never looked back.

That is when the tears would start to well up for Cole Watts. He replayed that story in his head that night while the others were treated with eager ears to Peter's own rendition of *The Giving Tree*. Cole had heard both stories many times before, but he always came back to that particular story, not for the fact that he helped inspire it, but because it always reminded him of the day he met Maddie, the day his horizons exploded and could never be turned back. He always thought back to those ground-shaking moments, letting them fill him with nostalgia as he cuddled up to her on this night; softly letting a layer of himself catch this moment to add to the others.

They all sat in a wide circle around the campfire Peter had set up, further up the ridge where lurking enemies could not see the light of the flames. There was a time when there was no fire, the fear was too great, but Peter took that fear away, and now he was center stage every night he had the chance.

"The tree survives, don't it? Like it grows back from being just a stump?" Lamar asked in reference to *The Giving Tree*, sitting up straight like a child in kindergarten. Ashton raised his hand and howled for that question to be answered.

Peter's arms played down their fears.

"Hush, hush." he whispered, taking his time, his smile always swelling just as he had them right in his hands. They always asked the same questions, and he always loved being the blanket of reassurance. "The tree does not grow back, but she is happy!"

Tom, Molly's love, now joined the others in sitting up with their legs crossed.

"Is it enough to be happy?" Tom asked.

Peter's eyebrows were raised to this, a slither of confusion escaping him. Tom never asked any sort of questions like that, in fact he never asked questions full stop. Taken somewhat aback, Peter turned to Cole, whose focus had left the group long ago as he gazed upward into the stars billions and billions of miles away, still thinking of that other story about the little bird with the big feet.

"Cole, would you mind filling in Tom's blank?"

Maddie tapped Cole on the knee and soon he was back in the campfire.

"Filling in what?" he croaked, his sight readjusting to the lit faces of the campfire.

Peter stared at him, as did the others, most of them disappointed that he wasn't as enthralled in Peter's story as they were.

"The tree does not grow back, but she is happy. Is it enough to be happy?"

Cole felt their expectations creep into him, but in that moment he wanted none of it. "Of course," he replied, before effortlessly sinking back into the stars. After a while he wandered back to the question. Peter was right: being happy was enough, and sitting beside the fire, bodies wrapped around one another, Cole knew this was it. This was enough. If everything could just stay as it was, right like this.

Stage III: Obedience

19. New-borne

He had that dream again. The one he had every night, and the one he always forgot. The sky was a dark gray, always teasing with the threat of rain while he stood in his usual position, elevated above the crowd that grew before him; completely exposed. They always started with the questions, first from people he knew. Their faces lit up among the crowd; there was Maddie, then Peter, his mother and father; the cruel pastor from his childhood. It was always the same, *"What should we do…"* over and over again. Before he knew it, the crowd swelled to over tens of thousands, and the same question rung through his body, echoing within his skin.

This time, when he saw Maddie, he closed his eyes and waited for the dream to die down. His hands covered his ears trying in vain to keep the questions from piercing his eardrums. "God dammit! Just wake up!" he screamed to himself, before he felt fingers surround his eyelids and pry his vision open.

Now Cole only saw Peter, blood dripping from the gunshot in his forehead, a wide grin on his face. Peter then whispered in perpetual delight to Cole, who was immobilized in reeling agony, *to finish his will.*

Cole uttered *no, no, no;* his knees giving out as he fell on his back. Peter advanced. Cole's arms feebly swung outward in defense as he closed his eyes, begging for Peter to stop.

Now Cole felt Peter, breathing heavy into his face, his fingers swirling like a million slippery tentacles latching onto Cole's eyelashes, ready to tear them open and let his body face the music. As the tentacles wrapped around each lash and begun the agonizing separation, the sound of the outside world beckoned Cole back to reality. The tentacles died off and Cole awoke to the rattling of his loosely bound corrugated iron sheet that settled for a door, as someone tried to squeeze through its awkward semblance.

Cole sat up in his ragged bed, scrubbing back up against the dirty, faded wall in the corner as a gun barrel poked through the crack. A hand quickly grabbed at the side of the sheet and pulled it down as it clumsily fell to the floor. Now Cole saw the man in his complete uniform. Army boots, army camouflage gear and a black gas mask that covered his whole head.

"Oh…my…god," the man whispered, before his assault rifle was raised at Cole's head. His grip on the gun was loose, his hands shaking as he kept stuttering to himself just what to say next.

"Um, uh… Foster!" he eventually yelled. The sound of footsteps running up the stairs soon followed as another person drew close to Cole's room.

"Max, what's the situation in there?"

His focus trembling as it held Cole's body within its sights, Max blurted out, "There's a guy in here. He's unarmed, I think?"

Max then stepped forward and, lowering his weapon by the slightest, sincerely asked if Cole had any weapons on him. Cole shook his head without moving his gaze. Following this, the other person slowly made his way into the tiny room, his gun held in his hand by his side; his identity also concealed by a foreboding gas mask. Max then backed up slowly next to Foster and relayed his thoughts of the situation in quiet whisper, just loud enough for Cole to hear. "I came in and he was just sitting there in the bed, looking all confused."

"I am confused!" Cole interrupted, his eyes wide in puzzlement. These guys looked military, but the trembling bewilderment of the kid with the rifle, the youthfulness in his voice, suggested otherwise.

Still facing Cole, Max leaned into Foster, and said, "He could be a newborn, from that guy out in the grass…"

When Cole heard this, he understood exactly what these men were talking about, what they thought he was. Cole was never usually one to grasp onto an opportunity, to jump into an ocean without testing the water, but in this moment he saw a chance at a new life—far removed from the one that had disintegrated right in his hands. To him it would be the only way to start again, to move on. All he had to do was forget.

Cole blinked. He blinked again. Looking around the room, he saw the grittiness of everything around him, many shades bleaker than the vibrant blue paint that once colored the room. Just as Max made his hypothesis Foster nodded in agreement and slowly stepped forward toward Cole.

"Son, I take it you must have many questions, but I have to ask some of my own in order to understand your situation."

Cole nodded. "My name is Cole. Cole Watts…sir."

Behind his mask, Foster smiled. "In any other situation I'd say it's nice to meet you, Cole, but in these trying times one finds pleasantries few and far between. My name is Colonel John Foster and this here is Sergeant Max Wilkins. We are soldiers of the Anti-Illusionist Front—the Resistance—if you will. Now tell me, Cole, who is Peter?"

Cole blinked once more, his face rendered in anxious confusion. How did this man know his friend?

"He's our leader, the mayor of Trent. Look, what's going on here? My room…it's different, faded…"

As Cole spoke he looked through the shattered glass that once was a window and witnessed the dull, colorless world outside. When Cole said this, Foster and Max both shot a look at one another. Foster took off his gas mask and Max followed suit. Behind the mask a rugged face appeared, surrounded by thick stubble of light gray hairs that played the same tone up top. Foster had baby blue eyes, the only part of him that betrayed the fact he'd been living rough his whole life. Max also held a layer of stubble, but was still more fresh faced than Foster, his light brown tangled hair held up from being suffocated within the gas mask. Foster put his handgun to his side and approached Cole very carefully. Cole shuffled further back against the wall. "Now, Cole, I believe this leader you speak of, this Peter, ran things around here because he was an Illusionist."

"An Illusionist?"

Foster looked back at Max and a hint of relief crept upon his face. They had never met a newborn in such shock before, a person in a state of foggy withdrawal after breaking free from the shackles an Illusionist had placed on them. For this kid to forget the very existence of these nightmarish mutations, Foster assumed the trauma of loss was severe. Despite this, Foster saw an opportunity. He saw this as another chance to espouse his take on the whole situation, right from the beginning.

He sat down on Cole's bed, the close proximity bringing Max to tighten his grip on his weapon just in case this worn-out Cole became feral.

"Cole, I don't know how much you remember, but the entire country has become the battleground for these people we call 'Illusionists'. They are a mutation of human genetics that allow an individual carrying the Type *A* version of the virus to greatly influence the perceptions and will of others carrying the Type *B* version of the virus. Essentially, they can control your mind; and they have destroyed this country trying to do just that."

Cole looked at Foster and Max in disbelief. There was a long pause.

"How long has this been going on for?" He stammered softly.

"Almost sixteen months," said Foster.

Cole's eyes darted between them both, and they in turn watched those eyes whimper *no* in disbelief. When Cole knew it was true, when the shock had taken itself in, he buried his head in his hands.

Foster stood up and motioned Max toward the door.

"We'll give you some time to get to grips with all of it," but before Foster could leave the room, Cole's voice stopped him in his tracks. "So this is why I feel this way, why I feel empty and cold, and everything is not the same, just *dead* looking?" he bemoaned as a great sadness began to seep from his confused face.

"Whatever this "Peter" person did for you, it wasn't real. You're now seeing the world without his touch," was all Foster could say. The room drew silent again. Foster stood awkwardly facing the door, eager to leave the room and give Cole space; time to think over the world he'd just been dealt, but Cole was more accepting of this change than Foster could realize.

"Where is Peter now?" asked Cole.

The both of them led him down the stairs and outside into the main (and only) street of Trent. Waiting outside was another soldier in full uniform, standing guard. Upon viewing the two of them without a gas mask the soldier began to remove her own, revealing a young woman, a beautiful woman of freckled cheeks and shoulder length brunette hair that had frizzled away in neglect. Her expression was one of agitation and when she saw Cole following behind them her rifle was thrust upward in fixation toward him.

"Kate, no!" Foster cried and she held off, only to respond, "What'd he tell you?"

Cole froze and found himself in a locked in staring match with Kate while Foster slowly approached her, feigning his arms downward for her to lower the weapon. She was now breathing heavy as he placed his hand on the barrel of the gun and eased its trajectory to the road on which they stood.

"Kate, look at me. He's a newborn. That was not his doing."

She couldn't help herself. "Well then what did he say happened to them, huh?" Foster's grip on the barrel tightened as he admitted that Cole had no memory of what had happened. When Kate heard this, she angrily tried to aim the gun back at Cole before Max stepped in to help subdue her.

"Well that's just fucking *convenient*!" she screamed at both of them.

After she had calmed down somewhat, Cole carefully approached the three of them, avoiding Kate's rueful stare.

"Did she say *them*? As in more?"

Holding back her mistrust and compelling accusations, Kate led the group in silence across the only street with three small shops on it to the hillside that overlooked Fort Collins and the other suburbs surrounding it at the foot of the ridge along the flatlands. A large mural lined the back-wall between the two buildings they cut through; depicting a scene of all of Peter's people huddled together around him, the words "In Peter's name" hanging above them. Cole saw himself in the mural, standing next to Pete, but looked away when *her* face came into view.

Trent was always a small town, if that. One of those out of the way stopovers for only those with ample time to enjoy the scenery on the way south across the Rockies to the ski slopes. Its existence was only the result of forgetful travelers picking up bare essentials. The playground the town had recently installed was for families with children passing through and any use was as brief as one would stay admiring the view. This was not a place for people to stay—yet Cole had done just that for the past fourteen months.

Cole smelt them before he saw them. Propped up against the railing of a swing set in the children's playground was Peter Storrs; his skin pale with a blood crusted hole the size of a penny sunk into his forehead. The sun had taken its toll and Cole struggled not to gag. The soldiers stopped their walk while Cole continued forward until he was only a few feet from Peter's body. He stood there for a long moment, just staring, just feeling the heaviness of it all weigh on his body. It was the sight of life-less feet in the corner of his eye that eventually broke his empty stare. He gravitated slowly toward her and with every approaching step, the memories started to creep back, to pull away at the future he was so desperately trying to jump into. A gun went off in his head before he strangled the past and swallowed it down once more. Madeline Bamsner, once the bringer of joy to many people's hearts, now stuffed in the playground's plastic house, her former self fully revealed to Cole when his knees gave way in a heap of misery.

He let out a long yelp.

She was Maddie. She was a caring soul, an opinionated soul—a soul of perfect imperfections. Now only he knew and this broke his heart. Fighting back the tears he felt the touch of a hand on his shoulder. It was Max, a flask offered in the other hand.

"Welcome to reality," Max comforted while Cole took a reserved swig between the growing sobs.

***

Eventually, Cole went in silence and found himself a shovel and started digging a few yards down from the grassy knoll where the ground leveled out for only a moment. Max and Foster helped him drag the bodies alongside the designated spots before Cole started digging while the others stood back and watched awkwardly, unsure of helping this man whose face seemed to be slipping into a full-blown collapse. Max decided to help anyway and while he did this Kate soon found her way over to Foster and began voicing her suspicions once again to him away from earshot of Cole.

"Those bodies are at least a few days old. He admits he knew them but he doesn't remember how they got that way. Don't tell me you buy that bullshit?" Kate vented in frustration.

"Kate, relax." replied Foster, whose attention was placed in comparing his map with the lay of the land they overlooked for miles on end. He didn't even look at her.

Seething, she continued her reasoning. "Don't fucking tell me to relax; He either did them in himself, or he's an Illusionist. *Those are the damn choices!* He's dangerous and you're trying to make friends with the guy."

Foster seemed to ignore her until she slapped the map out of his hands in anger. "He's got you guys under his spell already!" Kate spat, this time loud enough for Cole to hear. Cole and Max stopped their digging to look over and Kate looked away, fearful of catching Cole's gaze. Foster calmly picked up the map and then sternly grabbed Kate by the arm.

"Then why doesn't he just make you comply, huh? He's a newborn so his head is a little funny at the moment, but he'll remember soon enough. Kate, we need all the help we can get."

Knowing she couldn't reason with him, she muttered out a final objection, "I don't trust him."

Foster let go of her arm and followed through with, "Well, do you trust me?"

Kate stared directly at Foster, trying to remain strong under his piercing gaze. She was like family to him, and neither of them were saints. Foster had found her just after the peace had been broken. It was Salt Lake City and the Purification Front had been rolling eastward across the country. Their Illusionist claimed their vision was the work of the lord and their preference for Old Testament violence was prolific in their eastward expansion. Children were often used in their frontline attacks, causing hesitation in defenders opening fire. This hesitation would prove fatal, as these little monsters would not bat an eyelid in viciously murdering those who stood in their way; a lack of physical strength compensated by a resolute devotion to their leader akin to demonic possession. Foster had heard of these tactics being used in other cities and was quick to explain to Kate, then a twenty-two year old stranger to him what she would have to endure to make it out of Salt Lake. Foster had saved her that day; and it was this fact that made her equally uncomfortable in disobeying Foster as trusting Cole.

"Do you trust me?" Foster repeated the question.

"Yes," Kate lied.

"Good. We'll get to the bottom of this tonight. In the meantime, check on Daisy and watch the roads," he ordered. Kate trudged off, defeated.

***

It was afternoon by the time Cole had finally buried his two late friends. Sweat dripped freely down the sides of his face and rolled into his broken windows. The salt stung, but the pain was good; it took away from the knowing. His hands were blistered while his muscles ached from the weight they had carried. With Foster and Max standing over the freshly dug graves, they now stood unsure of what to do next. Foster asked Cole if he would like to say a few words.

Cole was hesitant for a moment before softly speaking, "Maybe just a moments silence." Max couldn't help but let out the slightest snicker at this. They'd already been in silence the entire afternoon.

As the sun began to set behind them, Foster was quick to conclude that they stay in Trent for the night. Cole was willing to oblige, showing them to makeshift bedrooms once home to Peter's followers; even offering supplies of canned goods kept in the former convenience store of Trent.

By sunset Kate had returned from her duties, still wary of Cole, albeit calmer around him. When they had all been acquainted with their beds (not a word spoken of who once occupied them) Foster insisted they eat dinner together as a way of getting to know each other. Cole agreed wholeheartedly, but then grew quiet as a mouse and requested they give him some time to be by himself, let the revelations sink in. Foster nodded and as they pretended not to keep a lookout, Cole shrugged off slowly up the grassy knoll, to the bench where he'd sat a thousand times before, this time alone. They watched his lone figure sulk from afar, as he tried to take in the pink streaks of a sunset that would never be the same.

When the sun had finally set, Cole took them to Pappali's, the only eatery in Trent and a small one at best. The place had been stripped clean, the paint on the walls worn down completely. All that remained were two large wooden dinner tables, with one whose table legs looked like they had been carved out from nearby trees.

"This was where we all used to eat, one happy family…" Cole mused.

"What happened then?" Kate asked accusingly.

Before Cole could answer, Foster diffused the situation by asking Cole where the chairs were. He checked out the back and returned with two chairs. "There's only two left," he said pulling them up.

"Max, get some of the foldouts from Daisy. Kate, you get the candles from our rooms."

"There are a few candles out the back," Cole interjected before fetching them himself. When everyone had chairs and candles were lit, they got to digging into their canned tuna. Cole ate like he hadn't eaten in days. By the time he'd gone through four cans, the questions began to flow.

"How much do you remember, Cole?" Foster asked.

Cole felt their eyes draw on him. He hesitated; he always did that. Choosing his words was always a difficulty for Cole, often weighing decisions but never making a choice, never putting his foot down. That's what Cole remembered, a lifetime of inaction…

But here in this room now, he felt more than ever the overwhelming need to speak with conviction.

"Not much; my memory seems to walk in and out of line. I recall watching a burning building before escaping Peter's house in Denver. I think it was…like a church or something, but I guess the sharpest part of it all is staying here in Trent, enjoying the sunsets."

"How long you been here?" asked Max.

Cole's eyes drifted off in their speculative ways. "I couldn't tell you, to be honest. A real long time, maybe over a year…"

"How much of it did you see?" said Foster.

"See what?"

Foster, Max and Kate shared a glance of weary eyes.

"The wars, the fighting. People tearing each other apart, this whole country falling to pieces."

"I don't remember much before Trent, why all this happened. From what it sounds like, things were terrible, maybe Peter just erased those bad thoughts."

"That'd be a nice thing to have, you lucky bastard," snarled Kate. There was an awkward silence for a moment, but this time Foster would not pull Kate back, instead agreeing with her.

"She's right, Cole. You missed a lot of bloodshed. I've been in Iraq and Afghanistan, and they don't come even close to what we've seen over these past sixteen months. It changes a person, right from the outset."

As he said this both Kate's and Max's heads fell in a sort of shame; feeling guilty in what they had to become in order to be sitting here, breathing in front of a man who had all those horrible thoughts just taken away, living in a bubble disconnected from the hardships they had to endure. They never spoke of envying those under control, but it always lingered along their surface.

"Well, what happened?" Cole asked earnestly.

Foster thought back to the beginning of it all, to when that first plane went down and he knew something was different. He always enjoyed putting his own opinion on ensuing events; it gave him a moral authority when he spoke of the Illusionists' failure to capitalize on their gifts, turning the possibilities of something great into an endless war for the control of our minds. But the preaching, he knew, was for a later day. He would stop himself short for now and just stick to the facts.

"I find it hard to believe you never saw anything up here, that no one else came to claim the view, because that one you have outside gives a nice strategic overlay of the Fort Collins below."

"For what?" Cole naively asked.

"To attack, of course."

Cole thought about this for a moment. Kate scanned his face for the longest time, trying to see something ignite behind those dark brown eyes; a memory he could share. She looked away when he replied though, still weary of his gaze.

"We might have, I just don't remember." Cole finally answered.

"This Peter, he must've protected you, kept you hidden," Foster suggested.

"Yes."

"How many were you before?" asked Max, his curious tone less threatening than Foster's probing.

Cole was more precise now. "There were twelve of us. We were just regular people of all ages, mostly strangers to one another, yet Peter brought us all together, and I got close with every single one of them over the past year." He paused but he wasn't finished. "The last thing I remember, I was out collecting firewood, and then I wake up in a blur with everyone I love gone or dead."

"Did you know her before?" Kate asked, this time the first sign of any sympathy escaping her.

"She was my girlfriend. Now she's dead, and I don't know why."

His face swelled at the coldness in his own statement. How could he say it like that, so bluntly? The reverberations began to shake inside him. He was ready to collapse again, but Foster held strong with the questioning.

"And Peter, did you know him from before?"

Cole's head dropped. "Since we were ten…"

They were unsure of what to ask next, and for a great span of time there was more heavy silence. Max returned to scraping his already cleared out spam, building up a collection of tiny specs so that he may indulge in one last quarter of a bite.

Kate tried to keep her guard up, but couldn't help feeling for Cole as he slumped across from them, sunk in a world of pain they all knew so well.

After a good ten minutes of sitting there in silence, soaking in his story, Cole slowly raised his head and began asking his own questions.

"What happened out there? Who did this to us?" he asked, looking specifically at Foster.

Foster decided to go from the beginning.

"I remember the news reports; it was on every channel: *Flight 34 from Houston to New York crashes well short of intended JFK, in downtown Richmond. More than one hundred dead…* We thought it was terrorists, but no one claimed responsibility. While they were still checking the black box of thirty-four there was talk of some outbreak, some strange happenings in California and Vegas. Of course, the government denied it all the way through. And by the time they figured out the two things were connected and they shut down all airspace the virus was airborne and the panic was everywhere."

"The virus you were talking about, right? That made the Illusionists?"

Foster sighed. "When the symptoms kept showing up all over the country, it became hard to contain the fear. Those that had the power—or *gift* as some called it—got caught up in the panic and freaked themselves out. Eventually they figured the downed plane was just infected people, the first cases. Mental illnesses became shared; you're looking at Alzheimer's, Dementia, Depression, and psychosis seeping into your brain without warning. Can you imagine living in a world unsure whether your own neighbor was controlling your thoughts, moving you about in ways you wouldn't intend? No one trusted each other and that's when the fights began. In the first two months people stocked up on weapons and food, while financial trading stopped. Money became worthless and it all just collapsed."

"What about the government?" asked Cole, now engrossed in this tragedy that had flown past him—*almost, at least.*

"When they finally did acknowledge the existence of Tyranto-cillous, they couldn't contain it. It was just too late. Martial Law was in effect a month after Flight 34, but how do you enforce it against people able to manipulate others like puppets? After that, well it depends who you ask…"

"What do you mean?" Cole asked.

"D.C. was nuked," said Max, and the fallout of his words were felt around the room. When it had descended like a mist, Foster added the grim speculation that relentless winds had carried the radiation northward up into the state of New York, where a dense population on the brink of collapse had no defense against the dying air. Foster's story was getting worse, but none of them could stop it. Cole could see all their hearts sink with the sullen look in Max's eyes bringing Cole to imagine a younger Max gripped to a news feed signaling a country that would never be the same.

"After it had spread to a national level, we thought it was only a matter of time before one of these freaks took possession of us. Then all sorts of people started to stand above the chaos, calming everyone down. All around the country you had every-one praising these average Joes for bringing back some form of authority to the situation—with not the slightest curiosity to how they were doing it. What was really happening was that they were able to handle the distortions in reality the virus generated in the mind, and that their brains were rapidly taking on the abili-ty to induce all sorts of controls on the minds of others."

"These are the Illusionists you talk about." Cole inferred.

Foster nodded. "At first they tried to rebuild what was destroyed in the panic. They tried working together to recreate the one thing that is the glue to society: trust. Some people likened it to the new wave of optimism in the late 60's, resurgence in flower power and the victory of peace and love. The Great Peace; that's what they were calling it. Kate got caught up in this and we were there to save her when this tenuous foundation collapsed. Not all of these Illusionists wanted peace, their love became a hunger for power and just when we thought the days would get brighter, all of a sudden we were plunged into a war; a war between Illusionists who use us as pawns in their endless power struggle. Now the main group in California, the Purification Front…"

The mere mention of their name caused Kate's face to drop in despair. Foster saw this and moved along.

"Anyways, we have very little idea how many in the population had the specific genes that caused them to become Illusionists, but through the few radio transmissions we've picked up in the past eight months we've heard numbers that could be as high as four percent. That's at least twelve million from the beginning."

Cole's face was growing in despair. Every so often his body would flinch in anguish, unsure of how to deal with the loss of the world he once knew and the new world he had awoken to. Frantically he searched for options of possible salvation—the might of the American military, the intervention of other countries—but Max shook his head with vigour.

"Most of the military got turned, just like that," said Max, clicking his fingers. "They're now just weapons at the disposal of those bastards who think they're gods. As for the other countries, *some* allies they turned out to be. They put up an international quarantine; who knows if it stuck, but they were ready to desert us from the get-go."

So there it was and that was that. All alone and at their mercy, whoever these monsters were.

Looking at their military attire, Cole got curious. "So, what's with the uniforms?" he motioned with his head. "If there's no army left, what flag are you still defending?"

Foster smiled. The conversation was heading his way.

"Cole, we may not look it but we're a lot stronger than you think. Because what we represent will never die. It does not need the brainwashing of an Illusionist to propel it. The thirst for freedom is in every animal, and those people out there under their control are caged and deserve the choice to break free. They need to have a choice, and resistance is the only way. We are just a few faces of the Resistance, Cole, and we'd all like you to join us in this fight."

Foster and Max's eyes gleamed at Cole, urging his concession, while Kate looked away in avoidance. She knew Foster's game. He would have Cole by the end of the night.

All Cole could muster after an agonizing wait was, "How?"

The others looked at each other in confusion. "How do we resist?" Cole elaborated. "I mean it seems a futile effort because from what you tell me, they sound unstoppable."

Foster's stare sharpened. He braced himself for the hook and went for it.

"Chicago. Two days ago, we received one last transmission, a radio broadcast. There's an encampment there just on the city's outskirts. From what it sounds like, they have enough resources to take out the Illusionists in Chicago. It'd be a start."

Cole studied their intent with a peculiar indifference. They called themselves soldiers and soldiers fought wars—that much was true. Yet to Cole, it still sounded like a fruitless endeavor.

"You still haven't answered my question. How? Wouldn't they get turned just as quick?" asked Cole, rising from his chair, startling everyone in the room. He had just been given a taste of this world and was already beginning to crack under the pressure.

Foster was resolute. "They've found the cure. It's the key to freedom. They just need help spreading it."

In those baby blue eyes, Cole saw a man ready to be free.

"We have it; Max, Kate and myself. It's in our systems. The madness has subsided for now, but the virus is still there, stuck in us, waiting. We need to get it out. And I know you know that you have it too. The only way to break this prison, to break the locks that keep us scared of our own shadow, is in Chicago. Do you understand, Cole?"

Cole did understand. He wanted it just as much as Foster, Kate and Max seemed to need it. But he was still skeptical.

"What if it's a trap?" Cole responded. This got Kate's attention; perked her right up—her words coming from *his* mouth. She'd brought up such a notion just as quickly in the dank cave in which they had barely scrapped by for over four months (during the harsh winter no less), cursing the monsters who pushed them into hiding, living quietly while Foster religiously assured them he would make those insidious creatures pay. Foster would beat himself up for everyday he failed to follow through on his words, to confront those bastards and deal with them like he would have settled problems back in the military. "We got more choices than those poor souls under their command, yet we keep taking the coward's way," he'd tell them whilst never being able to do anything about it. Foster talked less and less about the mission he once championed to Max and more about just getting plain old revenge, the failure of his mission to materialize weighing heavy on him.

But when he'd heard the broadcast while scouting the foothills around their cave—he'd found his salvation. The hope returned to Foster. It gave him a purpose he would give himself to fully without restraint. He'd approach it with as much vigour and determination as the will of an Illusionist's slave, if that is what it took.

"It's not a trap, I just have faith." was all he said, just as he had said to Kate. Even with this lackluster answer, it was hard to say no to his energy, to deny this man his hope.

Now it was time for Max to speak up. "Foster says we're strong, but we could use all the help we can get, to be honest. Plus, I don't know about staying here. The Purification Front have been patrolling round these parts for the past few weeks. Hate to say it, but it's only a matter of time…"

Cole slouched back in his chair and summed it up quick in his head. There was nothing here in Trent for him anymore and if Max was right, the Purification Front was going to get him, whoever they were. This new mission handed to him was almost as unreal as the world he had just joined. The Resistance, mind controllers and the apocalypse. It all seemed too fantastical to Cole, but like Foster, it would give him purpose—an escape from his broken cage. He knew he needed out of this place, as far away from the memory of Maddie, Peter, everything as he could. He had to leave, before that scent of hers suffocated him.

Cole looked in their eyes, both Foster and Max eagerly awaiting his confirmation while Kate slouched in her chair, preparing her disappointment.

Cole cleared his throat. "Well, seems there's nothing left for me here, so I guess I'll be Chicago bound." A sigh of relief shot through the room, stranger even that the tiniest smile emerged from Kate's hesitant face.

"With that settled, we'll make our leave tomorrow at 0800 hours," declared Foster in a formal tone that masked how relieved he was that Cole had joined their misfit group. Because for all his experience in the military and all their talk of championing the Resistance, they were a small-nit group in the middle of a large war, hemmed in by an oncoming wave of religious zealots and the great unknown they would have to cross to reach Chicago.

After dinner, Cole led them to their beds, all the while asking what he should pack and how they would travel, even offering the town's only car (they'd have to find fuel and a new battery first, of course). Upon hearing this, Max gave out a friendly laugh. "Tomorrow you'll meet Daisy, our ride. She's my baby. She helped us through the tough times and I owe it to her to drive her until she's bone dead. Heck, maybe even across this whole damn country."

Once they had lain down in their beds and Cole had left to pack in his room with the makeshift iron sheet door, they all fell asleep quickly, except for Kate, whose thoughts ran in their usual circles, interrogating this new character.

20. Chicago Bound

Cole woke in a sweat, the embers of his recurring dream dying with waking eyes. Attempts to grasp its trembling visions before they were vacuumed back in were short-lived. After a while, Cole just assumed it was about Maddie and decided it was good he hadn't remembered.

When Maddie was still there, Cole would ask her to listen to him sleeping, searching for words to bubble out in mutters that could give Cole a clue as to where to begin. But Cole always remained silent—if not restless—and the sweat-drenched awakenings were never understood.

Thinking back to those times, Cole was brought back to her, the way he clutched her when he woke, the sweat of his arms and forehead spreading to her skin, and her allowing it, even in the dead of winter. He thought of this, the way he'd always tell her it didn't matter, as long as they were together. He lay in his bed as those memories crept back, and when he regarded the rest of the room all he could notice was the smooth bedside table and the redwood chair, all hand crafted. He held in the pools beneath his eyes and let his gaze roll back to the ceiling. Keeping his eyes upward, he pleaded out a single wish: that he could go back to her, even if it were the worst day, all for just another moment.

***

Kate woke Max quietly, her hand cupping his mouth, motioning him to join her outside so they could talk away from Foster, who slept soundly in the corner. They tiptoed down the stairs, agonizing over ever creak before breaking out into the cool morning air that slapped them truly awake. Kate mouthed for Max to keep quiet until she was sure they were at a safe distance. They made their way up the knoll and over to the park bench where Max sat down and wearily asked Kate what the hell was going on.

"What do you make of him?" questioned Kate, her eyes expectant.

Max stared wearily at Kate. "You don't look like you slept well."

"How could I when that fucker is sleeping right there in the next room! Tell me you don't buy his story?"

Max looked back to the top floor above the eatery, to the window of Cole's room. He didn't buy Cole's story at all, and yet the guy seemed sincere in his grief. Most of all, though, Max didn't want to upset Kate. That was the last thing he wanted to do.

"I don't know, Kate. I mean, yeah, it doesn't really connect well whichever way you string it, but Foster seems—"

"—Foster! That's another thing! You ever seen him play so nice to a stranger before? Don't you think it's weird he tells us he wants to scout this dead area for a recon of FOCO—and we find someone? Of all the places?"

Max stood up and grabbed Kate by the shoulders.

"Okay, Okay! Yes, it's weird. It's definitely weird. But I think

221

we need to play it cool. I don't know what this guy's deal is, but I'd rather make him a friend than an enemy. I'm not going to let anything bad happen to you, Kate."

They regarded each other for a moment before Kate looked over to Cole's window, trying to calm herself.

"I'm not just looking out for myself; I'm looking out for you guys, too."

"I know. We'll both keep an eye on him. Just…keep it cool for the moment."

Kate put a hand on Max's wrist and gave it a reassuring squeeze, to the quiet delight of Max. "Sure."

***

Daisy was a beauty, or so Max thought. He'd picked the name when he watched Kate pick out a daisy, one of the last few left before winter came. It was just right out on the side of the road, before Utah met with Colorado. All her brothers and sisters in the shrub were long dead. Max didn't know what to think of the way Kate had twinkled it around between her finger and her thumb, her eyes trying to grasp at something. All he saw was that she was fascinated, and her fascination became his, because well…

Daisy was parked amongst some bushes half a mile up the road from Trent, just enough distance to scout the area and enough to retrieve her in a hurry. Foster told Cole this was standard procedure when passing a town. Max then explained to Cole that, once a basic black SUV, Daisy had been taken in by Max during the opening exchanges of the outbreak and had undergone some significant surgery under his watch. "Most of the windows are bullet proof; and I'll just point out the heavy duty bull bar," he said while proudly tapping the bar.

"Shut up, Max," Kate quipped as she loaded the food supplies (a day at the most, cleaned out from Trent) into the boot. Cole laughed awkwardly at Kate's remark, before meandering over to Foster who once again stood watching the flatland horizon of Fort Collins and beyond, lining up the landmarks on his faded map.

A treble of nerves crept in Cole's voice; here was a man weary of his own shadow. "Hey, I really appreciate you guys letting me come along. I wouldn't have known what to do with myself if you guys hadn't shown up…" Cole paused, glancing back at Kate and Max prepping Daisy, "…although, I'm not too sure Kate is happy with this whole arrangement."

Foster looked up from his map to greet Cole with a seriousness that shuffled Cole back just the slightest inch.

"Kate has her reasons and valid ones at that. We've got to be weary of newcomers and other groups otherwise we don't survive. That's the plain and simple truth."

This put Cole off balance and, mustering all his courage, he pressed the issue directly at Foster. "Well, do you trust me?" They stared each other down, Cole straining under the silence. Foster then chuckled and turned away. "Yes, yes I do."

The plan was to veer north and go around Fort Collins, then head northeast to Nebraska, which they would then go straight through, taking the I-80 (whilst avoiding former cities) and reaching Illinois through Iowa. It seemed Foster had this planned out in almost every detail, and Max remarked to Cole this was always Foster's way (if Cole hadn't noticed already).

***

Daisy glided seamlessly through the great plains of rural Nebraska, cutting a line carefully set by Foster in order to avoid as many townships and cities as possible. In the vast expanses of open fields, a cruel misunderstanding was felt by the lack of crops produced. When the virus had struck, food shortages ensued, as farming communities couldn't afford to share their harvests before a rough winter. Now in the summer months, nary a person could be seen out in the fields, tractors unused and rusted where they were ditched. The next winter would be worse if they ever lived so far as to see it.

As they hummed along, conversation was slow at first, kept to small remarks about the remarkable lack of people and the beauty of the green fields now untouched by man, while the grandness of the Rockies slowly receded in the distance. Despite the lack of crops, it was as if nature had flourished during this war, an indifference that spoke volumes of the insignificance of man and his petty conflicts. She would grow in his absence, no matter what.

Eventually, Kate got to asking Cole his story. "So, Cole, you live in Trent your whole life?"

Cole smiled, feeling a touch less interrogation and a growing sense of curiosity in her voice. "Nah, I was born on the outskirts of California; lived around there up until about three years ago when I moved to Denver, for college."

When Kate heard Denver being mentioned, her eyes lit up with interest. "Oh, I went to college in Denver as well! Yeah, CU. Fun times, right up until the Purification Front swarmed through. Destroyed everything I'd come to love. That was about eight months ago. Tell me, Cole, do you remember that?"

Her smile was sarcastic and her tone reeked of bitch and mistrust. Foster was quick to stop Kate, but she fired back mockingly, "I'm just trying to jog his memory."

Cole decided to go with her first question and hope it would quell her mounting spite towards him. "I don't remember; it's all still hazy. I mean, we ran north of Denver from Peter's parents' house, but that would have been more than eight months ago. Maybe I'm wrong; time was a different concept in Trent…"

Seeing she was getting nowhere, Kate opted to change the subject. "Well your memory can't be lost that far back, otherwise we'd be teaching you to eat from a spoon." (She had no scientific knowledge of memory and its processes.) "So what did you do before this all went to shit, huh? What's your vocation? Are you something useful, a mechanic like Max? Or were you training to be a doctor or something along those lines—I'll take a male nurse, even."

Cole's face became flustered as he sheepishly replied, "I'm a college dropout."

"Oh, terrific! I was just saying to Foster that we needed one of those!" Kate retorted.

A smile broke on each of their faces, including Cole, who stopped just short of a cackle of embarrassed laughter. In many ways he was lucky college hadn't stuck with him, or he hadn't stuck to college. Looking back on his past "career path", Cole tried to see the funny side of just how useless those skills were in this new world, a world where people weren't trying to sell you material goods or a way of life; just ideas which they needn't ask you to accept but merely tell you to think. Worst of all, you would love them for it. When it seemed Kate had given up deriding him, Cole returned to looking out the window, irrationally trying to remember those now useless skills and factoids, just for the sake of vacating a simpler time in his life where he held a small but safe purpose.

***

225

It had been almost an hour of driving in Nebraska before Max spotted them. Coming over the crest of a hill, he caught movement in the corner of his eye against a dead horizon. There were at least a hundred of them, wearing their plain gray robes, lugging around those big black crosses—the distinctive mark of the Purification Front. They were headed westward back to the Rockies, and from this distance resembled a flock of sheep. This flock was maybe over four miles away, but that was almost inconsequential. Once they locked onto you, it was only a matter of time. Kate slowed the car down and turned off the road onto the dirt. Everyone in the car had gone completely stiff, holding their breath while their heartbeats raged.

It was a good five minutes before anyone had the courage to speak.

"I don't reckon they saw us," Max hoped, his eyes fixated on the robed herd as it drifted away from them.

Kate whispered to Foster, "Gas masks?"

Foster shook his head all the while never removing his gaze on the sedating pilgrimage of their potential predators. "No, I don't think it's necessary. I think we're too far away."

"What are they doing this far out east?" worried Max, but his question went unanswered. Now there was just another long silence as they watched these people; not so much in fear but a kind of wonder, their mouths hanging open like tourists on safari.

Cole soon realized how he was looking at these people and tried to snap out of it. *These were people,* he protested internally. People who once had hopes and dreams just like him, only to now be considered somehow not entirely human anymore.

As the gray robes marched on into the horizon, it got to the point where Kate, Max and Foster had left the car and had placed their bodies prone on the crest of the hill, watching this migration through shared binoculars. Kate would later say it was to make sure they hadn't been made and that the gray robes were heading back to California, but Cole saw something else from the way they all looked at these people, even when they became ants in the distance. He felt they were attracted to the simple grace those people exuded, a jealous slant towards the simplicity of the flock's mindless happiness.

Once they had finished their strange fascination, Daisy resumed their travel eastward, where the questions about the Purification Front's movements began to swim at the surface in speculation.

"They were probably scouts," said Foster, "and they are coming back this way with a larger contingent to consolidate their new land." Kate and Max, with not much else to go on, nodded their heads in agreement. Cole, however, was not so sure.

"What if they aren't coming back? What if they were running from something?"

This sent a chill down the spines of the others. Foster tried to play down such a possibility, even going as far to suggest that it may have been the Resistance that had sent them back. But there was no chance of going back on Cole's brooding statement.

Foster was a little disappointed he hadn't considered such a thing himself, but reluctantly accepted Cole's theory and the dark implications. Cole saw he had made Foster look unknowledgeable, and having already recognized Foster's preference for always being the smartest man in the room, he decided to give some authority on the subject back to Foster.

"What I don't understand is the marching. Where are their vehicles? Surely they can't conquer the entire United States by walking distance?"

Foster sighed. "They march because it seems walking is the only acceptable form of transport in their new way of life, from what I've gathered."

Cole questioned the logic behind this, strangely recalling some documentary he'd watched (while high) about the hypocrisies of the Khmer Rouge in Cambodia, who had banned the use of modern machinery yet used guns to enforce it. Now, no one would blink twice at such a method, given this new climate of mass brainwashing. But Cole's comparisons were cut short by Foster's ultimate reasoning. "There are probably 30 million of them by now and nothing really poses a threat anymore, except maybe whatever sent them packing as you suggested was the case."

It was Max, however, who summed up the Purification Front perfectly.

"Backward ass-fucks."

They all agreed.

***

After the sighting of the robed wackos, the mood settled and a rhythm began of Foster checking his map and directing Kate through routes that avoided upcoming towns posing the threat of potential hostiles. In a day they had passed Nebraska, and now found themselves cruising into Iowa with little difference to be noticed despite the fading light of the sun, which tendered Foster towards deciding to set camp just after sunset.

Right as he said this, in the distance the shadings of two faint yellow arches crept into view next to the undeniable setup of a gas stop. Max exchanged a serious glance at Foster; every time they had passed one in Nebraska, Foster got the shakes and decided they keep moving on. Now with another day ready to be called, it beckoned to be realized that finding fuel just before setting camp would help them sleep easier.

"Make the call," said Max.

Foster looked at each of them wearily, leaving his gaze the longest on Cole who remained infectiously relaxed.

"Do it."

Daisy pulled up exactly between the McDonald's and gas stop. The gas stop was typical, boarded up and littered with signs that repeated "OUT" and "EMPTY" all over. The car park for the McDonald's was not entirely barren and a few road warriors were still parked within the designated lines. There was at least forty feet between the two. As they carefully scanned the windows, the empty silence made for high hopes. Foster produced two jerry cans and tubes and gave one to Kate and one to Max.

"Max, you and I will go to the gas stop. Kate and Cole, you two make for the two land rovers by the McDonald's."

The pairing incensed Kate. She figured Foster had picked a fine time for what he saw as a chance for a team building exercise, while Max was not exactly enthused with the decision either. They said nothing, letting their disapproval sink in with their inaction before Foster used that old voice of his to rile them out of the car.

"While we're alive, please," he grunted.

Kate threw the jerry can and tubing at Cole. "I'll be watching you with the AK," she explained.

With the sun almost through its descent, the cold air slapped them awake, Cole's cheeks flush pink as he dashed the 40 feet of open space before he hunched up next to the side of the building, doing his best to imitate the stealth of action stars in movies.

Kate walked briskly behind him, a finger on the trigger and both eyes on Cole. Reaching the edge of the restaurant, Cole's vision darted around the lifeless parking lot before sprinting off towards the first Land Rover. His hands shaking, Cole finagled the door handle ever so slightly, the ease at which the mechanism popped open stirring relief in his sweating scalp. Slowly creaking the door open, Cole was further pleased to find nobody in there, dead or alive. Pressing the lid opener, he then raced over to the ear that now protruded from the car. Funneling the tubing with the upmost care, Cole was all too weary of Kate's gaze that dug into his spine, waiting for him to fuck up as Kate made no attempt to hide the fact that the gun was always hovering in his direction.

Foster had checked each pump and the shitty Winnebago in a shade under three minutes. The signs told the bare truth. Kicking at the flat tires of the Winnebago, Foster restrained his mouth from blasting out obscenities, only to smack Max across the top of his long, tangled hair for already deciding the coast was by all means clear. The boy had his baseball bat out, smashing rocks out of the ballpark as he aimed for the home run yellow arches.

"What was that for?" Max bemoaned after Foster's smack was followed by that trademark stare.

"Go get Kate and Cole."

"Just a second, I'm trying to clinch game seven."

By the third car, Kate had lost sight of Cole, his eagerness to avoid the stare of that barrel sending him slyly ducking in the McDonald's as Kate searched inside the land rovers for anything useful. When she finally noticed, Kate stormed into the Mc-Donald's guns up. Cole stood at the counter deciding his meal. Arrested by this sight, Kate moved to ask him why he was in here, only to be struck by a whiff of golden fries. It only lasted a second, but in that moment the faintness of the smell grew pungent and the darkened walls seemed to show a glimmer of their former selves. As Kate suddenly found herself trying to suck in that smell, the spark of nostalgia evaporated just as quickly as it came, replaced by the smell of the dead manager sitting in his favorite booth just off to the right of Kate, his title still pinned proudly to his shirt. She was back.

"What're you doing?" she finally questioned Cole, his hands in the pockets of his grimy chinos.

Cole's hand waved briskly at the fading menu. "Just ordering a quarter pounder meal. Want my fries?"

Kate hid her surprised amusement, instead preparing her confrontation. "Look, those guys out there might play nice, but we both know your amnesia is bullshit… Why you with us really?"

Within the buzzing silence, Cole kept his stare on Kate, proving too much for her as her eyes darted away. His own did the same.

"The person I loved more than anything is dead. She's dead and every passing thought keeps whispering it to me. My feet just need to run and I got nothing else to do but let them. Can you see this, Kate?"

Before she got a chance to reply, Max had strolled in with all the confidence in the world, riding high on the back of his World Series title. He walked right up to Cole with his eyes firmly trained on the peeling golden nuggets hanging off the menu. "You guys ordered yet?"

***

Max, now driving, rolled Daisy a couple of miles away from the view of the arches before cutting off-road half a mile away from the empty highway. They drove through a clearing before finding a nice spot behind a row of trees and bushes that hid them from the road.

The group were quick to avoid the unspoken concern that echoed out in the wide-open expanse of nothingness they now occupied. They only had a fifth of gas left to get them to Chicago. Another gas run to an upcoming town beckoned in tomorrow's light, but for now they were all just relieved to comfort themselves with the star-filled skies of the Iowan night.

They gathered some small branches off the surrounding trees and soon had a small fire going. Max produced four cans of imitation-chicken stew from their supply box and everyone began digging in around the campfire, not saying much, just watching the stars that hung about the sky, looking down on them.

"Never thought I'd go to Iowa," remarked Cole. This drew agreement from the others with Max adding, "Shoot, I didn't think I'd have to go to Nebraska. I can now cross that off the bucket list thank you very much, apocalypse."

As they shed smiles at this, Cole found himself considering the word "apocalypse" and this got him wondering out loud if this really was the end. What if this was a chance to change everything? It all led Cole to one simple question: What would you do if you were one of them? Each of their eyes sparked up; it was a topic they always liked to muse on and Max seemed eager to answer right away.

"Well, for starters, I'd make sure everyone would take the time to watch and admire all this," he spoke in a giddy excitement as his arms motioned to the stars in the night sky and the rolling hills of nature that surrounded them. "It'd be part of my new learning curriculum. That, and everyone played baseball because they absolutely loved it."

"You'd be the best at it right?" Cole jumped in.

"Goes without saying…" Max laughed.

Kate snorted in joining laughter. "You can make people do *anything* and you make them play baseball?" Max had already told her this before and she had responded just the same, a joke presented for Cole's sake.

"Well, they wouldn't mind because they'd love it, because I told them so. In reality I'm not even really telling them, just making them realize the truth that's been there ever since Mickey Mantle beat Ruth's home run record in the World Series of sixty-three."

"At least make them play a sport that's good, like football perhaps," laughed Cole, bringing a smile across Kate's face.

"Exactly!" she agreed.

"All right, all right. I see how it is. Pick on the kid with simple dreams, sure. I'll remember that when I'm one of them and just letting you guys know it's going to be *clean Max's toilet day* for the rest of your natural-born lives! I kid you not, there will be an unholy amount of skid marks—I'll make sure of it."

Laughing this off, Cole then looked at Kate; her body slouched in the sagging camping chair while the fire danced between them. "What would you do, Kate?"

She sat up and her smile faded as she thought hard about the world she had begun building in her head ever since someone had asked her that for the first time. "Lennon's world," she eventually responded to the confusion of Cole alone.

"You know, *Imagine all the people…*" she began to hum which caused Max and Cole to follow suit. That warm smile of hers came back.

"I'd change some simple things, get rid of all violent acts, murder, rape, stealing and war—just run happiness on tap. And all we'd have to do is imagine it, just like Lennon did…"

Kate soon found herself melting back into the peaceful world she always dreamed about, if only for a moment, before Foster finally broke his silence.

Cole soon understood why Max had been so quick to express himself before; he wanted to get his two cents in before Foster struck him and Kate down. Cole knew Foster had hated the Illusionists because he had seen what they had done, but it felt as if Foster was unwilling to even admit the benevolent possibilities these people now had in their hands. It was probably because, unlike Kate, Foster had never been wrapped up in the warm fuzzy blanket of an Illusionist's touch, and he wasn't young like Cole or Max either, the optimism of youth still clinging on.

"Come on, Kate, if you were one of them you'd do all these great things—I mean how blind can you be? These people have had their chance to do all the wishy-washy dreams of life that you're all daydreaming about now and you know what they went ahead and did with that? CONVERT OR KILL anyone who doesn't ascribe to the bullshit they're feeding. You can't see that these utopias come at a price? They make us less than human; just feel good vessels with no moral choice of our own. You ever stop to think what happens when one of these people has a bad day? An entire society, relying on the whims of one person—tell me that's smart, tell me that'll end up *just great*."

The rest of them turned silent, their faces falling to the ground like children having disappointed their father, unable to look in his eyes from the shame they felt. In many ways, Foster was much like their father, not just in age respects, but also in his watchful and delicate authority over them. He had a voice that commanded the attention of any room, a trait that had served him well on his run up the military ladder. The armed services were always where he'd end up, even if there were a few bumps on the way. His granddaddy had served in the First and Second World War and his father in Vietnam. When Foster married and had two boys of his own he pushed as best he could for both to follow the tradition. Matthew, the oldest of the two, came the closest, studying Behavioral Psychology at West Point before changing schools and switching to the private sector. His youngest, Dylan Foster, was a flake, a college dropout who fought with Foster constantly over his lack of patriotism for America's foreign policy. His relationship with both reached boiling point when Matthew began to openly disagree with Foster's growing denouncement of Dylan. Foster hadn't seen either of them for three years, and ever since this whole shit-storm began, the two of them were in his thoughts constantly, as he silently rued the many failings he had gone through as a father and all those wasted chances to amend.

Now, sitting around these young people he considered like family, questioning their talk about the enemy—it brought him back to those recurring dinner table arguments he and Dylan used to have that would almost end in blows. He knew how he could push people away with his temper, he was very good at that, but he couldn't let them talk about the Illusionists this way because he had to protect them, keep them ever vigilant against an enemy who only teased them with the possibilities of peace. He had to protect them. They were all he had now.

"Look," he said, his face pinned downward as he stumbled through his apology. "I'm sorry I yelled, it's just we can't be talking in any way that humanizes these people, because they will use that against us. Kate, you saw how quickly things turned when they broke the peace. You mustn't forget this, or they will take your mind and walk all over you again."

They all locked eyes on Foster, willing to heed his words and for calm to be restored. The silence between the crackle of the fire was only ended when Max hastily remarked it was getting late. At this, they all awkwardly hurried off to their respective beds for the night, all except for Foster who stared at the dying fire, thinking of his boys.

21. Encounter

Kate remembered deeply just how it was when he first came running down that mountain, like Moses with the tablets proclaiming the good word.

The cure.

The sun shone bright through the leafless trees. She was reading an old gossip magazine she'd found and read a hundred times over, pretending not to notice Max who sat across from her, stealing glances, yearning from afar in his shy way as he pretended to tune a plastic toy guitar. They were both up on their feet when Foster had panted to a stop.

Could it be true? Kate studied that radio; certain she'd seen it dusty hours ago. Why had Foster decided to turn it on, bring it up on the mountain, today of all days? They hadn't used the damn thing since winter came and went. He'd been bitter the whole week—heck scratch that, the whole month. They all were. It was the dampness of everything seeping into their clothes and then their hearts, and even when the weather had gotten better as it was this day, there was still the constant hunger. Max had told

Kate he used to be chubby before the collapse. Used to be a big burger man (or boy as Kate saw him). Now he was just skinny like the rest of them. They had gotten lucky with a family of jackrabbits after barely eating for two days straight, and here was Foster, jumping up and down in pure excitement.

This was their mission.

This was the good word.

Kate didn't say anything at first. She was sure, almost certain, there wasn't a CDC center in Chicago, so how'd they come up with this tantalizing hope? She just watched Max and Foster dancing foolishly in upbeat frenzy. Their waiting was over. The time for action was now. As Kate watched them, she saw a fire of the spirit ignite in their faces. It was at that point she felt it true; it just had to be. She wanted to believe.

***

They all awoke to a sunny day, the heat bursting through their tents, slowly draining their energy to once again face their fears and travel into the unknown. Cole emerged from his tent to wipe his face in the morning dew that was fast evaporating in the building heat. There had been crying from Cole's tent throughout the night, but none had the courage to bring it up, for what could they say to a man trying desperately to hide his grief.

As they made their way around the dead remains of last night's fire, they were reminded of the heated arguments of yesterday that still simmered below the surface. There was little talk as they ate their canned tuna and whatever else had not become rotten yet.

When they had finished eating, Foster, without saying a word, started packing up his tent and loading it into the car. The others slowly followed suit, but stopped in their tracks when Foster began a weapons check on all the rifles. They watched on in silence as he checked the magazines of the Kalashnikov and M4 carbine, his face maintaining a great intensity throughout, avoiding their eyes despite making them know his presence. He then moved onto pulling apart each rifle using the bonnet of Daisy as his desk. Upon finishing the AK-47 he looked up at Max and Kate.

"You two: finish packing up Cole's stuff. Cole, I'm going to show you everything short of firing this baby," said Foster, his eyes wide and unblinking. Cole put down his folded up tent bag and shuffled towards Foster, his apprehension evident to all.

"Look, it's safe to say we may be expecting contact further east... We're going to need to make another gas run today and we can't count on another failed highway stop so that means going into a town. There could be people like us—scared, hungry and desperate. They will not think twice if you let them. Now, this Kalashnikov I hold in my hands may be the difference between life and death." Cole shakily grabbed the weapon and followed Foster's instructions.

"Press that to take out the magazine and pull that when you're ready to fire…that switch there allows you to alternate between semi or fully automatic…now firmly place the butt against your shoulder. The kick on this baby is worse than the carbine so if you do have to take out a target, either use controlled bursts or keep it on semi-automatic, because we don't have the luxury of wasting any rounds."

Cole held the weapon as he was told, trying hard to keep his hands from quivering. At Foster's word he aimed the gun at a bunch of trees and let his finger hover over the trigger. The butterflies in his stomach fluttered in their millions.

"Now obviously we can't shoot off a few here lest we want to give our position away," said Foster, much to Cole's relief before Foster leaned in closer, grabbing Cole by the sleeve of his worn t-shirt.

"But I need you to know these things, because they won't just be saving you."

Their eyes held a long stare before Foster let go of Cole's arm and returned to packing his stuff as if nothing had just happened. Cole glanced at the others who gave him sympathetic looks and no more. They didn't want to get involved. Nevertheless, Cole breathed easier the further away he walked from Foster.

When everything had been cleaned up they hit the road. There was no talking; only the shared dread they would have to face the closer the petrol dial sunk into the red. To speak of it and plan for it was practical, but their hearts and minds weren't ready. Trent had been a breeze compared to this, when Daisy still had the power to make a quick exit, but now…Kate was scared for more than just that. The only time she'd seen Foster act in such a way was the first time they'd met. Since then, encounters with hostiles had been scattered, but she feared that would all change soon enough. What worried her most was not that Foster was expecting trouble, but that he may actually be looking for it.

Max drove slower than he usually did, Foster's brandishing of rifles clearly weighing on his mind. They were now somewhere in mid-Iowa. Soon, the freeway they had been coasting along on became congested with more and more empty cars. Foster checked his map as Max parked behind one of the empties. They all anticipated a right turn somewhere up ahead as the right side of the road held green trees and scattered houses while on the left, hints of sprawling suburbs could be made out. Those suburbs would ultimately lead them to Des Moines, the capital of

Iowa. Foster mused on this for a while before bringing himself forward to the center of the car to point out to Max a possible exit hidden away behind a row of abandoned cars.

"There should be a left turn three hundred yards up ahead—I want you to take that."

Max looked at Foster, before turning to Kate, eager for a second opinion. Kate shuffled in her seat before turning around to face Foster. "Maybe I should look at the map as well, since I'm up the front and all," she suggested, her voice emanating like more of a desperate plea than she wanted to let on. Foster handed it to her, his stare burning her skin. She quickly turned back, her body tense as she frantically studied the map. Once she had spotted the exit he spoke of, her heart sank. The exit led to Holdsworth, an outer suburb that connected onto Des Moines. While fearful of his response, Kate knew she had to protest before it might've been too late.

"The exit leads us right by Des Moines, I don't understand why we need to go that close if we're just passing through," she asserted, knowing full well that these were the rules and disciplines Foster had instilled in both her and Max. For him to go against his own words was ample evidence that Foster was losing it (if he hadn't already). If they could remind him of this, then maybe Foster would relent and let them take a right.

Max turned to Foster, "I'm with Kate on this one; we can just as easily go right or even keep going straight for a little bit longer."

Foster tensed. He was losing them. He looked to Cole, who faced outward on purpose, avoiding the decision. Frustrated, he braced himself before speaking in a low, somewhat defeated tone. "We need to scope out the situation in Iowa, it just might be the case that it belongs to the Resistance, or at least give an indication of how they might be faring in Chicago—or the rest of Illinois for that matter."

The others were caught off guard. They figured he'd press the petrol issue, reminding them they had a greater chance of finding it in the towns. Foster pushed further.

"Getting into Illinois isn't going to be any easy feat either. We've got to cross the Mississippi, and I don't want to be caught in either Muscatine or Burlington when we're in the red like this…"

These were the facts they had to swallow. Of course, they could just ditch Daisy and find a quiet channel to swim across, but then they'd be truly vulnerable, and Max wasn't parting with Daisy just that easy.

Foster cleared his throat. "Don't want to be caught out like Salt Lake…" A blood vessel burst in Kate, her teeth clenching at his nerve for bringing it up the way he did. But her anger seemed useless, almost childish. Foster had been right so far…

Max eventually gave a sigh and started Daisy up again, moving around the empty car in front, flicking on the left blinker. In the silence its ticking echoed away in their ears. If you had asked Max why he did it, he'd simply tell you he was following orders, because it was easier that way. Even the more headstrong Kate felt some relief in resigning her fate to Foster.

The car slowly rolled onward before reaching the turn. Soon, the green trees that surrounded the freeway broke into growing pockets of rundown houses, most likely that way even before the war. The winds began to pick up. The sun that had baked them earlier in the day began to dissipate with the fast enveloping shadows of the clouds above. It felt as if time were speeding up through the changing weather, despite the fact they plodded along slower than ever, cautiously watching each empty house that went by. Where did all these people go? Did they cluster under a shared paranoia before spreading a panic that saw many to believe the other was mad? Some houses were completely burned to the ground, just ashes and a mailbox. *How crazy were these people that they burned their own house down? Were they inside when the deed was done?*

Was it like how Max, Kate, Cole and Foster had seen it, or were the people of Iowa spared because there was simply less of them to begin with? Putting down the window, Cole irrationally tried to hear for the sounds of people, people moving in their little circles. But there was only the sound of birds chirping and insects buzzing and the wind blowing. No people, just ghosts. The implications were hard to bear. If this was the fate of everywhere then their hopes were growing dimmer the closer they got to their destination. They would never make it out of this war with their minds intact—whether under the spell of the Illusionists or left to fend for themselves. They yearned for the freedom of their minds, yet what they saw could never give them that peace. *Was it all too late?*

Cole scanned each house and counted the one's that had their windows boarded up. It was a game he played, simply to keep his mind off things. It was a trick he had been playing ever since his youth, the easiest form of observation, or daydreaming as his parents called it. He would use it in long rides with his parents, or days at school where he didn't want to do any work. He was in many ways simply a daydreamer and a follower; that was how it went with Maddie anyways: Cole would take a whiff of her scent and with weakened knees would follow her to the end of the earth if he had to. All his life he'd been this kind of person, waiting for the answers and the shifting of shoulders in the right direction…

Eventually he stopped counting the boarded up houses. Just as a child the numbers would get too big and now every house was boarded up, and every one that wasn't boarded up was reduced to mere rubble, shells of a past world. Cole didn't want to count the rubble.

They were now well into the outer suburb of Holdsworth, with Des Moines and its potentially violent inhabitants too close for comfort. The now constant stream of destitute houses, some burnt completely to the ground, gave Kate reason to question Foster again.

"I think we've seen enough, maybe we should reconnect with the highway and head as far as we can to Chicago."

Even though the likelihood of finding something better in Chicago than the debris that surrounded them was growing slimmer by the second, Kate hoped if they got back on the highway they'd be safe for at least another day. Foster didn't have time to answer her. A lone car turned into their street only a hundred yards from them. Max hit the brakes hard in shock surprise, springing everyone forward against their seatbelts. The other car was old and run down—a beige Camry hatchback. Each car stood motionless in suspended silence, deliberating whether to make the move and present themselves as friends or treat each other as foes. Even if they weren't under the influence of an Illusionist, they could just as well be the paranoid gun-toting survivalists who didn't get this far by making peace. Daisy remained eerily silent, bar the faint whisper of Foster's voice murmuring, "What's it going to be, friend or foe?"

Without moving her gaze, Kate reached for her binoculars. Bringing them up slowly, she tried her best to get a glimpse of the occupants of the other car. She could make little of it, except for the fact that there was definitely more than one of them. Suddenly there was a burst of movement within the other car. As Kate tried to focus on what was going on, Foster had already reached behind him, sliding his four-gauge shotgun into his grip. When she saw the two in the front putting on gasmasks, a shot of relief rocketed through her body as she then relayed on the news to the others. They weren't out of the woods just yet, but it had seemed the other car was presenting itself to a peaceful outcome, whatever that may be.

The Camry's doors slowly cracked open. Out came a tall, heavy-set man, hidden behind a gasmask, wearing a trench coat. Even from afar, they could see his nerves wriggling away inside him, urging him to flee in any direction but theirs. After some clear hesitation, the man began walking slowly towards Daisy, his arms raised up and palms open.

Foster was the first to react. He put on his gasmask without saying a word to the attention of no one else, as they watched with intrigue this man that wore a trench coat in the growing heat. By the time they had heard Foster's door close, he was already in front of the car, walking out to meet the man who had now stopped in his tracks having seen Foster's shotgun. Neither was under the influence, but Foster's recent edginess kept Kate uneasy. Foster eventually halted his advance and they stood alone on the desolate street, no more than twenty yards from each other.

Not wanting to confuse his message, the man spoke in a slow, loud voice to counter the muffle of his mask.

"We don't want any trouble, we just want to pass through."

Foster didn't respond straight away, sizing up the man who quivered in his boots, his hands still facing the sky. Eventually, Foster's grip on the shotgun loosened and Foster repeated in kind. "We want the same thing… From where have you come?"

Both camps breathed a sigh of relief. It dawned further on Cole the depth mistrust could be placed in a person's heart and mind in this climate of fear. If there was no way of knowing if your thoughts were truly your own, anyone could be an Illusionist and one wouldn't know, one couldn't trust…

Cole realized that for those who weren't under the spell of the Illusionist—those who tried to resist it's all powerful control—would never really know what it was they were actually fighting against, no matter how much time and effort they put into it. To resist was to doom one's self to a life of second-guessing each idea, notion and purpose every second of the day. If this encounter was any indication of how the free men were, then what resistance could truly be held?

"We're just leaving Holdsworth," said the man.

"What's in Holdsworth?" Foster asked, taking one step closer. This sent the man one step back. The man reached for his gasmask and slowly took it off. This caused Foster to do the same.

The man was now exposed, the anxiety breaking through in his erratic tone. "On the outskirts of Holdsworth, there's a large contingent of refugees…well, larger than most."

"Military presence there?" questioned Foster.

The man hesitated. "There's some…mainly just regular folks with guns, but its mostly just families and anyone else that's made it this far."

Foster was getting tired of this man's cowering. He wanted

better answers so he kicked up his tone, putting a full throttle on that stern voice of his.

"How many?" Foster bellowed.

The man hesitated again, his feet inching backward, unsure if he should be talking further on the subject.

"Maybe about… four thousand," he said reluctantly.

The number took Foster by surprise. He found it hard to believe a number that large would escape control for long, but he wanted it so much to be the case, he was willing to keep an open mind.

"Why are you leaving?" Foster asked, but just as he asked this, the driver's door of the Camry burst open as a big woman emerged, running out to the man.

"Jesse, we gotta go! If we don't leave now, we'll never do it."

Foster moved to question what she was talking about, but the man cut his chance, grabbing the woman by the arms, "Becky, go back to the kids! I'm handling this, then we're done." Foster now saw the kids in the backseat. They were grasping the seats in front of them, gasmasks in their hands, trembling.

"Why are you leaving?" yelled Foster, this time raising his weapon. Becky shrieked but Jesse told her to shut it. He eyed Foster carefully before saying, "It's not safe there anymore. We couldn't live with all the kidnappings and seeing that face plaguing us every night."

Foster's eyes widened. "Do they control it?"

"THE SAVAGE KEEPS US QUIET!" Becky screamed in a tired voice, echoing her many sleepless nights. Jesse gave her another stern look before she turned back for their car without saying a word. Jesse turned back to Foster, ready to ask his own questions.

"Where can my family go, sir? We thought it was safe in Holdsworth, we thought all that running had come to an end and we'd finally catch our breaths. Families just like us, tired of constantly moving in fear… I'm tired of being tired, *so damn tired*." His body swelled in desperation at this admittance. He slapped his thigh in frustration while he looked to the sky, trying not to let the tears roll out, trying to keep it together. "We almost carved out a future in that town; a life just like before—but seems we dreamed too far again! Doubt there'll ever be another place like it. Last of its kind."

Foster saw the helplessness in the man's eyes, a story that would pain him to know. Foster decided to offer his advice first and then press the man for more information.

"All of California belongs to them: the Purification Front. They are marching east as we speak, so I'd suggest you steer clear heading west at any bearing."

The man nodded in gratitude before telling Foster what he needed to hear. "There's a doctor in Holdsworth, runs the whole joint, he'll tell you what you need to know about Holdsworth and…the Savage… Don't be staying too long though, or you'll get the fear like the rest of them, get trapped." At this, the man parted ways, breaking for the car, rushing to a relieved Becky. Foster fired off one last question to the man about the Resistance but he was ignored. He retreated to Daisy with shoulders slumped. This grand crusade he had led them on was losing its momentum; he was beginning to lose his fight. When Foster hoisted himself into the car, that maddened look he had woken up with was gone. Now he was just a broken man beaten by fading hopes once again. The Camry rushed passed them at this point, but neither had the guts to look the other in the face, their crossed paths seeming to head in dire directions.

Cole broke the silence. "What now?"

Foster contemplated his statement before raising his head, a slight smile appearing across his face.

"We need to see a doctor."

22. Holdsworth

Holdsworth was minutes away. Everyone in Daisy had put on gas masks. Ever since the outbreak, the image of a person wearing a gas mask was a sign of agency, resistance against the Illusionists. When it was announced over the Internet, radios and televisions all over the country that this virus was airborne, almost every second person scrambled to wear them. The army handed them out like pamphlets, sizes for all ages. Nobody knew if it really worked at all, but those who couldn't get masks were isolated like the lepers of old, observed with a watchful eye and ready weapon with the safety off at all times. Cole found it difficult breathing into this dark apparition, the way it stuck to his skin and made him painfully aware of each breath he took. Looking at the others, he saw their ease and familiarity seeing the world like Darth Vader.

They knew they had reached Holdsworth when from around a bend on the outskirts of the suburbs they were met with sandbags and high mesh fences draped with razor wire. Behind these walls of defense, in the sparse two-story houses along the street, men with guns held their weapons steady towards Daisy, all of them wearing gas masks. The car stopped twenty yards short of the fence. Everyone in Daisy clenched up, preparing for a tense confrontation once more. Foster motioned to Max who turned off the ignition. He then exhaled deeply and slowly opened his door. They could all hear weapons being cocked simultaneously. Foster's hands immediately reached for the air as he exited the vehicle, carrying no shotgun this time. Foster talked in a clear, calm voice so as to not confuse these soldiers, who although outnumbering them by at least six to one, were visibly shaking upon their perches.

"We mean no harm. We wish to barter supplies and information on the Resistance in Chicago. Specifically, I wish to speak to the Doctor…" at this he slowly removed his mask, causing surprise at his aged face. One of the men positioned on the street, crouched behind sandbags and a broken down car, stood and snickered at this request.

"We don't need anything of yours, and no one cares to hear about your 'Resistance' nonsense, least of all the Doc, you foolish old timer." The other men then began to snicker and laugh at Foster and his car.

"What do you think you're going to do, kill them with your walking stick?"

Others cried out, "This ain't no retirement home, gramps!"

Foster kept his feet firmly planted, waiting for all the wise cracking to go down. Kate, Max and Cole could do nothing but watch, a burning anger festering in Kate as she picked off each of these clowns one by one in her head.

Eventually, Foster started again, this time with more aggression in his voice, the gruffness down to an exact science.

"You're not so tough so don't bullshit me with all those guns you're fingering—I know chicken shit when I see it. You want to know how I know? I've seen the people you're protecting and they don't trust you a damn bit to keep them safe. Now I can see why! Seems none of you can help me, but maybe I can help you… Now tell me, WHO IS THE SAVAGE?"

They all froze. The very mention of his name tore through their nerves like a freight train on an unsuspecting squirrel. Foster could smell that instant release of fear. None had questioned how Foster knew of the Doc, but when he spoke of the Savage their hearts skipped a beat. Their change in attitude was immediate. The man who had first mocked Foster, the giant lumberjack of a human who dwarfed his fellows and had hairy arms the size of logs, was now on his walkie whilst conferring with his comrades next to him. He then motioned to the barricade and then to Foster. His friend, a short and stocky man in blue overalls walked to the gate and called out to Foster. "We'll open the gate, then you follow that jeep over there. They'll take you right to the Doc."

The streets they passed fell into patterns of broken or boarded up houses, thrown in with the odd bundle of camping tents on front lawns. Behind each of the houses Cole could see faint outlines of the mesh fence barricades that enclosed them. He could tell it was a highly compact community, adhering to the safety in numbers rule. Every couple of blocks men with guns sat around smoking cigarettes, their attention always turning to Cole and company as they drove by. By now the sightings of people became more numerous with maybe one in three wearing gas masks. People, especially children, would stop and point at their car before being motioned away by concerned adults.

Cole wondered if newcomers were a common occurrence, or just often bad news. The jeep in front came to a halt outside an enormous white rectangular tent, the size of over half a block. There was a constant stream of people walking in and out of the entrance. The tent was founded on what used to be a park, reasoned Cole, as it had been placed abnormally close to a set of swings and other colorful assorted playground equipment that children were gainfully playing on in the budding sun. Cole imagined them laughing, unaware of the dangers that lurked alongside them in the adult world, though he could hear nothing from the car. His mind drifted back to younger times when it was he on the play equipment and someone else in the car, carrying an insurmountable weight that he and all adults alike had come to know. The children's freedom and imagination was almost too liberating to look at, but as he did, for the tiniest of moments Cole wondered if their viewpoint, the innocent imagination of children, was somehow the key to fixing these things, this world he now belonged. That by feeling their innocence, the Illusionists could forget their differences and remember what it was and what it could be. Or maybe in some part of this now-rotting wasteland a child with the gift could make his moves to change the future for the better—a child that was incorruptible compared to the others. Cole sighed, maybe his imagination was too far off, and this child, like their future, would fade into nothingness.

These trains of thought were interrupted when Daisy was pulled away from the large white tent and playing children into a large three story compound, by far the biggest building in Holdsworth, second only to the great white tent standing opposite. Passing heavy black iron arches, they parked behind the jeep in the driveway before shuffling out of Daisy, only to feel the weight of their dead legs.

A young man in full police uniform, the shirt clearly over-sized, approached them from the lead car. He was fresh faced, looking just a little bit younger than Max. He was fumbling his words a bit, "Uh, the Doc is busy, he's, uh, still working in the Great White Tent, but they told me to get you to wait in his office for him—oh yeah! And weapons! I'm supposed to take your weapons, sorry! It's just for the time being…" They all nodded in understanding, although Foster would have felt easier if he had his .45 on him.

The compound was large and bereft of furniture, causing an emptiness that had a way of echoing. The young man seemed to pick up in his confidence, aptly giving a sweeping history of the house and its current function.

"The place used to belong to an old millionaire, owned some carpet franchise. He also donated that playground across the street. 'Course, it all made sense when they found out he was a kiddie fiddler. Conviction was eight years, but the monsters came in two."

The boy led them up the grand arching stairs with furnished banisters all the way up to the top. As they passed each level, people could be seen in rooms filled to the brim with papers while they wrote frantically in their journals.

"What're they doing?" asked Max.

"Sometimes its medical journals, other times its just crunching the numbers for running this whole place. I always see them busting away at their reports in a big hurry, heck I even heard that between the Doc and them, they've come pretty close to understanding the breakdown of a Controller's mind. 'Course, other people say we'll never really know…" At the top floor they were met with the large wooden doors of the Doc's office, the sun engulfing their sight when the young man parted its heavy doors. The room held one large windowpane that stretched across the whole wall. The room overlooked the playground and half of the gigantic white tent.

"It was probably his bedroom," remarked the young man.

"What's with the tent?" asked Cole.

"Oh, that's our town center. We call it the Great White Tent. The Doc set up an emergency ward in there. It's also where we have town meetings, and there's a small bar inside too, for when the meetings get people down."

"Looks busy."

"Yeah, unfortunately it is…"

The kid's trailing admission left them all weary of the view. They turned to focus on the room. Nestled perfectly center in front of this panoramic window sat an antique desk that was littered with stacks of papers and leather bound books. On the right side of the room in the corner, a psychiatrist's sofa had been placed with a pillow and ruffled bed sheets adorning it. The kid motioned to a stack of chairs in the corner on their left.

"Feel free to pull up a chair, I'll get you all a glass of water."

Before they knew it, he was gone. They looked over each other, trying to get to grips with the whole setup of Holdsworth. It had been too long for Kate, Foster and Max in their interactions with any sort of community larger than themselves and this left them feeling uneasy.

For Cole, scattered images flickered within him of the past he had carved out with the likes of Maddie and Peter. But this was not Trent, and those days and feelings of warmth weren't real. In this place the frenzy of activity made him dizzy, sending thick rushes of blood to his head and causing lightness in his feet.

They all turned to Foster, all sharing that gut feeling that they were out of their depth.

"What are we doing here?" asked Kate.

"We're here to help," said Foster.

"Help? We can't help these people. We have nothing to offer," Kate snapped back at him, her teeth lightly grinding away in frustration. Before he could get another word in she called him out on his original vision. "What about Chicago? The Resistance? We're no good to anyone unless we've been cured."

Foster was now trying to calm Kate down. "As I said before, we don't know exactly what the situation is in Chicago and we'd be fools to waltz in there without some knowledge of what's going on in the area… We might even be able to shore up our numbers."

Kate didn't trust him. "You can't offer our help when we're clearly out of our league here. You saw these people, none of them are trying to pick a fight; they're just trying to survive. I doubt any of them would want to join us."

"We need to make them see they can strive for more than just getting by, they just have to fight for it!" Foster shot back.

It was Cole who cooled their heads. "Kate, let's just hear what the Doc has to say, it may be worth the time." After hearing this Kate stopped grinding her teeth, all the tension dissipating. Cole was right.

Just as she had relented, the door opened and an Asian man entered the room. He held the door aloft for the young man who carried in their drinks. The man's face bore dark gray stubble, just like that of Foster's, and seemed of similar age—early fifties. The wrinkles under his eyes were much more than the old battering of age. He wore a hooded gray college jumper with the letters BYU marked across it in maroon letters. More noticeable were the dry bloodstains blotted on his jumper and khaki pants. He wore sandals.

"Hello, I'm sorry to keep you waiting, it's just that we've had an incident that has taken up all our time today. Now, our perimeter commander has informed me you were part of some kind of passing resistance?" He addressed the whole group but locked eyes with Foster, whom he had already identified as their leader.

Foster cleared his throat. "Informally yes; we were actually wishing to join the AIF contingent—the Resistance—over in Chicago. We were passing through and wondered if any more recent news of the east has been received by your people here?"

The Doc shook his head. "Haven't heard much about that for months now. I wouldn't waste your time on that, if I were you."

The others now looked at Foster, unsure how he'd react to such news. Seeming deep in thought, his face hid his disappointment. He changed tact and focused on Holdsworth.

"Seems you've made yourself quite a community here…uh," he spoke while extending his hand to formally introduce himself.

"Ah yes, Doctor Yuan. And you are?"

"Colonel John Foster, and these are my fellow travelers: Sergeant Max, Corporal Kate and Private Cole."

They all shook the Doc's hand, his skin as soft as a baby's while his grip was firm like a constrictor. Cole was first to speak up, asking the Doc about the incident that had occurred. The Doc was hesitant at first, restraining himself to choose his words carefully.

"We're not a military outfit; most people here are refugees in the true sense. These people only want to survive and live out what could be their last months in relative peace. That's what I thought of this place when I formed it, the last sanctuary. When we hit seven months, hope swelled among us and everyone started to cautiously dream of the future. We hadn't been rolled over by robotic armies or the lone crazies that littered the early days of the outbreak. Then, approximately three months ago, people started to go missing. It was only women at first, swept up in the middle of the night. Then the kidnappings got more frequent. It got up to three a week, and now it was both women and children. One of our border guards once saw a woman walking towards the barricade as if possessed. He tried to stop her from leaving, but she ended up breaking his neck."

"Is this the Savage?" interjected Cole.

The Doc sighed. "That's what most people have come to call him. From what they say, he looks like a Native American ghost, never all quite there, like his face is just a blur. Tall and muscular, he wears only a loincloth over his business. Of course, it's all speculation; you can never be too sure about the appearance of a Controller. I can only give you this description because three weeks ago he came into town in broad daylight, just outside this building in fact, and warned a large crowd, including myself, that if anyone were to leave, he would start killing us all by the hundreds each day…"

They all looked at the Doc in shock, Kate's hand gracing her mouth.

"But there are thousands of people here, many with guns. Why couldn't you have killed him then and there?" questioned Foster.

"He wouldn't allow that to happen. Anyone foolish enough to do something that stupid would have had their brains scrambled and fried a thousand times over before they even had their finger on the trigger. That's if they were lucky…fear is a powerful thing."

"He must live close by," mused Cole.

"Oh he does, yes, a couple miles northeast of here in the state forest. There have been two attempts to hunt him down, once by a passing AIF unit and another by our own men. The last time we tried that, he sent back one survivor, more or less as a warning, even though we couldn't get much out of him. The guy hasn't spoken since. That forest is his and there's not much that can be done about it."

The way he spoke of the Savage was much like the feelings shared by the rest of Holdsworth, a creeping shadow that hung over their heads. Holdsworth was under a mental siege, and in their frozen state, they were unable to do anything about it. *His* existence ran intricate, voracious circles around their minds like garrotte wire while the kids remained oblivious. The parents couldn't understand why the Savage had given their children leniency in this way and found it painfully difficult to hide their resentment towards the children's carefree life. There was also the terrible feeling that he preferred their children that way, whatever it was he was doing to them…

"What about this latest incident?" Max asked.

"Last night, a women and child were seen walking towards the fences in a trance-like state. A guard recognized they were under his spell—the guard then attempted to shoot them both with a tranquilizer gun we now carry to stop these kidnappings. Another guard of ours ran by just to see the man blow his brains out as the woman and child cut out a hole in the barricade…"

"Why did he have to kill the guard?" asked Cole, "He could

have incapacitated him any other way, sent him to sleep or something."

The Doc's stance changed. He walked over to his desk and clutched a framed photo that had been placed face down. He didn't look at the picture. He didn't have to. It was burned into his memory for the rest of his days.

"I don't know why he had to do it, believe me, I've read all the scientific journals and psychology books, trying to understand how these people think. Maybe they're too far-gone to be reasoned with. Or maybe the things they've done to us means we can never reason with them. I read in a book somewhere that cannibalism begets madness in the brain… People say that's what he does. They make up these stories that build this man into a monster and after a while I feel I have no reason to stop them from thinking this way."

Foster saw in the Doc a man broken by feeling powerless for too long. The cage the Savage locked everyone in that town in was only internal, but that's where the suffocating guilt came from: knowing you could do something if you just weren't so terrified. It was clear they all beat themselves up each time the Savage snatched another, and Foster, set in his ways, was determined to stop that.

"We can kill him," he boldly claimed to the shock of everyone in the room, all except Cole who had seen such a belief in Foster's face the moment he had heard of this monster.

Kate gawked. She was struck by Foster's sheer arrogance at so easily using the term "we" knowing full well whom that entailed.

The Doc was at a loss, too dumbfounded by the boldness and idiocy of Foster's statement to tell him why it was stupid. He was certain such a fact had already been established. "You can't kill him," was all he could produce.

"We can surprise him." It was Cole who spoke up this time. They all now looked at him, even more bewildered than when they'd heard Foster's claim. "You say he walked right into the center of town without a hassle. You people could have moved a long time ago and yet you've all stayed. Maybe he believes you're scared more than you believe it yourselves. If that's the case, he won't be expecting retaliation."

Kate wanted to punch him. Even Max wanted to tell him to shut up. Two days with Foster and this kid was willing to follow him into the thick forest to fight a deranged demigod.

The Doc was flustered by the audacity of what Cole was leading to, but his own response left him perplexed. "I guess he wouldn't..." he paused before trying to urge Cole back to the side of caution. "Like I already said, we've already marched on his grounds twice and nothing good has come of it. They were a hundred full the first time and around thirty of our own the second. Forgive me for saying this but you're four people who don't know the layout of the land, running on some bullshit optimism that just can't see the darkness right in front of you."

"I agree with the Doc," said Kate.

Foster turned to her with that stern look before shifting his gaze towards Max who meekly uttered, "Me too." Foster returned his attention to the Doc, seemingly ignoring the protests of Kate and Max. "We'll be needing maps of the forest if you have any—and any men you know willing to fight for their freedom of mind back."

The Doc was reluctant. "You'd hardly find anyone willing to partake in your suicide mission. I won't allow you to..."

"You're going to deny the people the power to choose their future for themselves? Isn't that what separates us from them?" Foster asked.

"Nothing good will come of it," the Doc repeated.

"You already made your bed. Tell me, this woman and her child that were taken last night, is their father here in Holdsworth?"

The Doc was incensed by where this trail was leading, they all were, and yet he answered him all the same. "Yes, he is."

"I'd like you to take us to him, if you'd be so kind," said Foster, who produced his warmest smile, an eerie front to his manic pursuit.

***

The man's house was several blocks away, on the outskirts of Holdsworth with the house backing out onto the mesh barricades. As they walked through the town, people would pass them, recognizing the Doc and then whispering to their friends about these new arrivals that followed him. They were all quick to reason he was heading to Bryan's place, the husband of Helen and father of Maggie.

Many of the townspeople had tried to sum up the courage to visit Bryan; to comfort him in his loss, just like the others who had their loved ones taken away by the Savage, never to be seen again, but they just couldn't this time. Kate didn't notice these people watching her move along the street. She had only eyes for Cole and Foster. She was fixated with the back of Cole's head, feeling a mixture of anger and disappointment. She was beginning to trust him, to accept him as just another kid like her, forced into a world they had no place in. His readiness to die for such a cause he had just only come to know was stupid to her, especially when she knew how Foster operated his bullshit.

Maybe Cole was suicidal. Kate got that feeling every time she braved those sullen eyes. Then again, maybe he was trying to atone. Make up for whatever he did to those two back in Trent. But he was sold and Kate knew exactly the angle Foster would now try to work on her—emotionally guilt her when she saw the despair in Bryan, the man who had just lost everything.

Guilt tied her to Foster. It was the guilt she felt when she had to shoot kids no older than twelve that Foster helped to take away, to rationalize. Now it was a different kind of guilt, to do the right thing. All that was needed was to put a human face on this suffering and Kate would buckle. What made her loath Foster was that he knew this would work. Once she was convinced, she believed Max would follow, because while he would never admit to it, Kate was all he had now. She always knew he had feelings for her, but she never saw him like that, never felt the same way.

Leading the group, the Doc drifted towards a house on the corner of the street, the mesh barricade directly behind it. A crowd of around twenty hung about the front yard and porch, some with their eyes dried out from crying. When one of them recognized the Doc, several stood up from the porch to acknowledge him while others walked up to the front gate to greet him.

"I'm sorry I couldn't come earlier, how is he doing?" He spoke to the people at the front gate, whose spirits were lifted by his calm demeanor.

"He's not doing too well. We're really glad you're here. Nobody really knows what to say, even after all the other—"

"I understand," the Doc cut him off from his weltered shame. The Doc took a deep breath and, reminding himself he had done this many times before, walked through the crowd and into the house, trying to ignore the shadow of Foster's group that hung disquiet over him.

Every corridor was filled with people, children sitting in the hallways, some playing with toy cars, each yet to truly conceive the adult world they would inherit. Muffled crying could be heard from distant rooms. When they opened Bryan's door, the people inside parted like the sea, revealing a distraught Bryan facing away from everyone as he sat on the side of the bed, his eyes staring at the window in vacancy. The Doc turned to Foster and insisted they let him speak to Bryan alone before Foster would make his case. Foster solemnly accepted this and took the others outside to wait. Now they stood alone in the corridor, bar a curious young girl, who kept peeking her head around the corner at them. Foster spoke to Kate and Max with a brash indifference to the mood of mourning that dulled the entire house.

"These people need us, and I need you. Guys, don't you see? This is the mission. *This is the way we resist.*"

Kate made sure she didn't raise her voice when she angrily replied, "Cut the shit, it's absolute bullshit that you threw our hands up for a suicide mission."

"We can't do it by ourselves, John," added Max, feebly trying to use Foster's first name to exert some control, "and I don't know its right us being here now, you know…recruiting."

Foster tore right through Max's words with a sworn look of determination reminiscent of the glare he gave Cole when briefing him on the assault rifles. He then turned, knocking on the door. It creaked open slightly and Foster walked into a room of silence and disgusted glares. The women in the room were seething in indignation at his nerve for showing his face at a time like this. It was clear the Doc had told the room of his intentions. Nevertheless, Foster passed through each of their burning windows of contempt until he found the ones that belonged to Bryan, any anger washed out with the depths of an infinite sorrow. He cleared his throat, making sure each word would hit Bryan in just the right way.

"I know it is not the best time, but I am afraid it is the only time we have now to save your wife and child. I know there is fear—there will always be—but the only thing we can do about it, is control our reaction to it. Now, you don't know me, and I can understand whatever skepticism these people may have placed upon you, but believe me when I say this: *We* are your *only chance* at seeing your wife again. And this is not a task we can do alone…"

The attention of the room gravitated back to Bryan who could only look away and bury his head in his hands. A middle-aged woman, repulsed by the smell of Foster's breath as he spewed forth these reckless claims of hope could take no more.

"How dare you try feed off the sorrow of a grieving man for your own nonsense!"

Many in the small room nodded in agreement.

"How do you know they're still alive?" spoke the Doc, aware he was trying to crush Bryan's hopes if only to save Bryan.

"I just have faith," replied Foster. The rest of them were gobsmacked at his lackluster answer, what faith could he speak of in a land that god had packed up and left? They were left reeling in shock when Bryan cracked, the writhing tension in his body proving too much.

"All right, I'll do it," he cried, a tired relegation breaking out of his dried lips. The same middle-aged woman, the one who had blared out her objections right in Foster's face, opened her mouth ready to plead to Bryan the foolishness in his endeavor. But she was stopped short as Foster began dictating to the Doc his requirements for this mission—the procurement of maps of the state forest and a place of rest for his team. The preciseness of his words that he parried like a sword sent everyone else quiet, afraid of him locking onto them and stabbing away. The Doc nodded with great reluctance before Bryan put up his own place for Foster's team to crash. "You can use the two guestrooms and there is a foldout in the lounge room."

Foster thanked him and made for the door, only to stop and ask the others in the room, namely the men, if they wanted to help Bryan. They turned and twisted in silence, avoiding the eyes of both Bryan and Foster. Finally another woman hidden away in the corner out of Foster's view reignited the middle-aged woman's protest by appealing to Bryan one last time.

"No one should help this man kill himself in the slightest. I'm sorry, Bryan, but I beg you to reconsider." Bryan glanced at her, then Foster, only to press a closed fist against his mouth, trying to keep the trembling from spilling out.

"I have to, Margaret. If there's even the tiniest chance their still alive…with Maggie—god they must be so scared…" At this he buried his head in his hands and those around him swooned to comfort his aching soul. Without saying anything more, Foster left the room.

When he looked at each of them and saw the embarrassment branded across their faces, he knew they'd heard everything. But this was to be shrugged off, given no consideration. The operation would go ahead regardless. Foster gave each of them the look that carried his *might* before settling on Kate.

"Bryan will be joining us. He's agreed to let us stay here for tonight. We'll get supplies from the car, brief the mission then look for something hard to drink."

"What time do you expect we'll leave?" asked Cole.

"Early morning. 0800 hours," replied Foster.

"Should we be drinking then?" Cole asked, puzzled by Foster's dead-serious eyes. Was the man capable of joking?

Foster grinned, a grin that Cole had already come to fear. "How else do you think we'll get to sleep? Alcohol will kill all those twitchy nerves one gets before a big day."

"And how can the Savage control us if we ain't got any brain cells left?" Max added in humor, hiding his sheer terror at joining them in the forest.

Cole laughed, felt like he had to. Like it would lessen the brunt of heaviness the whole ordeal would bring down on their tiny little heads. It dawned on him that he had helped push this, dragging Kate and Max into the thick of it. Once more, he told himself this was the right thing to do.

They walked outside to a hushed crowd. Somehow news of their crusade had found these people, with some giving them further looks of disgust while others looked away, in fear Foster would point them out and their cowardice would be known to all, exposed on a surface they all internally accepted of one another. It was not as if testosterone had ceased to exist. Unfortunately, very few of the group that stood before them were physically able, many too young or too old. They seemed like the discards of the Illusionists, unfit for the new societies envisioned. Nevertheless, Foster broached his way out to the edge of the porch and gave his impassioned call to arms, imploring nationalism and the human spirit when all else failed—and it did. The others were not bitter at the crowd's silence, but Foster took it to heart. His vigilance was his driving passion and he just couldn't comprehend how others could cower when they had the power to fight back. To Foster, it wasn't the American way.

Kate could see his failure and she felt as if she was watching him fall for the first time, like that first moment when a child realizes that their father isn't always right, that he too makes mistakes. It was at this point Kate was pushed over the precipice; she couldn't stand seeing him fall, even if it was clear what he was pulling them back into. She gave out a resigned breath. She would join them in the forest just as Foster had always known she would.

Max and Foster were her family now, right down to the end.

And she felt she knew a way to help them all. A way to return the fire to Foster's fight, keep it burning when so much was owed to him. As they walked through the disappointed crowd, Kate touched Foster on the shoulder from behind and softly whispered, "I will find us recruits."

***

The watering hole of Holdsworth was nestled in next to the town meeting spot of the Great White Tent. Later on in the night Cole would wonder why they didn't use the regular bar in town. Asking a 'local', he found it was much like the case of setting up the new town hall in the Great White Tent; there were certain smells and stains of war you could never fully get rid of.

Avoiding the stares of the few who drunk away their troubles, they saddled up to a table where Max scratched his head in the direction of the sole bar tender who stared back at their table just like the rest of the fellow Holdsworthians.

Max was unsure as to how they should pay for drinks. "I

think I left my wallet back in New Mexico…What can we get from Daisy that we won't need tomorrow?"

"There's that phony guitar you've been lugging around since Layton." Kate quipped.

"How was I supposed to know it was merely decorative?"

"It was made of plastic, for fuck's sake," said Foster.

"Well then it should've looked good if it was merely decorative… And no, we're not parting with *Trevor*. How about that sunscreen you've been forbidding us to throw out this whole time. Can you finally agree that the sun is the least of our worries?"

"Well, realistically how many beers does sunscreen get you anyway?" Cole joked.

"One and a half," said Foster.

Before any of them could take a reasonable shot at Foster's absurd measurement, a drink tray lined with cold Budweisers barged into their view as a young kid of no more than thirteen extended herself to slide the tray onto the high table they stood around. The very existence of the Budweisers was a true luxury in itself, dinosaurs of a forgetting era.

In a soft voice the kid stammered out, "Compliments from those gentleman over there," pointing to two old hounds who raised their moonshine glasses in acknowledgement; prompting Cole, Kate, Foster and Max to do the same. Kate asked the little girl when the bar got busy, if it did at all.

"Soon. Most of the adults need their medicine to help them fight the man in their dreams."

***

Jimmy Faulkner was a tough kid, always the first to scrap in any sort of argument. Back in school, kids would often make fun of a large, reddish birthmark that adorned the top of his scalp. Instead of letting his hair grow out to cover up this "disfigurement", Jimmy would purposefully keep it short as a means of giving his opponents ammo for provocation. It was what he lived for. Even when the kids in his neighborhood grew out of teasing him for it, he kept it short as a point of reminding himself he was the underdog, despite the fact that he would be the aggressor in most cases. But no matter how aggressive he puffed his chest; at a height of only 5'7 Jimmy relentlessly lacked any physical conviction in his talk. Bruises lined his knuckles, yet they were merely the result of poor temper control and an affinity for blaming inanimate objects.

When his eyes locked with Kate across the makeshift bar portioned off in the Great White Tent of Holdsworth, each saw different things in the other.

Kate had found her mark, a hothead who, along with his dim-witted friend, had just disposed of a drunk in a one-sided bar fight. They were ruthless and predominately unprovoked—the moral equivalent of sewer rats—but the only Neanderthals drunk enough to go for such a mission. The drunk they had smashed to a pulp was rambunctiously old, a former barfly in proper bars.

Cole, Max and Foster all thought about stepping in for the drunk, who although screaming strange obscenities and deft propositions, was clearly outmatched by Jimmy and his big (and rather portly) friend. Kate stopped them short of doing so, instead walking up to Jimmy's table and offering to buy him a drink.

The whole arrangement of the bar, the very notion of its strange existence in times like this brought Kate back to her days in college, days she understood. It was Jimmy's brash attitude, his cockiness apparent from across the dim-lit tent, that swept Kate back to those college bars where sweaty teenage hormones had once flushed through her. She could handle types like Jimmy Faulkner, her comfort bearing a smile.

This was not strictly business for Kate; she wanted it just as much as Jimmy was going to beg for it, and why not? This could be her last night alive.

She told herself all this, reasoning and justifying the inevitable coming together they were leading to, as she explained to Jimmy and his friend Kyle about the mission at hand. Jimmy laughed, bragged, beat his chest as the alpha male of the world who could conquer anything and was afraid of no one. His friend Kyle, who sported a copycat buzz cut like Jimmy, was less enthused and did require more convincing and soon Jimmy pushed Kyle just as hard as Kate while she teased Jimmy's thigh under the table.

After his friend was tied down to accept, Jimmy resumed his up-beat macho tales of survival since it all began. He recounted with blurred memory, the harrowing escape from Dallas during government clashes with fundamentalists that ended with the skies turning red in the horizon he was running from as thousands of ordinance fell from the heavens, enveloping his childhood state along with the government soldiers and all the others.

By the time Jimmy had finished that story, Kyle had left along with many of the others in the bar including Cole, Foster and Max who had retired earlier than expected. Since Kate had left them at the table, Max had feigned interest in Cole and Foster's discussion of the mission between putrid sips of moonshine, but found the talk of their imminent death a topic he could find no strength for while in the corner of his vision Kate got closer to

Jimmy.

There was an arm brush,

A flicking of her hair,

A smile Max had never seen before. A smile he felt would never be meant for him.

She had told them all beforehand why she was doing this. She was doing it for the group. But Max couldn't see that, he just saw what was in front of him, an almost wilful crushing of his soul. He led the quiet exodus just as Kate's hand reached for this boasting punk's thigh, staying comfortably in its purpose.

Max leaving was good for Kate. She wasn't stupid. She knew what she was doing. She knew it hurt him deeply. But it had to be done. It would help them all, right?

She'd felt it inside her when she first saw Jimmy. The bravado, back to days she understood; where she had a handle on it, some semblance of control. There were some very blisteringly cold nights in Eastern Utah; times when she'd considered Max—but had pulled away at the last minute. They were too close, she'd told herself. Now those times had passed, and in the light of tomorrow's dread, Kate saw the hours creeping slowly along. She felt it caving in all around her, the persistence of the moment.

So there it was, a flutter in the chest and the yearning between the legs. It had been so long.

As their physical touches became a steady motioned back and forth, Kate found the liquor easing her nerves, and opened up to Jimmy more about her experiences, her narrowing escapes; and then in the middle of it all, somewhere between the high-wire talk of fighting off wacked-out psychos and hunting former pets for food, Jimmy's tough guy shield was dropped as quickly as it was touted when he stopped her talking and looked her dead in the eyes. "You ever had to kill anyone?"

His face was now gentle, warm and reeling from past deeds he played to Kate in guilt-ridden eyes. Now Kate saw a person just like her; putting up a shield, hiding from a past they were fearful to even think of. In that moment she found a person to share that same feeling of guilt with, to find shelter knowing she wasn't the only one. She kissed him, just a peck at first, but it was soon drawn into a fit of passion. When she finally withdrew, she answered his question.

"We do what we have to, if that's what it takes to survive." And then she led him out of the makeshift bar.

23. Memories

Jimmy fell asleep soon after they had fucked. Kate sat up in the single bed, unable to sleep. It was quick, but just what she needed. Her body thanked her with gooey relief lingering all throughout. Unfortunately for her, this proved only temporary, as the minutes ticked closer and closer to tomorrow. Her connection with Jimmy had faded too quickly for her liking and was replaced with the growing acknowledgement that she had used him, played his character before she saw his real one, if only for a moment. The worst thing was, she knew she would do it over again if she had to. She tried to lie back down and find sleep, but couldn't find the space. Jimmy's peaceful face made her sick, the regret building with every slight breath she felt exhaling out slowly from his soft lips. Jimmy was no saint and neither was she, but he didn't deserve being dragged in with her—with the damned lot.

Then there was Max. Kate knew what she'd done.

Oh, Max.

But it had been so long, could they not see?

This went on for a long time, the circle of guilt and justification; plugging the leaks with desperate reason. Kate knew this circle all too well and now the option of leaving altogether crept in. It was practical; she'd have to leave otherwise she'd be useless tomorrow if too tired. But leaving worried her—would it sway Jimmy away from joining them, leaving the whole exercise enjoyable but fruitless?

The circle went round for a little while longer.

Eventually she decided she would have to take a chance and untangled her way out of Jimmy and out of the bed. Unable to find pen or paper to write a note explaining that she would meet him in the early morning, Kate had no choice but to leave without a message, fearing it would leave her empty handed.

Walking back to Bryan's in the lonely dark, Kate kept going back and forth in her mind trying to dispel the obvious possibility that Jimmy could just as easily back out and treat it for what it was: a one night stand while the world was slowly ending. His lack of contribution tomorrow could be the death of her, Max, Cole or Foster and in that way Kate felt she had failed as well.

Kate's footsteps plodded by their lonesome in the quiet night. It was curfew for everyone in town except for her group, as word had gotten round of their suicide mission. The guards on night watch knew this and didn't stop Kate, weary of just how nuts these people potentially were. When Kate finally made it to Bryan's house, the flame of a cigarette hanging above the porch caught her attention. Moving closer, a slouched Cole in a camping chair greeted her, his legs rested on top of the porch railing.

"I couldn't sleep," he said, taking a long drag.

"Neither could I," she replied, leaning against the railing.

"…Max seemed upset."

It felt like a harsh slap from an old friend. Kate dropped her head at this. " I know I…" she began but didn't finish her sentence; she just let it flow into a great silence.

Why would Cole understand? Why would any of them? There was nothing she felt she could say to explain herself; wasn't worth the effort this late in the game. But she did not leave Cole and go inside. She just stayed where she was and Cole didn't say another thing about it—because in truth, neither of them wanted to be alone.So there they sat in silence, and as they did, all those circles Kate had been running around for as long as she could remember finally caught up to her. Unable to hold it back any longer, she let herself go in front of Cole.

"I don't know whether to start praying…" she moped. And then she cried. It was quiet, there was no yelp, no sobbing, only the tears running down her face gave it away. Cole went inside and found a bit of cloth. Kate took it graciously and wiped her tears away. When she spoke again, she finally stared at Cole, forcing herself to hold his attention for the first time since they had met.

Right in the eyes, and her body quivered.

"I'm scared, Cole. This could really be it. We can't go into that forest—for fuck's sake he'll tear us to bits. I thought I was ready to go out there and fight them, but it's gone, Cole, there's no need for it now…" Cole didn't reply. He knew there was more. "I've seen some bad things, Cole. Done things I'm not proud of. I know if I go out there I'm not going to make it out. I need to survive; need to make up for the things I've done—just not this way, not like this."

Cole reached out and grabbed her by the shoulders. "You don't have to go, we'll be fine without you. Trust me. I will kill him. You don't need to go, okay."

He looked deep in her eyes. They were beautiful, even more so in their watery state. For a moment she followed him, but his own fear drew his gaze downward.

"I have to go," said Kate, "Foster, Max and *even you* are all I've got left. We need as many people as we can get."

Cole opened his mouth to say something but withdrew again. He knew it was the right thing to say—it was the truth—but he was too scared to say it, too fearful of how she'd react. Soon that moment was gone, and Cole swallowed its bitterness once more.

"Those guys you were talking to…they going to come with us?" He eventually asked.

Kate sat up further upright on the pole, now closer to Cole who now sat alongside her.

"I think they are, I mean I hope so…"

Cole finished his cigarette, then fiddle around anxiously with his hands, before deciding to have another one. He offered Kate one to which she accepted.

"Listen, Kate, I don't know who you guys are fooling, but you're not soldiers and neither am I—"

"And yet you're the one saying you're going to kill the Savage. Besides, you know Foster was an army Colonel. He never lets us forget that."

"He's retired," said Cole. "That's a huge difference; he's too old to fight."

Kate scoffed at this notion. "I thought this the first time I saw him as well, back in that tavern…"

She'd been hiding something in her past, too ashamed to tell Cole the things she had done and he assumed the worst. He knew the war had changed her, had shattered her trust in anything other than Max and Foster, and with Foster acting the way he'd been, Cole knew Kate's world was shrinking every hour, every second; soon it would be as empty as his. She'd been held together for so long, propped up by Max and Foster as best they could throughout the harsh winter. Where every night she shivered, didn't eat right. Faded away. Even when spring returned and the daisies grew round their cave, Kate kept her guard, for her soul was still stuck in that winter, perpetually frozen.

Cole had not wanted to know the past of Kate at first—he knew awful things lurked there, and he'd been all too overwhelmed dealing with his own demons. But now, as the seconds ticked away to a showdown they'd foolishly rushed themselves into, the Cole that wanted to help, the one that knew he could make a difference found his way from the darkness. Now Cole knew it was time to ask, to listen. To know Kate's pain like he knew his own.

"What happened that day you met Foster?"

Kate looked at him once again, his stare breaking down her walls; the ones she built within herself to block out those memories, to keep them inside and suffocate the very air out of them.

His stare broke down her walls.

"The tavern was still running for some reason; I didn't question it. A lot of people were in the place, keeping it warm. It was late November and outside was already freezing. There was an early blizzard of snowfall that had stopped the advance of the Puries momentarily, but this was receding and we were told we would have to pack up soon if we wanted to get out of town before they came through. I was very weak at that stage, my body was going through withdrawals after the Great Peace ended and we'd been hiding and running scared for two weeks. I had sought out Foster: he was the only one in military uniform. He told me he was retired and asked who I was with. I'd been surviving with my best friend and her boyfriend, and I told Foster that they were off bartering some goods near their car. Even though I knew we had to pack and leave, I wasn't as flustered or as panicked as when we had to leave Oregon. I asked Foster what he thought he was going to do from here, where he would go—I guess that's why I talked to him in the first place, he had the look of a survivor in him…"

Kate took a breath while Cole took a long drag of his cigarette. He didn't smoke often, though now seemed a good a time as any. "Where was Max in all this?" he asked.

"Max, as it turned out, was his driver at the time. Foster had found Max at the start of the war and asked him to make some specifications for which Daisy was born out of. I don't know the full details, but they were attacked and Max made the choice to leave with Foster, left his grandma behind. We don't talk about it much for that reason… I don't know, I guess it was the same deal with me, I was pushed to survive and Foster knew how to survive, we made decisions and the only thing we saw was that we got to live with them… Foster had started to tell me of the Resistance that was building in Nebraska at the time to eventually take back the West Coast, but he was interrupted by someone bursting through the tavern door, the light from outside blinding us. She was screaming that the radio reports were wrong and that they were already in Salt Lake…"

Kate went to continue, her heart beating faster, but stopped herself short, now more curious about Cole's story. "What about you, where did you come from, really? There's just something about you, like you just dropped down from space."

Cole chuckled at this, bringing a smile to Kate's face in the dark. "I guess I have been a bit aloof, a bit quiet. I've always been that way I think. I want to tell you more, but my memory seems to just come and go as well as it pleases since Trent."

Kate tried to hide her annoyance at this; Cole still wasn't giving her anything to go by, even though she was on the verge of giving up a huge part of herself, letting those memories find air. Still, she found herself deeply amazed by how relaxed he always seemed to be, no matter the situation. A part of her thought that maybe it was an afterglow of Cole's Illusionist still rubbing off on him. He seemed like the liberated man, the kind of person Kate and the others would become when the cure had cleansed their bodies after all this time.

It was clear her Illusionist during the peace was not as great as Cole's Peter. Sure, there were moments of pure ecstasy she could almost glimpse in recollection—but these were countered with the growing, piercing paranoia that swelled within her leader when he felt the truce would end just as it did. She was more certain of those anxious times; her psyche still recovering from the gaping holes it created.

"What did it feel like for you, being under control like that?" Kate probed.

Cole looked up at the stars in the clear night sky and in an out of focus gaze he was taken back to another place. "The times were good. There were moments in the day where the sun was everlasting; the warmth you felt would fill your body through to your fingertips. We would lie down in circles, watching the clouds listlessly go by, admiring the shapes of the clouds put into our heads. We would gather firewood and make bonfires, singing along to those cheesy camp songs. He'd read us stories, and he'd always tell them with such a burning passion. Some days, if he were feeling up to it, he would make the most dazzling and mesmerizing of fireworks that could go on for hours despite the fact we had no fireworks. Then there were the pink streaks, God's fingers, made in the afternoon where the sun would drift just the right amount over our heads and cause these striking-yet-soft streaks of pink across the sky... It was strange, in a way none of us thought it was real and yet we found it so easy to believe, all of it..."

Kate was now brimming with envy. Her period of peace was always interrupted, or so her friends had told her. There had always been something nagging away at the surface and even looking back, knowing exactly what it was, provided little closure.

"What about the Purification Front or any others, did they not pass through?" Kate asked. "Wouldn't the sound of fireworks attract their attention?"

Cole was deep in it now, right back in the bubble, and his voice perked up in defense. "He would've blocked the noise out, magic for our eyes and ears only. We were invisible to the outside world, ghosts..." Cole smiled, his mind still floating around in the memories in the warm bubble of Trent.

Kate was dejected. "You had it lucky, Cole. There's no doubt about it. I barely remember my Controller's name. It all just went away after I saw what became of those in control with the power." In the dark her eyes began to swell up again. Cole felt her trembling, her secret still bottled inside her; words on the tip of her tongue but acidic to her conscious self.

Cole knew she needed to let it out and so he pressed. "What happened, Kate? What is it that makes you so ashamed of yourself?"

Kate paused for a moment, and throughout her retelling, as the images of bloodshed were revisited, re-felt, the cumbersome weight she'd been carrying round got lighter and lighter; a spiritual knot in her gut untying like the bow of a ribbon.

"Moments after we were told they had breached the city, we started to hear gunshots in the distance. They were faint at first, but their frequency and volume grew louder every minute. I had frozen up. Before, when we heard all the news on television, when we knew it was something else, something huge; the shock of it all hit me in waves, a slow, dawning kind of fear that rattled my hands for minutes at a time. Oregon was blisteringly hot that summer but every part of me was chilled to the bone those first few days. I could deal with that, but this time—In Salt Lake—it was different. It was all of a sudden, right out there on the street where I could feel it, hear it with my own damn ears. Everything stiffened up, the hairs on the back of my neck stood right up. With every shot I heard, it occurred to me that one of those was going to be for me. I wondered whether I would hear the shot that would end it... Then Foster woke me, his hands gripping my arms so tight his nails dug into my skin. He looked me right in the eyes, bearing his clenched teeth, like an animal ready to kill. I'll never forget what he said to me in that moment:

"*'If you do as I say, you will survive this.'*

"He was hasty in asking me about my traveling partners, how close they were to the tavern. It took a while through the stuttered tears to tell him they were in a parking lot minding the car three hundred feet away. Foster asked what direction they went and I remember only being able to point, my finger shaking in the direction of the gunfire. Foster looked and knew what it meant; there was no way of reaching them. By this point, the tavern was almost cleared out except for a few stragglers like me who were being comforted by their surrounding family members to make that run outside, wherever they were going. Then I heard a walkie crackle from inside Foster's jacket; it was Max asking for a status. Foster looked at me then told Max to start the car and wait exactly eight minutes and if Foster didn't show, Max was to continue the mission. Foster then offered to take me with him."

I have to go, he'd said, *I don't know whether your friends are alive, but if you don't make a move soon you'll be dead. You can come with me, but you have to come now!*

"I couldn't make a decision like that so I did nothing but tremble and look down at the ground. He wanted to help but his patience was running thin so he made for the door and in that second I blurted out, '*WAIT!*' I'd known Sarah for ten years, we were best friends in high school and college and I knew what it meant when I called Foster back; that deep down I wanted to survive more than anything in the world. She was the first thing I lost that day..."

There was a lull, a pause in Kate's words while her lips quivered, and Cole understood all too well. He wanted to tell her about Peter and Maddie in her pause, to share his own pains, but he let her continue.

"When Foster came back, he told me to follow his orders to the letter and if I did that we would escape this place. I nodded, cleared my eyes and watched him produce a black handgun that he then placed into my open hands. He flicked the safety off."

Make no mistake. The kids would kill you just as quick as the adults.

Kate was now swept up in her own story, fully immersed,

recalling the outside glare of both the sun and the remains of the reflective snow whilst the chilly air made her cheeks flush a reddish pink. She was right back there.

"Foster examined the street, looking squarely in the direction of gunfire before turning his attention to the intersection a little closer to us, pointing and ordering that we must take that right up ahead of us and cut right across the line of the advancing crazies. It was half a mile of street to a tree line at the edge of town where Max was waiting for us. As we ran toward the intersection and the gunfire, the people running the other way—and there were a lot—would glance at us in puzzlement, if only for a second, before we'd never see their faces again. In each car that sped past us I looked frantically into the windshield, hoping to see my friends even though it was clearly not their car. I wasn't thinking straight at that point, just running on whatever was left. The closer we got to that piercing hail of bullets, the more I would see people, some alone and others in clustered groups, kneeling on the ground facing the sounds of the advancing monsters with their heads touching the ground in submission."

"Why?" asked Cole, intrigued by the odd image Kate had crafted in his mind.

"You've never heard of the tactics of the Purification Front, have you? I had heard through radio broadcasts and stories of narrow escapes that the Puries offered two options to their enemies: *convert or be killed*. From these stories, the method of signaling your intent to submit varied dramatically, but I instantly recognized what these people were doing. In that moment, I felt disgusted by these people who had given up and decided to take the easy way out. Looking back now though, I think I was really just covering up my own behavior; they were giving up their freedom while I gave up my friends—so I was no better, maybe even worse… As we ran along this street, the numbers of forced converts grew, along with everyone else running away in panic. I passed a car yard and watched as people beat each other with blunt objects to take their cars. I slowed down, wondering whether this had been the fate of my friends, putting the faces of Sarah and Justin on these people, hoping dearly that my eyes were deceiving me; that they got out alive. I hope they didn't wait; that they had made the same decision I had made. I looked back in the direction of where we had parked and soon my feet were carrying me back there, dragged by the guilt. That was when Foster grabbed me by the arm again. He knew what I was thinking and told me to stop it."

You need to focus on survival. Those thoughts will kill you now if you don't let go of them.

"I knew he was right. I told him I understood and then we ran, faster than before. By the time we had reached the next intersection I was struggling to breathe, my lungs working overtime while my legs were burning all the way through. It was always scary crossing the intersections; I never looked to my left, if it was going to happen I didn't want to see it coming. After passing several of these intersections I almost crashed into Foster who had stopped and crouched behind a rundown car abandoned on the curb. I crouched behind Foster as he peered around the corner, only to jerk his body backward. As we had run down this street waves of people and cars had streamed across us in desperate flight, but now the numbers came down to the last few and once we had reached this particular crossroad, for a split second it felt to me that both the gunfire and civilians had dried up. But it was only the calm before the storm, as bullets tore into the building opposite us, shattering the windows while dust from the bullet impacts sprayed along the shop. Then more of that insidious noise racketed through my eardrums like it was right on top of us now. Going against everything in my body I peeked around the corner to see retreating men and women in gas masks firing rifles at a crowd of sprinting youths; these tiny kids and large teens, brandishing all assortments of knives, swords and baseball bats they waved in the air while screaming a high-pitched yell, running full-tilt our way. It seemed physically impossible they could emit such hair-raising shrieks as they ran. I could see their breaths in the cold air, a constant stream while they ran on nothing and thought the same of it...

"Foster reasoned to me later that the ideas put into their heads would carry them forward no matter the physical consequences. Behind the youths, way far back in the distance, marched the adult members in their gray robes, sweeping any stragglers with precision shots of their rifles. The men and women in gas masks were the remaining numbers of Resistance Salt Lake had to offer. They had held on for as long as they could and in their retreat they were either shot in the back or swarmed by youths who would stab them until their blood hung in the air as vapor. I had my ears covered by my hands yet the sound of bullets whizzing past still deafened me. A soldier in the act of passing us made a sharp turn into our street to escape the sheet of lead that streaked along it, only to catch a burst of rounds in his back and he fell just a few feet in front of us. He cried in agony as he laid there, his hands too afraid to reach back and touch the pockets of flesh that blood was gushing out of. I was so distressed I looked away, wanting to just crawl myself into a ball and dream for it all to go away. I felt the presence of Foster leave my side and fears of desertion awoke me and when I opened my eyes to call him back I saw that Foster had dragged the screaming man behind the car amidst a hail of bullets. I thought Foster was saving the man but instead he took the strap of the shotgun off the man before snatching the gun itself from his weak arms. The man begged him not to, before Foster coldly said his only chance at making it was to surrender himself to them and they would not accept him if he had a gun. Foster turned to me and said we had to cross the intersection; that the car was only a hundred feet or so away. He yelled at me to run across the intersection and then cover him as he crossed. I hesitated after he yelled, 'Now!' only for him to push me out in the open. I thought I was going to slip, lose my footing and be mowed down. But my feet found purchase and I gave it everything I had running across. In the corner of my eyes I saw people running toward me, two of them turning in front of me to try and make for the safety of the corner I was also aiming for. Then a flurry of rounds hit the corner and three other stragglers on my left. I ducked my head and dived for the corner. I then shuffled back to the corner, lifted the gun from my jacket and started firing wildly into the street. I probably hit nothing but it was good enough for Foster to miraculously make it through, firing his shotgun from the hip as he ran. When he made it to me he screamed to keep on running. We gave it everything we had. He told me not to look back, but like a person told not to look down when facing a great height, I was driven to glancing behind us. There were now maybe ten or so youths, their screams now faded as their vocal chords had been completely shot through and yet they were as menacing as ever, gaining quickly on us, those footsteps thumping as fast as my heart was beating. We could see the tree line where Max was supposed to be waiting for us, but just as Foster pointed it out, the two people who had passed me on the corner were gunned down as they ran between the dirt clearing just before the tree line. Foster's radio then crackled, it was Max screaming to wait by the corner; that he'd pick us up. Foster did not respond, merely looking back on the youths that now closed in on us; hemming us in between the open range of the deadly adults and their pit bull youths. Once we had almost hit the corner, we both turned around to face them, Foster immediately firing his shotgun into the crowd bringing down at least three. But they still kept coming."

Shoot, Kate! Shoot!

"I raised my gun; my hands trembling. I saw their eyes, Cole—pupils so large there was barely any white in them. I wanted to close my own eyes, pretend I was somewhere else, but I knew I had to keep them focused to stop them, to kill. I looked down the barrel and aimed at the closest one: a tall, blonde haired beast of a kid, with hands that could crush my larynx in one squeeze. I fired the gun twice into his chest and yet he only stumbled, his forward momentum flinging him almost upon me. As his arms reached for me, Foster swung the shotgun like a baseball bat into his stomach, the force knocking him to the ground just short of me. Foster then swung at another youth, this one smaller than the large brute. The butt of the gun rocked his cheek, sending a splatter of blood shooting from the rat's mouth. '*Keep shooting!*' Foster screamed, as he narrowly avoided the blade of another one of them. I fired, this time at the kid's head. He dropped immediately, the explosion of blood exiting the back of his head and spraying a crazed girl behind him. As he fell, the girl came into Foster's range and he smacked her across the face before losing the grip on his shotgun. I tried to shoot the others, but my gun was already out of ammo. As I stood there frozen, Foster reached for the magnum in his jacket, but as he swung it out, a butcher's knife slashed his forearm, sending the magnum flying from his grip onto the ground in front of me. As I stared at its silver shiny body against the wet concrete pavement, the sight of two small boots overtaking its presence caused me to look up to a child of no more than ten coming right at me…"

Kate didn't say it, but those dark rings under this kid's eyes would forever be burnt into her memory. They went all the way round. In Kate's pause, her eyes pleaded with Cole to know that this was not a child anymore. It was a threat, something to be dealt with.

"Before I could fully process this thought, the kid's bat was coming down hard on me. I held my arm up to block it, the brunt of the bat hitting my wrist, sending an instant shot of pain surging through. My arm dropped and the child went to swing again. This time I stepped back and missed the swing, feeling the air of the swing on my face. Then with all my might I pushed the child with both hands, sending him falling backwards. I looked over to Foster, who now had four people on him as he tried desperately to defend himself. I picked up the magnum and saw the kid I had knocked was getting back up. I didn't want to shoot him, Cole, I really didn't but at the time I thought I had to do it. I couldn't help Foster if I had this kid throwing everything he had at me. I shot quickly and he fell. Swivelling the sight to Foster I caught the towering bully raising his butcher's knife on top of Foster while the other three held him down. I aimed at his chest and the magnum roared twice, the heavy kick of two shots recoiling against my tired arms. I moved to unload the rest of the gun on the backs of the vicious dogs but froze when I heard the chatter of automatics behind me. Forgetting Foster, I turned to see a large black SUV taking heavy fire, speeding straight at me before breaking hard almost on top of us. Max opened the door and fired on the youths at close range, their backs popping blood mixed with the puff of the wool ripped out of their clothes. Max then aimed the gun at me before Foster cried out, '*No*!!' Max understood, and as he did, I snapped back into action, helping drag the bleeding Foster into the car. Speeding off, Daisy absorbed a lot of lead, but that didn't really worry me by then. All I could do was look back at those kids on the pavement..."

She drew a breath. She was unsure what parts had been spoken and what had been kept inside of the story she played over in her head everyday since. Just how much had been shared was not easy to diffuse; yet Kate was overwhelmed with a sense that Cole had seen it all and was very forgiving. It was all out of her now; this cancerous memory that had grown inside of her since that day, eating her up and changing her to the point where she didn't look in the side mirror anymore, afraid of the girl that now inhabited her body. She was a college girl before the world collapsed; that was who she still wanted to be. House parties and organising socials were her game. But after that day, none of her old friends (if they were still alive) would've recognized her if they saw her now. That bubbly, cheeky and sometimes sarcastic girl was gone.

"It feels good to tell someone. I feel like I'm only now just getting used to this new skin I live in… Maybe it'll be too late come tomorrow," Kate spoke softly to Cole, the energy she'd used to tell her tale now completely drained as her lips quivered, ready to cry again.

"Kate, I don't know who you were, only who you are now; a survivor. And I know we'll both survive tomorrow, but only if you trust me."

Kate nodded, "I do," and it was then for the first time she realized Cole was holding her hand, giving her whole body a glowing warmth, and had done so the entire time she recounted her ordeal. She looked up and smiled at him, and in the darkness he smiled back. It filled them both with hope and contentment, and, if only for a second, there was no anxiety toward tomorrow, or no tomorrow at all for that matter, just this moment. As he lost himself into her, it dawned on Cole that Kate looked just like Maddie in this light…and like a cold snap, he pulled away.

"We should get some sleep," he said, to which they both did.

***

Cole gazed across Trent and into Fort Collins below. The air was warm and the smoke had cleared from the town as the crazies had settled themselves. Must've been summer he decided. Better days.

He took in her scent first; it made his knees weak—always did when he got that whiff. He was sitting on the park bench, the one they used to hold hands on while watching the sunset. They never talked when they did this, they didn't have to; their love needn't be declared at this point. Cole didn't look at her; scared he would wake up. Instead he slid his hand across the bench until it met hers. The moment his fingers intertwined with hers a silent earthquake shook all throughout him; he was really touching her! Feeling that warmth again. His hand clammed up and his grip tightened.

"Is this a dream?" she asked.

"Yes."

The seconds creaked passed. Cole had not dared look at her.

"I can't look at you," he said. "Can't look at your curly hair, your sweet dimples, those soft gray eyes. It'll wake me up; send me back to that world where you aren't there anymore…"

"Okay," she replied.

There was a soothing silence as they tried to take it all in. Large, soapy bubbles floated in the air around them—tiny rainbow smiles reflecting along their shimmering surface, gleaning the happiness, the color of past days. In one of these bubbles, Cole caught a glimpse of Maddie and when this happened, all the bubbles popped, as they all would eventually.

"What day was this?" she whispered.

"Could have been any of them. I made them all the same."

"Perfect?"

"Only because you were there."

They stopped talking and just took in the sunset. It was taking Cole every ounce of strength in him not to turn his head and fall deep into her eyes; trying to hold on, keep her alive as if feeling her touch would be enough. Even with this, without him looking at her, knowing every part that made her whole, their moment on the bench was slipping away, right through their hands. No matter how much he tried, how much he screamed inside realizing this very fact; the sun would set and it would all leave him, moving past at a speed he could never fully catch.

"If it's a dream, then does that mean you won't remember?" she asked.

"I guess so. It hurts to remember anyway."

He felt her soothing smile. "Then forget me."

"I can't."

There was more silence. Then a white noise flushed through

Cole's eardrums, sending him startled in his seat. He gripped her hand tightly. The other dream was coming back; the one that made him forget. The rubble was calling him to stand on it. They didn't have long.

"I'm so sorry," he cried. "You said to never leave you and I did. I saw it coming and I did nothing."

Tears rolled freely down his face as his insides choked up. A hand outstretched to rub away the tears. Cole was so desperate to open his eyes and see her, hold her one more time. Now they huddled together into one, clinging onto each other for dear life as Cole was beckoned to the rubble.

"You were the best thing that ever happened to me."

At this they brought their faces to meet, clenching each other's bodies, forcing the universe to see their love. Cole only had a few precious seconds to take in that face, that scent that told him he was home—to know her forever. And when the white light started to fill this moment, they kissed for the last time.

When their lips parted and the warmth left Cole, he kept his eyes closed; too broken to see her float away once more. All too soon, the ground beneath him formed into the uneven stones of debris: former buildings and foundations. And then the questions came.

24. The Savage

The people of Holdsworth were up and about before any of the members of Bryan's house had awoken. Most had packed their bags as contingency for when the Savage sought blood for being disturbed, while a small handful remained cautiously optimistic. Whether they were realists or optimists, a large group of both now idled around Bryan's house, anticipating the departure of their supposed saviors. The few that expected nothing but utter failure came only to snigger at the chest puffing bravado of Foster's claims, even if it meant their own lives.

The sky was almost completely clear, save for the odd cloud lingering about, while the morning dew was accompanied by the refreshing chirps of unseen birds lining the trees behind Bryan's house.

Lying on the floor in the upstairs bedroom Max had stayed in, there was a plastic guitar, sliced at the neck, broken in all places. Max awoke in his bed and lifted the pull down curtain above his head. When he saw the clear skies, he laughed to himself. *What a lovely day to die.*

Sliding off the bed and into his clothes, Max felt for the letter he'd sealed long ago and carried in his breast pocket, always for just in case.

Outside, the Doc made his way through the growing masses that encircled Bryan's house. For the many that saw him, a path was cleared until the Doc found himself next to the head of the guards, Renko the behemoth, who had taunted Foster earlier.

"Big turnout," muttered Renko.

The Doc sighed. "Well they have little to do around here but hope… I fear this last attempt will crush even that," he said, scratching at his stubble.

"Do you think he knows they're coming?" asked Renko.

"I'd say so. I guess we just have to hope he is too confident to think anyone is stupid enough to attack him, and they catch him off guard. Even then, they'll only get one shot."

Those inside Bryan's house groggily made their way to the dark kitchen where Bryan poured them cereal. All the windows in the house had their blinds drawn by Bryan who, upon being the first to wake, noticed people peering into the windows. As each came to gather around the white kitchen table, small talk was made about the mission while everyone thanked Bryan for making breakfast.

"We're pretty lucky here to have milk, Holdsworth is supplied its milk and beef by one farmer a couple of miles out of town. He does an amazing job with what he's got, I've been up there a few times to volunteer," spoke Bryan candidly, his mood vastly improved since the day before. While it puzzled everyone else, Bryan had concluded in his mind while wrestling with sleep that regardless of the outcome in the forest, he would see his wife and child again; dead, alive or in heaven as he joined them. He fantasized about asking the Savage if he could see them for one last time, one last moment so desperate was he to see their faces again. Foster, perplexed as anyone else by Bryan's swooning mood, tried to shake it off and focus everyone back to the mission at hand. "Everyone has studied the maps and knows their roles?"

"Yes. You saw us do it!" replied Max, agitated by Foster's nagging tone.

"Good. I just want everyone to be clear, we know what could happen if that wasn't the case."

"Yes, we know!" exclaimed Kate and Cole, almost in a joking, frustrated fashion.

While they chided about Foster's insistency, Bryan's demeanor dimmed, like he'd flipped straight back to that mourning state they'd met him in. "Did anyone dream about him…the Savage?"

They shook their heads before all eyes were turned to Cole. They knew about the crying in Cole's sleep, but Cole shook his head just like the rest of them.

"That's great, I guess. Means he doesn't know you're here yet. We still have the element of surprise."

Kate tried to smile. It was a small comfort.

After breakfast, Bryan informed the others that the watering system in the house was still flowing, even if there was only one temperature. Foster flexed off his usual tough grit, telling the group that staying frosty was in their benefit. They all took turns under the cold reminder, and when Max had finished his turn, he stepped out to find himself alone in the corridor with Kate. She'd been waiting for him. Her feet were shuffling, ready to speak of an unspoken charge that had built for too long. She tried, but couldn't meet his eyes.

"Max, I…"

"It's okay. We'll just forget about it." He then moved past her, up to his room with the broken fake guitar lying on the floor, to put on the clothes he just might die in.

As they loaded up their weapons in the living room, putting on body armor for some, there was a knocking on the front door. Bryan went to open it and returned with Jimmy and his friend, Kyle.

"These guys said they were coming with us?" said Bryan, unsure of what to make of the two.

Foster raised his eyebrows at Kate, interested by her answer. Kate cut a glance at Max before steadying herself. "Yeah, they are," she said, both relieved and embarrassed. "Everyone this is Jimmy and that is…"

"Kyle," responded Kyle, his cheeks blushing, his body already aware of just how out of place he was.

"There is *some* crowd out there," snorted Jimmy, "to watch us kick ass!"

"Are you serious?" Foster said to Kate, "*kick ass*? What is this kid, twelve?"

"Hey, wrinkles!" pipped Kyle, trying to assert himself. "We can fight, we know the forest—all them ins and outs, yo!"

"We need as much of that as we can get," Kate shot at Foster.

"All right, if you know the forest and a thing about guns," he relented, "but if you fuck up out there, make a twig snap when I don't tell you to, I'll wring your neck before the Savage has a chance to even think about you."

A gulp of anxiety shuddered under the surface of their throats. Despite the thinly veiled hostility of the others, Kate was generally relieved Jimmy and Kyle had come; it brought her hope that the cards she had played would save not just her but all the others as well.

Compared to the others, Jimmy and his buddy were essentially bereft of armor and weapons. "Where are our weapons?" Jimmy asked with a sense of entitlement.

"Kid, this ain't a fucking charity," shot Foster, his agitation growing with every word that broke from Jimmy's mouth.

"Hey fuck you, old man! Now we're decent enough to help out, the least you can do is spot us some heavy hitters, better than the .22 Kyle has and this snub .38 I got."

"You ever fired military-grade weapons before? Assault rifles, machine guns?" asked Max, keen to solve this situation before it got out of hand—even though the sight of Jimmy confirmed his worst thoughts about Kate.

"Yeah I have," replied Jimmy, his voice now calmer than before.

"Maybe Renko can lend you one," suggested Bryan.

"Nah, that fucking dickwad's got it in for me," Jimmy informed the group. Cole could see why.

"Then speak to the Doc, he'll sort it out," said Bryan.

As they left the house, the crowd stirred. The cool air was slowly escaping their presence as the sun began its climb in the sky. There were mixed emotions held by the crowd for each of the fighters. Many felt a great respect for Bryan, even though they worried for his safety. Some in the crowd had not even dared to fight back when the Savage had taken their loved ones. For the travelers of Max, Foster, Kate and Cole, the crowd acted indifferent toward them, hopeful they could do as they had promised but resentful they may cause the deaths of others as punishment for their retaliation. As for Jimmy and Kyle, little was felt for Jimmy while some pitied his buddy for being led down such a road. Jimmy cockily walked through the crowd until he stood face to face with Renko.

"I need a piece," he demanded.

"I'm not wasting shit on you," was the stern reply.

Jimmy then looked over to the Doc standing next to Renko. They sized each other up, Jimmy already keen to start the festivities of the day until the Doc relented and told Renko to give him his weapon. Renko looked at the Doc, clearly frustrated, before removing the MP5 sub-machine gun from his body and handing it to Jimmy without saying a word.

"Thank you," Jimmy said to the both of them.

The crowd made space as they walked to their cars. Foster turned to face the crowd and swell them up with hope, but cut himself short when he saw the man and woman—that Jesse and Becky—they had encountered just before reaching Holdsworth. They stood among the crowd, their children by their side, smiling at Foster. For a moment Foster was stunned, his eyes glued to their presence, before he turned away and tried to think nothing of it.

Bryan took his car with Jimmy, Kyle and Kate, while Cole went with Foster and Max in Daisy. Once they had passed the gates of Holdsworth they were treated to sprawling meadows of open field, the makings of a perfect day. As Max hummed along, he considered just driving the whole day, like the early days when his uncle would take Max and his cousins out for a picnic in the country; where in the afternoon the pink sunset would blend perfectly with the vast fields of green and illuminate the tree they played under. Today could have been like one of those, he wished.

As they topped a slight crescent, the treetops of the state forest came into view. Max tried to look beyond the first row of trees, through the thick brush where evil lay. The forest started as the ground began to incline, covering several hilltops that lined the area.

In the other car, Bryan and Jimmy speculated as to where the Savage lived. Their guessing left them somewhere over the other side of the hilltops where the land flattened out and the visitor's center was located, accessible through the other side. Kyle suggested maybe it could be one of the abandoned ranger cabins or just a shack the Savage had made himself.

"He only showed up during summer, he could have been camping this whole time." If that were the case then they could be searching for a while, or in the more likely scenario, they would have no trouble finding the Savage; he would subconsciously send them on a path that would lead them right to him.

Both cars stopped at the foot of the hill, right next to the abandoned tollbooth of the reserve's entrance. They all got out and stretched their legs and drank from their canteens. The yellow dirt road continued forward, snaking itself up the hill. The trees were slim but towered high in the air.

"It gets thicker once we reach the plateau," said Bryan.

"We'll cut through the loop. Kate, you lead on point," said Foster, as sweat ran down his face from the heat and heavy body armor he wore. Bryan, Jimmy and Kyle instinctively put on their gas masks. When Foster and the others saw this, they did the same.

The walk up the hilltops was vigorous. While the trees provided shade from the sun, the body armor and weight of the guns they carried saw their clothes cling uneasy to their bodies. With each movement and twitch of a tree, they would clutch their guns a little tighter. Bryan was the only one who noticed that the trees they passed weren't native to this region.

"See these plants right here," he motioned for the whole group to see. They were all led around to a beautiful flower that excited its white tips in their presence like delicate whiskers. "These are Native American Ghost Orchids. They're from Florida, and I hope I don't have to tell you those palm trees over there aren't exactly a part of *Tropical* Iowa."

They all looked at him, unsure of the point he was trying to make. After a while it was Cole who spoke up. "He means they are not real."

Jimmy was confused most of all. He touched the fern of the plants Bryan was talking about and to him they felt as real as it could get. "What do you mean, they're fake?"

"No. They're just in your head."

Cole looked around and started to notice all the little changes to the habitat Bryan had noticed first.

"So they don't exist unless we are here?" suggested Kate.

"They could be his sentries, cues that'll let him know we've stepped into his garden," Foster guessed, looking directly at Cole.

Cole's heart began to race, his consistent look of concentration hiding behind his mask breaking as the connotations of Foster's words crashed like a wave against him. All the plants and animals were like agents of the Savage, a million watchful eyes that missed nothing. "We'd better keep moving," was all Cole said.

They raced now, their boots thumping against the ground, sending the dirt floor swelling with each step forward. Everyone passed Cole as he struggled to run at full tilt with the gas mask on his head. He still wasn't used to it, his heavy breathing catching the attention of Max, who slowed down before coming level with Cole.

"The masks do nothing," he whispered to Cole.

"What?" Cole clambered in surprise. "Then why the fuck are we wearing them, in this heat of all things?"

"It's for them," Max replied, now down to a walking pace to distance himself from Bryan and the others. "Look, most people believe it helps prevent them from having their minds invaded, and it was a widely known belief, so we just roll with it."

"If it's a placebo, then why did you just ruin it for me?" Cole questioned to a stunned Max.

"Woops."

They had little time to dwell on it and soon they were off again. Cole wasn't mad at Max; he had no right to be. It was just an old habit, hard to kick—they were already sick anyway. The fact that people thought a gas mask would stop this kind of virus was ridiculous and Cole realized he should've known better from the beginning.

***

They stood around him in a circle. The first thing they noticed were his hands: gray and decaying with red sores around his fingers. Flies came and went from the blown-out eyehole of his gas mask, its rim lined with clumpy dried blood. A silver handgun lay in his lap, just shy of his right hand.

"Looks like he did it himself," said Cole. No one replied but they all seemed to agree, and now they were left to consider the sheer mental stress the Savage must have imposed on this man to force him to take his own life.

"Is he one of yours?" Kate asked Bryan. Bryan knew, just as well as Jimmy and Kyle. He didn't have to see the face; a tattered, red and blue woven bracelet hung around the boy's withered wrist giving it away.

"He was a good guy," admitted Jimmy.

Bryan and Kyle acknowledged this, before Bryan elaborated. "His name was Daniel Yuan. Like Jimmy said, he was a good guy, well respected in the community. He had a lot of spirit… The Doc was never the same after Daniel failed to return."

They let it sink in; let the possible fate of Daniel creep with cold fingers up their backs, all except for Colonel John Foster. For while he felt for this man's struggle, he knew the dead felt no pain and set about refocusing the group's attention to the task at hand. They regathered their pace and reached the plateau within minutes. Feeling their legs relieved from the strain of the incline, their breathing slowed, almost relaxed for that matter. They walked among the trees in a single file. The sun rode high now, the morning dew evaporated, leaving a dry dusty path they now walked over. Crickets clicked in the air against the slight treading of the group, while a light zephyr coasted across the forest.

Taking point, Kate was the first to see through the thick wall of trees—both real and imagined—making out the signs of a clearing up ahead. She looked upon this clearing and its place-ment with strange curiosity, drawn to its fairytale-like presence. How had this patch been created in the middle of this grand forest, completely untouched? Then she saw them: a young woman and a small child, kneeling before a man in a dark robe. Warm chills spread through Kate's body; she was awestruck at how peaceful they looked with the sun glistening on their backs, complete tranquility in the silent air, a picture perfect moment.

For a split second she forgot all of it: the war, the children she had shot, all the bodies she had stared at, fearful every day that it was a premonition of her own future. All these things in one moment had left her body, her mind and her soul as she felt a taste of his medicine. She wanted to walk over to him and kneel, join them in *forever*. For a split second she was whisked back to the meadows, Derek, everything.

And then the man in the dark robe looked up at Kate.

His face wavered and melted. His skin was brown one second—and ghostly white the next. Kate was seeing two things at once. The man's attention shifted from her to the others, who had just caught up to Kate and now stood paralyzed by what they saw. Without moving his lips the man bellowed throughout the forest: *Why are you here?*

This snapped Kate into action. The dark memories of the war flooded back and the sun and warmth that had filled her heart with goodness became cold and dim as she broke the trance of the young woman and her child who now turned their heads and stared at her in unison. Kate raised her Kalashnikov, the sights staring upon the distorted, perpetually melting face of the Savage. She fired three rounds into his face, the bullets snapping out the silence of the forest, and then lowered her weapon to see the damage. To all their horror, the Savage was untouched, the bullets passing through him as if he were a ghost.

Again his voice echoed, the same, *"Why are you here?"* reaching out to everything in the forest, sending birds reeling from their trees in a frenzy of movement. Then he was gone, disappearing into thin air. The others filled into the clearing, Bryan losing all inhibition and throwing off his gas mask as he broke from the group and ran towards his wife and daughter.

Foster's chance had been missed. The knockout grenade he'd readied, kept secure ever since those early days in the cave, had not left his belt.

"Surround the perimeter!" ordered Foster, and each of them spread out, covering the tree line, all except Kate who stood expectantly, her vision cat-like as she surveyed the still trees in front of her, certain the flicker of a tree or the brushing of leaves would give away his position. Just as she wanted, the rustling of leaves ahead resembled a moving figure, albeit invisible to the naked eye. Without thinking she quickly gave chase. Foster screamed for her to come back, but Kate was hell-bent on catching the monster. She was now out of sight of the others, darting between trees as she ran downward from the peak of the valley. The others stood their ground, unsure of whether to go after her while Bryan hugged his wife one more time than he thought possible. Only to him it was not the warm embrace he had imagined it to be. His beloved wife, Helen, and cheeky daughter, Maggie, eyed him with suspicion. He tried kissing Helen but she pulled away.

"Guys, it's me. Your husband; your father…" he begged, hoping desperately for their eyes to light up in recognition so they could be a family again. Instead, Bryan saw something much worse: hatred. Maggie stood and tugged on her mother's worn shirt.

"Mommy, I want to talk to Daddy."

Bryan held her, his eyes welling up, "I'm here, baby."

"You're not my father!" Maggie cried in soul-crushing spite.

Bryan glanced at the others who could not help but feel his agony. Helen got up from her knees and grabbed Maggie by the hand. "I'll take you to your father," she said, happy to leave this weeping man. As she turned to leave, Bryan pulled at her skirt in desperation, "Helen, don't go—I love you!"

Helen responded with a hard slap across the face, stunning Bryan who shrunk under her vicious gaze.

"Fuck off!" she yelled.

And as she did there was a change in the air; ever so slight, but enough for the others to realize something was coming. The hair on their arms stood up trying to run away while their cheeks flushed red as the chemicals in their body debated the old choice of fight or flight. Adrenaline shot through their bodies in heart-clenching overdrive as everything in their sight (the trees, the ground, the floating squiggly lines that swam about their own eyes) began to take on a sinister form, ready to advance on them. The light around them grew dim, the empty blue sky dissolving into dark clouds threatening the full wrath of Mother Nature. An invisible weight clamped down on them, sinking their feet heavy into the ground while their hearts beat like jungle drums in a native ceremony.

The trees began to sway. In between the leaves and branches, before their very eyes, faces started to emerge through the patterns of swaying. At first they were rudimentary, cartoonish faces, before they became fully formed people of the past that haunted each man, the wild gazes that stared back gripping their insides and forcing the truth down their squirming throats.

Max saw his grandmother, the movement of the branches contorting her mouth to ask him *why*? Why had he left her there in that home, all alone? She'd waited and waited for someone to come. She'd chewed off all her nails and then eaten them for food. She waited till there was no more of her, because he never came back.

Cole saw Maddie, blood dripping from her mouth and falling to the grass below. She laughed. *It doesn't matter because we're together—right, honey?* Just as she had come sweeping back from the dead, her face twisted, the leaves moving like schools of fish to reveal another face; a dying Peter, who had only just come to understand the true nature of their relationship and what Cole had done to him. Then the leaves parted and like mitosis, two faces were formed, Peter now grinning as he was joined by that old pastor, both holding hands as they each wore a wicked grin of betrayal that dug deep into Cole's insides. Filled with burning anger and guilt, Cole fired his rifle at their faces. As he did that the others fired away too, Jimmy's screaming embodying the madness that took them all. The trees around them shattered as leaves burst and dropped to the ground. When their clips had been emptied the realisation of what had just happened sunk in with the now silent forest.

***

Kate heard the gunfire but was so assured she had him. Her gas mask had been ditched early—it was too hard to keep her breathing steady in the thing. She managed to find tracks almost 150 feet from down the valley and persisted with the tracks. As she moved deeper and deeper down the valley, the shade of the dense trees cooled Kate, who held back her dread by maintaining her focus on the barefoot tracks she pursued. The tracks ended as giant rocks began to cover the ground in front of her. Walking over these rocks proved troublesome, as Kate had to keep her head up to watch for the Savage. The sound of water, most likely a stream, could be heard nearby. As she scanned her surroundings looking for the stream whilst leaning against a rock she spotted a dark object hanging from a broken yellow tree branch. Kate moved carefully toward it, her body crouching as she stepped over the rocks. When she was within five-feet the object became known to her; it was the dark purple robe worn by the Savage. She lifted the robe with the barrel of her rifle, curious as to what it could reveal about him. As she did that, a flicker of movement in the corner of her eye startled her. Kate switched her attention to the Savage who now stood patiently only twenty feet from her.

He was bare for all but a loincloth, his arms and legs covered in darkened war paints that ebbed and flowed, wriggling like strung-out earthworms along his body. They moved as if they were alive, trying to escape his body but cowering under his might. His face distorted like bad reception and melted with every passing second, the color of blue and green swelling like waves of the pacific as purple saliva dribbled from the bottom of his face. Kate noticed he had a thick ponytail that moved like a snake sniffing the air for prey. She knew he was staring at her, even if she couldn't make out his eyes. She swung her arms to aim her rifle, but the barrel was still caught on the robe. Kate fired when the robe was fully stretched, missing completely. The Savage, in a calm motion, retreated further down the valley. Kate scrambled to give chase but slipped on the rocks, smashing her knee into a small boulder. She yelped in pain, clutching at her knee. The thudding pain consumed her. She thought about giving up then and there, the swelling could already be felt. She was certain she had chased him off anyway. In fact, Kate felt that it was actually the Savage who was scared of her—her dogged determination throwing him off balance. Grunting through the pain, Kate picked herself up and continued further down the valley.

The sound of the stream grew louder and yet Kate could not see it. This puzzled her, and over time increasingly bugged her.

Before Kate knew it, she had forgotten all about the Savage and now searched fiendishly in all directions for the stream. She then saw the land drop off only feet from her. As Kate approached it she could hear the stream grow louder and louder like a gushing waterfall. She carefully made her way closer to the edge until she was able to peer over. There was nothing but a dirt ditch, six feet deep. Suddenly the sound of the stream stopped and she felt the presence of the Savage right behind her, breathing on her neck. Kate swung around to finally see those eyes, bright blue with heavy black rings encircling them, right before he pushed her over the edge. She fell backwards, landing on her right shoulder, the pain crashing through her body. Kate screamed in agony, her body crawling into itself. With tears blurring her eyes and arms feebly shielding her face, Kate glanced upward to the ledge, fearful of the final blow.

His figure shadowed her, his shape an eclipse. Then as the light came to the Savage, Kate saw a young brunette—her mother—standing in place of the Savage. Kate felt herself change too, the image of her mother bringing her back to a rainy day spent inside as a six-year-old. Her mother had just scolded her for doing something wrong. Standing there trembling in front of her mother, all little Kate wanted to do was cry, to make the world go away. But she didn't want her mom to hear her cry. It was not how her mother wanted her to act; her mother wanted her to be tough. Instead, Kate ran to the bathroom to cleanse herself with a bath. And soon it came to be that whenever Kate was sad and felt like crying she would take a bath. It became her sanctuary. She spent a lot of time in baths as a child, escaping the bitterness her mother had held for her that day. She had forgotten those days, had grown; lived a thousand lives never again looking back at her mother that way, a child scared…

In a bolt, Kate was back in the forest, only now the white porcelain of her bathtub surrounded her. Kate looked up at her mother who held the very same expression of contempt she had given Kate as a child. Kate's mother then turned and left the edge. The tub was now gone. The stream sound returned like a piston; this time all around Kate as the ditch began to fill with muddy water. Kate screamed for her mother to come back, save her—tell Kate she was sorry, but her mother never returned and Kate's pleas were drowned out by the sickly water that enveloped her.

***

Back in the clearing, the smoke from their weapons filled the air around them, the burn of gunpowder still hanging in their nostrils. They looked at each other; cautious about asking the other what they saw whilst dreading what came next. Helen, who had taken cover lying down in the grass during the shooting, came to life and immediately went straight for Bryan's face. She tackled him to the ground and started punching, clawing and biting. Maggie joined in too. This snapped Foster into action as he came running to Bryan's assistance, knocking Helen out with the butt of his M4 carbine. With the assistance of Cole and Max, he then ripped Maggie off a terrified Bryan.

"Tie them both up," ordered Foster. Bryan protested weakly but knew they had little choice. Foster searched through his several pockets until he produced (to the surprise of Bryan alone) plastic cable ties.

"These will do for now," Foster said to Bryan as he handed him the ties. Bryan's hands shook and a look of trembling fear erupted across his face. It was too much; he couldn't tie them up—it was all too much, too illogical for his sliding moral groundings. Seeing this, Max pushed the screaming Maggie over to Foster, before he snatched up the cable ties and did it himself. As the plastic was applied tight into their wrists, Foster set about rounding the others into action.

"You two," he gestured to Jimmy and Kyle, "Keep an eye out while we sort this out."

Shaking in their boots, they carefully turned outward to the forest that wanted to eat them alive.

"We gotta get the fuck outta here," Kyle hissed to Jimmy. Jimmy looked him over and agreed wholeheartedly before hesitating; he was too full of pride to scram just like that but he wouldn't let Kyle leave if he stayed. "All right," Jimmy said, thinking aloud. He glanced upon the tying of Bryan's wife and daughter.

"We'll offer to get them out of here. Then we'll split!"

As the two planned their escape, Cole considered a similar retreat. "Foster, we need to get Bryan and his family out of here."

Foster knew he was right but held such a grasp on finding the Savage he stubbornly shook his head.

"We're right in his heartland! Right on his doorstep, ready to finish him and you want to leave? We only have one shot, if we can't get him now—then when? His retaliation will be bloody for everyone in Holdsworth, not just us!"

They stared each other off, both aware the other had valid points. Watching the argument unfolding, Kyle saw his only chance to get them out of there. As he started to move toward them, ready to agree with Cole, Jimmy watched his friend come to his rescue once again. Theirs was a relationship of power: Jimmy had it and Kyle followed. Jimmy was tough, but he knew that was all he had. Kyle was often the voice of reason, cooling off the situations where they were hopelessly outmatched. Jimmy was the mess that Kyle helped to prop up. He was liked much more than Jimmy, and Jimmy knew it. Yet through all this, Kyle remained loyal, forever Jimmy's best friend. Goose bumps began to line Jimmy's skin, reflecting the genuine respect he felt for Kyle…or so he thought.

It was strange.

At first it was a notion, then it snowballed, sweeping up everything Jimmy had ever known, consuming all his previous conceptions to inconsequential dust. All that remained in Jimmy's mind was a single objective: To serve *Him*. Jimmy's body reacted to this decision as if it were the only thing it had ever known. He flung off his gas mask and then the machine-gun was drawn up to his shoulder, his face absent—eyes cold.

Cole turned to see Jimmy's snap, while Kyle, his only true friend for over twelve years, never saw it coming. The burst rang out across the forest, sending Cole and Foster diving for cover on the ground. Max had no time to connect the two bloody dots that wet his face. As Kyle fell, Max locked eyes with Jimmy who now aimed the machine gun at Max. Max tried to react but was hit with a burst to the chest before he could raise his own weapon. Jimmy then turned his attention to the helpless others who lay sprawled along the ground. There was no time to aim their weapons; all that talk of survival and being the Resistance till the last breath was lost on Foster, the weight crashing down on him like raining bricks. He was tired of fighting and thought of death now as a bed of permanent creases he was all too happy to fall into.

Jimmy raised his gun to finish them all in one final spray, his face twitching before a wry smile appeared. That wicked smile burned into Cole's mind as he closed his eyes for the last time, ready to accept it and remember the good parts. The sound of gunfire rung through the valley once again, its short burst followed by nature's silent reply.

But Cole felt no pain from his tense body. He opened his eyes to see Jimmy lying face up on the grass, smoke seeping from the holes Max had put in him.

"Max!" Foster exclaimed, the idea of accepting death evaporating in that very moment. Max dropped his Kalashnikov and let his head faint to the soft grass below him. His body armor had absorbed all but one bullet that had entered his left shoulder. Taking off his gas mask, Max coughed as he clutched his chest with his right hand, the brunt impact of the bullets also fracturing his left rib cage.

Foster clambered up and rushed towards Max—but without realising it—had pulled out his switchblade mid-stride, his grip solid as if to finish what Jimmy had started. In the split-second Cole had seen this, he screamed out, "No!"

Foster, unable to remove the knife from his own grip tried to stop his feet from reaching Max. The knife came down hard as Foster fell, narrowly missing Max, who gasped at this second attempt on his life within a matter of seconds. Foster threw the blade away, unsure of what had just taken over him.

It was Cole's defiant "No" that had broken Foster's trance.

When they all came to realize this, Foster, Max and Bryan were drawn to the only possible conclusion. They all watched on in silence as Cole removed his gas mask, wiping off the sweat that ran down the side of his face, now standing in the fresh open. Foster did the same, taking off his gas mask too. When Cole spoke again they clung onto every word he said as if it were their own breath. His voice echoed through their minds, resonating in their memories as a higher authority. Here was the real Cole, the one he could hide from no longer, looking into each of their eyes, taking the reigns.

"We need to get you guys out of here. Max, you need to help Bryan get his family back to the car."

Max, who had strained his face as the blood oozed from his shoulder, forgot his pain in an instant as he realized his duty. Cole then gazed up at the trees around them, his eyes squinting, checking for the slight flicker of their reality altering. "Foster, when I find Kate I want you to take her back to the car. As soon as you're all there I want you both to hightail it back to Holdsworth and tell them to shore up their defenses in case I fail." Foster nodded, but a part of him wanted to stay, to fight and help Cole kill the Savage. Maybe it was his pride or Cole's nerve-racking fear of facing the Savage alone, but without words exchanged Foster stood his ground, ready to fight alongside Cole to the end. Cole accepted this and before he motioned for Max and Bryan to start moving, the deep running concentration in his face let up and he spoke from the heart.

"I hid this from you because it destroyed everything I once knew. I tried to keep it from myself because it destroyed me. But now I know I have to accept it, and I'm sorry I was too scared and weak to come to that conclusion earlier, before I put you all in danger." There was nothing to say because Cole didn't let them answer; it was said more for himself than anyone else.

With his unhurt arm, Max grabbed the resistant Maggie who screamed and spat at him, her vicious face growling like a pit bull. Bryan, with all his might, picked up his petite wife and carried her over his shoulders. Before Max and Bryan made their way back up the hill, Max took one final look at Cole.

Please save her.

Cole nodded, trying his best to let Max know that he could do it. That he could make everything right.

I will.

Cole now stood in the clearing with Foster who studied Cole, who kept his eyes closed as he strained himself searching for the pulse of Kate's mind. Cole remembered her touch, her eyes—the few times she had smiled at him. Slowly but surely, Cole became one with her brain until he cast out along her memory banks and traced the path she had taken. There was a flicker of Kate's mother and a sharp pang of guilt that wrapped tightly around Cole's head.

Cole opened his eyes and saw a wild-eyed Foster waiting in anticipation, holding his M4 at the ready.

"She's in a ditch, five hundred yards that way," he said pointing down the valley. "She's unconscious. The Savage has done something to her."

Foster was worried the Savage would catch him before he could get to her, but Cole intercepted these thoughts and threw them away like scrunched up paper, hastily reckoning, "Okay. Think of an egg, keep that image in your head and if he were to enter your mind, the egg will break. If I know the egg is broken I will rid you of his presence. I may have to control your mind at some point during all of this, but it is for our own survival." This relieved Foster and he was soon bolting off after Kate. For Cole, the whole business with the egg was just to calm Foster down, the idea of a figment of an egg alerting Cole to Foster's sense of mind rather over-elaborate compared to Cole simply telling Foster not to worry about it. He felt he had to make it sound more complicated than it actually was, to give it credence in his mind and Foster's.

This was all a moot point anyway. The Savage was much stronger than Cole, his mind more in tune with the gift each had bestowed upon them. Cole felt rusty, he had tried to avoid using it since the day his peace ended, and now it was weaker, cumbersome in its flexibility. Even if Cole could see that Foster was under the influence of the Savage, there may have been little he could do about it, especially from further away.

Now the only person left in the clearing, Cole set about searching for the Savage in his mind. It was hard going for him; he could only concentrate on one thing at a time at first, the pieces swooping like fish in a stream. He closed his eyes to help him focus, but this just made him feel naked—totally exposed to an attack if the Savage lurked nearby. Brushing aside this fear, his vision became a tunnel, picking up tiny thoughts the Savage had left scattered around the forest. It ranged from the introspective to acts of extreme brutality. A peaceful observation of a butterfly became violently intertwined with scenes of ritualistic sacrifice, rape and the bloody disposal of those who had fought him in this forest before. This included the Doc's son Daniel who had been told there was a bug in his brain he needed to kill.

Cole dug deeper, looking for a time when the Savage was not a savage, when he had a name before all this mess; but there was only darkness, memories the Savage had forgotten on purpose. There would be no reasoning with him. A sharp pain then shot through Cole's head and he left his trance. He clutched at his head in agony. His powers had withered in their self-imposed dormant state and now the Savage was fending off his incursions with great ease. The strain on Cole grew immense, his jaw clenching down hard. He had rarely used his powers in times of such stress and now up against a powerful enemy he felt hopeless once again. The lingering feeling that he was not a leader, not the hero, took a hold of him. He wanted to leave this place, to not make the hard decisions, to fall into Maddie's arms and forget. But he knew there was no going back and if he allowed what had happened in Trent to happen again; to allow death to come where it was in his power to prevent, then he was nothing, pathetic.

Cole dropped his rifle and sat down, trying to calm himself in the process. He threw away the negative thoughts that clogged his arteries—like the fact that he could've prevented all the deaths today—in order to save those that remained. Endless images of the forest flew through his mind. These images that he didn't recognize soon came to him at such a rate it felt as if he were watching a movie. Slowly but surely, the shrubs and thin trees became familiar to him. As his vision became one with the Savage, he saw him running higher along the plateau in the direction of Max and Bryan. The Savage was darting through his violent garden at a frenetic pace, the feel of something heavy in his hands. Cole tried to get *him* to look down but this seemed to catch the attention of the Savage who echoed *LEAVE US ALONE*! This stopped the vision completely. Cole stood quickly and sped off in the direction of the agile Savage. As he ran, he called for Foster in his mind. Foster was halfway upon reaching Kate when he received Cole's voice and instantly turned back for the clearing as soon as he heard it.

***

Bryan and Max had been hobbling down the hill, with Helen still unconscious and Maggie as stubborn as ever. Helen's weight bore down upon a tired Bryan who had to put her down every five minutes. Max wanted to help but his hands were tied up handling an aggressive child who feverishly bit his hands and hurled abuse at him worse than most adults. Max wanted to ask Bryan where his daughter learned such language, but instead opted for suggesting he knock her out just like Helen. Max then added it was in her best interest, hiding the fact he wanted to hit the little shit anyway. Bryan gave him a look that said: *this is my daughter you're talking about.*

"Fine," said Max, "it was only a suggestion."

"It's a shitty goddamn suggestion! What did you think I would say?"

"Well I don't know who taught her the word 'cunt'," replied Max.

Bryan threw his hands up in the air. "Are we really going to talk about this here? You're going to question my parenting skills while I try rescue my family from a telepathic madman in the woods?"

Max knew he was right; it was stupid to have this conversation here—besides, she probably learned it from TV.

"Let's keep going then," Max relented. Bryan agreed and, wiping the sweat from his brow, readied himself to pick up Helen, before the voice of Cole echoed through their minds at a weak frequency.

The Savage snuffed out Cole's words—but the warning was clear.

Max let go of the girl and raised his Kalashnikov while Bryan swung his Uzi in a frenzy of all directions. For them, behind each tree lurked a dangerous enemy. The sound of grunting foot-steps coming straight for them from all directions filled their ears as they studied the ground only to see everything remain dead still. Max fired back up the hill helplessly, praying he would hit the Savage by some random luck. Suddenly the sound of footsteps stopped for all but one pair, coming straight towards Max. He turned to fire but as he did a sharp pain ran through his trigger arm, paralyzing his fingers. He looked helplessly down at his dead hand, which clung to the gun in a clumsy manner. When Max looked back up, the Savage was upon him, and his last seconds of life, of knowing this world, was feeling the hard-swung hatchet tearing through his soft neck.

Bryan sprayed the Uzi hoping to hit the Savage but found his arms forced too high up in the air to hit nothing but tree branches above him. Before he knew it, his clip was dry. He scrambled to reload as the Savage reappeared from behind a tree, an evil grin of yellow fangs emerging from his shape-shifting face. He walked slowly towards Bryan, blood still dripping from the tip of his hatchet. Bryan's hands grew sweaty as he fumbled around to reload. He tried to place it back in its position, but as he did his sight became blurry. Everything then went dark for Bryan. In blindness he placed his hands forward, trying to detect an attack, but stood no chance as the Savage struck him down with the butt of the hatchet. Wincing through the pain and with tears running down his face, his last words were begged.

"Please, don't hurt them."

While Bryan did not see the busy hatchet come down on his life, Cole felt it break the innocent flesh as he hurdled himself toward the scene. In an instant, Cole saw the whole thing play out and he couldn't help think of what he could've done differently.

He could've reversed the hysteria put into Helen and Maggie, that way they would've made it to the car in time. He could've checked the location of the Savage before they had left. He could've told them he was an Illusionist from the start and they never would've gone into the forest. He could've told Maddie and the people of Trent the truth. He could've saved her. He made mistakes and people were killed. Was all this his fault?

Tears started to run from his eyes as he ran. They merged with the salty sweat. The sting of it was blinding, but it changed something within him; he felt the rage begin to take a hold. He wiped it all out from his eyes. Now his vision became more focused, his breathing more rhythmic. Below him the grass was soft and his feet seemed lighter, his legs given a jolt of energy. Cole could now feel the Savage and tweak the machinations of his gift while running at full tilt.

The Savage felt Cole coming at him like a freight train and left Helen and Maggie, sprinting across the hill away from Cole whilst Maggie declared her love for him in the growing distance. Over and over the Savage screamed in Cole's head to leave him alone. Cole switched his direction and came up with a plan. He left the Savage's head and entered Foster's.

"The Savage is flanking us. Turn to your right and be ready to shoot. He will be invisible, but I will make him appear at just the right moment." Foster had just passed the clearing and now dropped behind a clump of shrubs. He leant on one knee and aimed his rifle at the trees. If he didn't hit the Savage, it was game over for Kate and him. The sight of the gun shook as Foster's hands trembled under the pressure. He had no idea how Cole would reveal the Savage to him, let alone in time.

Cole had some idea—well, sort of. He'd seen the blinding, paralyzing, effect the Savage had poisoned Bryan with and figured he could apply something similar. He re-entered the

Savage's skin. The Savage tried to fight back by sending sharp pains throughout Cole's body, tried giving him fake heart attacks, shatter his will, scream in him all the mistakes he made—choke him with the past—but Cole's mind persisted through all of this, breaking through at every wall. Digging deep, Cole narrowed his thoughts to just one: a bright and blinding light illuminating the Savage's skin. He thought of every time a light had shined upon his face, bullying his pupils into tiny dots, smaller than a grain of sand. The light began to fill the Savage's entire body. It consumed every single pore, crevice, hair and freckle. In haste the Savage put all his power into ridding himself of this cursed light. It was in this distracted moment the Savage's invisibility left him, and upon seeing a flicker of light followed by his tanned body between the trees, Foster did not hesitate. The burst tore through the side of the Savage's stomach, sending him flying into the vegetation.

He yelped like a dog. Blood was coughed from his mouth. He felt at his wound, his fingers warmed and shaken by the blood that covered them. His eyes, if ever they existed, looked up through the canopy into the sky above, asking in ventriloquist rigor, *why have you allowed this?* As these words echoed through the forest and came to Cole and Foster, the righteousness in them shone through; *He has allowed it because it was just.* Seeing the Savage down—crawling scared, they now moved in for the kill. Foster stepped carefully toward the Savage who clawed further down the valley in Kate's direction.

Suddenly, two arrows flew through the forest, both striking Foster's heart. Foster gasped. His heart started to break down, to feel heavy. He struggled to breathe as he collapsed to the ground. As Cole made his way through the plateau he saw Foster lying there, clutching at his heart. He ran to him and lay down beside Foster whose body went into wild spasms. Foster's eyes were wide open as he stared at Cole while running his fingers against the wood of the arrows that breached his heart. He really believed he was dying. Cole hurriedly placed his hand over Foster's heart where the two arrows should have been. This confused Foster who struggled to come to terms with the fact the pain was all in his head. With a calming jolt from Cole, Foster's breathing slowed from its rasping ways.

Once making Foster realize he was going to live, Cole rose back to his feet and, with a cool head, set his gun sights in the direction of the Savage, who desperately crawled away through the brush. Cole scanned the ground in front of him, searching for the tiniest of movements only before the ground in front of him began to move in waves, coming to life in spasms of wriggles. The dirt started to breathe, a strange funneled sound escaping it. Cole's feet drew loose as they lost touch within its surging vibrations—his balance beginning to fail him. As Cole passed an oddly thick tree, the sight of the Savage scampering away from him came into view. Cole's gun swung up and found the center of the Savage's bare back. Cole squeezed the trigger and a flash of lead cracked through the air only to go directly through the Savage, who kept running off into the distance, completely unharmed. Cole's eyes opened wide in shock horror while a grinning Savage appeared from behind the tree and, with his last ounce of energy, swung his hatchet into the back of Cole's neck. The hatchet sliced through his neck as if it were thin air and hacked right into the thick tree, the blood-soaked head caught. The Savage gasped as Cole's body disappeared from right in front of him. Less than thirty yards away, a patient Cole softly exhaled his breath before popping the Savage's head like a watermelon. As the Savage's body slowly collapsed into a slump against the tree, all the tension in Cole was lifted, the rifle slipping effortlessly out of his exhausted reach.

It was over.

Cole slowly eased his whole body into the soft undergrowth, ready to relax all those bones that had been so heavy for too damn long. He yearned for rest; eager to just lie in the soft vegetation and let the insects and nature reclaim his spent energy, but his mind refused, the synapses in his brain now firing quicker than they had ever done before. He could see everything at once; all the tiny inputs of life passing through him like a busy highway. It urged his legs to get up, to take all of it in. It was the gift, infused into all his brain cells. Cole wept at this. No matter how hard he tried to hold it all back, keep it dormant, he knew it would always be there, waiting; an eternal hunger that needed satisfying.

25. Homecoming I

Standing over the Savage, lingering memories were slowly absorbed into Cole, as Cole caught the Savage's life flashing before his eyes. There were many questions the Savage had asked, yet even at such a peak of evolutionary engineering, could find no answer. The question of desire and its limitation filled the mind of Cole. Cole considered it for a moment; but passed it off as only some Buddhist quandary the Savage had toyed with. Besides, there were more pressing matters. The forest was quiet now, the brief periods of extreme violence subsiding under a peaceful drone of crickets. Many of the plants that the Savage had generated were now gone. To Cole's surprise, this saddened him. Seeing into the Savage's world in that brief flash, Cole had grown a fondness for the Savage's garden even he couldn't quite grasp.

Foster lay sat on the ground and stared at Cole when he reached him. Foster had many things to say, but felt that Cole knew them all. There was no going back for either of them. For the moment, Foster's eyes told that he did not want to talk, only to collapse into deep sleep. "Let's get Kate," Cole said, as he helped Foster up.

They made their way down the valley, calmed by the cool shade they felt on their backs. When Foster saw Kate he rushed to her side and checked to see if she was breathing.

"She's fine, well, alive," said Cole.

"What happened to her?" asked Foster, as he held her head and brushed away her ruffled hair. Cole stood in quiet contemplation for a moment before rousing his lips. "She's suffered some severe mental trauma. Her ankle is sprained and I think her collarbone has been shattered. She believes her mother tried to drown her. The Savage was playing on a childhood guilt she had once forgotten."

Foster stared into her face, annoyed he could not see into her worries like Cole, but grateful Cole was there to open such a window. He then remembered the tale of the catatonic sole survivor of the last expedition to these parts. He feared Kate could share the same fate, but Cole hushed such an idea before it was spoken.

"I will fix her, I promise, but for now we'll just get her back to Holdsworth and assess the damage there."

Foster was relieved and greatly comforted by this new Cole.

This relief would change when Foster asked about Max and Bryan.

Max.

Foster would swallow each tear. It would all be silent. A quiet despair of grief that would break like a tide when Foster allowed it; when the walls could withstand no more. But this was not now—it would be kept in until Foster was left lying in the dirt on the side of a road, broken and beaten from every angle. Standing in this forest now, the grave of many, Foster thought about everything else but it; a temporary agreement between the universe and he: that the death of Max, the death of a son, was not to be acknowledged—it couldn't possibly have occurred.

Because he knew who was really to blame.

A truth was unravelling slowly in the skin of John Foster.

They picked Kate up by her legs and shoulders (despite the likelihood of causing further injury) beginning a slow, dogged march up the valley back to the cars. Cole sent for the help of Helen and Maggie with Helen helping them carry Kate and the bodies of Bryan, Max, Jimmy, Kyle and Daniel. Despite her petite frame, Helen did most of the heavy lifting without fuss, all her bones and strength of will taking to Cole's task as if it were all she knew.

Cole made sure Foster didn't watch Max's lifeless body taken into the car with the others. Foster's eyes pointed outward, like a scared animal trying to sniff out greener grasses.

When it was done, Foster asked Cole if they should bring the Savage's body as well. Cole stopped instructing Maggie to collect the scattered rifles and walked over to the Savage's body. He watched the face become more human to him.

The Savage had been a white loner before the war, a misunderstood former resident of Holdsworth. His love of nature, the peaceful serenity it brought him, caused a radical desire to seek the comforts of another culture he believed to be more in tune with his love. It was only in having the gift he was able to externalize such an image. It wore him down to maintain it, to keep his manifestations of the forest running, and Cole saw this in the tiredness of his once-wired eyes, the dark rings a sign of the physical toll his induced hallucinations had on his body.

Watching him, Cole felt this would be the way of all Illusionists: the rapid expansion of the mind and the body's inability to withstand it. Limitless ability and unlimited desires would drive each Illusionist to their own death in the end. They would never be content with the reality they made for themselves.

"Leave him," said Cole, his voice emanating a slight sympathy. "The others will come through here to search for the remains of their loved ones later. They will deal with the Savage, though I have a feeling they will find him strangely underwhelming in this state."

When they had finished loading up Bryan's car with the bodies of the recently departed, Cole offered to drive Bryan's car, as his body could easily block out the thoughts of riding with the dead. As Helen and Maggie made their way into Daisy, Foster took Cole aside.

"What are you going to do about Kate?" he whispered, an unease of anticipation creeping into his voice.

"I haven't figured it out yet, but I'm sure I can reverse the damage; maybe wipe those memories and replace them with happier ones. It'd be like she never went into this forest."

Foster waited for Cole to finish, but only to rephrase his own question. "I mean, will you show her who you really are?"

Cole was taken aback, unsure of what to say.

Foster pressed on, a hint of nervousness in his voice that left Cole confused. "Look, I know you have the gift to make her accept you, but if you don't do that and you just tell her you're an Illusionist, she will never forgive you. She will blame you for everything that has happened to…Max and the others. I need you to understand this, because I know what I stand for. People, our friends especially, should be given the power of free will—that makes them who they are. I know you think this too, that's why you didn't tell us, because it would have changed how we felt about you and you would have bent our wills reluctantly. But this time… I'm asking you, for your own sake—and mine too—that you make her accept it, forcefully, if that's what it takes. It must be done, in order to preserve her sanity and trust in us. You've got to do it for the both of us…"

Foster's last words puzzled Cole at first, yet the more he thought about it, the more something grew within him, a fact Cole had hidden from himself the day he met Foster. He'd been so caught up in believing his own lies that he missed the straight-arrow truth that was right there all this time. All those looks Foster had given Cole, those glances seeking approval before they did anything rash…

Cole's eyes lit up in shock. They were open and reeling, lost for words. There it was, out in the open, the cruel truth: Foster had already known Cole was an Illusionist. Their meeting was not by chance.

As this all came to Cole, as Foster knew it finally would, Foster walked away, his head in shame as the guilt bore in. When Cole told Kate, Foster's knowledge of the fact would become known and she would never trust Foster ever again. She would hate him with every bone in her body. Cole now understood why Foster pushed so hard for them to go into the forest. He swallowed his mouth, trying to hold back the rage.

"You…YOU knew what I was and you used me for your own fucking war! You used me—just like Peter!"

In between the retching anguish, with his back turned to Cole, Foster blurted, "It was the right thing to do! *It was the right thing to do…*"

Cole wanted to crush Foster's throat. He wanted to so badly that Foster began to feel the invisible fingers of Cole wrap around his neck and choke him. Foster dropped to his knees, clutching at his throat, unable to plead for mercy. He then fell backwards, and upon seeing the pain in Foster's face, Cole stopped short of taking his life. He'd seen enough of that today.

There were obvious questions to be asked, questions that would keep any person up, completely obsessed with finding the answers, but today had been too much for Cole; his sponge wrung thoroughly dry. He just wanted to sleep and felt he had the power to do so. He had the rest of his days to ask those questions, and such a time would come tomorrow.

Once Foster had recovered his breath he moved dejectedly to Daisy. Realising there was nothing more to say for now, Cole dragged himself over to Bryan's car and followed Foster back to Holdsworth.

***

They had been watching the forest with their binoculars and their telescopes since noon. As the sun dropped in the sky, the movement of two cars along the road filled the guard who first saw them with giddy excitement. By the time they had rolled up to the front gate the entire town had crowded behind sandbags, eagerly anticipating the news they waited on edge to hear.

While the Doc and Renko remained grounded, setting up defensive positions lest it be a cunning trap, there was not a single person amongst the crowd that didn't think the tyranny was over; they wanted to believe it true, make it true with the sheer weight of their combined will. Floodlights now illuminated the street as the sun began to disappear. As their cars rolled up, the guards became shadows to Cole, surrounding the car, looking in to see who made it while the steel gates opened up. Both cars stopped in front of the crowd, held back by struggling guards relying on the heavy sandbags they kept getting pressed into. The buzz in the air was electric, the full expectation of praising returning warriors like in the times of ancient Rome.

Cole felt Foster leaving his car and did the same. They were both hit with the blinding burn of the floodlights. The crowd set itself, ready to hear the words that would set them free. Helen and Maggie stayed in the car, scared and confused, Cole having not yet snapped them from a trance since Helen was sent to work carrying the bodies.

Fighting through the oppressive lights, Foster turned around trying to see Cole, whose reignition of his gift left him feeling overwhelmed. Cole now saw more than just the faces of the crowd. All at once their names, their memories, hopes, fears and dreams became open to him. He felt and heard each heartbeat and with each beat his own became faster. While the crowd only produced hushed murmurs now, Cole could hear much more as the thoughts of everyone collected in his ears, piling on and suffocating him. Cole leaned heavily against the side of the car, barely keeping upright.

He wanted only silence, and in an instant, it came to fruition. Like a switch, the murmurs and the thoughts all became mute; the floodlights were dimmed and time became frozen.

Foster saw Cole was in distress and raised his hands to calm the now robotic crowd. He looked back at Cole, whose cheeks had turned a bright puffy red. He asked for Cole to give the crowd his attention, to which Cole weakly obliged. The crowd's eyes now turned to Foster in an eerie synchronized fashion, his hands still raised.

"The Savage is dead!" Foster shouted. As he spoke, Cole released his grip on the people.

There was no confetti, no absolute hurrah of gratitude. There was only a tired relief, released in long outpourings of breath, as it slowly dawned on them that they could rest easy. They could finally rest.

But this was not how Foster expected them to react.

He expected confetti. He expected yells of howling love, roaring out his name in his victory. He had met their hopes and he wanted to see the fire light up in their eyes. Grand expectations more befitting the war he had just fought for them.

And without realising that the hands of Cole were still temporarily his own, he got his wish.

Their eyes lit up, every single pair, and Foster felt the surge before it had happened. The crowd roared—confetti sprayed out like fire from their mouths—filling the air with colorful joy. It all reminded Foster of a homecoming celebration before he was swept and surrounded by his new fans. They grabbed him, patted him on the back while cheering his name, and in the midst of it all he caught a glimpse of what Cole feared: A power beyond one's wildest dreams that would consume everything they knew. Adoration; love—all now artificially inserted into a reality that was once only imagined, but accepted all the same. They shoved drinks in his face, told him he was their hero; that they owed him everything.

It was only for a moment, this grand surge—this tiny taste of Cole's gift. And while Foster feared its dizzying heights, the feeling was instantly missed the second it left him.

Foster then watched as the Doc made his way through the fanatical people who now began to hug each other and celebrate with other loved ones. The Doc's face remained emotionless, there were to be no congratulations shown to Foster. They shook hands, but the Doc's expression remained like stone. "Where are the others?"

Foster was annoyed that the Doc hadn't truly acknowledged their great victory, but he refocused on Kate. "Kate is unconscious, and Helen and Maggie are still under some sort of trance, so you've got be careful with them."

When he heard that Helen and Maggie were alive, the Doc's face perked up, only to be struck down again when he asked about Bryan and the others. Foster said nothing; he didn't have to. The Doc then ordered his nurses and assistants to take the rattled survivors to the Great White Tent. Foster then scanned through the blurred masses of people for Cole, but couldn't see him. With tired feet, Foster followed the Doc over to the Great White Tent.

The Great White Tent was split into two sections: a general space that included the makeshift bar and meeting hall, and the hospital that filled up the opposite wing of the tent. Foster maintained a close proximity as he watched Kate being stretchered into the large hospital room, while Helen and Maggie stuck together and walked at their own pace, fearfully conscious of their bright surroundings. The hospital was one giant room of twenty or so beds, crammed in tight. A light cloth separated each bed, giving the patient's the barest of visual privacy. Over in the far corner a few more private blocks were held, their walls assembled from what looked like cubicle dividers. Kate was taken to one of these while Helen and Maggie were herded into another next door to Kate. Foster watched from the door as her meek body was switched onto the hospital bed before being fixed up to a machine and put on a drip. When the Doc had finished, he came up to Foster, and suggested they talk in his office. Foster asked if Kate was going to be fine, and with the Doc's reassurance that she was stable, he agreed to talk.

They left the hospital in silence, savoring their words for when they entered the room. From within the crowd of frenetic partiers, a line of stretchers bearing body bags broke out. The lead man, Fleming the mortician, saw the Doc and confirmed that he would examine them in the morgue later.

Outside the large three-story compound, the young man who had first led them to the Doc's office greeted them. He rejoiced in the presence of Foster and lamented the fact he could not fully celebrate that night because he was taking the frontline defense shift in the morning. "But I'll face that forest tomorrow with little fear thanks to you, boss!" he revealed in admiration.

Foster smiled and thanked him for his exuberance, politely declining to retell the events of the day. When they made their way into the Doc's office, the Doc turned on the lamp in his desk before closing the door.

"Drink?" he offered.

"That'd be great, thanks," Foster grunted, easing as best he could into the foldout chair.

The Doc opened a drawer in his desk and produced two glasses and a cheap bottle of whiskey. "You'll have to forgive me. This is all I have here. All those fine luxuries like a good scotch were all drunk up, with not a single thought of appreciating their value. Just pissed away in the first few months when people really did think it was the end…"

He poured Foster his glass and Foster leaned forward to receive it, sipping it with a tepid face. The Doc then continued.

"Of course, it was not the end. Here we are sixteen months later, still surviving, breathing the air of freedom we once took for granted, only by running away from the nightmares that are the Controllers and their armies. Yet you sit here, having walked into the very heart of the hornet's nest and slain the hornet when we could very well consider you and I as both ants in comparison. It begs the question, how? How did you do as you have so claimed you would?" Foster ran his fingers through his graying hair, his eyes fixed on the Doc's. He shrugged his shoulders, still strained by the Doc's incessant nature.

"I don't understand this animosity directed at my group. Sure, we lost people, friends of yours and friends of mine. People *very* dear to me…but through their sacrifice we were able to kill a great scourge that has plagued these lands."

The Doc was growing impatient. Foster was stalling, unsure of what would happen if he revealed their greatest weapon.

"My animosity is well justified. I feel the need to assuage my fears that we aren't just swapping one tyrant for the other. I'm grateful for the service you have done. I've lost many men in that forest, not just with you, and I think I am entitled to know what made your trip so…successful. I think we both know there is only one thing that kills a Controller…"

Foster held off on answering. He knew exactly what the Doc wanted him to admit. Instead he went a different way.

"Your son, Daniel, we found his body."

The Doc was shocked. The mere mention of the name was a slap that woke every fiber in him. His muscles tensed as he stared to choke up; the hanging cloud of his son's fate finally dissipating with the winds of closure, something he believed he would never find. In this moment, Foster saw the Doc's human side break through that calm and composed face he put on for the town every single day he had to. Seeing the Doc break down, not as the head of a community, but as a father, moved Foster. Foster immediately regretted the way he'd broke it to him so coldly. He knew what it was to be torn up inside not knowing the fate of your children. Foster decided to tell him about Cole. He told him about how he found Cole in Trent with two bodies—Cole's lover and best friend—and despite all this, defended his innocence because he knew that Cole was only misguided. As Foster spoke this, he couldn't hide the hypocrisy in his words, defending an Illusionist, but he knew this only scratched the surface.

"Cole doesn't want to cause harm. That's why he was there, in the middle of nowhere. He isn't like the others, those maniacs on the West Coast. I could tell he was lying about the bodies, but his remorse; it was so real, so believable."

The Doc's tears were wiped away by this point and his tone was back to business.

"That's probably what he wanted you to think!" he exclaimed, reaching for the walkie-talkie on his desk. Bursting upright, his face pouring out violent heat, Foster slammed the talkie back to the desk, recoiling the Doc's fingers. "Look! I trust him. He didn't keep it from me. He kept it from himself!"

"How did you know then?" spat the Doc.

Foster walked away. "He was scared to use his powers; he fears them the same way I do, scared he might turn out like one of the others. Don't you see? His reluctance for all of this is what saves him. I've seen him fight the evil. He means well."

"So you suggest we side with the good ones and discard the bad? Have you forgotten that what we consider good and bad is seeded from their manipulation! You of all people—wanting to lead the Resistance against all Illusionists—and yet you are willing to compromise when it comes to Cole just because he shares your ideas about free will. You've seen him fight evil? You must know that Illusionists kill each other all the time. They are the natural competitors of each other to attain more control!"

Foster turned around to face the Doc, whose rant had left him breathing heavy.

"Where is Cole now?" The Doc demanded to know.

Foster was perplexed. The Doc seemed ready to expel Cole from Holdsworth, but they both knew he could do nothing if Cole said no. "What are you going to do with him?" asked Foster.

"I only want to talk to him… If he is as you say he is, then he will be able to be reasoned with." Foster reluctantly agreed, but admitted he had not seen Cole since they were swarmed with the townsfolk. "I'm sure we will find him when he wants us to," is all Foster said, before he left for Bryan's place, everything in him exhausted. The front door was locked so Foster broke in through the window. He checked to see if Cole was there and when Foster found no one he hit the mattress like a ton of bricks.

26. Aftermath

Foster awoke the next day, guided by the presence of a sombre Cole who beckoned Foster in a dreamlike state to meet him by the river. Just as Foster was collecting his senses, there was a knocking on the front door. Foster threw the covers off his bed and scampered over. The Doc waited at the door alone. His face was uneasy as his feet paced back and forth along the porch. "You felt it too, right?"

"Yeah."

The Doc led Foster through the quiet town, all its inhabitants nursing the bruises of heavy celebrating. When they reached the mesh fence border, it was only just ticking over to nine-thirty in the morning. The guards standing by the gate were the first people they saw. The Doc moved to explain himself, but the guards were already opening the gate before he said anything. As they walked passed, the Doc looked into the eyes of each of the two guards standing at attention at each end of the heavy gate, both staring off into the distance as if no one was home.

"Is Cole doing this?" The Doc asked Foster, who was still

trying to rub the sleep from his eyes.

"Probably."

They walked for a short time along a road of abandoned houses with burnt-out cars lying about every few blocks. They didn't speak, Foster content to just absorb the disheveled shells of what used to house life, assured they were drifting effortlessly towards a waiting Cole. They found him on the other side of a hill, sitting next to a small bridge; the scenery of suburban remains replaced by dead yellow grass and leafless trees. Cole did not turn to greet them, his eyes observing the weak trickle of a small river on the verge of running dead dry. They watched on as Cole's mind played with what water still remained, bubbled letters dancing about to produce the word *"Cole"* in the water for a few restless seconds before the tiny stream would shake it all away like a computer glitch, only for his name to slowly return again, the glitch in an endless repeat.

"There was no need to bring a gun, Doc. I have no intention of harming you or your people."

The Doc's cheeks flushed in embarrassment as Foster looked at him in surprise. The gun was concealed but remained utterly useless.

"Then what are your intentions?"

Cole turned to look at both of them, his face drawn in bitter conflict with itself.

"That's the million dollar question, isn't it? It wasn't that long ago I had only myself to look out for. What I did had no consequences but for me alone. Now it seems everything I do affects everyone. I know I can't run away from this anymore, it's just a question of finding the right direction… There is something inside me that feeds from it, needs to feel more of it. Ever since I killed the Savage, it has come flooding back to me all too willing. I can feel its eagerness to take over once more, and now that it has tasted blood, I fear that it will be completely different to the way I understood it in Trent… There's something else, too. I've seen the Savage's life flash before my eyes. I've learned his instincts, and sometimes I feel his urges, as if they were my own. My mind is becoming the weapon you pushed me to be, Foster, and now I'm scared I may never be able to turn it off."

Both the Doc and Foster grew uneasy, believing they were witnessing a transformation to a darkened mind, a path that many Illusionists took in the end as they threw countless mind-controlled slaves at their enemies to wipe each other out as these slaves spouted off about the great divine will of their leader.

They watched on in horror, as the water from the river in front of Cole became an intense, thick layer of blood, bubbling away at the surface ready to boil—before a face, the one Foster recognized as Peter Storrs shimmered upon the surface of the water. The Doc noticed Cole's body tensing up, a silent explosion playing out in him before it eased up, and as Cole finally came to relax, the bloodied water of the river slowly subsided back into its normal form.

"It's funny. Every day without exception I see her face. I see it in mirrors, in the sky, when I close my eyes. I even see her in other people's faces, if only for a moment. I saw her in Kate. It is the only remaining image of a perfect day where the sun shone in just the right way and made her curly hair glisten. I had the gift then, but in that moment I'm certain I didn't use it. There was no need. It was perfect all by itself. And then her face becomes *his*, and *he* smiles. It is not the smile I knew growing up, but the one I saw on his last day, sinister in every inch. We knew each other since we were little kids. He was always the cool one; the one everyone looked up to, the one I always followed. He would always be full of these great ideas that we'd recklessly explore before laughing for hours on end about our great intentions becoming laughable failures…"

Cole paused. He was smiling, but knew the next part would take it away just as quick as it came.

"When the Illusionists first appeared and Peter found out I was one of them, he took charge of a group, including Maddie and myself, leading us through the carnage of Denver until we ended up in Trent. I resented using my powers, but Peter was persistent in asking for me to help him lead the group, swaying them his way when he felt it necessary. It was strange, the more he asked of me, the more it fed his own belief that *he* actually had the gift. I knew he was becoming this way, his ego growing beyond measure. I told myself; if I was the one who did this to him, I could just as easily cut him down a peg. But I never did. I just let him run… There were eight girls in our group and while most of them had boyfriends and husbands Peter still slept with most of them and then made me assuage their partner's anger if they found out. They were all devoted to him by the end—even Maddie—but despite his intentions I never allowed him to touch her in any way…" Cole stopped. The way he talked of such things made it seem like this was years ago, not just a few excruciating days.

"Like a child that only wants what it can't have, he pined for her. One day, on a chilly afternoon he asked me to fetch some firewood. We had been caught out due to a cold snap. I didn't have the energy to warm the group's bodies psychologically so I agreed; thinking the short walk to the woods would keep me warm. As I walked, I sensed something was wrong. I tried not to believe what I felt was happening as Peter made his way to Maddie who sat on the swings of the playground by the grassy knoll. I kept walking to the woods, blocking out his thoughts that confronted me with the raw nerve of it all. I told myself I was just imagining things, just paranoid, some kind of stupid excuse for my inaction. He started to grab her, force himself on her right there on the swings. She pleaded with him to stop, tried to push him away. They both fell to the ground, her scream sending me running back. When he reached for his gun I knew I had held out too long. I tried to stop him with my gift, but he was too far-gone. If he couldn't have her, he wasn't going to let me. The gun went off and the pain shot through me as I felt her heart collapse.

"Just like that. No more…

"By the time I made it to the playground everyone had surrounded her, looking at Peter, expecting him to explain why she had to die. When I locked eyes with him, he gave me that *fucking* smile. That smile that said he was convinced beyond a doubt I would forgive him. That he would tell me it was all right and that I would accept it, just like that. *Just like that, just like that…* I remember my hands clenched up and tears were streaming out of me. I held out my hand and Peter, still smiling, handed me the gun. I didn't hesitate like I had before. I shot him. I shot him in the head, and everyone backed away…

"Oh, they wanted me dead, you should have seen…

"They saw *me* as the monster. But the longer they thought about it—the more it dwelled in those brainwashed heads of theirs—this feeling crept among their surface that something had fundamentally changed. It was this tiny, infant doubt that had always been picking away at them like it had been doing to me, that just exploded into this gigantic truth that was now banging on the doors of their souls, demanding to be screamed into them. I didn't have to say a thing and yet they came to understand the way I felt. They saw Peter for all that he was: a puppeteer I let out of the box. The warmth and all the love they experienced now just seemed like it was manufactured cheap—all of it just this big fucking lie. They would forever look up at the clouds and be reminded of everything I had done for them, but know it was all bullshit—the faces that smiled at them in the clouds would do so no longer… In an instant, paradise had been taken away from them. They pinched themselves, taking in a coldness that grew deeper than the weather. The memories of all the bloodshed they had endured in the war; the hangings we witnessed in the sub-urbs, all those memories I had kept from them now came back, covering their skin, hanging under their noses with the stench of death. It was too much for Ashton. The shock gave him a heart attack. Kelly was a doctor, but it proved no good. He was dead within minutes."

Foster and the Doc sat down on the dry grass; Cole's retelling having placed them in Trent as if they were standing right in the crowd that day.

"How old was he, this Ashton?" asked the Doc, calculating as to whether such an incident would repeat itself whenever the truth of an Illusionist was revealed to weaker hearts.

"He was only forty-two," replied Cole.

Foster thought back to when he first met Cole. At that stage, the street of Trent was completely empty. "Where did they all go?"

Cole shrugged, the disappointment clear in his voice.

"Most of them headed west to join the Purification Front.

When the warmth left their bodies and reality hit, they all begged me, some of them on their hands and knees to make it better, return things to normal. They didn't give a shit whether it was Peter or me. They were too attached to this world of controlled happiness to go back to the old times, where they had to think and fend for themselves. When they knew I would never do that, all they were left to feel was losing Maddie, the guilt. The darkness that hung in my heart would spread to them and take us all down. So they went west, to fall under another spell. To taste a simple, happy, mindless existence once more."

There was silence as they all pondered what Cole's failure had meant for all their futures. Even with his best intentions everything he had done to help the group in Trent had turned to complete shit. It spurned the belief that no Illusionist could produce or maintain the peaceful outcome they intended. And yet despite this, it still it remained; that nagging quality of all humans that was the source of any spirit. Hope. *Cole was young. He could mature. He could get better…*

The Doc picked himself up, brushing off the grass that clung to his pants before turning the head of Cole who watched him, eager for him to make his case, to compel him to stay.

"Now I know Foster wants you to follow him on some cross-country crusade to liberate us all from the tyranny of other Illusionists, and that is all well and good, but I don't think it's really what *you* want, and I don't believe it's a plausible path. Most people will only learn through pain what matters most to them. Cole, Trent is yours to learn from. This town needs you, not as a fighter but as a healer. You can make a difference here, a real one. All the other Illusionists—the power hungry—they dream so big their own sense of reality becomes too distorted and they crash. The one problem we always blamed for the war's beginning was that the Illusionists could not satisfy themselves enough, they always wanted more. I believe there is hope if you use your gift sparingly. You can make a smaller—but real—difference here. Stay with us, Cole. Learn the art of limiting the negative effects of your condition. I can help you if you let me."

Cole absorbed this offer and daydreamed the rest of his life in Holdsworth. Settle down and try start again with Kate. Maybe have kids. Carve out a peaceful existence for his fellow townsfolk and slyly deter any unwanted traveling armies from finding Holdsworth. It could be just like Trent he reasoned, the old times only better managed. Cole knew it wasn't right to only help these people and ignore the pleas of others who ran or died at the hands of the Illusionists, but the Doc was right, he was but one man, and he saw no wrong with trying to enjoy however long his life remained.

He looked over at Foster and regarded his weary eyes and cracked lips. Foster was just as worn down as Cole was. Sure, he'd huff and puff his chest up about the Resistance, but he was getting old and inside he just needed to slow down, retire. Still, Foster was going to go to Chicago, because he had to know...

Foster cleared his throat, ready to ask Cole to see this journey out with him—only to have Cole cut him off.

"I know you have to go to Chicago," Cole muttered to Foster. "I know you have to go because your son is there. Matthew."

Foster was taken aback. The very mention of the name...

"What's he talking about?" The Doc asked as Foster stood frozen, the truths he held deep within him now tumbling out in the light breeze.

"There is no Resistance. No cure that he so professed about

finding. Foster's son is in Chicago," said Cole.

"How do you know this?" The Doc asked Foster, who was still lost for words.

"Because his son is like me, he's an Illusionist." said Cole.

Now Foster was back in his cave, taken back to the time he'd heard that soft voice, barely a whisper one morning many months ago while he brooded over striking back at these cold-blooded tyrants that had stripped him of everything. He was dismantling his rifle and putting it back together for the millionth time, his focus twitchy as he dreamed of finally using it on one of them. But then there was that voice, soft yet commanding, the tone he recognized as his son, Matthew. The voice beckoned him to go to Chicago but Foster had refused; too scared and not convinced enough that it was real, that it wasn't just a trick of the brain.

He didn't hear that voice again for a long time. And while he tried to pass it off as his own imagination, in his spare time he would map out routes that could lead him to his son once more. When that voice returned, many months later, his concerns over making it there alive were dispelled.

Foster trembled. "He said: *Find a broken man in the town of Trent. He will guide you to Chicago, where I will fix you both.*"

"I know what he said," bickered Cole, thoroughly incensed that he may have been no more than a babysitter for this family reunion.

"And?"

"I think I am fixed." Cole triumphed. Without saying it, he gave Foster two choices; stay here or go there, but don't bring the rest of Holdsworth into your troubles. For a long time there was a silence only Foster and Cole understood.

"I have to see my son. I just have to know," Foster eventually chose; a choice Cole had already known he would make. His gift was growing back much quicker than he thought and in this knowledge he sulked. First it would be reading thoughts, then controlling conversations, behavior, and eventually beliefs. He'd seen too many dark, twisted things in this life, and he knew Chicago and its violent palette would send the gift's insatiable taste further beyond into the darkness.

Each passing second was sending Cole further and further into staying in Holdsworth, it was the only chance to reverse his slide into the black maw. It was the new light with the familiar warmth.

"So be it. I wish you all the best," Cole replied with utter indifference.

Foster was distraught. They had been to hell and back and this was their goodbye? He had to console himself. Of course Cole was still bitter, and to be honest, Foster was expecting a physical outburst from Cole. He'd half expected the dying water of the river to rise like a snake and tear out his soul for the lies and the blood that now covered his hands.

But nothing came of it.

The Doc was fast in interrupting their cold and awkward farewell, asking Cole what his first order of business would be.

"I'm ready to start the healing, first of all with Kate."

***

The night they killed the Savage, Cole was screaming at the star-filled sky, trying to tear it apart, repeating over and over between the spit, "I'm just a fucking kid. I'm just a fucking kid."

***

Inside the Great White Tent the air was much cooler, the constant drumming of the once abundant comfort that was air condition-ing the only sound besides the odd errant cough. As the Doc led them past each patient lying in their beds, he began to give Cole the rundown of the litany of issues Cole was able to fix; a man dealing with his paralysis, a woman left distraught by a still-birth—before the Doc stopped himself short, realizing Cole was still a work in progress who would need time to get into the thick of things.

Cole assured him it was okay, that he would pick it up quick-ly; such was the nature of his gift.

"Once it's all in motion, the tide will have no break wall this time," he said with a heavy heart. When they reached Kate's room, Cole asked to see her alone. Before he opened the door, Foster's hand grabbed at his arm.

"Think about what I talked about. You aren't doing her or yourself any favors if you let her react her own way. Let yourself make her accept it. It's the only way for a clean start."

Cole looked at Foster as if to ask why he wasn't in Chicago already, yet Foster's advice still stood there, a clear possibility—though to Cole the easy way out.

"You could've told them long ago, Foster. But you were too scared. You wanted to keep them angry, just like you, because deep down you didn't want to go peacefully. Look how that turned out…"

Foster's eyes immediately drew away, before dropping his head in shame.

Cole's face clenched up, and he swallowed down the pressure that was building up in him. "A clean start can only happen if I tell her the truth. She deserves to know. We have to accept that it'll take time for her to forgive us."

Before he could back out of his decision, Cole briskly walked into her room alone; ready to reveal his true self to Kate for the first time. The room was thick with her odor, a scent that was more familiar when she called her home a series of cave systems. Kate opened her eyes as the door behind Cole shut.

"Sorry if I woke you," he spoke softly and carefully, his words already brimming with nervousness, but she paid no mind.

"No, it's okay," Kate smiled at him. "The nurse says you guys killed the Savage, it's unbelievable!" Her voice had perked up and he knew she would start asking for the details she had missed. His nerves began to freeze up—he wasn't as ready as he thought he was. Cole thought of trying to shy away from it, working his way up to it.

It should've been simple. He knew the words that could make it right, and yet looking into her eyes, feeling his body quiver, Cole could only draw a blank, before inexplicably letting the stupid out from his fumbling breath. He asked her what she remembered from the day. There wasn't even a *how are you feeling*.

Taking his question in earnest, Kate tried to remember and as she struggled to grasp its elusive nature—it dawned on Cole that her own mind had already blocked out those memories, the ones he had replayed to himself dozens of times over among all the other trains of thought that passed his station that day. As Cole thought about those memories Kate's brain had fogged out, his face became transfixed in one twitching motion. Kate started to frown, but it was not in confusion, more as if she were seeing what he saw in her that day. She began to tremble all over. First it was her lips, and then her whole head before it shivered down into her arms and legs. Cole stepped back. He had unintentionally re-transmitted Kate's mother drowning her in the tub back to Kate. Cole was lost for words—he hadn't meant to do that, he couldn't understand it. Nothing in this situation had gone to plan.

"No, no, no…" she started to utter before her bed became the pure white porcelain bath she found herself in back in the wicked forest. Kate started to scream as Cole frantically lifted her from the bed that filled with muddy water. He emptied his head and the bath disappeared while Kate fell on top of him against the weak wall, taking her drip tube with her. The door swung open immediately, the Doc and Foster running into the room, standing over the top of Cole and Kate.

"IT'S FINE!" Cole yelled. "It was only a flashback." *Only?*

The Doc was confused. "You haven't told her yet?" he questioned in his abrupt manner.

"Not yet, I was working up to it—or at least I was trying to. Fuck, I don't know what happened!"

Kate looked at Cole, confused. "Wait, tell me what?"

Cole turned back to Kate. He tried to slow his breathing, to keep it together. He held her hands, summing up the courage to tell her how he killed the Savage, killed his best friend and was responsible for losing the best thing that ever happened to him. But just like before, his mind did the talking before he could. As it happened Cole was struck by an inability to comprehend why this kept happening but the more he looked back on it, there was something about Kate that made her special, something that connected them. It was a worn-down guilt that made them fucked up together. It was a guilt that needed to be shared. He had never told Maddie about his gift, and this was something he needed to rectify with Kate.

In a lightning flash Kate saw it all and then some. Her hands clenched harder on Cole's as a trembling rage boiled within her. Kate's hands shook as she saw what happened in the forest (mainly Cole's inability to act) and finally understood why he had tried to tell her she didn't have to go into the forest, the words setting off thunderous jolts of molten clarity in her head. She watched like a fly on the wall Cole's most intimate moments with Maddie in Trent, his reluctance and eventual reliance on his gift to make her happy in the sick world that surrounded them. Kate saw him beginning to feel the same feelings he held for Maddie forming for herself—but such a fact was useless now as it all summed up to one thing: Max was dead.

Max was dead and Kate was too late to realize her own feelings.

Max was dead and Cole was the closest to blame. Kate broke free of Cole's grip and started swinging, Cole's arms meekly blocking her frenzied rage—the pain of her injuries momentarily forgotten. Tears swelled from her eyes as she kept repeating, *"Why, why, why did you do this?"* She moved from his body to his face, striking at his nose and lips till blood ran from them. Foster and the Doc wanted to hold her back, but Cole willed them not to, believing Kate needed to get this deserved fury out of her system. Kate stopped striking at his face, but then threw her hands around his neck, ready to squeeze. He looked into her heart to see if she would do it. She wasn't going to stop. Her hate for him bore down like the hottest of the sun's rays; burning his skin the further he struggled through her hate. When Cole could take it no more, when those nails dug fiendishly too far into his trachea, he did as Foster had suggested in the first place, zapping a calming wave throughout Kate's body. Her nerves went dead as the grip around his neck loosened.

Foster, the Doc and any nurse tall enough to peek through the open door watched in astonishment as a smile emerged from her once stricken face, the blood in her cheeks fading unnaturally quick.

"I'm sorry I hit you," said Kate. "I understand now why you feared telling us. I will get over this, because I think I'm falling for you," she put bluntly to Cole in words he knew, because he pulled all the strings to make those robotic gestures spout from her mouth and make her believe them all the same. While it wasn't ideal (the very fact that he'd succumbed to Foster's advice churned him inside), the violent anger had subsided for the moment, a gasping Cole reasoning that he would have to release it from Kate in controlled amounts until she would come to forgive him in a neutral sort of way.

The tension off his mind, Cole picked Kate up and helped her back onto the bed. Her eyes closed, ready for sleep as a slight smile lifted her face. He then looked at the Doc and Foster, the relief clear in their faces. A squeamish nurse behind them in the corridor screamed in shock, "Oh my god he's one of them!" before fainting whimsically into the arms of her peers.

Standing there, rocked by his unintended release, Cole tried to go back to his day dreaming of his future in Holdsworth. He needed to reassure himself what he did—and what he was going to do—was right. And in his fruitful daydreaming, the prospect of peace spread slowly but surely throughout the hospital. Other patients joined in Kate's peaceful smile, some humming soft tunes of summery days. It really did seem like the beginning of a new chapter, an aftertaste covering the already jovial spirits of the people now that the Savage was dead.

Cole kept his hold on Kate's hand, and as he did this, like he had done when he heard her story, a warmth was transferred, but it was not Cole's doing. Now the room was only her hand, and Cole was gripped. Watching Kate in the last moments before sleep took her, Cole was left floored—blindsided by a thought that left him wondering. For every time he'd looked at Kate Brewer, he'd seen another person, a girl with curls that were curtains to her smile—standing beneath the skin, hiding in the eyes.

So Cole blinked.

And then he saw Kate for the first time.

It washed over him. His eyes boggled. He drew a breath, the cleanest one yet, and he fell to his knees as he buried his head into Kate's chest. Her eyes still closed, she hugged him, softly repeating, "*It's okay, it's okay.*" And in those words he felt an ocean of peace, for he believed her. This feeling would carry them through.

It would all be temporary, of course. There would be no peace for Cole, not if the world had its way. In an instant the cocking of a rifle shattered the tranquility they had just dreamed up. It was two hundred yards away, outside one of the eastern gates into Holdsworth. The guards, watching from the windows of the border houses were taken by complete surprise at the convoy of black SUVs that appeared out of thin air against a lifeless horizon of open ground. The convoy had already stopped in a defensive formation before some of the watchmen had time to reach for their weapons or even know they would have to do so. By the time Cole had felt the cocking of the rifle by one of the many armed-men from the convoy, the confused shouting quickly escalated into gunfire.

Breaking from Kate's intimate scent, Cole led Foster and the Doc quickly to the gate, joining up with other guards who were rushing to get there. The exchange had only lasted for a few seconds and by the time they had reached the scene, one of the guards, the teenager who had shown them to the Doc's room when they first arrived—the kid in oversized police uniform— had been shot in the chest and was fast bleeding out next to the upstairs window of the house that overlooked the gate.

Cole kept calm, the storm in him holding beneath the skin. "The kid is dying, Doc. He's upstairs in that house, go and save him while I deal with this."

As the Doc ran into the house Cole walked up to the gate, scanning the people of the convoy until he found their leader. He motioned for the guard nestled behind the sandbags next to him to open the gate. The guard did as he was told. Cole strode confidently toward the convoy, his stern face causing every armed member of the unwelcomed guests to tremble each time he took a step closer. Cole stopped only ten yards from the cars positioned like an arrow pointing away from the gate, ready to send them back to wherever the hell they came from.

"You have spilt blood and now you cannot enter this place. Leave now or I will kill each of you, one by one, slowly."

Silence hung in the thick morning air, making itself known again after the bullets had made their screams. The men of the convoy all wore the same black military garb, and if their explicit single mind scared Cole, he didn't show it.

In a flash, one of the men broke focus; his itchy trigger finger believing it was quicker than Cole counted. He was wrong. The man's rifle was swung upwards to his own chin, Cole freezing him in that position. Cole studied the others to see if they held fear, only to be shocked that their uniformity was snapped back into place. No more itchy fingers, yet still no fear.

The opening of a door from the furthest car revealed the

leader of this intimidating pack: bald and dark-skinned, sporting a long, black duster jacket. The leader looked over at his man still holding the rifle against his chin, and then the leader raised his eyebrows at Cole with an expression that asked, *why haven't you done it yet?*

Before Cole could react, the leader made sure the man's itchy trigger finger was finally scratched. The shot rang loud, and the people of Holdsworth shrieked.

Satisfied, the convoy leader then walked calmly toward Cole, who stood frozen by the man's cool presence, until they were standing face to face.

"The shooting of the young one was an accident. Your people fired first and we had no choice but to retaliate."

Cole's eyes squinted in growing anger, but when he searched inside for the truth he found the man had already spoken it.

"What is your business here?"

The man smiled. "I have been sent here to bring you and John Foster to Chicago."

Cole was stunned. A million thoughts blurred past his ever-growing mind and each one had him stumped even though the answers seemed obvious. He looked inside the leader for more information, but was met with a dark wall of nothingness. The man began to laugh, further confusing Cole. "My mind has been trained to only disseminate information my leader wishes to disclose, an inbuilt system *he* has placed into most of his subjects."

Cole, with panic clear in his face, desperately looked over to the other soldiers and was now met with the same wall of darkness.

"Then again, you could just ask me," the man continued, the same smile reappearing on his face.

A disappointed Cole relented. For a sly minute back there, he was kind of enjoying the fact he was the only *special* person in town. "Okay. Who has sent for us, and why?" he asked like a grumpy child who didn't get his way.

"A dinner invitation, courtesy of his son," the man said, motioning to Foster, who stood behind the fence, pistol raised. Cole watched Foster, who looked back at Cole, trying to decipher just what the hell was going on. Cole knew that Foster would go, he'd said that much himself, and once again Cole got the gut feeling that his presence with Foster would inevitably be forced on him again.

And despite all that Foster had done against him, Cole did want ensure that Foster saw his son again, though Cole resented having to leave Holdsworth, the dream dying just as he had given life to it. In this resentment, Cole asked what would happen if he refused.

"I will kill you and then slaughter everyone else except John Foster."

Cole considered him. He wasn't kidding.

"On the decree of Matthew?" Cole pursued with caution.

"Only if he has to." The man's warm smile was now long gone, replaced with a fierce threat Cole knew he could carry out. *Does that mean he's like me, one of us?* Cole wondered, quickly deducing this guy was a whole other level of not to be fucked with. Cole scratched away at his troubled head, turning in a slow drunken circle, taking in the people behind the fence and the people who compelled him to join them on another far-fetched crusade. As long as he allowed people to influence him, his gift and thus his life would always be forever trying to please the wishes of others.

"What about Kate, can I take her?" he asked the man, assuming he already knew about her.

"It would be advised by myself and my leader that it is safer for her if you were to leave her here. Chicago is not pretty this time of year and Kate has no place there in her condition. You will be able to return to Holdsworth shortly, my leader only wants to invite you to dinner."

The man believed everything he said but Cole wanted to call bullshit. No one was going to let him return to Holdsworth, there would be no peace for Cole Watts. He'd be strung along, forced to fight wars for demented causes until he was finally killed or did himself in.

"I'll tell Foster what you have said," relented Cole.

"He will accept."

"I know he will!" Cole snapped back, fuming at the whole situation. *That bastard will be fucking joyous.* He then walked away frustrated. The man was both stern and playful, confusing Cole as to what kind of operation Foster's son was running. Was Foster's son anything like Foster—*what a pleasure that'd be!* While Cole wrestled with this, he relayed to Foster the "great news". Foster really took it to heart when he knew his son was alive and waiting for him. Not just a voice in his head, but actual confirmation. He held back the tears as all those niggling unknowns fell to the floor around him, finally giving him some breathing space; there would be an end to his search, an end to his journey.

Foster thought little of his son being an Illusionist, it was a fact he had learned to accept over the many months he struggled to temper his hatred towards them all. Now seeing Cole the way he was, maturing into a decisive young man of much promise, he held higher hopes than the anger he spewed forth back in Nebraska and all those other instances with Max and Kate back in the cave, when all their comfort was a hard dirt pit of despair. The hypocrite in John Foster was dying, and now all he hoped for was that Matthew had kept his brother, Dylan, alive and well too.

From what Cole experienced briefly as a fly on the wall to their relationship, Matthew wasn't Foster's favorite. In fact, from the way he treated both, it seemed neither was the winner of such a meekly coveted title. Cole would press Foster for more information later on the drive to Chicago, but he also knew too well about strained family ties and withheld his curiosity for the time being.

The Doc appeared from the street behind them, his shoulders sunk and his clothes bloodied. The teen had died just outside the Great White Tent. The Doc didn't have to ask to know the dream was over. When they met up close there was little Cole felt he could say and little the Doc felt he could do.

"Will you say goodbye to Kate for me?" asked Cole.

"Why don't you tell her yourself?" replied the Doc, a sting in his tone he couldn't help, upset by the uncertainty of what now held for his people.

But Cole couldn't face Kate again today, the shame propelling him to make up for it in the future. "Please, just tell her I will come back for her—all of you," he said, his eyes tilting to slide the conviction in his words that put the belief back in the Doc.

Foster and Cole left Holdsworth shortly after that. They were husked away in one of the black SUVs with nothing but their ragged, foul-odored clothes on them. Foster made the comment that they were riding in Daisy again; such was the similarity of the SUV they rode in, but found the comparison dragged them back to the person most attached to Daisy.

The crowd that had gathered round the gate now looked back on the Doc, searching for the answers to what had just happened, why their warriors had run off with these intruders. The Doc calmed them and began to proclaim the promise that they would indeed return to protect them once more. Filled with hope by the news, they started to chant the names of their saviors until the convoy disappeared into the forest.

Stage IV: Oblivion

27. Six Days Ago

His brother had told him not to go into that building. He'd said it was a trap. Said it in that all-knowing voice of his—the one that could command a million fates and melt the minds of enemies with just a single thought. There had been many close calls before, and whenever it got real hairy, that all-knowing voice would always find him and draw him back to safety. But Dylan had gone too far this time. And when his brother, with that crisp, alluring voice that never waivered, tried to call him away from that building, Dylan had not listened. Because by then Dylan was convinced, beyond all logical reasoning, that this rickety building barely standing before him was the key to winning this war. That somehow, from one of its many broken windows, lay the gift of a perfect vantage point; where Dylan could see all those horrible vermin—those slaves to an empty ideology—ripe for the killing.

By the time Dylan Foster had rushed inside and the reality of the situation became clear, Matthew, his brother, was given a choice: *Let me take him or the C4 blows.*

There was hesitation, a rare thing.

There was guilt, a thing long gone.

And in this all-knowing, all-seeing mind where wars were waged and grand futures were written, this moment had been enough. In this moment, Chicago itself became too much.

What Matthew did next was eventually passed off as a knee-jerk reaction. An unintended cry for help from a man of pride caught hopelessly out, wondering what his father would say…

But as Matthew searched into distant lands for the wisdom of his estranged elder, yearning to seek a forgiveness of sorts, he was instead drawn to a young man, a Cole Watts, screaming on his knees in the middle of a street, completely annihilated by the love he had just let die.

It was in watching this young, gutted soul that Matthew saw great potential, and so a destiny was prescribed.

***

Dylan was gagged, cuffed and blindfolded, but not before he watched his men die. He began to resist when they'd taken him down the stairs and left the building. After his wild kicking finally connected with one of the many captors that surrounded him, they got a dog leash and tied it to his neck, dragging him that way for over a mile.

Sebastian was never much for taunting. It was often too risky giving away a peak of his operations. But for that one, vicious mile, he was willing to let Matthew watch.

When Dylan settled down and was allowed to walk upright again, the screaming of hundreds of voices attacked him on all sides as he was pelted with rocks and any other debris worthy enough for the brother of the great nemesis. They led Dylan into another building. He was walked down many hallways. The screams he'd been hounded by in the street were now replaced by cries of anguish, most likely his brethren suffering exquisitely at the hands of well-equipped converters. After many blind steps, Dylan was finally taken to a quiet room, where the outside sounds of terror were shut out.

There they left him, alone, for what felt like years.

And after time and darkness had twisted beyond his comprehension, after the infuriating quiet had killed his sanity a thousand times over, Dylan's gag was lifted, and his blindfold was untied, only for a blinding light to be shone upon his face.

"Felt like a long time—years in fact—didn't it? Ah, don't worry! It's just a neat little trick, brings the conversion time right down..."

Dylan squirmed in his chair as the light burned through his closed eyelids. He gritted his teeth.

"It cost me a lot to get to you—just to even get close, in fact. Had to let you take that warehouse, slaughter one of my battalions, merely to get the ball rolling. Then I had to let you capture those ammo dumps, get that confidence overflowing inside, blocking out those logical thoughts that said this was too easy... Let you get closer, too far away from him to protect you. Let you feel like victory was in reach if only you had got to that building..."

Dylan felt a hand draw upon his arm. A friendly, warm hand unlike the mind it belonged to.

"You should've listened to him, you know. He's been a tough one to crack, the toughest yet. But they all fall, Dylan. They all have so far..."

Sebastian paused, a question popping into his head. A question that could've made him look weak, but one he asked nonetheless. "Tell me, Dylan. Does he sleep well?"

The light was turned out. Darkness again. Dylan stopped squirming, but now he was breathing hard, as if his eyes had needed air after holding their breath.

"Is that a *no*, then?"

When Dylan stopped seething and was finally able to speak, he made sure to try and spit at Sebastian first (if the shadow that stood in front of him really was Sebastian).

"You think that by taking me, you have a hostage?" Dylan raged. "You can't use me as your protection, or to cease this war. I won't allow it. My brother will wipe you and your vermin—your slaves to an empty ideology—off the face of this earth and I will happily die knowing this!"

Sebastian grinned. Those venomous barbs of hate Dylan pitifully hurled at him sounded amusingly familiar.

"Slaves to an empty ideology, that's a good one, never heard that one before!" Sebastian chuckled. "Now, if you're done being all uppity about your dear, sweet brother, I'd like to correct the assumptions you have placed upon your fate, Dylan. I don't want you to die. I want you to kill."

28. Reunions

The dense forest that had almost become their grave was now peaceful. The light of the sun breaking through the trees reminded Cole of the youthful sun he caught when he was a child playing among the grass with Peter on a Saturday, then escaping church the next day to explore the dirty undersides and plumbing of a building he readily discarded as unimportant. These were the memories he now clung onto, his own light show he played to himself as they circled around the heart of the forest and the scenery began to draw dimmer.

The further east they were chauffeured, the grayer the skies developed. Once the thick underbrush was well in their rear view, the road drew flatter and more and more houses began to pop up. Not a word had been spoken up to this point and while Foster was curious to see which bridge they would end up using, it was neither Muscatine nor Burlington or even Davenport. Instead, they pulled over by the side of a road parallel along the Ol' Miss. She was calm and endless, her skin a light brown. They were ushered downhill through the long, thick swirling grass that lined her sides, then onto the muddy bank where an old man in a small, rickety wooden dinghy stood waiting. He was barefoot, with raisin skin and pure white hair only just sticking out of his sun hat. He had barely any teeth and those that remained were black at the gums and wildly slanted at the tips. Foster thought he could make out Muscatine in the distance, the steel bars sticking straight out where cement used to make a bridge. He asked what had happened to the bridges. It was pointless but Foster had to know anyway. Maybe it was just to entertain the possibility of Daisy fulfilling Max's wish one day, making it across to the East Coast. The leader of the black coats was abrupt in his answer.

"The bridges were blown. Isolation purposes," the man stated, before ushering them into the dinghy with the smiling old man. All the black coats' rifles were then stacked into the boat. The dinghy took five. Foster was not impressed. Where was the naval fleet? A motorized boat at least. The leader did not respond, and Cole tried to relax Foster. They all sat down in the wobbly boat as the old man started on his only job left in life, his seasoned arms gliding gracefully in a way that betrayed his age. Cole turned around and watched as those men who could not fit in the boat (all seventeen of them), with their skin-tight black fatigues and boots still on them, wade into the water before their heads were bobbing up and down like frogs, effortlessly. Foster had turned around as well at this point and they watched the line of pure obedience follow them diligently to the other side where identical SUVs were waiting.

They passed towns without the fear or hesitation they once held. At first, there were handfuls of people they passed, many of them dressed for farmhand work, but these numbers soon grew in the hundreds. In the distance, Cole witnessed large food crops being worked on by many busy workers. Those workers close enough to the road would stop what they were doing and salute the convoy. The sightings of people grew more numerous and soon they were greeted by an almost forgotten condition of the past, traffic. Endless lines of huge sixteen-wheeler trucks; transporting food, guns, explosives and all other sorts of supplies, lumbered in front of them until the convoy made the move to overtake. Something much bigger than Cole expected was happening in Chicago. He shifted uncomfortably in his seat. He was over his head on this one.

"Have you been to Chicago before?" he asked Foster.

Foster, still looking out the window, gruffly cleared his throat. "Yes, I used to live here for a couple of years before Matthew was born; before I joined the army," he recounted, the nostalgia building in his voice. "I met Joyce, his mother, there, maybe only thirty miles away from here in a bar I was drinking myself stupid in. I'd just lost my job at a newspaper delivery business for reading too many newspapers I should've been delivering. I was reckless in those days, stubborn as all hell. I'd constantly bicker with my colleagues over the politics of the day. Then one day I went overboard and got physical proving a point. They fired me, and I was staring down homelessness in a week's time during an icy winter. When the barman kicked me to the gutter I thought I was at my lowest point, the beginning of the end. That's when she found me, at first mistaking me for a bum when I was only soon-to-be. She only approached me because I was her age, bless her soul. The pity she held blossomed into a love that I kept with me every day since, especially on those dark days in the service where I only had to think of her to know there was another side to me that existed."

"Where is she now?" asked Cole, aware of the answer but feeling Foster needed to say it himself.

"Melanoma. We found it too late," he said swiftly. "Never been whole since…" Foster then went quiet, content to dwell on the life he made with Joyce. But he couldn't. As the houses and buildings became more prominent, so did the signs of war and destruction. They were back in it. Foster couldn't help wondering how much of all this carnage had been directly the result of his son. He made crass assumptions of what his son was thinking, fearful he was past a point of no return and that when they would finally meet face to face, he wouldn't even be able to recognize Matthew. He knew Matthew was a very logical and practical thinker, often polite, yet prone to exhibiting coldness in calculated decisions. He wondered, like Cole, just how far his son's reach had extended and the dark, bloody actions he'd taken to get there.

"You and Matthew…you guys weren't exactly best buds, were you?"

Foster had seen this coming, had known Cole would peek in. Cole would've been a fool not to after all that had happened. Still, a sense of violation creased Foster's insides.

"I was away a lot, with the military… I wanted them to be strong."

***

They reached Chicago late afternoon. Already they could hear the faint language of gunfire in the distant southeast. Riding up on an overpass they were given full view of O'Hare International and were stunned by the amount of wrecked planes, scattered across its many airways like swatted bugs. The people in the streets they passed were now armed with all various sorts of weapons; ranging from baseball bats to heavy machine guns being lugged along. Their clothes were all worn out, grimy, and their faces were stern, eyes focused, carrying on their backs the burden of endless war. Despite this, Cole could sense they were all well fed, and glimpses into their souls gave Cole the impression these people were extremely content—unnaturally so. The more he looked into their minds, the more he heard a strange voice that kept dropping in and out, little excerpts of a speech by someone he assumed was Matthew Foster. Cole looked at Foster who began to hear the speech himself.

"It's my son, but where's it coming from?"

Cole tried again to read the mind of the driver to see where they were headed. There was still a blankness he could not seem to break through, until a fraction of an image sparked off in a split-second motion, where green turf met sandstone dirt.

"Wrigley field!" Cole exclaimed. "We are going to Wrigley Field."

Throughout the rest of their ride into the city, Cole watched on as thousands of men and women would rush past in front of their convoy, followed by several armored vehicles, including large green tanks that slugged their way toward an enemy they hated (without truly grasping the real reasons why, Cole imagined).

"*There is conflict, both internal and external,*" the voice of Matthew echoed in their ears.

"*We can only progress so much before our petty differences consume us. The next step in evolution dictates the need for only one ideology, one leader, one direction.*"

In the words that drifted in and out of Cole's head, Cole felt he could hear tiredness in Matthew's voice, and wondered if others could hear this too. Even though this seemed the case, Cole felt uncomfortably swayed by Matthew's words, like his body was already in the process of easing into the creases of a familiar couch. Before he could dwell on it further, the car pulled up next to Wrigley Field, just as Cole said it would.

The streets were packed now but movement was orderly. The eyes of each soul that passed him were possessed with an air of purpose, a willingness to do whatever necessary to please their master. Without effort, the crowd reshuffled their walking patterns, opening up a clear path to the back entrance of the stadium. Cole was sure this pathway was intended for his group and yet the people who made it did so for reasons completely unbeknownst to them, the only reason being a voice in their head compelling them to do so. That was all that was needed now.

The leader of the black coats came up swiftly behind Cole and Foster to take the path created for them. As Cole and Foster moved along, each person they would've run into on the left would mechanically change course; walking away from the stadium until they had passed Cole and Foster to which they then resumed their original course. They did not deter their gaze when they did this, to Foster there was no one at home for any of these people, while Cole could only see purpose and contentment but nothing else. (As if more was needed.) It was life choreographed perfectly, and Cole and Foster were the audience, the only people who didn't know their lines.

Through the back door was a light blue tunnel that led them to a flight of stairs which they climbed until the loud booming of hundreds of thousands of people in mass unity was brought to them in the open air as they walked out with a miraculous feeling of freshness into the stands just above center outfield. It was packed; every seat and foot of field filled with a dedicated member of Matthew's legion. They were dead quiet though, the booming sound only resting in Cole and Foster's ears; maybe it was their heartbeat, all synched up as one? The crowd hung onto words Cole knew he would be surrounded with shortly. The two bits of standing space they now filled were definitely reserved just for them; the last pieces to a puzzle that made the jaw drop in sheer disbelief at the size of the crowd and their eerie stillness.

On a small podium at home base, a single person stood. When Cole and Foster both saw this, their ears were inundated with Matthew's speech, only this time there were no pauses or cut outs—just his crisp, smooth alluring voice echoing out across the stadium.

"Brothers and sisters, we have fought tirelessly over these past six weeks against a nemesis whose sole desire is to destroy us. He has sent his planes into our people's hearts; he has tried to trick us, to make us believe we are alike. The same words I speak come from him also, yet his words are empty—damn empty I say! Because he believes in them not! To do this is a mockery to the truth we follow. He cares not for the future, because he cannot see past today. All you however, do see the future. You see because your belief carries you there. I tell you, the foundations I have set—that we have built together—will last for a thousand years…and then a thousand years more!"

They were all buzzing, twitching in anticipation, waiting for him to release their subdued states so they could cry out his name in joyous agony. Cole and Foster were not immune to this, their own bodies filling with a rush of fervor they struggled to contain.

"Those standing here today are the beginners of this dynasty, the first steps on the path to paradise. And though you may only ever have a taste, your young will dine forever!"

Those few who weren't already standing, the blood in their

legs gone from waiting seven hours for him to speak, leapt back to their feet and joined in the ground-shaking applause of Matthew's vision. Goose bumps ran all along their arms and the back of their necks. Foster turned to Cole, wanting to confirm what they were feeling: *this great sense of purpose*! Cole had goose bumps too, but he was shaking; disturbed. His senses heightened, just like back in the forest. His eyes darted around frantically. No one else felt the rumble in the gut of approaching death. Was it someone in the crowd? His head bopped up and down, searching for any signs of dissidents but only saw smiling, oblivious faces.

"What's wrong?" asked Foster.

"Someone's going to attack. We're all in danger!" exclaimed Cole; his dread sending a sharp jolt through Foster's entire core.

"Where's it coming from?"

"I don't know, it's just…"

Cole stopped himself mid-sentence as his gaze turned to the sky. It was unmistakeable in its shape and speed, but Cole had never seen one from this angle before: a Boeing 747, hurling directly at the stadium, ready to kill everyone in its final flight. Cole's mind raced, he couldn't get a read on it and began to suspect it was empty; its pilot dead with the controls jammed into crash sequence. The blood rushed to his head. It filled his sight with thunderous wobbles, the gift urging his legs to flee as far as they could carry him. He grabbed Foster, who now saw the approaching dot in the distance, coming down hard on them.

"We've got to get the hell out of here!" Cole cried out to Foster as his legs had already taken to the task. But Foster was bound to his place, the overwhelming sense of joy at seeing his son keeping him tied down, already dismissive of Cole's warning. Cole held at a railing just before the stairs, trying to override the mechanisms that sent his legs in the other direction towards safety. He now saw the cockpit, the dials reading a cool 385 miles an hour, coming in directly from behind Matthew, ready to burst through the stadium wall like it was paper.

The pilot's mind was now clear to Cole: he was not dead, his kamikaze stare honing on his grip on the stick. Cole looked over toward Matthew searching for the fear he expected to see. The people in the stands all around Cole must have seen the plane torpedoing in and yet they wavered not in the slightest, following the calm demeanor of their leader. Now Cole found himself standing back out there beside Foster, curiously fixed onto a man he was sure had all the answers and solutions—even to missiles the shape of Boeings.

Matthew's face twitched and the pilot's demonic grip on the controls jerked sideward, sending the 747 careening overhead into Lake Michigan, missing them all by a shade over a hundred feet. The passing wind rattled Cole's insides and he would've been knocked over had he not clung onto the railing in absolute fright.

There was no applause for this near miss. Everyone was oblivious to the loud thud of the plane taking the top off a small building before causing an earth-shaking splash.

Cole studied the faces of the crowd, still keenly focused on the little spec of a man who filled their hearts with all they needed, all unaware just how close they came to annihilation. Cole tried to get these people in the crowd to notice, to replay the moment they almost burned, collapsed, and fell on top of each other to their deaths as the plane had intended. And yet Matthew's grip kept them blissfully ignorant of this fact, easily overshadowing Cole's plea for them to open their eyes.

Matthew was so cool with it all. A little too cool…

Was it all a show, a mere chance to display the all-encompassing *might* of his gift? Cole looked around and noticed the little things of people around him: a redneck stood side by side with a black man, a paraplegic crying in her chair with absolute joy, a blind person who could now "see", former lovers reunited. These were contrasts of the past thrown in Cole's face, as if to show him that this was the future, this was how we all learned to get along. He looked back at Foster who swallowed it in all too happily as "Matthew" flowed through all his senses.

Matthew's voice was now only a muffled drone in Cole's head and as soon as Cole had realized this, his temporary sense of "better than" quickly evaporated with the sound of someone talking to him from behind.

"Close call, closer than usual anyways. The controls and the pilot were deliberately jammed at 30,000 feet and I only had a few seconds when he came into range to force him to override the jam and go for a swim. The key is to make my nemesis believe he still has control for longer than is true. Most of the time I would get them to land the plane and then turn the pilot, but there wasn't enough time for this. Pity really."

Cole did a double take. Once at the Matthew standing on a podium in front of a hundred thousand people, and once at the Matthew standing right in front of him with a wry smile and a third eye (of a deeply piercing blue) imbedded into his forehead; a physical manifestation of his mind's eye. He wore a white robe, and his head was beautifully bald and mesmerizing, just like every other part of him. He wore sandals.

This god cleaned up nicely.

Cole motioned to Foster to turn around and when he did, all

that awestruck inspiration Foster had been consumed with only moments ago was gone, the sight of his son up close and personal bringing him back down to earth, paralyzing him with shaken uncertainty.

One always wonders about these kind of reunions; will the bitterness of their past be washed away in the moment, celebrated with hugs; or will healed wounds be opened up, just as fresh as the day they were cut? Surrounded by a sea of people still infatuated with "stage Matthew", Foster was speechless, his mouth trembling as the words became stuck in his throat.

"Hello, John," sneered Matthew. Open wounds it seemed.

Without letting too much silence fill the space between them, Matthew reminded them they were hungry. "Let's take a walk."

The trio were soon out on the street, cutting easily through a tide of fanatics wishing to get in and see Matthew dazzle them with his mere *everything*. Stranger it seemed that not one person recognized Matthew up close, complete unaware that their god walked among them, right within touching distance. As Matthew led Cole and Foster in stride, so too did he address their rolling questions that pushed and demanded answers, scrambling to take hold of their mouths.

"I have to be in many places at once, to break up the source of my gift in order to deceive my nemesis of my true location. You are right to doubt if I am even walking with you at all."

When he blinked, his third eye blinked, but not all the time.

Cole and Foster stopped, unsure of how to react to this. "Well, I wasn't going to say anything…" chided Cole, pretending he had always considered that a possibility, despite the fact that pretending was a pointless gesture in front of people like Matthew, if there were people anywhere close to being like him.

Matthew smiled at Cole's childishness, the same smile he used on countless others with the same exact result each time: a relaxing of the body, the ship of the mind in calm waters aware that this man controlled the wind. This eased all the tension off Cole's shoulders and he breathed easier. He was a follower again, free of indecision for as long as he hung by Matthew.

Still standing in his spot, Foster was now peeled back, unsure of whether to follow this man who was his son with three eyes and a leader of millions. *So is it you, or not*? Foster demanded to know with raised eyebrows, tired by the revelations of the day.

"Even if it's not me, rest assured there is gold at the end of the rainbow we walk upon. Let me ask you, when was the last time you had your favorite meal?"

29. Home front

Up and down, little valleys and mountains. Fifty-eight beats a minute. Stable.

These were Kate's vitals. They had her hooked up again as soon as the Doc had returned from his fruitless efforts saving the kid. Another kid lost. Kate was a priority, the Doc said so himself. Whether she knew it or not, Kate had become a key part of the survival of Holdsworth, if only for the way Cole felt about her. On the surface she was a sleeping angel, but many of the nurses had seen the demons lurking inside and most were too afraid to approach. They swore on giving her the best help possible, but had all the orderly work passed down to Yolanda Flores, the only nurse who hadn't seen Kate's crazed attack on Cole before he had her purring in his arms.

"Now, Yolanda," they insisted, "Kate is with Cole. You don't want to upset Cole do you?"

"No, miss, of course not."

"Then you make sure she doesn't stray from fifty to seventy-six. You do this, and Cole will be very proud of you."

Yolanda's eyes lit up; undeniable sparks from youthful vigour. Yolanda hadn't bothered to ask why an inexperienced person such as herself had been given such an important task and this left the head nurse quietly relieved. It was overdue. She'd handled too many shocks for the day already and her heart was still too aware of the edge it had been dangled over.

"Well, last we checked she was sleeping it off. So your job should be pretty straight forward," the head nurse reiterated, eager to conclude this passing of the baton and make some distance between her and the sleeping basket case.

Yolanda nodded. "Ms Kramer, I won't let you down."

***

A canyon. It was like falling into a canyon. The gushing of wind ruffling her hair while her brain sent dreaded messages all over her body to brace for the impact, but it never came and as this dawned on Kate, the air around her grew quiet and she became suspended in darkness. She kept touching her shoulder blade, expecting it to crack like glass before she just went all out and brushed her entire arm off her wilted body. But there was no pain, and even in her dream, Kate was gripped with this underlying feeling that Cole was the reason she couldn't feel the pain. He was the comfy landing. Kate tried to find Cole in her dream and around a corner she found him with open arms, exactly as she had remembered him when his hand warmed her body on that porch—only this time everything was illuminated in a bright light and she was certain she was on the precipice of knowing precisely everything in the universe. All she had to do was look in his eyes, stare right into them and take a swim in their deep, dark waters. A rattling of a food tray in the outside world shattered this chance however, sending Cole scurrying away. Kate frowned as she reluctantly returned to the surface, where the pain became known again.

Her eyes opened to a young Puerto Rican woman, around the same age as her, balancing a light blue tray of a bowl of soup and a plastic water cup. Yolanda was tiptoeing her way towards the bedside table. When she crossed sights with a blinking Kate, Yolanda froze mid-stride, the soup swirling unsteadily as her statuesque form was cemented. Kate was lost for words at first, thinking her only available method of communication should be a strained smile, unsure of how much energy she had. Instead, the pain in her shoulder amplified and she winced in pain, sparking Yolanda into action as she rushed to put the soup down and tend to her patient.

"Oh, baby, try not to move! They said you fractured your collarbone. And there are some other things…" Yolanda scrambled while flipping through her clipboard to accurately depict Kate's ailments of which she was already painfully aware. Still wincing, Kate tried to resettle herself into a more comfortable spot, trying to sink into the upright bed with upmost caution.

Yolanda rushed out of the room before bursting back in just as quickly, a dampened towel ready for Kate's sweat-lined forehead. "Hush, hush," Yolanda beckoned as she carefully laid out the towel onto Kate, who never took her eyes off Yolanda. Feeling its warmth drenched Kate all over as the pain subsided and her head started to gain some traction on where she was.

Kate steadied her back before asking Yolanda with a dry, raspy throat where she was exactly. Yolanda held the cup of water up to Kate's mouth as she reiterated what had been told to her between the nurses and everyone else in Holdsworth. "Well you know, honey, that the Savage is dead, and he ain't coming back."

Kate nodded, "I know. Cole killed him." At the mentioning of his name, a spark was lit.

Cole.

"He sure did!" said Yolanda, now swaying backward and forth, remembering just when the news was broken to her, and how she was just overcome with the deepest gratitude for Cole, Mr Foster and Kate.

"You such a brave girl for going in there. To be honest, we thought you were all cuckoo for trying. I swear, I had my bags all packed up, but then it happened and we were saved! You saved us!" Yolanda was now holding hands with Kate, bobbing up and down, as giddy as a child at Christmas time. Bedside manner was her forte (so thought Yolanda) and thus the words came gushing out, mostly concerning the aforementioned savior, Cole Watts.

"So, you and Cole, huh. You two a thing?"

This got Kate smiling, with a faint tingle of a blush.

"Well," she started slowly, wanting to be cautious but soon found herself wrapped in an infatuation that ballooned well beyond her control.

"We have held hands," she swooned. "And I think I'm falling for him. Yes. Yes I am. Just when I was looking at his eyes, oh it was so blissful. It's like I'm young again, like I feel I can be pure; cleansed from all this…"

Her eyebrows furrowed, as the true, desolate state of things crept back into all her mirrors. Yolanda was quick to spot this and nudge Kate back to thinking only about Cole. His quiet soul, those dark brown eyes, and a slight smile that never went full bore…

"He's just got this air about him—like a bubble—I just couldn't put my finger on it at first; maybe because when we met

I didn't trust him, but it was all just a big misunderstanding I'm sure. I just get these tingles now, can you feel?"

Kate held her arm up and ran her other hand across the tiny bumps that lined her skin, that told her something was growing inside her; that sweet little tang of all-encompassing love.

"He loves me, I just know it," Kate repeated as Yolanda gave her arm a slight feel, now a little apprehensive about continuing the conversation. This Kate had clearly been through a lot and as she struggled to get her breath back after her flurry of confessions, Yolanda tried to restore calm, keep Kate relaxed. Not get her too worked up.

"Girl, he sounds lovely. There ain't many good guys like him out there right now, I guess you could say I'm a little too aware of that right now…"

"Where is he?"

"I don't know, honey, but Lord knows I've been looking… Oh! You mean Cole. Yeah I was told he had to go away, fight more bad guys I'm pretty sure."

Kate smiled, "That sounds like him, always protecting us… Do you know when he's coming back?"

"No, honey. I don't. But I'm sure he's just fine. Gonna come back real soon."

"Yeah, we're in love." Kate decided. "So he will."

Yolanda couldn't help but admire Kate's astute conviction, even if it was clear she'd been knocked around the head a few times too many. Feeling some of that magic rubbing off onto her, Yolanda eased up in her apprehension, patting Kate on the forehead, ready to treat her right, so that Cole could say she'd done well. "Well, I tell you what, when Cole does return we can't have you smelling like that ghastly forest now can we? I'm going to talk to the other nurses, see if we can't get you in a bath so you be all fresh and beautiful for when he gets back and you know what, I can personally see myself doing something with that hair of yours, just have to straighten it out and…"

Yolanda had to stop in her blabbering track as a look of pain was thrust onto Kate's face. At first it was just a slight twitch, before it became clear to Yolanda a dawning darkness was setting in Kate as she began muttering something under her breath. Yolanda leaned in closer, her eyes squinting just trying to read Kate's lips.

"*Ba-Ba-Ba-Ba,*" repeated over and over was all Yolanda could make out, her arm firmly trying to squeeze Kate's arm, snap her out of it. Kate's whole arm began to shake before it spread to her whole body. Now clinging onto both arms, Yolanda asked desperately what was wrong, right in Kate's face as the "*Ba-Ba-Ba,*" continued its trail till their eyes met and Yolanda finally understood what Kate was trying to get out of her.

Bath.

Yolanda was now out the door screaming for help as Kate thrashed around in her bed, trying to avoid the surging water of the porcelain bath that filled her with guilt. Now the white coats poured into the room, scrambling to stabilize Kate. They had straps thrown around her arms while a needle was prepped for sedation. The on-call doctor (who was more of an orthopaedist) yelled at a frozen Yolanda to get the Doc.

***

The Doc had looked up the address for the Holdsworth mortuary a couple days after the Great White Tent suffered its first casualty. The place was tiny, in its last legs leaning towards completely defunct—the coroner usually sending the rare, suspicious fatalities along to either Des Moines General or Polk County Mortuary. Yet now, its claustrophobic walls were kept busy as Fleming (a mortician before the epidemic) occupied himself daily, studying away at fatal gunshot wounds, stabbings, broken necks and now the infamous Savage.

Fleming always got worked up in his usual eccentric state when it came to discussing the brain and body of the true terror, feverishly expecting an Adonis of insanity—if it were even possible anyone could get close to him. And then that group had shown up, made a bold claim, and in all the faintest possibilities of the world they'd slayed the beast and made all of Fleming's wishes come true. Even though he provided autopsy after autopsy for the victims the Savage left in Holdsworth—this including Max, Jimmy, Kyle and Bryan, whom Fleming knew quite well—the prospect of studying the Savage still gave him a sense of wonder, a glimpse into an alien (at least the closest he would ever get). Fleming struggled to hide his excitement at the prospect.

He had three hours with the monster all to himself, but wrote up an autopsy report in less than one. When the Doc finally made his way into the pocket of humming, cold blue light that Fleming called home, barely a word was exchanged as Fleming handed him the report, attached to it a letter, before excusing himself just as quick.

Clean exit wound, right through the forehead.

That Cole sure was some shot, thought the Doc.

Two 5.56 mm rounds lodged in the lower right ribs. Incisors: as normal as any other human—definitely not fangs. Muscles weak, fairly timid. Unattended scratches all over skin, most likely from passing branches and other foliage. Deep rings under rest-

less eyes. Signature ponytail that hissed like a cobra: machetied off as a souvenir from one of the clean-up teams.

The sweeps had gone out hungry to the forests in the early morning, led by a determined Renko. The Doc recalled Renko's voracious claims should he ever get his hands on the body: Renko would desecrate every inch; mutilate every inside. Chop off those cruel fingers one by one… The thing he'd always put the heaviest details into were the teeth—oh he'd smash those front bastards in good with a wrench and then pluck the molars out, one by one. There'd be no more fangs to scale his terrified skin in those dark dreams he'd endured.

Then, after Renko was finished exacting his own; hang the remains up just outside the Great White Tent on a large post, guts hanging loose, before the whole town joined in communal singing as they burned any evidence the Savage ever existed, hopefully extinguishing those nightmares he once tortured them with.

Kumbaya my lord.

But none of this fevered revenge fantasy had come true, only the cutting of his ponytail was allowed by Renko as the men stood around the meek shell of their devil, a silent reverence taking over them. It was Renko who explained all this to the Doc, having entered the blue darkness of the morgue quite some time after Fleming had left. Without making eye contact, Renko struggled to let the words come out as to why he didn't go through with the mutilation he'd planned over and over while drunk, all to a Doc who seemed to understand his reluctance, despite the fact his son lay still in the next room.

"Because he's not what you expected. He looks nothing like the monster we all saw him as," said the Doc.

There was a long pause before Renko agreed. "Yeah," he uttered before seeing a folded sheet of paper in the Doc's left hand. The Doc's thumb had been rubbing up and down its crumpled surface ever since he came to know of its existence. When the Doc noticed Renko's eyes drawn on the letter he quickly retracted it back into his breast pocket, before realizing the burden of carrying this information around was too much to bear at a time like this. It had to be unloaded.

"It's a letter, addressed to Kate."

"From?" Renko inquired, already puzzled by the resonance of the Doc's tone.

"That boy over there." He said without looking, pointing to the lifeless Max in the other room. "Fleming left a post-it note on it, leaving it to me…"

Renko shuffled forward. "Love letter?"

The Doc nodded slowly, his eyes keeping vacant on the body of the Savage. "That's what I'm guessing. It's pretty worn, as you saw. Feels old; feels like he's been carrying it around for a while."

Renko tried to brush away the fact the Doc was never like this; never one to dwell on the squabbles of young love—he was too serious a person to even be considered being young once—and yet here he was, clearly distressed by a letter that had nothing to do with him.

Renko knew it was really about Daniel, had to be. The two boys looked about the same age.

"Well…when you gonna give it to her?" Renko eventually let out.

Now the Doc looked up at Renko and gave him a true look of loss, before returning his pained eyes to the floor that could not judge. "I'm wondering if I should do that at all… I mean, if you saw the way Cole put the spin into her…it seems she loves him now, whichever way that is, and I think…I think this letter will just complicate things."

"It may be the last wishes of a dying man," Renko pointed out, now getting a sense of the Doc's state of mind. He was suddenly relieved he wasn't the one holding the letter.

"I know, and we should uphold it, that's what's been done; that is our tradition as people, since always, but I just don't know if I should…" The Doc's knees felt weak; he wondered if Renko noticed, if Renko saw his soul hanging by a thread, too tired and broken to make a choice he'd been given the power to decide.

"A happy Cole means a happy Holdsworth," the Doc eventually let out.

"Then let him decide." Renko stated, hoping the simplicity of his answer could lift the weight off his friend's slumping shoulders.

The Doc had already considered this; he'd already considered a whole lot of things he could leave up to Cole as he mulled over the Savage's body. But for reasons unknown to him an old feeling kept creeping up in him that Cole had no right to decide this one, no say.

Renko was now certain it was about his son. Renko was never great at talking about these things, he left them out of him, and he figured he'd gotten away pretty clean, considering the things he'd seen.

Renko gazed into the next room, and from the open door he could just make out what he assumed was Daniel's bare foot.

"Do you want to talk about it?" he asked timidly, knowing full well it was never brought up when Daniel didn't return. There were just extended periods of silence. Not even the drink would let the Doc's emotions slip, and there was always a torrent of it being self-administered those first few weeks. That's when Renko took the reigns for a while; always reminding everyone he was only a caretaker in the interim.

The Doc kept still as he'd always been this entire conversation, and just as Renko had decided to pull in his empty line, the Doc started talking, once again in that slow, pondering linger of his.

"I just wished he'd left something behind, like this poor kid. I wanted it so bad; just to hear his voice from his own writing, rather than whatever pictures I still have the courage to look at… Then there are those made-up reunions I play in my head, over and over."

Renko remained silent as the Doc trailed into nothing but dark thoughts, stretched too far. Renko surprised himself when he found the words, the best he could do.

"Maybe Daniel didn't need to. Maybe he already got to say everything he wanted to."

The Doc was snapped from his fixation with the floor and drew eyes with Renko; genuinely touched as a rare smile, ever so slight, creaked its way the surface.

Without a word, the Doc then sagged his way past Renko, walking out of the dark blue light, through the empty reception and then outside into the warm sun and the sound of chickens clucking as an old lady in rain boots fettered out seed to the squawking birds. The Doc settled himself on a bench outside the mortuary in tired disarray, Fleming sitting quietly on the other end, neither wanting to speak while the old lady stopped her feeding to stare at the Doc, sympathetic to his lackluster spirit.

Renko drifted into the room where Daniel, Max, Bryan, Jimmy and Kyle had been kept. Absorbed by the stillness, he carefully removed the large white sheets draped over each. Fleming was decent at making them look shades better, and he was sure Fleming would step up to the plate for Daniel, but Renko had already decided the whole affair would end up being closed casket. Then there would be the whole ordeal of getting the Doc courage enough for the final goodbye. After all that, there was sorting out the business of rehabilitating Helen and Maggie, and who knew how long that would take without Cole…

Renko sighed, already drained by the tasks that beckoned. He re-draped the sheets over the bodies once more, even giving that punk Jimmy a meaningful look of sorrow. He was just a kid after all.

Then Renko's walkie buzzed, bringing Renko back to life.

***

The Doc burst through the crowded room, only to be greeted by a calm and soothing Kate, all thanks to mother morphine. Nurse Kramer stuttered away as she tried explaining what had happened, taking the Doc back out of the room when she relayed the word 'Bath' to the Doc, fearful of another episode. There were ten coats outside, eight nurses and two other doctors of varying trades. They couldn't help but notice the Doc's usual straight-laced demeanor leaking at the edges; his skin pale, with sullen bags of purple under his eyes.

"God dammit, Kramer, I specifically told you…" he seethed; his dictating hand clenching in a tempered rage as he tried to let the anger in him pass through and wrestle it out the other side where it could never see the light of day. With his other hand he palmed the air outward, towards the exit. They got the picture—well, most. Yolanda stayed put, even as Kramer tried to rush her away. She knew the Doc was tipping away on a ledge that kept getting smaller, but still she had to ask, because if anyone was to know, it was going to be him. "She keeps asking when Cole will return. She's not the only one. When will our saviors return?"

The Doc edged his way into Kate's room. Kate's cheek warmed as she smiled dopily and stretched out her arms to hug him, oblivious to his hollowed appearance.

"How are you feeling?" he asked softly, trying to crack a smile, repeating the mechanics of the smile he played to Renko while the truth sagged heavy in his breast pocket.

"I'm feeling good, Doc." She replied sitting up, seeming to be more aware of her surroundings, her tongue more lucid in the texture of her tone. "I just wish Cole was here. I really miss him. Do you know where he is? We really love each other you know!"

There was that rabid trailing Kramer had warned him about. Kate was definitely in a fix and it wasn't just the morphine. The Doc reached for a chair in the corner of the room and planted himself down. He was at a loss of what to say. Kate kept her eyes on him in expectation, a twitch in her eye urging his reassurance to wrap herself around, go back to her gooey bubble.

Oh, Kate, why had they played your mind the way they did? Was it the beauty that compelled them? Turned you this way, an inability to be anything but their whims. They said it was to protect you, but I know it was just the image they wanted for themselves. I didn't know you well enough; only knew you tried to be brave.

The Doc, like Renko, searched for his words of comfort; the one's he felt they'd been telling Kate all her life; trying to stop the putrid black shit of the world from touching her. He avoided those puppy eyes that seemed to know no wrong until his own found their way to the heart monitor they had her hooked up to. It was still beating…

The letter…

"I don't know really," the Doc uttered, but Kate did not register this answer. She ignored him. "He's coming back, right?" Then came a spark, "Of course he will! We really love each other you know!"

The Doc reached out for her hand, and was taken aback by her warmth, the life that flowed through her.

"I hope so, Kate. I really do."

Renko was waiting outside the room for the Doc.

"Poor girl," the Doc remarked.

Renko waited for the conclusion, but it never came. "Too late for the kid?"

The Doc shot a look of lingering defeat. "Cole will decide."

30. Fancy Dinners

One had to wonder why Foster asked the question, his own concoction nonetheless. But surely, even if it was just a lie for him—the red herring he injected into himself and swallowed as the god's honest truth—there had to have been some progress made. Somebody out there, in all this madness, must have found the answer, the cure. Foster couldn't believe it was just the remnants of that red herring leaving his system. He couldn't accept that the mission he always swore about was just the ramblings of a washed-up colonel.

Matthew answered Foster's question on the imaginary antidote he had cooked up with a brazen laugh.

"If there was one, why would you need it?"

"To have the ability to choose!"

"You cannot fight the future," declared Matthew.

Chicago was a purring beast. They walked along the pavement now, out of the way of the masses in tattered clothing. Cole wondered why these people didn't change their clothes? Would the clothing not rot away and leave a pungent whiff hanging around. But there was no smell, because Matthew said so, and according to random sprawls of graffiti that covered the walls and windows of now pointless shops, *"WHAT MATTHEW SAYS THEREFORE IS TRUTH."* Instead of the word "therefore" however, was the math symbol of three dots that formed a triangle, the shorthand means of explaining proof, all too similar to the three windows that were always open on Matthew's face. Most of the cars had been swept aside for junkyard endeavors, their purpose now to serve Matthew in whatever shape he had so wisely decreed. A few buildings had been smashed in by artillery strikes, but on the whole it seemed rather clean for a war zone (so far). Everyone they passed carried with them this intangible fire that even Foster could feel beneath their cold eyes. It was one of passion, and they both knew it was all aimed toward Matthew. So now the question begged, what did Matthew want from these faceless masses, the one's that scurried along this wide street and all the other streets of Chicago, tools or weapons in hand, ready to work on the machine of war he had them all riled up and hungry for?

"Keeping them busy," Foster remarked. As they walked along, a girl of no more than eight bolted passed them. Cole caught her thoughts and was stumped by their complexity. *Help Nathan recalibrate the engines to the half-tracks, Pick up a trolley for the boxes then take the ammo from Walters on Huxley Avenue and redistribute to Mackey's machine gun nest. All for Matthew..."*

When Cole snapped his head back to Matthew, he asked with his eyes, *how old?*

Without looking at him, Cole sensed that third eye flicker, seeing the answer but struggling to believe it. She was five and a half and already a cog. Cole's eyes followed the street along, watching others; their clothes all a dry brown, their figures lean, as every muscle was expanded and contracted, every thought in its most prodigious efficiency all put in place like gravity around Matthew and his wants—and in Chicago this was becoming clear to Cole in a term he'd half perused way back when in the time before, where things were laid out into periods of no more than an hour; a half-awake Cole listening to his history teacher, Mr Derkins, talk about the concept of "total war". The hawks (as Derkins had put it) had always called such a concept nearly impossible in reality (despite their wet dreams for it), and yet here it was, right before their very eyes; the movement of millions of pairs of legs, eyes, ears and hands working steadily towards annihilating Matthew's nemesis. No one was absent. The pregnant women worked just as hard as everyone else and when their children were brought into the world, they would already know the basic principles of life: the love of Matthew and the love of the gun. Matthew had scientists studying the virus, looking for better ways to spread it (as if its reach hadn't taken everywhere already). He had them working like the clock itself, endless in trying to fully understand the nature of the original specimens that were buried under rubble somewhere in West Texas and the USAMRIID labs in Fort Detrick.

There were no more bureaucrats, no red tape, no arguing against the facts of Matthew.

There was no second-guessing.

In the far distance, Cole heard the light humming of exchanges between Matthew's legion and the people of his nemesis. Cole felt the smile creep underneath Matthew's face as his greatest work, the giant, swelling machine of total war was presented in its efficient beauty to Cole and Foster, who seemed the only one's cognitively available to recognize such a fact.

***

Their walk ended in front of a small, dilapidated green grocer, the windows barred and glass shards surrounding the now door-less frame. It had once been an old relic amongst the other modern giants that surrounded it by comparison. Yet now, the scattered strokes of war had camouflaged its decay well, blending into the gray and dusted war zone that was Chicago. So unassuming it was that the mind could easily skip past it, never knowing it had ever held any life to begin with. Even though Cole had spent many a days working in an eerily similar shop, he saw it as a void in all of existence, something to be overlooked and never considered twice. It was for this reason that Cole began to see why Matthew had chosen it above any other place to settle as a home.

Even an Illusionist would think nothing of this place.

Matthew led them in, and without bothering to turn the light on, guided them into the pitch-black store through to a door that with a few drops of stairs opened up into a large underground hallway of many rooms. The walls were all painted a light blue and blended with the humming of the lights to calm the nerves. The treatment of the place was unmistakeably new, a recent addition and an easy feat considering all those hands available. All doors were open and empty of inhabitants; but empty bunk beds in each corner suggested this would be a temporary instance. When they came to the end, the rooms had opened up to be much bigger and Foster was given a fright by a woman and man sitting in a chair behind a desk in opposite rooms respectively. Each was devoid of any proper thoughts, sitting dormant until their master called for them. Behind the woman along a shelf were large plastic storage boxes labeled *dental, vitamins, pain* and *sleep*. Next to the woman was a hospital bed, perfectly made, though Cole felt it had been rarely used. To the right in the room where the man sat, a miniature pristine kitchen was guarded next to a heap of boxes laying stacked at stomach height all along the floor. The last room in the hallway; the largest of all, was set up as a dining room, a dark mahogany table centering the mostly empty room. Matthew motioned to the man in the kitchen who immediately became full of action, first lighting the peach candles in the dining room before setting off to make their dinners.

Matthew motioned for them to sit opposite him in the dining room and they did so with dawning wonder in their stomachs. Their mouths began to salivate at the prospect of seeing, feeling, tasting and savoring their favorite meals; a succulent roast lamb lathered in gravy and sided with vegetables for Foster; and a bucket of fried chicken garnished with the colonel's secret eleven herbs and spices for Cole. At this point, who could blame them for expecting it? Matthew was treating them as guests of the highest honor, and this they soon grew to expect from him: a rapid ability to meet their every whim that assented and dug into their brains like a cancerous parasite, though a comfortable one nonetheless. It was a burden Matthew had come to take on from everyone he influenced, a clear impediment to his final plans he had never addressed. How could his ideas about the direction of humanity be realized when the pieces on the board sucked ferociously on his teat for happiness?

As Foster looked around the dim-lit room made visible by these miniscule candles on the table, the dullness of his surroundings disappointed him. His image of his son had been blown into gigantic proportions as his own seed held a stadium captivated, and now they sat in the living quarters of a second rate lieutenant in a Berlin bunker waiting for the Russians to come. *Where was the extravagance?* Foster sulked. Chandeliers, gold platted plates, throne chairs? Sure the table was nice but the chairs were creaky and dust settled heavily in each corner. Cole felt this too and to a point agreed with Foster, only for Cole's attention to switch onto a pressure-cooked Matthew, whose blood began to boil at Foster's unspoken disapproval.

Matthew finally exploded after the food was brought out to them, a sloppy mountain of gray goo that looked like off-oatmeal. Cole tried to understand this, had Matthew forgotten to morph the look of the food? Looking into the many eyes of Matthew he saw that this was on purpose, tipping Foster's disappointment to a point Matthew felt justified in spraying his father after all these years apart. The explosion was calmer, more controlled than Cole expected, yet both he and Foster carried the heat of each stinging word till the hairs on the back of their necks had been thoroughly singed.

"I'm sorry father; Cole. If this was not what you have come to expect, please understand this. Right now I am making two hundred and twenty five thousand and four people believe the gruel they are eating is even better than the taste of their favorite dish, which they thought they had last night. I'm organising battle manoeuvres and giving courage to my soldiers who are facing a dogged enemy that will stop at nothing to kill them. I'm helping to produce the new broadcasting program we will be putting into place around the country whilst giving the sleeping enemy nightmares and the sleeping ally the best dreams they have ever had. I'm influencing other Illusionists in proxy towns, keeping

a close eye on other advancing armies. I'm giving my people
fascinating light shows in clear skies that are altogether kept blue
by my will alone—that's right, I'm controlling the weather—in
a manner of speaking. I'm doing all this while stopping my
nemesis from reading my mind and converting the minds of my
followers. I've been living on two hours of *much* needed sleep
a night for the past three months and going through how I will
deal with the other threats both domestic and international in the
future. I'm sorry if this room is a little dirty, but I'd like you to
consider that *maybe I have other things on my mind...*"

Cole and Foster were gobsmacked; terrified. Despite this,
Cole felt the immediate backlash of Foster building in his throat
and could only close himself off when Foster retorted back with
bloodshot eyes, "Why don't you just get one of your servants
over there to do it..."

Foster wanted to continue, mocking, "Controls millions of
people and can't get one of them to clean his dining hall..." but
Matthew's third eye boiled red as it bulged to the size of his forehead and swallowed Foster whole.

"EAT YOUR FUCKING DINNER!" the eye bellowed as
Matthew's fist struck down on the table. In a sudden whoosh the
room was filled with classy candlelight that swooned ambience;
on each wall priceless paintings of renaissance royals stood so
eloquently in their conceitedness. The dinner plates were now of
solid gold, and the sloppy gruel that had almost driven the hunger out of them was now the roast dinner and bucket of Kentucky
Fried they had wished for without asking. They first prodded it
with their fingers, bringing their heads down to its level to let
the smell warm their cheeks and when they took that first, gentle
bite; a glance was shared between all three of them. Cole had

never been able to change food anywhere remotely close to this, and found himself examining the crumbling crusty fried texture of the chicken more so than eating it.

When he finally gorged on its unfathomable nostalgia, he found that each bite was better than the last; Cole's mind orgasming each time he ripped into the flesh. They both knew it wasn't real, yet ran freely among its flavors. With their final mouthfuls swallowed down heartily, Matthew's servant came and dropped off cups of golden beer that was drowned out quickly in admiration. They slumped back in their chairs, never having ever felt satisfaction like this.

As the taste subsided, the knowledge that this was only gruel slowly worked its way back to Cole. Against what he had just felt, Cole knew he had to ask why? Why go to all the trouble of making everyone's food taste better when Matthew should have been more focused on the war he was waging.

"Because I can," Matthew smiled before Cole could even ask. "Because I believe this gift is meant for the betterment of mankind. If you had the power to help people, to make them happy, as you do, Cole, then why not use it? I find the more I do this, the easier it comes and the stronger I grow. The people here in Chicago will not see the end of my dream, they will lay their bodies down for a future they will not see and I feel giving them the most succulent of meals each night is the least I can do. A taste of what their grandchildren will feel forever."

Foster was indignant. The rumbling of cogs positioned for argument struck Cole as odd, how could Foster be so quick to anger after such an experience? But alas, it was in his nature, a repeat of all the old habits of pushing his son to be better—pushing so hard without looking to see its actual effect.

"What future?" he grumbled, his body now upright and leaning towards Matthew ready to grab him by the scruff of the neck. "From what I've seen these people are fighting and dying for nothing. This whole country has gone to shit because people like you set out these grand visions of how things should be and you force others to think like you. It's pure fascism. And how do you know what people need, can they not make that decision for themselves? I'm pretty fucking sure they know better what it is that makes them happy; god knows we've been at this for over two thousand years—let us get there our own way!"

Matthew stared him down like a snake, waiting patiently to strike.

"A man can only do his best with what he has been given," Matthew said calmly, regaining the trust Cole had given back to Foster in his tirade. "You see, John, the thing of it is, is that I know it doesn't matter what philosophy these people adhere to. Whether it is the religious Illusionists of the west, the south—or even the nihilists up north, the people would be just as sufficiently happy following any one of these 'messiahs'. What it really boils down to is who gets to preach; who becomes the hive mind. For too long conflict has been in our nature. Like all of nature it has been the source of our rise to the top of the food chain, the key to our progress. Yet it is because of conflict and its aftermath that we see a wall of irreversible destruction to the very planet we inhabit. Our desire for more will always produce conflict and thus propel us toward an unsustainable level where our very species will eventually become extinct. I am not an environmentalist and I am not anti-human, but I recognize that with this gift lies an opportunity to scale back our endless desires and to thus resolve human conflict for all time, both internally and externally.

This may come at the cost of innovation, but in this new world we can create, one cannot better perfection."

When Matthew had finished he watched them closely for reactions. For Cole, the whole speech had been blurred out; its content stored away to be analyzed later. Cole's real focus was on understanding Matthew's mind to better grasp and feel his means of influence, his gift. To his surprise, Matthew's power seemed non-existent, suppressed. At first, he put it down to Matthew's superior ability or his desire to hide his presence from his nemesis. But this did not seem right; Cole felt it strange that he felt no strings attached to the words sprouted forth, no hint of manipulation. Matthew's powers were beyond measure; that much was true, but there was something else that nagged at Cole. And then it came to him. Could it be that Matthew was sincerely speaking from the heart? Was he were seeking their approval in an unaltered way because it was not them he wanted to convince, but himself? Maybe Matthew needed to reassure himself from a feeling he couldn't possibly reflect on from his countless "yes" men: the feeling of doubt. And when Cole saw he had it, all the preconceived notions he had built up about the ideal Illusionist were shattered. They were still for the most part human, doomed along with those they called lesser to share the same fate, unable to truly believe their own words, the ever present knowledge that what they presented to others was never and could never be for them.

If Matthew did succeed in his vision he would be surrounded not by people but by automatons, his achievement a lonely one. The fears, the anxiety, the desperation; all these things Matthew would wash away for all the others he could never clean from himself. In a way he would become the last real human. It left

Cole disappointed. Matthew was the man with all the answers. *He had to be*, or else what was all this for? For only a moment Cole was allowed to consider this great loss of hope, before Foster's voice brought him back to the room.

"Conflict?" Foster scoffed. "You say you want to end conflict? Son, if you're so aware to the make of things—as you readily claim—do you not notice that you perpetuate the very conflict you seek to eliminate?"

In all his power, Matthew was still only a son in his father's eyes, a boy that would always need direction.

"You always did have to be right. Some things never change…" Matthew responded calmly. "But in this instance, your vision falls a few yards short of mine. In order for me to address the eternal issue of the internal struggle I must concern myself with the more physically brutal outcome that is our violent nature. When the source of power and knowledge comes from only one, the creation of a hive mind will destroy the niggling differences we pick that draw us to war. There is no need for ideological differences to co-exist with the rise of the hive mind."

Foster wretched inside at Matthew's eloquent vomit. He could now see he had no power over his son anymore, no ability to reason or change his will; only to pester him of the ways it used to be. There was no way to beat this, and now the questions that Matthew wanted to answer came without much resistance.

"Your nemesis," Cole began, "what does he believe?"

"I'm glad you asked," grinned Matthew. "My nemesis has no real fixed ideology that he prescribes to. To my knowledge, with the prisoners we have captured, I have ascertained he is willing to compromise where he sees fit. It is in his ability to adapt that has made his followers harder to crack, the very reason why so many of his captured are not yet converts and it has taken over six grueling weeks to push him to the brink of defeat. I will admit his ability is far beyond the minds of those zealots of the west and that bitch Queen of Texas."

"You mean the Purification Front?" corrected Foster, his strained cheeks and thinning eyes almost offended Matthew had not given them the proper respect they deserved as a threat. Matthew brushed this off however, mentioning the ease to which he turned around all movements eastward by the wack jobs without a shot being fired. "Their numbers are great, sure, but the quality of their influence is too far spread, allowing those on the fringe of their sphere to be quickly converted. *Backward ass-fucks* I believe a former member of your party considered them. This is unlike my current nemesis. He has mimicked my effort in placing many layers of detailed influence within the souls of my followers, hardening their willpower like armor plating. His people were also survivors in their own right before the war, survivors of the early flu and the fallout in the Northwest States."

"So it is true," Cole interrupted, "D.C. is no more? And New York too?"

At this Matthew closed his eyes, all three of them. In the dropping of his lip one could feel the sullen weight such a memory brought down upon him.

"Was it this man—your nemesis—that did it? Did he start this whole thing?

His nemesis had begged him the opportunity at great distances to be there when it happened. His nemesis wanted to witness the justice—as a native of New York he felt he had the right. But Matthew couldn't trust him, no matter how much he also deserved to be there. Matthew's weapon of choice required the upmost attention. And with this in mind, the threat of his nemesis killing two birds with one stone was too great to allow...

When Matthew's eyes finally did return to the world, his stare with Foster left them all lost for words. Eventually he spoke up, his voice sullen. "It was not my current nemesis. It was Senator Richards."

"The fat cowboy asshole?" asked Foster.

"The very same." Matthew dejectedly confirmed.

Cole felt Matthew's grip on the table tighten by only the slightest. Yet it was enough for him to ask with his eyes, what his mind already figured.

"I dealt with him correctly." Matthew let slip. "The matter was...personal."

Foster had not yet asked Matthew if he was still with that wife of his, and would never for that matter, now sure her fate had been spoken. They sat in silence for a long time after that. Soon, both Cole and Foster were waiting in hope for that cool, soothing Matthew to return to them, confident that all things were at his fingertips.

"Was it the Senator who started all this?" Cole asked after a while.

"The Senator did not start this great change, no, but he was in league with the one who did. That person was a scientist, a brave man who sowed the possibilities I will be forever grateful for, despite the pain it has caused me."

Foster recoiled. "*Brave*? You're calling him brave—and saying you're *grateful*?"

"Why did he do it?" Cole interjected, wanting to stop the conversation from exploding once more.

"Yes, *grateful*," Matthew directed at Foster. "He did it for the same truths I have already spoken. He did it because he saw what was becoming of us. He saw we needed to change not who we were, but what we are. He saw this virus as an opportunity. A chance to simplify us, to reset the system and recreate."

"He caused the deaths of millions," said Cole. "I can't see how you can cap the cowboy and then call this other guy brave. He deserves to die too."

Foster nodded in approval, relieved that Cole had finally agreed with him.

"Christopher Jenkins has already paid the price for igniting this vision. Your Purification friends took care of him—very early on, in fact."

"And when will you take care of them?" asked Foster.

Matthew smiled softly. "All In good time, John. All in good time."

It was then that Matthew drew distant. His eyes dazed off. A thin glaze appeared in his third eye. He was off somewhere, organising war. Cole and Foster shared a glance, unsure whether to interrupt him. For a while they stared at his third eye, mesmerized by how real it looked. Eventually, Cole decided to break Matthew's trance.

"Before, you were speaking of your nemesis?" Cole hinted.

"Yes," Matthew awoke, the pupil of his third eye expanding once more to encapsulate the room and all its subjects. "Tough bastard. As it stands, it takes roughly four days to process one of his into mine, and approximately six days for him to convert one of my own, which brings me to Dylan…"

The very mention of this name brought Foster's whole body forward, clutching the table in anguish. Any shred of sympathy left in Foster for Matthew's wife was already gone. "Dylan! What's happened to him—is he okay—god dammit what have you done?" roared Foster, already presuming Dylan's predicament was the fault of his brother.

"Dylan has been in the hands of the enemy for almost a week now. Before that he served with honor in the frontlines alongside Julius, my dear friend who escorted you here. My nemesis has claimed that Dylan will be the one who does me in. A far-fetched plot, but one I'd rather avoid."

Foster was livid. "How could you let this happen? Your own brother! Why did you let him go to the frontlines?"

"Because he wanted to, Father! Because I listened to him and asked him what he wanted—not like you! He believed in the cause, long before this war began. We grew to think much alike since he left home, left you. You had no idea how much we both tried to make you proud. It truly broke him when you distanced yourself; why do you think he started to act out? We were always your second family!"

"I had to put food on the goddamn table!" Foster banged the table once again, the motion sending the empty plates rattling. "I paid both your ways through college—at least I would have if Dylan had bothered to stay. I made sacrifices; don't you dare think I didn't want to be there with you—I just couldn't!"

Foster was now on his feet, yet their grip on the ground was feeble at best, his disgust at himself pumping through every blood vessel inside him. His eyes swelled with liquid regret that never quite breached the surface. In exasperated mouthfuls, he managed to utter, "You may think you know everything now, that you don't need this old fucking stain of a dad… I know I wasn't always there, I made mistakes like everyone else—but what do you know about being a father? Those people you say you care about, they're just toys to you! Chess pieces! You're playing to win only for yourself."

The room dropped to an unnerving silence, the heat leaving as quickly as Foster had played his hand. He had seen his son and was ready to leave just as soon as he'd come. There was never going to be the reconciliation he had hoped for, imagined, everyday he moved closer and closer to finding Matthew.

Matthew was composed in his reply, patiently spreading the flow of information that would break his father, if only to offer him something to live for. "I am the father of an ideal world, but as I have come to learn, as has Cole, that the meaning of my words only persists in the minds of my followers until another Illusionist is able to do the same with their own thoughts. The continuation of my world can only be found in the controlling of other Illusionists who share such ideas to the letter of the law. These Illusionists must be fed solely on such a diet, bound to its preservation by the most natural of institutions…that of *family*."

When Foster connected the dots he started to choke up. "You're…a father?" he said, the words struggling to leave his rasped lips.

"Yes," said Matthew, this time smiling. "Thirteen of them, each just under four months old. They were all healthy but only one has what I need."

Foster exploded. "You monster—they're children for god's sake—not some experiment for your demented social project!"

Matthew knew Foster was right, and although it hurt him, Matthew showed no emotion, reminding himself long ago that he'd made this choice for the good of the future.

Foster paced around the room. Nothing here was as expected,

as hoped. He wasn't the guy that wanted gold plated plates and comfy chairs, those things had never mattered to him before, so why now? He was the man who needed little, who could survive rough. Or had he done that for too long? There had been no lifting of the unease he yearned for—not just for himself, but for Kate and Max too. This place was doing things to Foster, confusing who he thought he was, if he was sure he knew. Chicago was a lie, and he'd lost everything trying to get here.

Damn this wretched place.

Foster looked at them both; these newly appointed grand champions of the universe, while he was just one man, stuck in between; a toy that didn't know his place.

He felt very stupid. And then there was the anger.

"Where are they?" snarled Foster, his patience spent.

Without a word spoken, the location of the children was revealed to him. His form stiffened. He gave his son one final look of disappointment before he was out the door. The room remained silent as they both listened to the sound of maddened feet that ended with the slamming of the bunker door for the outside streets.

Matthew was not worried. To Cole it seemed it was all part of a plan—*It had to be, right?* Matthew simply stretched his arms and relaxed himself. The polished veneer he had surrounded them with at the request of Foster slowly began to disappear, Cole hovering his hands above the table watching all the shiny accoutrements vanish before him.

Matthew smiled. "*Expectations.* They can ruin even the most pragmatic of men."

Cole shrugged. "Well, if anyone could deliver…"

Matthew chuckled. "So, what is it you expect of me?"

"What can you deliver?"

"What do you expect?" Matthew quipped, clearly enjoying himself.

Cole sighed. "I expect you want something from me."

"What do you believe you can deliver, Cole?"

"Nothing; but I don't think that'll matter."

"Oh, and why is that?"

Cole's eyes narrowed. "Don't tell me I have a choice here. That you'll just let me walk away from whatever this is. You clearly want something from me. I have nothing to offer. You don't need my help."

Matthew drew a deep breath. "You mistake me, Cole. You do have a choice. You've seen how it can go so horribly wrong. You've seen the madness of being alone, trapped in a forest, the sanity peeling slowly off the skin. You've taken lives and let their memories entwine with your own. A hard thing to process—I know from my own experiences…"

When Cole made the connection, his whole body clenched up. Rage built steadily in the back of his throat, ready to accuse, but Matthew continued his declaration before Cole could let fly.

"Cole, you can go back to Holdsworth, unprepared for what the gift burns in you, doomed to repeat the past like all the other humans; Illusionist and infected alike. Or, you can stay here and find your true function, learn your new self, and change humanity for the better. I don't need your help, Cole. I'm offering you mine."

Cole was breathing hard. Seething. "The Savage…*you knew him*."

There was that smile again, complimented with the alien focusing of the third eye. "As much as anyone who reads people's minds in a matter of nanoseconds can. When I saw what he was doing to the Holdsworth catchment and processing area, I came to him in a dream and gave him instructions to keep the people of Holdsworth tied to their post as watchers of the west and to process members of Resistance traveling through. He knew enough to follow my words."

Why have you allowed this? Those words echoed through Cole now just as they had done in the forest, chilling his skin.

"But he killed children—raped mothers and daughters! Was this part of your instructions? Your plan?" Cole raged, fully incensed by Matthew's seeming indifference to the blood on his hands.

"They were only a few of the many he sent to us; I never had complete control over him, my eyes were trained on matters closer to home. As for the blood on my hands, there is a purpose. You must understand I am trying to build a better world."

They could've been killed in that Forest. Cole. Foster. Matthew's very own father. What would be the point of sending them along for some grand scheme if they never made it? Then Cole saw it in that third eye again—the truth, plain as day. What use was Cole if he could not tame the Savage? And Foster, he dies just the way he wanted: in a final battle, the warrior's death.

This burnt Cole. Made him sick to his stomach. He had more questions, an endless list. He could've stayed there all night and Matthew would've gladly answered each one concisely, tying back all his endeavors to the greater good. He could've asked what happened to the government, how many Illusionist factions were still left destroying the country—or fixing it, as Matthew decidedly put it—and what was happening to the rest of the world while this virus tempered its arteries. Had the madness spread? To understand the fundamental shift in how humans would forever interact, or remain ignorant to maintain some semblance of sanity.

In this world Cole had a gift, an opportunity to lead. But Cole was a follower and he knew this. Matthew knew this. Resisting it felt pointless.

"Why have you brought me here?" Cole eventually relented, ready to accept a mission he had not been told about as of yet, but one he was sure he had been groomed for. Despite the earlier doubt he felt from Matthew, Cole still clung to the idea that there had to be a reason for all of this. There had to be a reason and Matthew had to have the answers, for who else would?

Matthew's first statement was bold. "I can see the future, Cole, because I make the future. It is determined through manipulating the most important variable of all: the human variable. With the gift you and I share, we can guide this variable to its upmost potential and realize the utopia we could only dream of before."

Cole was unmoved. Matthew had already won him over, yet he continued to dance around, unsatisfied with Cole's submission.

"I see your frustration, Cole. Your whole life you have followed others and you see me as just another master. This is different; it's a war of the mind and you're my surprise soldier, an ace in the hole. I need you to truly believe in my vision without all the illusions I cover it with, so you stand some chance when my nemesis tries to take you for himself."

Cole was getting more uncomfortable in his chair, each nerve pinching him; making his blood run hot. His mind was swiftly splitting dangerously into two. Before him sat a man he was willing to fight for, yet each passing second spent in Matthew's presence made Cole's body twitch in growing anger. It started to dawn on Cole that this could be a side effect of the gift, the aspect that pushed all those with it to conflict, in order to realize a single viewpoint. Maybe Matthew knew this and needed to show it to Cole.

Cole tried to steady himself and move things along. "I said I was going to play ball. I intend to play it for your team."

Matthew smiled.

"I want you to retrieve Dylan for me. Though my nemesis is on his dying legs, his threat still rings true. And when he finally concludes defeating me is a task that will never be completed, it will be the case that he takes it out on my brother, an event I'd rather like not to occur."

"How am I to undergo such a task? If you see the future the way you describe, surely telling me how to do so will move things along more smoothly."

"I'm well aware you feel that way, in fact much of the dialogue we have engaged in in at this dinner has followed my script. Unfortunately for you, it is more secure to the cause if you discover the path yourself."

While this agitated Cole, he knew he had to agree. What was the point of arguing?

"Seems like a cop out, but I'll bite." Cole then felt a yawn coming on, and wondered how late it was. At this the bags under his eyes grew thick, as a fried clot emerged behind his eyeballs. Thoughts of sleep began to caress him before a sudden clarity shot through his tired frame. *The dreams*! How could he forget to ask? Why were they only a black fog when Cole knew there was more, a vivid portrait that sent reverberations all over? Why did he wake in a layer of sweat every night? Was it Maddie?

He looked expectantly at Matthew, expecting an answer that could tie everything together neatly, a diagnosis of the mind only a person like Matthew could conduct. A revelation to dispel the slip of doubt Cole had witnessed this dinner. But in Matthew's face, a tingle of disbelief broached his frown. Matthew did not know, or he didn't want to admit he couldn't see. His eyes were tired too—even the third eye that rarely blinked, started to drift off every now and then.

Be grateful you sleep at all, it whispered to Cole. And that was that.

Dejected, Cole then asked where he would be sleeping. Matthew, his mind forgotten of that unanswerable question, described the dirty bed available in a room on the second floor of the green grocer. Cole didn't question why he couldn't sleep in one of the many well-made beds in the underground rooms. Matthew snickered, his eyes latching onto Cole's unspoken observation, "It's for Foster's sake. You can enjoy the view of Chicago better…" Cole did not ask what was for Foster's sake, too resigned to the stars now to second-guess their trajectory. Cole nodded then stood to leave before Matthew stopped him.

"Don't you want to know your reward for completing this mission?"

Cole turned, and with tired eyes sarcastically questioned, "What else other than serving your lovely cause?"

Matthew laughed. He hadn't heard sarcasm in too damn long.

"In helping my cause you will help the people of Holdsworth stave off the brutal carnage my nemesis would bring upon them. A stronger Cole ensures their long term survival."

"I could just as easily return to Holdsworth and protect them myself," Cole claimed, though he wasn't sure how true this was. "Besides, I thought you said victory was assured." He started to leave but was stopped again.

"There's more, Cole. I can help take away the memories you yourself are not able to destroy; Madeline and the pain of Trent will exist no more and then you can start fresh with Kate. There will be no past to shadow over you while the others play in the light of the bliss you provide them."

For a second it was considered. The slightest of seconds but who could blame him? Every waking moment since was a constant circle of Cole wanting to put her back together, twisting things around so she was there, breathing, right next to him. Everything back to the way it was.

But this was not the answer. Cole wondered why Matthew offered him this if he knew his response. "I needed those mistakes, no matter how painful, to learn from the past."

He clutched the doorframe as a shimmer of Maddie crossed his sight. Before Cole left for good, he had his own question, one last one. "Do you really believe that what you're saying about all of this is true, or do you just make it true?"

This gave Matthew a satisfaction he hadn't felt in a long time. "After a while, what's the difference?"

Cole left the cold bunker, and as he walked up those rickety stairs in the dark, the words of Matthew began to roll around in his mind, the setting of motions Cole could never fully comprehend, just latch onto for dear life and hope for the best.

There will be little sleep for you tonight. Foster will knock on your door bearing a baby.

31. Wander

Climbing up those dark stairs, the reward Cole had been offered swelled within, tantalizing the part of him that yearned for simpler times, happier days.

Cole wondered if he even needed help; he was sure he could block out the memories of Trent if he worked tirelessly at it, if that's what he wanted. Erase Peter, his best friend for almost fifteen years, and Maddie, the greatest thing that had ever happened to him. He'd done it before—maybe not to such a cruel extent—but then there hadn't been the need. He remembered nothing of Denver and apparently he had hidden from his very own eyes and heart the fact that Foster knew he had the gift. Still, the offer made him curious as he lay down in a stained mattress with no covers, certain he would hear Foster knocking just as Matthew had told him.

Lying there, in the dark, Cole wondered if Matthew had done the same treatment to himself—the forgetting trick. But this was not the case. It was in the eyes. That soul could not let go, and Cole decided neither would he.

Cole heard Foster's approach from two blocks away. Foster's pace was frantic as he held baby Eve in his stiffening arms. Foster kept checking all around him expecting a pair of hands to snatch him up in the darkened street and take Eve back to her crib with the others. When the hands never appeared Foster eventually found himself at the entrance of the decrepit grocery store, surprised he had gotten this far, yet unsure whether to take the next step. Knowing it as inevitable, Cole gave Foster a scent of his location and reverted Foster back to the purposeful, almost-robotic Foster that had stormed off to see his grandchildren.

Cole opened the door before Foster could knock.

There was no hesitation in Foster's grand statement. To him, it was now or never.

"I'm taking Eve back to Holdsworth. She can't be used the way he wants her to be. She can't grow up in a war zone." Cole disregarded the fact Foster had gladly done the same thing with him and struck him from another angle.

"What about your other grandchildren?"

This disturbed Foster, turning him toward the open window where the dim streetlights illuminated his face. Cole studied his eyes and felt the guilt that Foster kept trying to hold back, to swallow and keep down there for only him to endure. Cole wanted to tell him he was just as bad as the son he derided, but he could only see a bitter old man trapped in his convictions, and that truth seemed too painful to inflict.

"What do you want me to say?" pleaded Foster, spit leaving his mouth, as he held a baby who remained relaxed, unbothered by the darkness around her. "I can't carry them all, Cole. I'm sorry. I know it's wrong, I just…" He turned to Cole who sat in a fix, struggling against the weight of his decisions.

"Holdsworth is still in his reach," Cole finally spoke, "they are proxies—Matthew's watchmen—even if they don't know it. He told me after you left."

Foster's breathing drew heavy. The walls were closing in once more. "Well…well…it's got to be safer than this sick place."

Cole looked up at the desperation pouring out of Foster, melting his bones, urging him to collapse.

Cole would forgive Foster; he felt he had to. He'd help take the other children and see that they all made it safely back to Holdsworth. He'd help take care of Eve and marry Kate, settle down and build a small paradise to the best of his abilities. Go back to simpler times. It seemed so straightforward and yet the decision to leave Chicago, Matthew, a purpose he had only just come to see… Running away from it all felt like he was missing the defining moment of his destiny; or was that just what Matthew wanted him to feel? Cole dug into himself, wanting to ask Matthew for guidance, but he only felt the man smiling at his indecision. As much as Matthew infuriated him, the notion that he could help him forget certain events and people was still there, tempting him. Madeline Bamsner was a ghost he knew would haunt him for the rest of his days, even in her sweetness.

"Will you come with me?" asked Foster, shuddering Cole back to the cold dark room.

"I'll get you out of here. I'll even help you take the other grandchildren you were willing to leave behind. I'll take you as far as the edge of the city, but I will meet you in Holdsworth only after my purpose is complete."

"What purpose, Cole? We have no place here. He's just going to use you."

"He wants me to save your other son, and then it's done."

The edges were peeling off Foster as his movements, his whole existence, dangled by its hinges. "Cole, please you won't be able to save him!"

The words shocked Cole to the core. There were depths Foster was going that Cole could shed no light on.

"You don't even want me to try?"

Foster didn't have to respond. A glint in his eyes told Cole everything: that Foster couldn't lose him, that Foster saw a son standing right there in front of him. He'd already lost Max; his real sons were too far-gone. But Cole could still make it out.

Foster turned away again, wiping his eyes on his free shoulder. Cole slid off the bed and walked over to the frail man, putting his hand on the now damp shoulder.

"There are only a few things in life you see to the end, and for me I think this is one of those. I mean, I don't know if the reason why we're here is divine or man-made, but it's bigger than us, and I know this place is the final destination of this journey. It's something in me that won't stop until I find it. Now, let's get your kids to safety."

As Foster relented and was led by Cole to the door he had one last thing to say, lamenting his sorry role in Cole's affair.

"If I knew what my son was, I never would've pushed you all to come here."

"Maybe you weren't supposed to know," responded Cole, who in his heart was beginning to build a strengthening appreciation of the grandeur he was walking towards.

They then slunk their weary feet down the rickety stairs, sensing each heavy step was bringing them closer to a resolution, the end of a journey that began in the west.

***

The streets of Chicago had the appearance of inaction in the dead of night, dressed in a cloak of static. The constant gunfire had drawn silent—but in this silence, an electric charge was building. While Foster could only see empty streets, Cole saw into the hearts of all of Matthew's disciples behind closed doors, motionless yet content as each body was smoothened out by the soft reassurance of Matthew's voice. It was all they needed now; the modern forms of colorful distraction just a distant memory they would only recall as meaningless (if there was anyone left to ask such a question).

Foster walked the dim-lit streets with less panic in his legs than before, Cole's presence allaying his fears that Matthew would change his mind about letting him take Eve. Still, Foster kept telling himself it was the best thing for Eve, desperately hoping Matthew would somehow come around to Foster's side if he hadn't already. Cole did not share this fear, instead growing certain that assisting Foster's exodus would somehow lead him to a sign of how to save Dylan. He even went so far as to believe that Matthew had implanted this notion in him; a thought that gave him further confidence in his stride.

They walked for almost a mile in a straight line in the pure dark before stopping in front of a heavily fortified medical center, barbed wire hung over the top and sidewalk around sandbags, while several men in black uniforms, the same uniforms worn by those who had escorted them from Holdsworth, stood guard by the door. Foster began to tell Cole that when he had come by before, these great big floodlights were cast upon him from surrounding rooftops—but was interrupted when they were blinded by great big floodlights from surrounding rooftops. When the cocking of weapons followed, Foster held Eve, wrapped in her tiny brown blanket, tighter, but Cole was unmoved. Without saying a word, Cole had the floodlights dimmed and the weapons lowered simultaneously along with reassuring both Foster and a now awake Eve that there was no cause for alarm. Cole then nodded to one of the guards and in a flow-on effect there was movement from within the medical center until twelve babies, each fast asleep, were carried out by nurses and soldiers alike, and carefully placed into a van and SUV that had pulled up just as the first baby was exiting the building. One of the nurses came up to Foster and took Eve from him with little resistance offered from his dazed hands.

He looked over to Cole who simply shrugged. "He was willing to let you take her, it makes sense that he would provide you with the proper security."

"So you didn't do all this?"

"I told them to," replied Cole, "but I figure they'd only oblige my orders because Matthew would allow it."

A soldier opened a door to the SUV and gestured for Foster to hop in. He was not ready to say goodbye. "Well, it's not too late to join us," he quipped.

"Come on, John, we'll see each other again when I find Dylan..."

So this was it. Foster had gotten his battle—his mission—his last swipe at the Illusionists like he said he would. He made sure of that, and Max paid for his ticket. Kate was crazy. His son thought he was a messiah—a messiah with a fucked up dad. Things you can't undo...shall I make a list, Max?

Unable to leave it all, Foster pressed Cole. "Know how you're going to do it?" he asked, hoping to stump Cole. "You just going to stroll over enemy lines, ask where they keep the prisoners?"

The question was completely ridiculous, masterfully absurd, but it got Cole thinking.

"No, but I could ask some prisoners on this side of the fence..."

"If Matthew can't break them, then what chance do you have?" Foster cautioned, eager to shoot down this idea before it swung in full motion, but he was too late.

"No," said Cole, his eyes moving left to right in a trance as he fleshed out the legitimacy of his ability, his confidence growing. "Matthew couldn't do it because he could never fully give himself to cracking them. He has battles to wage and people to feed. As for me, I don't have to worry about that. I can apply all my will power to retrieve information it would take Matthew four days to extract."

Foster saw the perkiness in Cole's eyes intensify as he got caught up in the intricacies of his craft, and Foster couldn't help but feel pride in seeing this young man mature in his gift, even if in many ways it terrified him. "I'm coming with you then."

"No, Foster. You've got some kids to raise."

"I only want to see if you can do it," said Foster, clinging onto the close of his adventure.

Cole thought about this, looking at the door still being held open by the soldier who stood blank-faced and motionless; he would do that indefinitely unless Cole said otherwise.

"All right then," Cole relented, "but as soon as it's done you're going back to Holdsworth."

"Where we will meet again, I hope," John said with a smile.

32. Prisoners

It took Cole little time to find where prisoners were being held. He simply walked along the streets closer towards the enemy-controlled territory, scanning the inhabitants that dwelled within all buildings nearby, looking for the faintest sign of dissatisfaction.

They soon found themselves in front of a battered down Chicago precinct. Eyeing its walls, Cole's brain connected and encircled the dissident brain cells that urged to break free from their surroundings and cause righteous mayhem.

All up, he found several guests being held against their will. He made a guard standing outside take them down to the holding cells where both Cole and Foster came face to face with the "enemy". The cell was brightly lit and permeated a pungent smell of two-day-old shit lining the far corner of the dank cell after the broken toilet had its fill. Cole filtered this smell for Foster and himself before beckoning the prisoner to come forward. Summing up his thoughts, Cole was aghast at the mental and physical state of this shade of a man who wearily shuffled forward, the bones of his legs growing brittle through their dragging.

"He hasn't eaten for two days while they pump him full of drugs and brainwash him with a pamphlet of your son's literature," Cole said in a matter of fact way to Foster, who kept his distance, finding it all out of his depth.

"Well, were they close to breaking him?"

Cole eyed the two guards playing statue at the door, feeling for how much persuasion Matthew had been giving them to work on this prisoner. "At this rate he's closer to dying than cracking."

"Maybe we could try another person."

"No, this is perfect," said Cole, holding out his arm to stop Foster. He approached the cell until he was only inches away from the rusted bars. At the same time the prisoner shambled his way closer, the abscesses growing all over his face and arms becoming more defined in their crusted texture the closer he got.

"What is your name?" asked Cole in a relaxed tone.

"It's irrelevant," rasped the prisoner, scratching away at the scabs of his folded, bony arms.

"You don't know your name, or you don't have one anymore?"

"It's irrelevant," persisted the prisoner.

"Your master made your name irrelevant, didn't he?"

Before the prisoner could respond, there was forceful surge from Cole only the prisoner felt. The prisoner clamped up as if he were being choked. Then Cole released him.

"He said not to tell," relented the prisoner who then immediately cupped his mouth, overcome with guilt. Cole retracted these words and carried on as if they had never been spoken, leading the prisoner to forget he had said anything in the first place, the guilt in him vanishing.

"What is your master's name?"

"He said not to—"

The prisoner could not finish his standard response as Cole made him dig his own fingers into one of his open sores just under the ribs, twisting and cutting through deeper with every little twitching motion as the man's body tried to defend itself. Tears began to stream down his already encrusted eyes. Foster flinched just as much as the prisoner, but Cole remained firm in his stare.

"What does he say about us?" Cole demanded, his voice still eerily calm.

The prisoner's eyes trembled, he wanted to close them and wipe away the tears that blinded him, but Cole would not allow his eyes to shut. He would only let the prisoner wipe away the pain with fingers currently inside him.

"WHAT DOES HE SAY ABOUT US?" Cole roared.

The prisoner held for as long as possible before blurting out, "He says you are monsters—brainless automatons! Slaves to an empty ideology!"

"And what does that make you?" Cole pierced without missing a beat. "What does your master stand for?"

The prisoner was more lucid now, his voice finding itself after days of silent loyalty. "The pursuit of the ideal human who can only exist in a society without difference!"

It was trumpeting the party line, spoken with a military authority, but his master had broken him in to a point where that was all he knew.

"And what are we to this plan?" asked Cole, his hands now clenching the bars.

"You are the enemy! Vicious cretins who will stop at nothing to— arrrrrrgggghhhh!"

The prisoner's words were cut short by his fingers digging further into his bloody wound under his chest, a line of blood now running down his body and covering the floor that his emaciated shell then collapsed onto.

"You hate us, don't you!" yelled Cole. "You hate us more than you love him, don't you!"

Foster tried to grab Cole, thinking he had gone too far, unsure of where he was going with this, but the prisoner's emphatic blurting of, "Yes, yes, yes!" made Foster think otherwise.

"WHAT IS HIS NAME?"

"SEBASTIAN! ...Sebastian," the prisoner repeated, absolutely devastated before he threw up blood and bile, just missing the tip of Cole's worn shoe. Then just like that, Cole brought the man closer to death than he could possibly go without falling onto the other side; a suffocation that clamped the ribs, twisting them into daggers as they turned on him and tried to rip out his own heart. As the drilled in structures of discipline instilled by Sebastian were picked apart and the prisoner's life flashed before his boggled eyes, Cole was there to capture the moment this man, Harold Panowski, believed he met Sebastian in the flesh, and finally the face and name of Matthew's nemesis became known to Cole. The room got very quiet with all eyes on the slumped body that then jerked upwards, breathing heavily after being dangled over the edge.

When Harold managed to wipe the tears away he found himself staring at the master who was everything to him, just as he had remembered. The other prisoners now came to life knowing full well that this man was not the grand Sebastian, their fearless leader. He wore thin rimmed glasses, had the look of an intellectual and a dark gray coat that stretched down to just above his knees. The other prisoners cussed and rattled the bars screaming imposter to all who would listen, but it fell on deaf ears for Harold Panowski, who saw his savior standing before him.

"They are monster, aren't they? Look at what they've done to you."

Harold crawled towards "Sebastian" and held his knees close to his chest while his tears soaked Sebastian's thigh.

"They…tried to kill me…make me betray you…" he exhausted between his runny nose and the tears that blended with the drippy mucus.

"There, there." comforted Sebastian as the hounding objections of the other prisoners were simply muted from all existence. As far as Harold was concerned, it was only Sebastian and he, in what might as well have been the greatest place on earth. Sebastian then leant down until his face was level with Harold, light shining from his face, enchanting him with a divine glow.

"I know a way we can get them back; a way in which you will be serving me *and* avenging the pain you endured at their hands."

Harold had already forgotten such pain, so enraptured was he with "Sebastian".

"The monsters we keep on our side, there is an important individual among them whom I want you to lead me to. I have a question I want you to ask him…where do the most important prisoners go?"

Harold didn't notice the holes in the question, the only logic being to answer it, to please his master. He knew exactly where they took the few prisoners that were caught, East Chicago General, where the monsters became cured. Cole read his mind before he had opened his mouth and saw what Harold saw in earlier days: the long march through packed streets of flying spit and filthy abuse as they were taken to the hospital to be fixed. Cole hoped that among those taking this torrid march was Dylan, for at least he knew where to start looking.

The next time Harold blinked, Sebastian had disappeared and he was back in his cell, face to face with the *enemy*. Before Harold could vent his anger at his own betrayal a vessel in his brain clotted and he was dead within thirty seconds. They all stood back in shock at the sight of this man squirming on the ground, the throes of life leaving him with each jerked movement of his body until it moved no more. A stunned Cole shuddered when Foster drew a hand on him, each looking at one another, Foster fearful of how just how far Cole had gone.

"Was that you?" he asked.

Cole's face went ghostly white. "It wasn't me," he murmured as his hands trembled.

"I'm just scared it was someone else."

***

On the corner of Haight and Sullivan Street stood two guards of Matthew's Legion. Once known as Leonard Wright and Carl Crundwell, they overlooked the battered bridge that led to a waiting enemy hunkered down along the other side. In the dark waters of the Chicago canals below them lay the bodies of people from both sides, many driven there under the guise that the enemy was waiting under the water for them at the canal's floor. It had been a quiet night and the two guards stood behind the mount of an M-60 machine gun nest made of sandbags and other junk scraps in comfortable silence. There was little to say now, but in another life these two were the best of friends, living only a block away from each other as kids and going to high school together. One had been the best man at the other's wedding and the other had helped fund the other's web business. Their greatest moment together was when they starred in their team's tightest victory against their pesky rivals, the Riverside Bobcats, in water polo. These memories were distant specks of the horizon now, only reflected on in the spare moments when Matthew did not have their ear—and even then they were perceived with an air of indifference; like watching the model cavemen at the natural history museum. It was all overshadowed by the internal contentment Matthew had bestowed upon them.

So there they stood, staring into the darkness of the other side, bathed in soothing silence.

But this was not to last.

In an instant, the calm static that radiated from the air was transformed into the explosive, hungry monster of war. They first saw its terrible face in the skies above them: transparent lines waving about that formed into tentacles from the sky, soon reigning down upon them. The M-60 was thrust upward and the heavy chatter of its voice (along with their screams) echoed throughout the night. No matter the ferocity of their firepower, the tentacles cut through the tracers and engulfed them until every orifice of their body felt like the air had been choked right out.

Support teams were drawn to the shooting but were only witness to the two bodies. This was followed by the sound of thousands of feet sprinting toward them. Before they knew it, their throats were slit by an advancing army of invisible men flooding across the bridge, headed straight for Matthew.

33. The Nemesis

He had waited for Matthew for a long time. And now, face to face, after the bloody road he'd taken to get here, he knew he was losing. His machines were failing him. His body, while used to the toll of war, was being pushed too far.

He was getting desperate.

They'd come all the way from New York, him and the original people that were his. Not that where they came from mattered much anymore, as long as they were his to play with. He'd strolled through Pittsburgh and Toledo to get to Chicago. That'd been a cinch compared to that "detour" to Philadelphia to crush that Randall Flagg.

He'd taken over ten after the Great Peace ended, and that wasn't counting their followers—in the hundreds of thousands, and sometimes in the millions. Some were part of the good ones, the builders of the Great Peace, but Sebastian was always good at making his reasons, telling himself what he was doing was necessary—that this was the world he lived in now, either me or them. And there was a light at the end of this tunnel. There was a reason for all this. He knew it, Matthew knew it and all the others still left, they knew. They all wanted the same thing, the idea finding its way into all of them eventually: to be the last, the last voice.

And those machines of his, the tanks and the planes and the helicopters and the artillery and the weapons that spouted great fires of lead—all taken from the army before—they cut through everything and everyone. They'd gotten him all the way to Chicago, but now they weren't enough.

Sebastian hadn't concerned himself with a home like Matthew, who fortified himself in Illinois, or that Queen down in Texas. (He'd have to save her for last). There was no point in having one. Sebastian was willing to adapt to any condition possible, so long as he was still alive. And so his people moved like a destructive wave of fish, an unending terror that gained as much as it lost: the equilibrium of Sebastian. All across the Northeastern States his natives laid waste. He'd lost four hundred thousand (like a bad hand in a card game) in less than two weeks against Flagg—but once he got him, once he'd taken the life from the one he once considered a brethren, those that were Flagg's were now Sebastian's, one of his natives.

Now he was losing, and badly. Matthew's legion did not turn as quick as the others; his legion withstood the mental whips Sebastian flogged tirelessly at them. They'd been at it for six weeks—day in, day out. An endless stream of lead crossing this way and that, tearing flesh but never the resolve. When he tried to push past the canals Matthew would take his men by the head and drive them into the lake. He'd tried sneaking in through underground systems but Matthew had those routes caved in while his natives were still inside. He took to the air, but the closer his pilots got, the more the orders they'd been given were twisted, and Sebastian's machines became Matthew's. Before, he'd never have to have gone anywhere near as close to the frontlines as he had done this past week, but the power of Matthew dictated it necessary, and so both had edged closer each day, the buffer of protecting bodies drawing ever so thin.

It was non-stop, and while Sebastian, with his weedy frame and rimmed glasses was never the most physically imposing, the lack of sleep had drained what little was left of that.

Sleep. What a jolly fucking luxury. Before he knew it was time to go after Matthew, Sebastian had been living on four hours a night. That had been comfortable. Someone once, in the time before Tyrantocillous found America, had said that sleep was essential to helping the brain learn by giving it time to recuperate and connect the dots of the day. But that was for humans, a category neither Matthew nor he could say they belonged to anymore. Those four hours he could allow in Philly against Randall Flagg and in Hartford against Shannon Miller were very much days of the past—now it was two hours and slowly shrinking. For the longer he was awake, Sebastian could defend, keep his people's minds under his command, and the longer he slept, the greater chance Matthew had to attack.

How long do you sleep, Matthew, because I can do the same, I CAN, I CAN!

Sebastian had learned to copy Matthew. Whatever Matthew did, Sebastian had to match. He had to think the same in order to guess where Matthew was moving his pieces next. And even then, Matthew had suffocated him out, almost encircling him like a trapped animal. But Sebastian, like Matthew, was never going to give it up. He'd made his bold claims of killing Matthew with his own brother, and he'd given up far too many to catch Dylan. He would not give up the sworn oath he'd made months ago to his people, the original natives: That justice would be theirs.

***

Sebastian hadn't always been like this. And they hadn't always been enemies.

Sebastian was once a college student, just like Maddie, Kate, Peter and Cole. He was a former member of the student union but when he was no longer a student, Sebastian became lost, a faceless member of the real world. When he joined a bigger union to help the workingman, the upper echelons of the Docklands Union were quick to cut him down, seeing his temperament grow unruly in youthful ways they had no time to nurture. He spat at those degenerate runners who paid too much lip service to the fat cats who wanted to trample his style. Too radical they thought he was, well fuck that noise.

Needing a fresh start, Sebastian had tried to find it in the Big Apple, finding himself a one-bedroom apartment in a black ghetto, a fine place to rally the disaffected he thought. Yes, Sebastian had big plans, and wanted to tell them to the world, drawing up lines of "us" versus the "one percent". That was in 2003 and after a few failed starts at re-invigorating several retail unions, Sebastian found the apathy too much and his goals shrunk out as the part-time Kinko's job he held turned to full-time and Sebastian Kruger settled; joining the masses in accepting their fate. When the GFC hit and the Occupy Wall Street movement tried to shake things up, Sebastian did lift his head if only out of some past interest. But he was too jaded to change the world now. Or so he thought…

When people started getting sick, Sebastian was untouched,

relaxed even. When the fallout swept through a frenzied New York, Sebastian had noticed it before anyone else around him; somehow he'd felt the vibrations in D.C. hundreds of miles away. He didn't know how he knew, but his words among the panicked masses united small pockets of people, the scared ones, and soon Sebastian gained that hope again. The hope that he could change things, that he could be a force for good.

When the Great Peace came, they all regathered. They all looked inside and wanted to start fresh. Their bond was cheerful in the beginning, they helped each other rebuild, all actions motioning like cogs towards the greater good. They got the electricity running again. Services were set up and connections were made between the once lost. For the first time in a long time, Sebastian was lifted in pride; he was a part of this healing, just as much as Matthew and the others who could speak out across great distances.

At first they had wanted nothing to do with righting the wrongs of the past, so busy they had been with rebuilding, discovering the nooks and crannies their minds were opening up to like great big sponges. But as time went on and safety was returned, shelters secured, that creeping desire grew back, the unsettling wriggles within that called for action, an opportunity to use what they felt what was in their hands to the full extent.

It started as a need for justice—or the desire for revenge— whichever way it was reasoned. It was claimed that they could only go forward, progress, if those responsible for this monstrous change were held accountable. They wanted the man who started it all—some science jerk-off—but it turned out that he'd already been taken care of by some religious army building in the west. So it followed that the culprit of the mushroom cloud would be their first; and it soon became obvious which of the powerful ones had done the deed. They chased him all over, and in distant cries he screamed witch-hunt. Told them he wouldn't be the last, that the cleansing wouldn't end with him, oh no. He told them the kinship wouldn't last. Sebastian had discounted this, just like the others. They were different from Senator Barclay Richards. They were good.

When Matthew had captured Richards, Sebastian had begged, incessantly, to do this cowboy in with his own hands, but he was denied. When he asked, respectfully, to watch this despicable piece of shit have the life taken from him, he was denied.

By the time Richards was dead, the peace was well and truly over, the bloodlust too great and invigorating to shy from. So Sebastian waited. He built his natives, the ones who had their justice denied, and he grew in silent wanting with them, so that one day he'd take that memory from Matthew Foster's brain and make it his own.

And when he saw "himself" in a run-down prison cell, a Harold Panowski clutching "his" leg in desperation, Sebastian knew it was now or never.

34. Seven Minutes

Seven minutes. That was all it took. Thirteen months spent developing himself; fine-tuning his brain to bring others to build a dream he worked every second towards. Seven minutes, a miniscule lapse. 6, 035, 212 followers at his disposal and another estimated 2.5 million he stood to gain once he had taken his nemesis by the throat and squeezed the life from him.

Matthew punched the walls and kicked at the legs of his mahogany table. The anger in his mind boiled the room, the paint on the walls melting as flames began to spread like weed in a deliberate snake-like motion, engulfing his surroundings. He slammed his fists on the table.

Seven minutes.

Matthew retraced his thoughts right up until the moment he closed his eyes, confident everything was put in its rightful place. Now he feared a seven-minute nap had taken everything away from him, all those carefully placed pieces he'd put on his table now blowing away in a gale force wind. He kept coming back to the blame he had inflicted upon himself. His ego had gotten the best of him and he knew it. He slowed his breathing and saw the flames begin to die down. He had to figure out what had happened and what to do with the advancing enemy that gained yards on his position with each passing second.

He held his chest and once his breathing drew steady, all fire in the room was extinguished. A line was made in his mind, splitting his focus into two. While one side organised wave upon wave of followers to defend him, the other occupied itself with reconciling the mistakes that had led him to this point. How had Sebastian found him? He had closed his eyes just as Cole had seen the precinct where the key prisoners were being held. He screamed through clenched teeth. Why hadn't he stayed up to see Cole retrieve the information? Was it something in Cole's methods that alerted the attention of Sebastian?

Matthew replayed the extraction through the minds of those who oversaw it, while he tried desperately to ignore the image of his past self, sitting comfortably in his chair like a true king, the confident smile he wore with pride now a burning reminder of a future that was rapidly disintegrating right through his hands.

Then Matthew saw it: Cole's impersonation of Sebastian, an act that no doubt would've raised the attention of his nemesis. Of course, this may not have been it, his position could have been given away as soon as Cole appeared in Chicago; the presence of another Illusionist ally on Matthew's side prompting this Hail-Mary assault that now had every chance of turning the tide.

Matthew's whole line about keeping Cole in the dark for his mission was supposed to be security against plans being stolen from Cole. There was also an enjoyment to it, a child-like desire to toy with Cole, keep him uncertain, because sometimes that feeling of control was just what Matthew needed. But now that the obvious opposite had occurred—with Cole practically giving away his (and therefore Matthew's) location—it was glaringly painful to Matthew how short-sighted he had been.

The very thought of it churned Matthew's insides, his teeth grinding away in an uncontrollable rage. There was no hiding from his mistake. The fires in the room were burning again. The pestilent bug of regret was gnawing at him as he kept finding himself going back to that lapse, to curse those seven minutes. And while this poison seeped through him, Matthew began to hear the thumping feet of forty thousand pairs of boots surging through his frontline within the confines of only three parallel streets, climbing over cars and each other to feed from his heart. They were now closer to him than they'd ever been and behind this blasting wall of bodies came the undeniable presence of Sebastian himself—as if to beckon Matthew into a frontal confrontation.

It was working.

All the time he had spent building layers between himself and his nemesis, the effort he put into splitting his presence all around his territory—all of it useless now. His ego was crushed. *He*, the one who saw everything, the one who controlled all the variables, had never seen a kamikaze attack by Sebastian himself as a possibility, and now it bore down on Matthew hard, tugging at his spine, releasing an animal of pure rage within his core. All that work destroyed in seven cruel minutes.

He would have to retreat, lose ground, up to a million assets and then the sleepless nights could go on for many months to come. He needed that sleep, he craved it wholeheartedly, but his mind was always moving, always fixing away at the tiniest of nuances that his followers were reliant on. To rebuild would be a failure, yet it was the smartest option available to the smartest man left…

But as men of pride seldom back down, retreat was never an option for Matthew. He sent his eyes out to survey the scene from soldiers closing in on this swarm of forty thousand pests and tanks that punched through the gut of his defenses. At this rate, Matthew's Legion wouldn't be able to effectively enclose Sebastian's advance and Sebastian would reach Matthew's position with most of his assault force intact. Unless of course, if Matthew had anything to say about it.

Before Matthew walked out into the cold dead of the night, he called out to Cole and Julius to join him in the fight for their lives.

There was something else in Matthew's choice he couldn't deny, ever since he'd seen the great white flash and learned its manner. There was a peacefulness inside it, an end to it all, a sleep with no end. Matthew wanted that. He wanted the oblivion.

***

It was only moments after leaving the precinct that the thunder of gunfire invaded the ears of Cole and Foster. The sound was both terrifying and a little bit exhilarating, filling the street with its monstrous roar. It took one look in his eyes and Foster knew that Cole would be called up to fight, and Matthew's voice in Cole's head confirmed this. They regarded each other; both knowing the time had finally come to go their separate ways.

"If you were Matthew, what would you do?" asked Cole. Maybe it was the wrong time to ask such a question, but to Cole it seemed his last chance, a last bit of advice from a father to a son, from the old to the young.

"I'd give it back to the people, for better or worse."

Cole smiled. "I'll see you in Holdsworth," he promised, his mind pushing such belief into Foster who could only smile back, now confident he would be seeing his friend again. Foster started running back for Eve, while Cole drew a deep breath before making his way toward the thunderous rounds of lead being exchanged en masse across the city.

Chicago had come to life. From lifeless buildings hundreds and hundreds of people leaked, all with weapons in hand scurrying like ants to catch the harvest of war. Some made war cries; others simply drew cold killer stares. When Cole read their minds all he heard was, "Protect Matthew," murmured over and over to the beating of their hearts that readied them for carnage. He became one with the masses, his head bobbing up and down as they did, straight lining it in the dark towards the muzzle flashes eight or so streets over. His heartbeat soon began to pump at the same rate as the others who crowded around him like the big pack in a marathon.

Just as he was getting into rhythm a sharp pang pinched him at the side of his head. Wincing, he stopped and dropped off to the side, almost falling headfirst into the side of the front steps of an apartment block, just in time to miss the hail of streaking bullets that struck the crowd, causing them all to run for cover. The chippings of cement and brick fell on Cole's head like rain as a line of bullets sunk their teeth into the building. He clutched at his head feebly trying to protect it, before a more composed Cole took the reins, knowing full well staying there would get him killed.

The attack had come from a platoon of Sebastian's men who had surprised the group from an intersecting street, wiping out many in the crowd. Those of Matthew's people still standing returned fire but were crushed under an intense sheet of firepower. Cole thought frantically about making himself invisible and slipping past the platoon, but the intensity of their armor piercing rounds that searched for his body foiled such a method of escape.

No, he had to fight them.

He summoned a thought of only silence and cast this idea out to his enemies who suddenly felt a burning urge to hear only silence. With the sound turned down for only a second, Cole pinpointed the weakest willed of the group hanging at the rear, the owner of a Rocket Propelled Grenade launcher. The man's comrades never saw him pull the trigger; Cole clearing their sights before the ground was lifted up from beneath them.

Cole didn't look back. He had done what he had to. Besides, the heavy chatter of gunfire welcomed his attention up ahead. He slowed as he neared the next intersection, only to see an armored car hit with an explosion as soon as it came into view. Men and women from opposing sides now swooped in after the explosion, clashing in vicious hand-to-hand combat, clawing at each other's faces, trying to rip the limbs off one another.

They were fighting to the death over hashed lines they were told they believed in. It was a paralyzing sight for Cole, unsure exactly how he was going to pass through. Once again there was no way to get past without killing; Cole hadn't the skill to do so. And yet on the other hand, he knew that those with the skill to incapacitate without causing actual harm wouldn't bother in the first place; all too easily passing off killing as necessary to their ends.

Cole wasn't scared of dying, that had passed long ago. It was the path that scared him, the path where he'd grow to find taking another's soul came easier with practice.

Still trapped by his moral reproach, muscles stuck firmly in the headlights, Cole was stunned to see the man who had taken them to Chicago, Julius, along with his men in their distinctive black coats, swoop in like a flock of ravens and take control of the intersection within a matter of seconds, brutally executing all of Sebastian's natives within range. For Cole, whatever was blocking the thoughts of this man before had been lifted and now Cole could read Julius as an open book.

While Cole had plied his gift for peace and hiding, enjoying the pink streaks in the sky, Julius had spent the same time becoming war. He was the soldier every person in Matthew's legion was modeled after. The experience of twelve years of military service, four different theaters of war and forty-three confirmed kills was instilled into the heart of a person when they became one of Matthew's children, all thanks to the memory of Julius Banks. Friends at West Point before the war, Matthew betrayed Julius when he discovered they both had the gift, intentionally stunting Julius' development to a point where Julius could only ever be Matthew's right-hand man. Yet there was no bitterness, the instilling of love paving over such broken roads of the past.

Would the same fate be handed to Cole? Maybe, he thought. It could already be happening, but the time to dwell on such things was not upon him.

Cole called out to Julius in his mind, and after the man had broken the jaw of a bewildered enemy, he locked eyes with Cole from a great distance and nodded. No words were said, but a call to arms was beckoned and understood. Cole ran to Julius' position, covering the rear of his death squad as they continued their rendezvous with Matthew. Together they decimated whoever feebly tried to stand in their way, Cole letting go of those moral quibbles that clouded the instincts his gift urged him to devour. Every thought that passed him now drew blood. He followed Julius like an apprentice eager to follow in his ways. He'd watch Julius reach into the soul of a man, twisting and stretching it to places of horrific imagined pain, before decisively destroying the brain to the point of immediate organ failure. Julius was controlled in his methods, they wouldn't cry out but sure enough he'd give them the fear their master had taken away. Just by watching each successive display of brutality, Cole tried to emulate such puppetry in his own attacks, but came off as crude and sloppy, judging from the blood-curdling screams of hell he sent their minds gushing through like cows to the slaughterhouse. Somewhere along the way in this thick haze of murderous rage, Cole had picked up an assault rifle and began firing it at enemies he rendered defenseless with his paralyzing stare. When he ran out of ammo, he was taken back to the days of childish games of war in the backyard, and started to pretend-shoot his victims, their hearts playing along as their own minds pulled the plug.

All those inhibitions were dropped like the shackles they'd been, as Cole became a pure animal, so free—and righteous too! *Remember, boy, all of the sinners the same!* Bloodlust lit up his eyes, surging through, becoming forever a part of him; forever tempting.

By the time the last enemy within eyesight stopped breathing, the cold air blew across Cole's face, bringing him back to his naked, exposed senses. He looked over at Julius, a touch of heaviness and shock in his eyes as his hands trembled, his grip on the blood-marked rifle and reality extremely threadbare. As members of Julius' black coats returned to their rescue mission,

Julius showed Cole he knew well the mental realm of heightened bloodshed and its toxic effects on one's sanity, but was firm in his reminder that their mission was not over, and they would have to endure more of this violent circus until the deed was done. A heart-pounding Cole agreed in such an assessment, taking a deep breath before he and Julius resumed their course towards Matthew, now only four blocks away.

35. The Stand

The sounds of war beat with the rhythm of precision held in Matthew's heart. Matthew licked his lips; all too familiar with the tangy taste of taking lives, which he welcomed like an old friend. Walking out onto the street where he would throw it all on the line, Matthew inhaled the chaos that stood before him, only to exhale the focused demeanor of a cold, deadly tyrant ready to bite the head off the fool who awoke him from his slumber. The night was receding and with the slow rise of dawn came the imposing sight of forty thousand dogs of war only four hundred yards away. The majority of Matthew's defenders on this street had already rushed this swarm at full force only to act as speed bumps to Sebastian's stroll down murder lane.

Matthew cut a lone figure in the street and Sebastian pulled the reins on his forces that snarled and growled and itched to be released upon their most hated enemy: the cause of all that was wrong in this world.

Matthew's third eye blinked slowly, cheekily enticing Sebastian to come play.

On seeing this, forty thousand dogs were released, the first few waves sprinting like crazed animals screaming for blood as they waved their weapons in the air. Their run was short-lived however, a single twitch of Matthew's emotionless face and a twinkle from his third eye made their skin feel as though fire had engulfed every pore, while white phosphorous napalm seeped into their brains. Others had their bodies invaded by invisible spiders and serpents that descended from the skies, causing them to collapse and writhe around in a state just short of death. The squiggly gel of transparent lines that floated around aimless in the eyes were turned back on their owners, blinding their sight, causing them to trip over the stumbling others in front. For the lucky few, their end came quickly with the simple shutting off of the brain's central nervous system.

Attempts to retaliate were thwarted by Matthew's tweaking of each shooter's aim and as he drew ever closer, his control of them grew with each calm, precise step forward. He felt the gushing of wind from surrounding lead zip past his head but never pierce the skin. This kept his wicked grin. The small arms and mortar fire was slowly encroaching its way towards eventually making its mark and a stray bullet was all it would take, but this was not a possibility Matthew had decided and what *Matthew said therefore is truth.*

Within seconds, the ordinance of Matthew's own artillery provided him covering fire, the coordinates of each target flying through Matthew's mind, which were then being transmitted in nanoseconds to artillerymen miles away at O'Hare airport. The shells would sink into the surrounding buildings, the falling debris crushing soft bodies below. Matthew soon found himself weaving left and right dodging the falling debris Sebastian's tanks countered him with. He was only two hundred yards away now.

Sebastian's army struggled forward to a point where bodies had to be hurdled and crawled over. When they had gotten to within only a hundred yards of their target, the sound of blades above distracted them as Matthew's entire apache and fighter jet fleet came swooping in to rein down hellish fire upon them. The chain guns of the apache gunships tore straight through the flesh, separating limb from limb while the F-16s released their payload right in the middle of the pack. Sebastian was forced to strain himself to make the pilots avoid his trajectory, which then gave Matthew more moving space to eliminate Sebastian's men at a higher rate.

Once the F-16s had passed, Sebastian regrouped; reaching out to the pilots and making them crash far away into empty buildings. Sebastian then turned his attention to the apache gunships still engaged in strafing runs against his quickly depleting army. Sebastian's few Javelin missiles rocketed through the air, hitting an apache hovering just above Matthew, the explosion rocking him and sending him rolling for cover, a foot of rotor shrapnel missing the back of his head by inches.

While Matthew was knocked down stunned on the ground, Sebastian's swarm made valuable ground towards him; their feet running hard as they sensed that final kill. In a daze, Matthew slowly got to his feet and was finally hit with a ricochet just under his left knee, bringing him back down in excruciating pain, his legs in a tangle.

The inevitable odds of getting hit had finally caught up with him, the only bullet of thirty thousand rounds to hit. But instead of giving up in a heap, overwhelmed by the mental marathon he'd been making for himself around the clock for thirteen months straight, all Matthew could feel was rage. It was this fury that would overcome any physical pain he would have to endure in order to bask in the moment where he wrung the neck of Sebastian with his own hands and felt that last breath duck out to an irrelevant world.

The first of them were almost upon him, their faces red from all the pure adrenaline pumping through their veins. Matthew tripped the one who almost brought his axe down on his head. He then instantly unplugged the systems of others and made those with guns assured they could not miss from such range turn the weapon on themselves and blow their own brains out. He could not do this forever, their hate overbearing as they just kept coming by the thousands, ready to inundate his veins with their teeth, but Matthew was looking beyond that, through the masses of blood-thirsty monsters, squarely at their ringmaster.

Matthew had one last weapon; the weapon he used against the culprit of the mushroom cloud. It had taken Matthew over four months and five and a half million of his people to surround that despicable vermin. There were countless others Illusionists, the good ones from the beginning, all lost trying to capture this devil until only Senator Barclay Richards and Matthew Foster were left. Matthew had Richards tied up and spent days tormenting him with his own medicine. It pained Matthew just as much as Richards to go back to that moment, to feel the thermal burns shriek the skin off bone, as he ensured this cycle would become Richards' hell over and over till the memory drew deadly. He made Richards pay for what he did, and now with his remaining energy, Matthew would hit Sebastian with his most powerful weapon. Sebastian was a longer shot of course, much further away than that trembling Richards, tied up in pleading horror, but this was Matthew's only chance. He screamed in pure rage, his mind's eye filling with the confused last few seconds of life his beloved wife saw before a blinding light took her from him.

It was the flash of pure death, the splitting of atoms and the destruction of all existence and in Matthew's mind this bomb fell gracefully onto the street.

Those around him were knocked from their feet as the awe-struck reality of total Armageddon engulfed their brains, the flash of a billion memories passing through a needle. Sebastian raised his hands as he screeched, doing his best to repel Matthew's full focus of the blast. Matthew's last memory was firing everything left in his armory at Sebastian's last known location: a carpet of artillery and the last few missiles of what remained of his apache squadron. There were explosions all around him, and once the light of the nuclear blast had found its way through every living soul that Matthew could reach, there was only black.

***

The sun had risen by the time Cole woke to its bright rays; his eyes crusted over from a deep sleep. He was surrounded in the open street lying on top of other unconscious bodies of both Julius' death squad and the mangled, ragged bodies of Matthew's enemies, some in deep comas while others read no pulse. Attempts to recollect what had happened were soon overwhelmed by the onset of a pounding headache that brought Cole to sickness. He tried to find open space on the ground to leave his vomit but the cluttered sea of bodies around him gave him little choice but to throw up on a motionless woman. His eyesight was blurry while the sharp jolts that echoed through his head sent cold chills down his spine.

Fighting through the pain he tried to survey his surroundings to gather his bearings. The streets were dead quiet, the sounds of war long gone with only the ringing in Cole's ear to remind him of their grandiose absence. Cole then felt someone moving and turned his head to see a blood-stained Julius dragging himself to put his back up against the wheel of a destroyed shell of a car. When Julius' dazed eyes rolled over to Cole's, there was little explanation to be found. Mustering all his strength, Cole suggested they search for Matthew, before he started scanning for Matthew's brainwaves himself.

Around the corner, one hundred feet away from Cole, Matthew's eyes began to slowly come to life. Buried under all those who had tried to kill him, he fought through the jackhammers that pounded his skull to slowly free himself from the tomb of comatose shells. Getting his left arm free helped him to angle and roll over the two lifeless people who pinned down most of his right side. Eventually his right arm was freed and he shuffled himself till he lay on his front side, waiting for the blood to return to his arm. When it flowed back and he felt he could move it, Matthew stumbled upwards before vomiting blood. Looking down at the blood that slowly dripped down the back of another body, Matthew felt for the wound on his leg.

As painful as it was, he started to laugh, taking in all the debris of buildings left and right that should have crushed him as it had done to hundreds of others mere feet from him. He looked up into the sky and held his hands out in exalted joy, basking in the open sun that flooded through the street; exposed by the shattered concrete surroundings that were now reduced to rubble. The belief in his prescribed destiny had faltered truly, but now it warmed his body stronger than ever. Everything but the kitchen sink had been thrown at him and yet he still stood; his survival a testament to the fact that *his* ideas were meant to survive, just as nature dictated.

Matthew sent out word for medical assistance and started some medic who had not been affected by the blast wave on her way towards him. He then turned, gazing down the direction from where his foe had come to stand toe to toe with him. The sight of endless piles of quiet bodies and burning tanks and apaches made Matthew grin. There was no lone figure that mirrored him, and Matthew was convinced Sebastian would never rise thereafter.

His ego swelled and as he relaxed he called out to Cole and Julius eager to confer his survival to them.

He had won.

But it was the flicker of a grin that caught him off guard, sending his knees weak. The grin belonged to Sebastian and now Matthew beheld the unsightly lone figure standing among the destruction, Sebastian's grin a frozen nightmare Matthew endured for over fifty lifetimes in a state of utter hopelessness.

How?

His ego had gotten the best of him again, shattering his world. There was no fight back this time. The pulling of a trigger from a high-powered rifle four hundred yards away saw Matthew watch his own face give up through the scope held steady by his brother, Dylan. And as the bullet passed through his brain—taking his third eye with it—Matthew's empire of thoughts, dreams and ideas collapsed along with his tired body.

The shot echoed through the ears of Cole and Julius who now stood immobilized in terror, the hair on the back of their necks now awake and stretching in a desperate attempt to escape the torture their bodies would soon endure. There was to be no mercy, no chance to surrender and submit to *his* will, Sebastian whispered—*as if he were right up in their ear.*

Then came the sound of footsteps, each one bringing dread to Cole and Julius as Sebastian strolled toward them, hands held behind his back as he whistled a tune from his demented soul. The medic Matthew had sent for jogged methodically past them, disappearing around the corner to square up against Sebastian. The snapping of the medic's neck was a sure sign of things to come.

By now Cole and Julius were side by side, their hands shaking as they put them into closed fists, if only to look like they were ready to fight.

Cole turned to Julius, ready to grab him by the arm and ask his big brother to fight the approaching bully.

"W-w-w-what are we going to do?" Cole stuttered, hoping Julius had something up his sleeve, an ace in the hole that would stop the whistling monster that made his way toward them, one delighted step at a time. Looking into Julius' eyes, Cole dropped his hopes like a bag of bricks.

"They were practically the same," Julius muttered. "There is no chance."

Julius then picked up a Kalashnikov from the stiff dead hands of one of his men, and aimed it half-heartedly towards the corner that death approached from, ready to die. He was simply out of ideas, but Cole saw something in Julius' defeated words that gave him hope, gave them a chance, if only that. If Matthew and Sebastian were practically the same, then it was possible their weaknesses were shared. Cole replayed Matthew's death in his mind, watching carefully that face of utter shock, and felt that

Matthew would've moved if he hadn't seen Dylan behind that rifle, a paralyzing puncture of realising Sebastian's promise coming to fruition; sending a man who believed he could engineer the future to a point of total loss.

Cole's body stirred, his plan rousing him to believe it could work only on the basis that both Julius and himself believe it with everything they had left. Julius sensed the hope vibrating throughout Cole and turned to him.

"Julius, put down your weapon and listen to my words carefully."

Julius, still focusing on Cole, lowered his weapon.

Sebastian had only thirty feet between him and the corner at this point. He could've attacked them right then and there, but he had his own preconceived notions about their fate—notions he would've preferred to explore with Matthew had he ever gotten within such distance. Besides, there was little to fear now and he could take his time.

"Julius," Cole continued, "**Matthew killed Sebastian**. Sebastian is dead, and he is never coming back. The person who will walk from that corner is Matthew Foster, your greatest friend for five years, and our great leader. He will walk to us, and tell us that we have done him proud, and we will say the same of him. *Matthew lives*, Julius. *He lives*."

Cole then turned to face Julius, his face doubtless by his words, and from this Julius began to believe.

"*He lives*," Julius repeated, throwing his weapon away, and then they watched the corner as the sound of feet ticked away the seconds to when they would see their Matthew again, if only for the longest second.

Sebastian stopped just short of the corner and looked out

yonder past the bodies to where his defeated nemesis lay still among countless bodies. A smile blossomed from his face as he fantasized about desecrating Matthew's face inch by inch. *Your brother is one hell of a shot*, he thought to the dead man. When he finally walked out into the view of Cole and Julius he expected the fear of god to be plastered deeply into all the tiny crevices of their pathetic cowering faces. He expected they would bow down to him, beg and grovel, and he'd give them a far spun hope—only to crush it with all the satisfaction in the world. He'd expected a lot of things, but when he saw those stern faces with not a drop of fear perspiring from them and he gazed upon their minds for the first time, everything in him seized up. For when he looked through their eyes, it was Matthew who stood before them and not the great Sebastian himself. Sebastian held his hand to his face and was so gripped in the reality they had set, that he felt his features had changed.

And in this small moment of doubt, he saw Cole send a signal off, the two words "*He lives*" echoing like a bullet to a waiting Dylan, who still in his obedient state, cocked his rifle and once more fired at "Matthew". Sebastian's disciplined instilling of the one mission Dylan would obey indefinitely had been used against him. Sebastian turned towards Dylan to command him to stop, but the bullet had already left, missing his head and shattering his collarbone instead.

As Sebastian fell, he reached his hand out to crush Cole's heart. This snapped Cole from his intense concentration, pulling him forward onto the ground where his heart felt insidious fingers trying to rip through it.

Seeing Sebastian distracted, Julius dived towards his discarded weapon and from a prone position fired off a spray of lead.

Sebastian was able to misdirect the majority of Julius' spray, except for the first bullet that careened into the side of his stomach. With Sebastian grasping at his stomach, Cole became free from Sebastian's grip and lifted himself up, staggering towards his downed enemy, ready to finish the job.

Cole imagined knives being slowly entered into all of Sebastian's limbs while hands dug deep into the back of his eyeballs and slowly twisted them out like light bulbs.

Sebastian used all his remaining strength to fend off these excruciating manifestations, shutting his eyes, straining to stop those hands from taking them out. Sebastian imitated replications, as best he could, of atomic blasts exploding inside Cole just as Matthew had done, the flashes bringing back those dreaded screeches.

And then just like that, the pain was gone.

Sebastian opened his eyes once again in surprise, but now he saw something more ghastly than the pain he had just experienced. Standing over him, a smiling Matthew laughed in a muted fashion before thrusting both hands down like piranhas to a bird that had fallen in dark waters. It was just as how Matthew had promised him throughout their entire war, repeated in echoes across great distances, only to now become a reality as Sebastian felt the breath of Matthew, the smoothness of his thumbs as they dug in deep into his trachea; the complexion of his skin now seen for the first time as Sebastian's consciousness faded in transit.

In a desperate last attempt to fend off his destiny, Sebastian rasped out a single word, "Dylan."

The rifle was cocked for the last time, and as Sebastian waited for the bullet to strike his attacker, the pressure on his throat subsided and the weight of Matthew's body seemed to lift all at once. With his right hand Sebastian swung at Matthew's face, only for his hand to pass right through. The last thing he saw was Matthew smile, as a bullet snapped directly through both their brains.

Cole, still standing ten feet away, dropped to his knees before hitting the ground completely and losing consciousness.

36. Decisions

The sound of sparrows wrung in Cole's ears. They chirped playfully above the long oak tree in his backyard, tending to each other with their own rules and customs. Cole sat on the back porch watching them, ever so keen to just be the fly on the wall that just floated about, never a hard decision to make. He did this every Sunday before church, wearing his Sunday best while his parents got ready. He never much liked church of course, the rigid uncomfortable perfection of his clothes always reminding him of where he was heading, where he had to make that first choice, the one of God. He'd sit in his pew surrounded by his parents, his best friend Peter Storrs just a few pews in front of him, fidgeting away in his equally uncomfortable uniform. When they found themselves out of sight from their watchful parents, they took the opportunity wholeheartedly, off like the wind.

When Cole, urged on by Peter, told his parents he didn't want to go there anymore, they were furious, threatening this and that, reminding him of the eternal burning of his flesh and soul. It was the first act of defiance he had made against them, his first real choice. Cole felt the weight of that one choice throughout the rest of his life. He was just a kid of ten years, but the guilt stayed with him and just like an animal hurt once by a trap, he became very conscious about making decisions, too afraid to accept the consequences. He never watched the sparrows on a Sunday again after that; the echoed feel of a tight collar, tie and scorched wrist reminding him of that first defining place his choices had stung him.

***

Cole had that dream again. Standing above them, the rubble his podium, he watched their faces call out to him once more, asking him what they should do. They were all there again amongst the growing crowd: Maddie, Kate, Foster, Peter, Max and now Matthew; a bullet wound centered perfectly upon his forehead where his mind's eye used to stare. Yet this time the dream was different, more lucid and less like the creeping terror of indecision that plagued and eventually fogged up his dream. Their faces were crisp, more defined than ever before. Cole himself felt more awakened, even feeling like he could find his voice and speak to them finally, but what to say?

***

Cole woke up, the aching in his head wiped clean. Julius knelt by his side, a bottle of water in his hand extended to Cole. It was a pre-emptive gesture of saying sorry; Julius had contemplated for the slightest of seconds to crush Cole in his sleep, but immediately rubbished the thought, urging away the natural instincts the virus had invigorated in him.

Cole drank from the bottle then let out a laugh—the best he could do. Julius helped him to his feet, keen to make up for his most ugly of thoughts.

"We can't help it," said Cole. "At least that's what Matthew reckoned. Maybe he was wrong; maybe he made it a truth. Either way, think nothing of it. If he was right, if we are driven to kill each other, we simply acknowledge it and walk away."

Julius smiled. "Agreed."

It was a simple idea, but it filled Cole with confidence in the ease in which he decided it. They then settled themselves and without saying a word, made their way over to Matthew's body. The rising sun revealed all the devastation Cole felt he had helped create. Matthew's ideas had made this a reality, and Cole felt within his bones the price of pursuing the utopia of one man. Sure, Matthew was a powerful man, a god in many ways, but ultimately he was still human, still prone to the corruption power brought to him, twisting his rationalizations to extreme ends. Now that he was dead, his bullshit was aired out, completely exposed; and all that nonsense Cole had bought in Matthew's destiny game was worthless. He thought of the future and the endless bloodshed that would ensue in order to achieve this utopia, and knew he hadn't the heart to take Matthew's place on the throne.

There was no destiny, no purpose to this power that Matthew had promised. If Cole took the helm, he'd become just like them; just like Matthew, just like Sebastian and just like the man that dropped the nuke.

Just another monster, slowly but surely.

The dejection Cole felt was soon confronted with more questions as he turned the corner. When he looked towards the rubble Matthew had climbed down before his death, it was then and there that he saw everything he needed to see.

He realized he had seen this place before; it was exactly as how it was in the dream he had every night since he arrived in

Trent. Julius stopped in his stride when he felt the dawning revelation in Cole brew. With great intrigue and a light sense of deja vu, Cole took his place atop the rubble and slowly did a complete 360, eyeing each single stroke of his vision until it was aligned perfectly with the scenes of his sleeping states. When this was done, Cole perched himself down and sat on his throne, waiting for the people to come.

He did not need to beckon them; they were drawn in after being snapped out of the deep grasps of reality Matthew and Sebastian had painted for them. It was mild at first, a slight dissatisfaction that snowballed as the receptors in their brain ran plump out of the love that once held them together. They shivered away, mucus drooping down their noses, the muscles growing sore all over—all of it happening too abruptly. Their bodies ached in yearning for such control again, and so they began to flock from everywhere, some in mid-fight miles away, others waking from the severe brain trauma Matthew had put them through when he released his most painful memory.

As they came from everywhere, so did the question. What to say? Cole now had the voice, the power to sway the hearts and minds of a growing contingent of god knows how many people—maybe four million—but for what purpose, war against the other Illusionists until there was only a utopia of one?

How long would this take, this bloody path set for him? Only moments ago he had discarded the very possibility and yet the dream brought it all back; like he was meant to lead—the doubt he felt just remnants of his former indecisive-self leaving his body. If that, what goal was this? No matter the power he possessed, he knew he had no right to control these people, despite what Matthew had said.

His conscience clung to him, desperate for him to walk away.

Worse still, he knew the answer. How long it would take. He'd seen it in Matthew and Julius, whose bodies thirsted for it, even if they never admitted to it. He'd felt it himself, if only for a brief moment. How long the war would last inside, how long he'd have to fight before he gave control back to the people. The answer was spoken in Matthew's voice and it was terrifying:

"When they know better."

The crowd was growing larger with every passing moment and each of them became more restless without the soothing mindless massage that familiar authority filled them with.

What would happen to them if he just walked away, told them to live freely like it was before? He peeked into each of their souls and saw that all were too far gone; they wouldn't go back to living free, pursuing happiness as individuals; they would spread as far as possible until they found themselves in the arms of another Illusionist who would gladly take them in and reprogram them. While silent at first, the restlessness only in their shuffling of feet and shaking of their arms, the crowd began to find its voice, to murmur and then plead for direction.

"Tell us what to do!" they cried.

"Make the sky shine like heaven again!"

"Give us the warm blankets of love!"

These were all the things Matthew had done for them, the same cries Cole had heard before in Trent. It was a vicious cycle that was breaking him. He yelled for them to stop and they did so immediately, the eerie silence sweeping through the streets of Chicago. Then, just like in the dream, their faces were slowly plucked from the crowd. Foster, Peter, Matthew, Max, Maddie, Mom, Dad and Kate.

Kate.

There was a future there. Somewhere, far down the line, it was possible: a shot at feeling the warmth again.

Just walk away and have the life he wanted to have with her in Holdsworth. It wasn't too late to start again, to feel the sun's rays as they ran through the grass in the day and sat idle when it set. Was it selfish to want this? Did he deserve a second chance?

He could have a child with Kate, the one he wanted with Maddie, and together they would make their own utopia, in the here and now, while the world collapsed around them. It was overwhelming in its beauty, its simplicity, and for the first time since he lost Maddie, Cole knew he could live with the sparrows once more. As he took to this notion, this sweeping urge of walking away, letting go of the controls, it dawned on him that he had never actually asked Kate if she wanted this; in fact no one had asked Kate what she wanted this whole time. He had barely asked Maddie that very same question…

And then he knew it. Just like that. Why his mind had spoken the truth to Kate, before he himself could announce it. Because the truth would give her a choice, and that would make her a person again, free like she always wanted. And Cole wanted that Kate, above all else, even if it meant she didn't want him.

At first stunned, this obvious oversight gave him a light chuckle in front of the swelling crowd. All his pores drew open as he saw the colors of this new world, this new shining truth. He had time. *He had a second chance!* The truth would set them both free. But then what? What if Kate hated him for it, what if those hands tried to strangle him again for letting Max and the others go into that forest—all like she rightfully should. Would he handle it gracefully? In that moment, Cole decided he'd have to. And if she were still willing, if she could forgive, he'd play the old-fashioned way, maybe starting out with a picnic in the field with the daisies…

Yes, this was it. This was his chance. He smiled at all of them in the crowd, every pair of eyes and beating heart, ready to be happy again. As he did this, a sunny breeze of possibilities was caught by each of them, releasing a sea of blossoming souls. Cole then picked up Julius' scent. Julius remained in the bustle of people, reading Cole's thoughts, unsure of what to think of them. Julius had seen Cole's dream as well, and believed that Cole was brought to them to carry on Matthew's idea. But Cole had other plans, Cole would leave and Julius would take over; it would all fit together perfectly.

And for a moment, Cole's story played out. He found himself with Kate, their eyes growing old together as their skin wrinkled and their smiles managed to keep. It took a while, but they found it again; they made something from their broken pieces. This world Cole dreamed was the world he lived.

But only for a moment.

As Cole extended his idea to Julius, something stirred inside of him, something buried very deep, hidden to everyone, including himself. It had been waiting, incubating itself until the perfect moment when it would break free into the world. Cole's head began to feel heavy, like cement was being poured into his brain. His hand, extended out to Julius as a gesture of his idea being shared, was quickly withdrawn. An internal struggle soon developed and the crowd watched on, confused by the crazed twitching and spasms that rung through Cole's body. This invisible intruder, triggered by the fulfilment of Cole's recurring dream, flooded through his brain, eager to consume the masses of souls that stood before him. Cole shivered and strained, desperate to fight off this sudden enemy, his whole body contorting itself, wrenching his organs to and fro. He threw himself to the ground, clawing at his suffocating head while his eyes rolled into the back of his skull. He screamed.

***

The last thing Cole saw before it had total control of him was a fire, burning bright. It was just out of East Denver, a few blocks down from Peter Storrs'. The fire was in the process of consuming a church, just like the one Cole turned his back on as a child. An old rustic place of the wooden variety, the windows barred from the inside. It had only taken a matter of minutes for its walls to collapse and its occupants to take their final smoky breaths.

Cole had been racing back to Maddie and Peter who had bunkered down in Peter's house along with Claire and other survivors, keeping as quiet as mice like the many other residents who hid in their homes while the outside world burned. Denver had become the battleground for three of the gifted ones who waged petty war against each other, either unaware or uncaring of the Purification Front that swelled in numbers all over California. Cole had just come back from California. He had snuck past the army's severely depleted lines, spread thin and pointless across the Rockies and then through Utah and Nevada, all to find his parents, if only just to learn their fate.

He was witness to those big black crosses that lined the Hollywood Hills and all the lands around them; their outstretched metallic arms ready to curl sharply inward and snatch him up at any moment. He'd seen those particular crosses before, and deep down knew whom they belonged to.

But he could not accept this. He didn't want it possible.

Like a careful ghost he had observed the ruthlessness of the Purification Front first hand, swarms of their number rapidly adopting the feared gray robes they became known for; dragging those hiding in their homes out into the street where they were judged on the spot, the two outcomes of conversion to the Lord or execution. And it wasn't long before they started putting all those big black crosses to use.

Returning to his parents' house he found nothing but distant memories and dust-lined surfaces; they were gone. His search pointless, Cole chalked up their fate to the gray robes, converts he was sure they had become. While he simply walked passed patrols, completely invisible to them, an old man he had not seen for many years felt his presence and took a deep interest in Cole's journey. And it was watching this fire consume the church and swirl about in its naturally destructive ways that the old man's face appeared once more before Cole, those eyes wild in their conviction, just how Cole remembered him all those years ago.

Pastor West.

In that one moment, a belief was buried deep within Cole; the equivalent of years of intensive indoctrination, rammed down his throat in nanoseconds and forgotten by him just as quickly, waiting patiently for the right moment to expose itself to a vulnerable environment: when Cole Watts had finally assumed control of a large enough population. The pastor had seen something in Cole as he followed him all the way back to Maddie and Peter. He saw a reluctant Illusionist. A rare form that would fly under the radar to other Illusionists, one that could gain their trust...

***

Cole stopped twitching. Collecting himself, he stood up again, but there was an evident change in him. A transformation. Julius saw it, but by the time he realized Cole was not "Cole" anymore, hands were all around him, clutching at his legs, his arms, his body, his face. Julius scrambled to stop them, to push them away with his mind, but the hands were persistent and soon hands became knives and Julius was stabbed repeatedly in the neck. The members of his very own squad had done the deed.

Now finished, those who had just murdered their former master turned in silent obedience to their current one. Cole looked out among the masses, his voice swelling to booming monolithic proportions as the words of his new master became his own.

"ALL HAIL THE PURIFICATION FRONT!"

And eight million souls responded in kind, their perfectly synchronized cries echoing across the whole state of Illinois.

37. Homecoming II

Along an empty stretch of flat road, only a few miles from the border of Illinois and Iowa, two cars cut through the open, lifeless stretch of landscape. In the backseat of the tail car sat Foster, little Eve in his arms. There had been no sleep for Foster and with the morning sun climbing in the sky, the bags under his eyes tendered his whole body weary. Eve had never left Foster's arms since they escaped Chicago in the dark of night, Foster never loosening his grip as he held her future in a delicate balance.

Her father would come for her; Matthew would change his mind, this Foster was sure of. But if he worked at it, Foster could separate the two just enough so that her footsteps would not walk down the same path he had driven his son down. He'd been a lousy father, but he was determined to change this. He would have to change if it was going to work with Eve; and he promised he'd do whatever it took to make this happen.

While his whole body clutched at Eve like a safety blanket, Foster's mind kept drifting back to Chicago, desperate to know the fate of Cole and his sons. He kept repeating the same hopes in his head of seeing Cole walk back into Holdsworth, the reassurance that Chicago was over; that none of its cold grasp would reach Holdsworth anymore. Every time Foster did this, he would put the thought away as final, conclusive in its reality. But his recurring trips into this fairytale bore even greater doubt with each visit.

The quiet burdening of his pain was causing him headaches. He had no one to speak to. The two soldiers claiming the front seats were drones; any attempts at learning the fates of those left in Chicago were met with the ideological vomit of, "There can only be victory," and, "You worry too much, sir. Your son will do you proud."

Disparaged by their mechanical responses, Foster began talking to Eve; telling her about the nice place they were being taken to, where she would grow up like a normal kid doing childish things, completely isolated from the madness she had been destined to inherit. He gazed into her big blue eyes and waited for that smile she'd already perfected; the one that made him warm and cuddly all over, the one that made him know she was the one Matthew had spoken of. But there was no smile this time, Eve's whole face a ghostly white. Her whole body started to warm up and Foster began to panic, asking Eve what was wrong. She didn't say anything—she couldn't, she was a goddamn baby—yet a concept had struggled itself free from her face, summed up into a single word that startled Foster.

Danger.

Foster reached for the handgun in his jacket, and looked frantically out the windows in every direction, looking for the *danger* Eve had definitely warned him of. But the landscape remained unremarkably lifeless. He looked back to Eve, ready to shake her, to understand the *danger* he was so certain she was in. Her face remained aghast, on the verge of tears, and now Foster moved to tell the drones in front.

"Guys, I think we're going to be hit here," he yelled, but they seemed to take no notice of him this time.

"Guys?"

The brake lights of the van in front appeared through the windshield, quickly followed by Foster's car applying its own breaks. Looking at Eve one last time, Foster finally understood the *danger* and fired two shots into the front passenger as the man spun back onto Foster, his weapon drawn. Foster then fired through the seat in front, hitting the driver, blood splattering across the windshield. With the driver dead the car drifted off the bitumen road, careening into a bushy ditch by the side of the road as Foster covered himself over Eve.

Dust swirled in the air both inside and outside the car as Foster regathered his stricken nerves, first making sure the two drones were dead, then making sure Eve was fine. Tears dripped from her eyes as Foster placed her on the floor of the car, bracing himself for the *danger* that still persisted.

From the van in front, two more men dispersed; the beads of their rifles drawn rigidly against the wreck they approached with cold precision. Suddenly, the side door creaked ajar, and they fired off their rounds sporadically. Popping out from the far side of the car, Foster caught both of them in the chest, their bodies dropping in unison. Seeing them still alive, Foster rattled off the last rounds of his clip, sending one of the men fatally still. He then slid back behind the back of the car; reaching for another clip only to have his shaking hands drop it onto the dirt ground. Cursing, he recomposed himself and reached for it, this time making sure his grip was firm as he slid the clip into his gun. Slowly peering up above the boot, he saw the last man stretching desperately for his rifle. Seizing his chance, Foster sprung out from the cover of the car, rushing the man as he fired away at the rifle the man could almost grasp.

Foster was soon upon the man, beating his dying face in with fists that trembled uncontrollably with rage. When Foster stopped, the man gasped for what little air he had left. Foster grabbed him by the collar, shaking him violently.

"What Happened in Chicago? Did Sebastian win? Tell me you fucking bastard!" Foster screamed right into the man before collapsing beside him in a hopeless heap. The man was dead, and Foster was left with only speculation.

It was then and there that the walls of John Foster finally collapsed.

Dirt covered his face as it stuck to the gushing tears that broke uncontrollably for Cole, Matthew, Dylan, Kate and everyone Foster couldn't help. Everyone he failed. He turned on his side and let the sun beat down on him, the morning heat drying away his crusted face. It was all too much. Didn't God know he was just one man—*just one fucking man!* He cried till his lungs hurt and the coughs drew in dirt, which made him cough all the more.

***

Foster lay there for a long time, wallowing in agony. When the tears had dried and the heat bore down heavy on his face, he knew he had to get up. Regaining his composure was difficult at first; all things were, it seemed. But Foster knew it had to be found, because there were still the questions, the never-ending tasks. He hated the prospect of running again; if Sebastian had won, were the others in Holdsworth now Sebastian's? Maybe they were too far away; Cole did refer to them as proxy towns, unaware of the roles they served. If this was the case, and indeed the best-case scenario, then yes, these old legs of his would have to run again, run till his legs were worn to the bone and his heart ready to give in.

Still sobbing, he heard Eve, who cried out to him in a more natural way, like a normal baby, and not the most dangerous creature this planet had witnessed thus far.

She lay on the floor of the car, halting her cry as soon as Foster appeared through the window. When he picked her up, the warmth of her body spread through him, and he was given hope again. He realized nothing had changed in his purpose; Eve and the other children were now his life, and he intended to follow this cause till he could give no more. There was power in purpose as he had learned from Cole, watching him transform in these past few days, once a grieving boy riddled with indecision, to a man who took charge and was ready to accept the consequences, even if the path wasn't the one Foster liked.

Looking into Eve's big blue eyes, tiny lips and radiant smile that bubbled, John Foster found his strength—and he saw that resistance was still possible, just as men will always dare to dream. If a man chooses his own purpose and pursues it, then that is the freedom he lives and dies by. His family (as it should have always been) was that purpose, and Kate Brewer was a part of his family. He'd tell her the truth and accept the consequences; it was the right thing to do, the right way to start again. And who knew what would happen after that? Maybe, just maybe if he tried, if he persisted, he could help little Eve bring them a beginning they all prayed for, a world just like Kate had imagined.

Wiping the dirt from his face, Foster walked briskly over to the other van, a swelling confidence building from his stride. He put Eve in the front and she instantly hushed the crying ways of her siblings. With his keys in the ignition, Foster glanced back one last time to the horizon that held Chicago, and then set off for Holdsworth; fears of what he might find there repelled by the little bundle of hope that sat riding shotgun.

<u>Acknowledgements</u>

I'd like to first thank my parents for putting up with me and encouraging me when I needed it. I'm also in deep with my first readers (Peter, Lucas, Ed, Beth & Chris) who are bastards that really don't know what they're on about (except for most of the time). And finally I'd like to thank my inspiration, an author and dear friend, Elisabeth Storrs, for giving me invaluable pointers along the way.

About the Author

Aden Simpson grew up in Sydney, Australia. He completed a degree in Commerce but then thought: "Nuts to that, I want to be a successful writer."
He is still working on the "successful" part.